Dreaming
of Heroes

Dreaming of Heroes

American Sports Fiction, 1868-1980

Michael Oriard

Nelson-Hall [nh] Chicago

Lines from the following poems are quoted by permission:

"Autumn Begins in Martins Ferry, Ohio"
by James Wright from *The Branch Will Not Break*. Copyright
© 1962 by James Wright. Reprinted by permission of Wesleyan
University Press.

"Cobb Would Have Caught It"
by Robert Fitzgerald, *in The Rose of Time*. Copyright
1943 by Robert Fitzgerald. Reprinted by permission of
New Directions.

"To an Athlete Dying Young" from "A Shropshire Lad" —
Authorized Edition — from *The Collected Poems of A.E. Housman*.
Copyright 1939, 1940, © 1965 by Holt, Rinehart and Winston.
Copyright © 1967, 1968 by Robert E. Symons. Reprinted by
permission of Holt, Rinehart and Winston, Publishers.

LIBRARY OF CONGRESS CATALOGING IN PUBLICATION DATA

Oriard, Michael, 1948-
  Dreaming of heroes.

  Bibliography: p.
  Includes index.
  1. Sports stories.   I. Title.
PS3565.R5307   813'.009'355   81-16877
ISBN 0-88229-588-8 (Cloth)   AACR2
ISBN 0-88229-796-1 (Paper)

Manufactured in the United States of America

10 9 8 7 6 5 4 3 2 1

The paper in this book is pH neutral (acid-free).

Contents

For Julie and Colin

Acknowledgments

I wish to thank a number of people for their help in the writing and publication of this book. William Chace and George Dekker of Stanford University and Eric Solomon of San Francisco State University offered much needed advice and sound criticism of early drafts of the entire manuscript. My colleagues at Oregon State, David Robinson and Anne Taylor, read and commented on portions of the work. The late Claude Simpson kindly extended to me use of the facilities of the Huntington Library in San Marino, California to study Frank Merriwell in the *Tip Top Weekly*. Anton Grobani most generously sent me his own typed copies of his *Guide to Baseball Literature* and *Guide to Football Literature* before those excellent bibliographies were published, greatly facilitating my initial explorations of an uncharted field. The Oregon State University Research Council and the College of Liberal Arts provided me with time through a grant and with typing support for work on part of the book. And the editors and staff of Nelson-Hall have been most helpful in their dealings with me during the preparation of the manuscript for publication.

Portions of the book have appeared in the *Journal of American Culture,* the *Jack London Newsletter,* and *Critique.* I thank the editors of those journals for permission to reprint the material.

It is appropriate at this point, it seems from my reading of so many other authors' acknowledgments, humbly to credit these men and women for all of the book's virtues, but take full responsibility on myself for its faults. Such disclaimers have long seemed to me too much like the false modesty of the star quarterback in schoolboy football novels who responds to congratulations, "I owe it all to my parents, coach, and teammates (if not to God and country also); what I did was nothing." Of course I am responsible for the book's faults, but for some of its virtues, too. Nevertheless, I am very grateful to all those who aided in its conception and execution—for their kindness as well as their wisdom.

Autumn Begins in Martins Ferry, Ohio

In the Shreve High football stadium,
I think of Polacks nursing long beers in Tiltonsville,
And gray faces of Negroes in the blast furnace at Benwood,
And the ruptured night watchman of Wheeling Steel,
Dreaming of heroes.

All the proud fathers are ashamed to go home.
Their women cluck like starved pullets,
Dying for love.

Therefore,
Their sons grow suicidally beautiful
At the beginning of October,
And gallop terribly against each other's bodies.

—James Wright

one

Introduction:
The Field
Defined

And somehow one does not associate
professional baseball players with
the graver problems of life.
New York Times Book Review
(21 October 1923)

I n 1970, 9 billion American man-hours were spent watching
football on television; 70 million viewers watched the Super Bowl alone; a single sixty-second commercial for that Super Bowl cost advertisers $200 thousand.[1] That professional
football in America thrived during the seventies is attested by
the fact that in 1980 the television audience for the Super Bowl
had increased to more than 76 million,[2] while advertising
costs had soared to $234 thousand per thirty-second spot.[3]
During the decade, ten new stadiums were built at a cost of
over $500 million, increasing the capacity for weekly attendance to 1.8 million fans;[4] paid attendance for all NFL regular-season games reached a record 13.18 million in 1979.[5] But
football did not eclipse other major spectator sports by any
means. The National Basketball Association drew an all-time
high of 9,937,575 fans during the 1979-80 season,[6] while attendance at regular-season major league baseball games in
1979 reached yet another record, with 43,550,398.[7] At the
beginning of the 1980 seasons, there were seventy-seven professional teams in the national football, basketball, and baseball leagues, some valued at well over $20 million and all
followed avidly by millions of devoted fans. The impact of

1

sport on American life is virtually incalculable; it has provided countless words and idioms for our vocabulary, revenues for our economy, and recreation and entertainment for
our leisure.

Such has not always been the case. Organized sports became a significant American institution for the first time only
after the Civil War.[8] Prior to that national turning point, Americans had little time or need for organized recreations.
Seventeenth-century Americans had been burdened not only
with the Puritan indictments against foolishly wasted time,
but also with the fact that survival was a full-time occupation,
leaving little opportunity for sport. In the New England colonies, Puritan and later Quaker leaders opposed games on the
grounds that man's energies should earnestly serve God, not
frivolity. Within a year of the landing of the *Mayflower*
Governor William Bradford objected sternly to boys and
young men playing on Christmas, that Roman holiday, while
others worked. "If they made ye keeping of it mater of devotion," said Bradford, "let them kepe their houses but ther
should be no gameing or revelling in ye streets."[9]

One can too easily overstate the Puritan opposition to play,
but certain facts are irrefutable. The 1648 *Laws and Liberties
of Massachusetts* declared that no person "shall spend his
time idly or unprofitably," and in 1653 the colony's General
Court made sport on the Sabbath a misdemeanor.[10] From
1657 to 1786 regulations were passed in Boston that banned
football, sledding, and gaming for money, among other pastimes.[11] Although the initial fervor of Bradford and the first
generation of colonists could not sustain itself long, revivals
of religious enthusiasm such as the Great Awakening invariably retarded whatever openness to sports and games had developed. Nor was it only Puritanism that opposed such activities in the North. The Quakers who settled Pennsylvania may
have disagreed strongly with their Massachusetts brethren
on theological questions, but William Penn spoke as Bradford
might have when he exhorted his followers not to "eat, drink,
play, game, and sport away their irrevocable precious time,
which should be dedicated to the Lord, as a necessary introduction to a blessed eternity."[12]

Southerners were more open to sports from the beginning.

Calvinism was the foremost religious influence in the South as well as the North, but it was tempered by a simultaneously thriving hedonism.[13] When King James I published the *Book of Sports* in 1618, following the *Basilikon Doron* of 1603 which had positively enjoined his subjects to exercise with running, wrestling, tennis, horseback riding, and other recreations, the Puritans who later settled Plymouth and Massachusetts Bay colonies were appalled and resistant, but the Virginia colonists who founded Jamestown in their king's name were much more open. The Virginia colony was not immune to Puritan restrictions, but the less austere Anglicans engaged in sports more readily than did their Puritan counterparts in Massachusetts.[14] Hunting, horse racing, and cockfighting emerged as the most popular sports in Virginia in the seventeenth and eighteenth centuries. Earliest sport in the South was a function of class, and in these recreations Southern planters emulated the sporting customs of England's aristocracy. The lower classes were not able in many cases to share the sporting enthusiasms of their better-born or wealthier countrymen. In York County, Virginia, in 1674, a tailor, James Bullocke, was fined one hundred pounds of tobacco and cask for racing his horse against that of a wealthy planter, "it being contrary to Law for a Labourer to make a race, being a sport only for the Gentlemen,"[15] according to the court's judgment. Throughout the colonies, members of the lower social ranks were restricted to ball games, running and wrestling contests, and crude frontier diversions such as "gouging," "corn-shucking," "driving the nail," and "barking off squirrels." Only after the Civil War did sport for the masses truly emerge, with an impetus from many sources: urbanization, industrialization, technological advancements, the shrinking of the frontier but retention of the frontier virtue of rugged individualism, the movement away from Puritan orthodoxy, the example and influence of England, waves of European immigration, and the efforts of enthusiastic promoters and sports journalists.

Baseball led the way in creating sport for the masses. Its origins can be traced to the ball games of antiquity, to the British game of cricket, and more directly to boys' games of "town ball," "rounders," and "four-old-cat."[16] First organized by the aristocratic Knickerbocker Base Ball Club in New York in 1845, the game was quickly taken over by the immigrant working class. The Civil War introduced the primarily Eastern game to the South and West, and as early as 1866, baseball was being termed "the National Game."[17]

Football was more directly an import from England.[18] Also of ancient origin—the Spartans played a game called *harpaston,* similar to modern rugby—football has been played through the ages in many forms. As *calcio,* the game was characterized by its formal elegance and was patronized by sixteenth-century Florentine noblemen, but in England, where the earliest written record of the sport is 1175, football was a widely disparaged, often outlawed sport of the lower classes.[19] Once introduced to the United States in 1869, football became the preeminent college game; the professional version, begun in steel and mining towns for the workers, acquired wide popularity only in recent decades. The difference between amateur and professional in all sports has not been so carefully maintained here as it was in England; the United States lacked both the inhibitions and the aristocratic tradition of the British to restrain commercialism from entering sport.[20] But vestiges of the British prejudice against professionalism appear occasionally in American sport, and professional football was fully accepted only recently.

Boxing—together with footraces, probably the oldest of all games—survived illegally through most of the nineteenth century as the least reputable of American sports, but it flourished in the early decades of the twentieth century.[21] In England, the sport had been practiced by men of the lower ranks for the amusement of the aristocracy, a tendency continued in the American South, where plantation owners wagered on bouts between their slaves. But in the North, and elsewhere in the country after the Civil War, boxing was performed by and for the lower classes and was considered depraved by respectable society until well towards the end of the nineteenth century. It was not adopted as a spectator sport by all classes until the twenties, the decade of Tex Rickard's first milliondollar gates. Participants continued to be drawn almost exclusively from the lower social ranks, but the bouts were patronized by the social elite as well as by boxing's traditional clientele.

Basketball was the last of the major American sports to develop.[22] Conceived in 1891 by Dr. James Naismith, who nailed two peach baskets to the gymnasium balcony at the International YMCA Training School in Springfield, Massachusetts, basketball was originally intended by its inventor to provide the physical activity "muscular Christians" required but could not find outdoors during the winter months. The new game caught on slowly, first in high schools and then in colleges; not until 1946 was a strong professional league formed. Basketball also evolved in ways its founder never imagined— from a rugged, cautious, tactical sport characterized by scores of 8-7 and 14-12, to the run-and-gun game of great artistic beauty and style dominated today by blacks. The last developed of the major sports, basketball was also the latest to become widely followed, but it has emerged in recent years as the most popular American spectator sport.

These four—baseball, football, boxing, and basketball—are the sports which have given us almost all our sports fiction. In order to discuss this type of American literature, I must define sport much more narrowly than Johan Huizinga's concept of "play," which is the basis for all culture,[23] and more narrowly than Roger Caillois' definition of "game," which includes gambling, mimicry, and vertigo as well as competition.[24] I must even exclude much of what is termed "the sporting life"—hunting, fishing, and riding—which characterizes most of early American sport, but whose purpose was primarily recreation or maintenance of class distinctions. I am limiting "sport" to exclusively human games: organized competitions involving tests of physical skill, pitting men against men, without extraordinary means of locomotion. I thus exclude hunting, fishing, horse racing, and bullfighting—"sports" that have their own substantial body of literature—as well as yachting, auto racing, polo, crew, and others. I am interested in this study in sports whose overt origin was in competition and playfulness, not survival, improvement of a breed of animals, or technological advancement. I am specifically interested in sports popularly dismissed as "mere sport," that

have no obvious purpose beyond the rules of the game—sports
that are clearly separated in the American mind from serious
activity or work. Boxing is a partial exception: its origin is undoubtedly a playful reenactment of the basic fight to survive,
or to assert one's superiority in primitive tribes. But boxing is
a purely human competition, in which rules are clearly defined and rigidly enforced. Thus, although it resembles hunting and bullfighting in some ways, it has popularly been considered a game.

The fiction dealing with these sports is largely a product of
the twentieth century, although its origins are in the nineteenth. The body of sports fiction in this century has grown so
large that it clearly defines a subgenre of the novel, as the
political novel, sea novel, or war novel can be thought of as
subgenres. In imitation of Irving Howe's definition of the political novel,[25] I define the sports novel simply as one in which
sport plays a dominant role or in which the sport milieu is the
dominant setting. A seemingly small, and maybe obvious, but
important addition to this definition must be made, however.
A sports novel is not a novel that happens to be about an athlete; rather, it is a novel that finds its vision of the individual
and his condition in the basic meaning of the sport he plays,
formerly played, or watches. The sports novel can concern
any of a number of popular American sports: golf, tennis,
track and field, swimming, and so on; but, in fact, almost all
our sports literature concerns baseball, football, boxing, or
basketball. The first three of these sports have elicited the
bulk of our sports fiction; the contribution of basketball is
very recent and not yet substantial. The most important reason for this is undoubtedly the early and continuing popularity
of baseball, football, and boxing—hence basketball, due to its
current popularity, is emerging only now as a dominant subject for sports fiction and will undoubtedly soon produce a
substantial literature of its own.

There are other reasons less obvious than simple popularity
why baseball, football, boxing, and basketball should receive
particular literary attention. Each of these four offers the
writer a vehicle for a distinct representation of reality. Baseball is our most pastoral game and combines most obviously

to the spectator a balance between offense and defense, individual and team, organization and individualism. Football is more complex, employs attack and defense motifs more clearly than baseball, and represents most obviously the subservience of the individual to the team effort for the common good. This emphasis on teamwork makes football perhaps the most middle class of sports; but it also has a reckless, desperate quality, and a certain grandeur, which perhaps accounts for its great popularity in the South now deprived of its blood sports.[26] Boxing represents most clearly the pitting of one man against another in a stark, impersonal environment; it is the most primitive of all sports. And basketball is the most artistic of our national games, the one allowing the most creativity and spontaneity by the players. Thus baseball in literature produces most often either a nostalgic remembrance of the past or a representation of the American innocent confronting complex reality; football becomes a ready metaphor for violence in all its forms or for the stifling of individuality by corporate America; boxing becomes the naturalists' representation of urban dehumanization; and basketball exemplifies the life of the individual ill-suited to regimentation and control.

All four sports are ideally suited to the technical problems of writing fiction. Sport solves a persistent problem for the American author by providing a center in this vast and heterogeneous country—an ordered universe like Melville's *Pequod* or Twain's Mississippi River—that can comprehend all the varieties of American people and ideas. Sport also provides other specific advantages to the writer of fiction. The duration of a single season, a single career, even a single game or fight with its preparation and aftermath all offer a distinct beginning, middle, and end for the construction of a novel. Conflicts, tension, and climaxes are built into the framework of sport, ready for translation into fiction. Each sport offers a ready-made cast of recognizable characters which writers can easily manipulate. The game itself establishes a focal point around which the characters cluster and in relation to which they reveal their personalities and opinions. Even the division of a novel into chapters can be dictated by the nine innings of a baseball game, the four quarters of a football contest, the ten rounds of a boxing match, or any of a number of other such natural components.[27]

Sport even offers specific advantages to the writer of experimental fiction. No human activity is more thoroughly regulated and ordered than sport, so the author's imagination can strain against this natural order of the material to produce a controlling tension. Because the mechanics of the sport and the stereotypical sports figures can be assumed by the author to be the common knowledge of the book's readers, he or she need not establish a normative model before beginning to deviate from it. Moreover, few activities so combine reality and fantasy in such paradoxical ways as does sport: the realities of hard work, business practice, discipline, and failure; and the fantasy dreams of freedom, perpetual youth, and heroism. All sports epitomize American dreams, fears, and obsessions; qualities like rugged individualism, teamwork, striving for the pinnacle of one's profession, self-reliance, fair play, and fear of retirement or failure are as intrinsic to American attitudes towards life as they are to sport. Sport is both a metaphor for American life and an escape from the banality or complexity of life. It is an expression of values fundamentally important to the American people, a reinforcement of those values, and at times an illusion that certain of those values—like equal opportunity—truly exist in the society. Sport thus offers the writer an ideal microcosm for analyzing and criticizing these American characteristics.

It is, therefore, remarkable that sport has so long been denigrated as a subject for serious literature. There is obvious justification for this snobbery regarding the bulk of sports fiction, but not regarding the entire possibility of sports fiction as a genre. Early sports fiction in the nineteenth century includes no literary gems. The earliest writing of this type in America is largely found in dime novels and boys' weeklies.[28] *St. Nicholas* (1873-1930), the best and longest running children's magazine of the era, contained many sports stories, as did Street and Smith's *All-Sports Library* and Frank Tousey's *Work and Win, Pluck and Luck, The Young Athlete's Weekly,* and *Wide Awake Weekly.* The earliest known novel incorporating baseball activity is William Everett's *Changing Base*

(1868), and the first novel devoted entirely to baseball is Noah Brooks' *Our Baseball Club* (1884). Football arrived a little later on the literary scene; one chapter of Mark Severance's *Hammersmith: His Harvard Days* (1878) describes a football match. And Richard Harding Davis' "Gallegher," found in *Gallegher and Other Stories* (1891), is among the earliest fiction to describe boxing. Although the first of the major sports to appear in America, boxing was late in providing a literature. The supposed (and often real) depravity of the sport kept it out of even subliterary genres until Jack London gave it literary respectability in 1905 with *The Game*.[29]

The real father of American sports fiction, however, was Gilbert Patten who, under the pseudonym "Burt L. Standish," published a Frank or Dick Merriwell story every week in Street and Smith's *Tip Top Weekly* for sixteen years (1896-1912), with total publication as high as 500 million copies.[30] The early writers created simple stereotypical characters and predictable plots without any notable stylistic skill. Patten and his imitators—Ralph Henry Barbour, William Heyliger, the writers in the Stratemeyer syndicate, and the other authors of schoolboy stories—did not even aspire to high art, but they did establish the traditions of American sports fiction within which and against which serious authors wrote.

Although these men were typical writers of sports fiction, they are by no means the only practitioners of the art. Unfortunately, "sports fiction" to many readers means nothing more than these clumsy oversimplified stories. Of the hundreds of writers who subsequently wrote sports novels, only Jack London, Ring Lardner, Bernard Malamud, and perhaps Robert Coover and Philip Roth are widely read in American universities; and their sports fiction is rarely the source of the selections read. But the number of "major" American writers who, while not writing straight sports fiction, included sport in a minor way in their work is considerable and impressive. Frank Norris played one year of football in high school before a broken arm ended his career, and Richard Harding Davis played the game in college. Both contributed short stories about sport to the more substantial body of their nonsport writing. Norris's "Travis Hallett's Half Back," "Shorty Stack, Pugilist," and "This Animal of a Buldy Jones" concern a foot-

ball player, a boxer, and a baseball player respectively. Added
to his sports reporting for the *San Fancisco Wave,* they reflect
Norris's considerable interest in sport. As early as 1894, he had
described in his fiction the clichéd idea that sport was a valuable testing ground for the later rigors of life. Davis was more
active as an athlete himself, and many of his tales in *Stories
for Boys* (1894) are concerned with sport. The rest provide in-
cidentally some detail of sporting life.

Sherwood Anderson played baseball, as he records in his
Memoirs (1942), and he writes in *Beyond Desire* (1932) of
Red Oliver and Ned Sawyer, two ex-ballplayers. Sinclair Lewis
and John O'Hara satirized the country club businessman-
athlete, and Elmer Gantry and Judson Roberts from Lewis's
Elmer Gantry (1927) are ex-football heroes. F. Scott Fitzgerald played football, basketball, and baseball, although "his
athletic career was an unbroken series of unadmitted defeats."[31] Despite these failures, his capacity for hero worship
never diminished: one hero—Hobey Baker of Princeton—appears in *This Side of Paradise* (1920); and athletics figure
prominently in the Basil Duke Lee stories (1928-29) such as
"The Freshest Boy," as well as in the characterization of Tom
Buchanan in *The Great Gatsby* (1925).

One of Thomas Wolfe's most memorable characters is Ne-
braska Crane, the baseball player in *You Can't Go Home
Again* (1940) and *The Web and the Rock* (1939). The latter
novel also mentions Jim Randolph, an ex-football star, and
chronicles the Dempsey-Firpo fight. James T. Farrell—like
Anderson, a former player—has the heroes in his Studs Lonigan trilogy and Danny O'Neill tetralogy "move from early
romanticizing of sports and its heroes to a disillusioned realization that this early overvaluation of athletic endeavor has
helped to ruin their lives."[32] In addition, at least half of Farrell's short stories contain some reference to sport,[33] particularly baseball, and he published his own baseball reminiscences in *My Baseball Diary* (1957).

Ernest Hemingway elevated the sportsman to a code hero.
Among his writings are short stories on boxing; the characterization of Robert Cohn, the ex-athlete of *The Sun Also Rises*
(1927); and Santiago's veneration of Joe DiMaggio in *The
Old Man and the Sea* (1952). William Faulkner was less in-

terested in sport than Hemingway, but he created the football players Labove of *The Hamlet* (1940) and Charles Mallison of *Intruder in the Dust* (1948), and made a trip to a baseball game in *Sanctuary* (1931) the original escapade that leads to the action of that novel.[34]

The character of Bo-Jo Brown in J. P. Marquand's *H. M. Pulham, Esq.* (1941) is intended by the author in his preface "to be recognized at once as a familiar type formed by college athletics." Both Robert Penn Warren in *All the King's Men* (1946) and William Styron in *Lie Down in Darkness* (1951) utilize football scenes. James Jones' hero of *From Here to Eternity* (1953), Robert E. Lee Prewitt, is a boxer. And John Steinbeck's Victor in *Burning Bright* (1950) is an ex-athlete.

While this list could be broadened, it already encompasses a significant number of the important American writers of the twentieth century. If we add dramatists who use athletes or ex-athletes in their plays—Robert Sherwood (Boze Hertzlinger of *The Petrified Forest* [1931]), William Inge (Hal Carter of *Picnic* [1942] and Turk of *Come Back, Little Sheba* [1940]), Arthur Miller (Biff Loman of *Death of a Salesman* [1939]), Eugene O'Neill (Bill Herron and Jack Townsend of *Abortion* [1914], Gordon Shaw of *Strange Interlude* [1928]), Tennessee Williams (Brick Pollitt of *Cat on a Hot Tin Roof* [1944]), and Clifford Odets (*Golden Boy* [1937])—the list is indeed impressive. Three recent plays—Howard Sackler's *The Great White Hope* (1968), Jason Miller's *That Championship Season* (1972), and Jonathan Reynolds' *Yanks 3, Detroit 0, Top of the Seventh* (1975)—are particularly notable because sport is central in them, not peripheral.

Even without these familiar names, straight sports fiction comprises an impressive body of work that stands on its own merits and failures and needs no apologetic reference to Hemingway or Faulkner. The prejudice against sport as a subject for serious fiction is truly surprising, as is the fact that sports fiction, with few exceptions, has never been truly popular. The most consistently popular type of sports fiction has been juvenile literature. No one has ever matched the popularity of Frank Merriwell, but Barbour, Heyliger, John R. Tunis, and others have had fairly large readerships, and juvenile sports novels taken as a body have been well read—several are published every year. This is sports fiction for boys, however, and herein lies the root of the failure of adult sports fiction to attract a wider audience. The prejudice has long endured that sports are mere boys' games. Adults play sports, too, but the consensus of American adults who consider these things at all would echo the Puritan distrust of games and claim that sports is play and, therefore, by definition not serious. Work is the American adult's primary concern, a source of values, measurement of success, and identity as a person. Professional sports are also work, of course, but professional athletes are actually just entertainers, not true professionals—so the argument seems to go.

The few writers of sports fiction who were popular can be quickly mentioned. Jack London was the most popular writer of his time, but his boxing novels were not prominent among his best sellers, and he is not widely read today. Ring Lardner, according to his biographer Donald Elder, in 1926 was among the ten most famous men in the United States[35] and admired by the critics as well, but he suffered doubly from the prejudice against sports as a good writer's subject for fiction. Even the critics who admired his work impatiently awaited his turning away from his apprenticeship as a mere sportswriter to the true talents that his artistry predicted.[36] Even more sadly, he himself became disillusioned with sport, or rather with the athletes and fans who distorted its simple purity, to the point that he received little pleasure or satisfaction from much of his writing.

No major writer reentered the sports fiction arena until Bernard Malamud wrote *The Natural* in 1952, because writers who aspired to great artistry undoubtedly were aware of the widespread debunking of sport. Malamud was not yet a major writer when he wrote *The Natural,* his first novel. In fact, several of the superior sports novels were early novels by writers who then moved on to other topics. In addition to Malamud, Mark Harris turned early to sport with a trilogy of baseball novels: *The Southpaw* (1953), *Bang the Drum Slowly* (1956), and *A Ticket for a Seamstitch* (1957). In an interview eight years after the publication of the last of these, Harris cites the frustrating limitations that a semiliterate athlete-narrator imposes on the writer and implicitly dismisses his baseball novels as a stage he had to pass through as a young writer on his way to more serious fiction.[37] Despite such disclaimers, two of his baseball novels are better than anything he has written since, and the recent publication of a fourth baseball book—*It Looked Like For Ever* (1979)—suggests perhaps a change of heart about baseball's possibilities for serious fiction. Frederick Exley's first novel, *A Fan's Notes* (1968), recounts his fascination with Frank Gifford of the New York Giants and establishes the narrator as a vicarious, not an active, participant in life. The theme is repeated in his next novel, *Pages from a Cold Island* (1975), about the critic Edmund Wilson, but not so successfully.

Recent writers have been liberated, however, by the shifting awareness of the importance of sport in American culture. Robert Coover and Don DeLillo wrote sports novels as second novels, but Coover has also written other sports pieces as well—"McDuff on the Mound" and "Whatever Happened to Gloomy Gus of the Chicago Bears?" (1975)—and DeLillo focuses on games or sports in parts of four of his six novels. These examples, and the fact that Philip Roth was already an established and important writer when he wrote *The Great American Novel* (1973) (he acknowledges that the examples of Lardner, Harris, and Malamud suggested the possibility of writing a good novel about baseball, although for a long time "a certain snobbishness about the material held my own imagination in check"[38]), indicate that sport has now been accepted by the arbiters of literary quality as an acceptable subject for fiction.

Although this one hurdle has been cleared, the other remains—none of these novels has been truly popular. The only recent popular sports novels are *Semi-Tough* (1972), a legitimate "best seller" by Dan Jenkins, and to a lesser degree *North Dallas Forty* (1973) by Peter Gent. It is a long time from Lardner to Jenkins, and the elements of the latter's novel that made it popular are quite obvious: humor and sex. Gent substitutes drugs, violence, and a tell-it-like-it-is style for Jenkins' humor, but between the two writers, we have the five elements most likely to attract a popular audience. Subsequent sex-and-violence sports novels have not captured the same wide audience, however, and it is possible to conjecture about the dilemma of the sports novelist. *Semi-Tough* and *North Dallas Forty*, in addition to having the proper ingredients for becoming best-sellers, were favorably and prominently reviewed. In order for a relatively unknown author to attract a large audience, the book must be well reviewed. But most of those books which are praised by the critics—*The Natural* (Malamud 1952), *The Universal Baseball Association* (Coover 1968), and *End Zone* (DeLillo 1972)—do not also have the ingredients the mass audience desires for leisure reading. To both please the critics and satisfy the canons of popular taste is difficult.

The writer of sports fiction is thus affected by prejudices in the marketplace over which there is little control, but the writer is also caught in a dilemma created by the subject. The mass of Americans who are most interested in sports prefer to play them or watch them, not read about them. Sport means entertainment to most Americans, and reading about sport would simply be less interesting entertainment—it would have the illusion of immediacy rather than the real thing. Nonfiction sports books are more likely to be popular—Jim Bouton's *Ball Four*[39] is a good example—because such books satisfy the sports fan's desire for information, particularly exposés, about the athletes he or she follows. If we compare sports fiction to either science fiction or detective fiction in this context, the disadvantages of sports fiction are obvious. No one can live in the year 2000 or be teleported to distant galaxies; few can solve mysteries or coolly confront brutal danger and survive. But a great many ordinary citizens could hit a home-run in the bottom of the ninth to win a recreation league softball game, and everyone can watch actual sports heroes on television for many hours every week. The pleasures offered by science fiction and detective fiction can only be received from books—they are necessarily vicarious pleasures. But the pleasures of sport can be gained more intensely outside of books; to read sports fiction one must seek the pleasures of reading.

A person who is not interested in sports is even less likely to want to read about them. Even a serious student or connoisseur of good literature is less likely to read a well-reviewed sports novel than a well-reviewed novel on another subject, unless the sports novel is acclaimed so highly that it cannot be ignored. Once again the writer of sports fiction is caught in limbo.

It is easy to predict optimistically the continued appearance of exceptional sports fiction in the wake of the fine novels of the past quarter century. Scholars in many fields—historians such as John Rickards Betts, sociologists such as Jack Scott and Harry Edwards, psychologists such as Arnold Beisser and Susan Dorcas Butts, and even philosophers like Paul Weiss and Michael Novak[40]—are revealing the critical impact of sport on American culture and on the American individual. Writers of fiction will surely respond to this growing awareness of the importance of sport, but unfortunately it is not so easy to predict that these novels will necessarily be popular. This new attitude toward sport will possibly educate a large audience who will then want to read the latest fiction on the subject, but it is more likely that the popular sports novels of the next several years will be thinly disguised romans à clef about the incidence of homosexuality in pro football or about the sexual gymnastics of jet-setting tennis pros. It is quite possible that the joining of popularity and quality in a sports novel will continue to be elusive—more elusive than in other fiction. It is a strange anomaly that the literature about one of the most popular activities in American culture is not itself popular, but such is the case.

The inevitable lack of popularity, however, does not detract from the accomplishments of the authors of sports fiction who have written in a rich tradition. "Adult" or "serious" sports fiction began later than the juvenile origins of the genre and was influenced by frontier literature as well as by the juvenile fiction.[41] With the notable exception of Jack London, the earliest sports fictionists in the twentieth century were to a large extent sports writers, and even London did *some* reporting of boxing matches. Sports journalists in the 1880s, particularly in Chicago, developed a style in their columns that stressed humor and ingenious use of sports slang rather than mere factual reporting.[42] The first leaders— Leonard Washburn, Peter Finley Dunne, and Charlie Seymour—evolved the style that later served Ring Lardner, Charles E. Van Loan, Damon Runyon, Heywood Broun, Ru-

pert Hughes, and other early writers of sports fiction. These
men were themselves sports reporters, and this dominance
of the fictional writing about sport by the sports columnists
is seen even today in such writers as Dan Jenkins, Tex Maule,
Frank Deford, and Jack Olsen of *Sports Illustrated*, as well as
many others. The early tone established by the sports journalists was sardonic or frivolous, and their use of language was
wildly inventive. The excesses of their originality with language were so evident that they received satiric treatment in
Owen Johnson's *The Humming Bird* in 1910.[43]

These early sports reporter/fictionists knew each other
and promoted each other's work. Van Loan, for example, was
instrumental in having Lardner's earliest work published in
the *Saturday Evening Post*. This period marks the beginning
of a conscious sports fiction tradition of which Lardner was
the most important early figure. Both Hemingway and Farrell consciously imitated Lardner's style early in their careers, and, as late as 1958, Farrell acknowledged Lardner as
the author of "the definitive work of fiction on baseball."[44]
Mark Harris was likewise aware of following Lardner; and
Philip Roth recognizes Lardner, Harris, and Malamud as his
predecessors in writing about baseball.

Baseball was the sport of the early writers, followed by boxing. Short stories were more common than novels, as one
might expect from writers whose profession teaches the importance of concision, the sharply drawn image, and a swift
pace. The twenties, thirties, and forties were dominated first
by the college football novel and a bit later by the boxing
novel—the work of the naturalists. The fifties saw a return to
baseball as a primary topic with the postwar boom in interest
in the game, and more recently the professional football novel
assumed the leadership in quantity if not quality of output. In
the past decade, basketball novels have made their most significant appearance. Artistically, the crucial history of the
genre focuses on Jack London, who identified the primary
themes that future sports fictionists would probe; Ring Lardner, who with greater artistic skill used sport as a microcosm
of American society; and Bernard Malamud, who freed the
genre from the limitations of strict realism and prepared the
way for Robert Coover, Don DeLillo, and other superior

writers. Quality novels have come from all four sports: Budd Schulberg's *The Harder They Fall* (1947), W. C. Heinz's *The Professional* (1958), and Leonard Gardner's *Fat City* (1969) are the best of a generally routine lot of boxing novels; the best football novels are *A Fan's Notes* (1968) by Frederick Exley and *End Zone* (1972) by Don DeLillo; and the best baseball novels are Bernard Malamud's *The Natural* (1952), Mark Harris' *The Southpaw* (1953) and *Bang the Drum Slowly* (1956), and Robert Coover's *The Universal Baseball Association* (1968). Basketball has been most distinguished by John Updike's *Rabbit, Run* (1960), a novel which has little actual basketball action, but which uses basketball impressively as a central metaphor. Baseball has contributed more good novels than the other three sports; because of its pastoral origins, its mathematical symmetry, and its obvious mythic quality, it has attracted more fine writers. In addition to the novels just mentioned, Ring Lardner's *You Know Me Al* (1916) and Philip Roth's *The Great American Novel* (1973) head a list of other significant baseball fictions.

On subliterary and nonliterary levels, the varieties of sport art have had a consistent but limited popularity. Juvenile sports novels have had a constant readership after the initial Merriwell mania died down and have figured importantly in the childhood of millions of Americans. Such sports pulps as *Sport Story, Fight Stories, Baseball Stories, Exciting Football, Popular Sports, Thrilling Sports, Super Sports,* and *Dime Sports* had their vogue in the twenties, thirties, and forties, although they never were as popular as the westerns or romances. Cartoon strips were made of "Frank Merriwell" and "You Know Me Al." In addition to the earliest strips—"Mutt and Jeff," "Joe and Asbestos," and "Barney Google"—that centered on horse racing, others have concerned sport as I have defined it: "Curly Kayoe" and "Joe Jinks" by Sam Leff, "Joe Palooka" by Ham Fisher, "Ozark Ike" by Ray Gotto, and "Big Ben Bolt" by John Cullen Murphy.[45] Sports movies have been produced by the hundreds, but with the notable exceptions of comedies starring Charlie Chaplin (*The Champion* [1915]), Harold Lloyd (*The Freshman* [1914]), Buster Keaton (*College* [1917] and *Battling Butler* [1926]), and a few others, the vast majority of the early films were dreadful.[46] This trend has shifted abruptly in recent years, however. Film versions of good sports novels have proliferated; in addition to movie remakes of such British works as *This Sporting Life* and *The Loneliness of the Long Distance Runner*, a number of fine American films have emerged including *The Great White Hope, Bang the Drum Slowly, Fat City, The Bad News Bears, The Bingo Long Traveling All-Stars and Motor Kings, Slap Shot, Rocky, One on One, North Dallas Forty* and *Raging Bull*. The unpopularity of sports fiction is starkly contrasted to the popularity of many of these films. Perhaps movies provide the sense of participatory spectatorism that the sports fan requires and that fiction does not provide. Sport has also spawned a great deal of music, although few notable songs. The earliest tunes—"The Base Ball Polka" (1858), "Home Run Quick Step" (1861), and dozens of others—as well as songs of more recent vintage, have long been forgotten. Only Albert von Tilzer's "Take Me Out to the Ball Game" (1908) has survived.[47] The popular theater and vaudeville presented such temporarily popular plays as *A Base Hit, The Girl and the Pennant, Body and Soul,* to name but a few, but no masterpieces.[48] With the few exceptions noted earlier, legitimate theater has largely avoided sporting themes, but other high art forms have not been so restrictive. Winslow Homer, Frederick Remington, Thomas Eakins, and George Bellows head a list of painters of sporting scenes, and R. Tait McKenzie was the most prolific of the sculptors of sport.[49] These artists, perhaps better than anyone else, have recognized that sport itself is art.

It is primarily in literature, however, that the broad range of athletic themes and styles is explored. The variety of literary presentations of sport is indeed remarkable. Fantasies such as H. Allen Smith's *Rhubarb* (1946), Valentine Davies' *It Happens Every Spring* (1949), Douglas Wallop's *The Year the Yankees Lost the Pennant* (1954), Bud Nye's *Stay Loose* (1959), Paul Molloy's *A Pennant for the Kremlin* (1964), Marvin Karlins' *The Last Man Is Out* (1969), Hal Higdon's *The Horse That Played Center Field* (1969), and Paul Gallico's *Matilda* (1970) are so numerous as to define a subgenre of the sports fiction genre. Another subgenre might be termed the sports-mystery novel, which dates at least to Cortland Fitzsimmons' *70,000 Witnesses* (1931), *Death on the Diamond* (1935), and *Crimson Ice* (1935), and that has been very evident in recent novels of terrorist attacks at sporting events, such as Thomas Harris' *Black Sunday* (1975), George La Fountaine's *Two-Minute Warning* (1975), and Russell Braddon's *The Finalists* (1977). Jack London's "The Mexican" (1913) is a propagandistic revolutionary tract; Martin H. Greenberg and Joseph D. Olander collected stories that combine sport and science fiction in *Run to Starlight* (1975); Robert Coover's "Whatever Happened to Gloomy Gus of the Chicago Bears?" (1975) is political satire. The short story in general is a mode of fiction ideally suited to the treatment of athletics because most sports hinge on crucial moments that can be perfectly realized in the short story form.

Poets have not neglected sport either. Kenneth Koch has written an epic poem about baseball, among other things, titled *Ko, or a Season on Earth* (1959). A great deal of doggerel sports verse has been written, but there have also been poems by writers such as Carl Sandburg ("Hits and Runs"), Marianne Moore ("Baseball and Writing"), Edwin Arlington Robinson ("A Mighty Runner"), Vachel Lindsay ("John L. Sullivan, the Strong Boy of Boston"), William Carlos Williams ("At the Ball Game"), Rolfe Humphries ("Polo Grounds"), Robert Fitzgerald ("Cobb Would Have Caught It"), Robert Wallace ("The Double Play"), and James Dickey ("In the Pocket"); as well as the better known "Casey at the Bat" by Ernest Lawrence Thayer.[50] Walt Whitman's "The Runner" could even be included in this list.

A great many fine writers have obviously written briefly about sport, but the main focus of this study is sports novels— full-length works that probe deeply into the meaning of sport in America—and it is possible to make some generalizations about this fiction. Sport means many things to many people; to Michael Novak, for example, sport represents the celebration of physical capabilities, mental discipline, and emotional spontaneity—a true religious experience, the fullest expression of our humanity.[51] Against this ideal of what the games are in themselves or what they can be, the reality of owners, players, and fans often intrudes to distort or pervert its value. Walter O'Malley taking his Dodgers to Los Angeles from

Brooklyn, where they had literally been the heart and soul of the community, and leading other owners to do the same; players sacrificing loyalty for the enticements of the marketplace; fans hurling bottles at umpires or spitting on players— these are too often the realities of sport in America. There has been little sports fiction that emphasizes the positive aspects of sport, with the exception of simpleminded novels that simply do not acknowledge any criticism of their sport, and which celebrate essentially spurious or fictitious values in sentimental or melodramatic ways. For example, a novel that describes the unimpeded rise of a disadvantaged youth to fame and glory, as well as to moral maturity, too often celebrates the ideal of sport without acknowledging at all the intrusion of a less-than-ideal real world. The majority of serious sports novels emphasize the negative impact of sports on individuals or on the culture—the fact that sports heroes are often self-centered and infantile, that sports corrupt innocent virtues, that they grind individualism down into corporate sameness, that they incapacitate athletes for any meaningful relationship with women. The essential conflict between the game itself and the individuals who play, watch, or control it makes sport as susceptible as other human institutions to corruption by excess, but these criticisms are but one side of sport. Babe Ruth may have been a self-centered bum, but as a sports hero he was also a vital source of cultural value and community identity. Sports can retard maturity and obstruct the athlete's ability to function in the real world, but they also celebrate youth, the spirit of play, sportsmanship, camaraderie, and immortality. Team sports—particularly football— may too often crush individualism; but cooperation, commitment of self to a larger idea, and willingness to assume a supporting role can be positive virtues necessary to even the most utopian of societies. Sports can reinforce destructive sexual stereotypes, but the supposed "masculine" qualities of sport —mental and physical toughness, even competitiveness and aggressiveness—would be sorely missed if removed from our culture and are cultivated in few places as fully as in sport. As we become more comfortable with acceptance of sexual differences that don't impute superiority to either sex or required behavior to any individual, we may find the survival of these "masculine" ideals particularly important.

Sport is all of these things, the best and worst in American culture, because it is at the center of American experience. This study may appear to emphasize the negative in sport nearly to the exclusion of the positive, because that is what the fiction largely does (our definitions of "realism" unfortunately demand this). But the best sports novels—those by Malamud, Coover, DeLillo, Exley, Updike and others—deal more subtly with the complex reality of sport in America. Even in their nay-saying, these novels by implication reflect what might be or might have been. Although the reality of sport culture can be brutal or dehumanizing, in their essence the games celebrate life, the vitality of the spirit, and human potential; the best novels understand both sides well.

Within the diversity of forms and the various styles utilized to express them in fiction—Lardnerian satire, Hemingway's clipped prose, journalistic reportage, and the convoluted complex styles of recent mythic novels—a mainstream can be defined in the sports fiction genre. The themes most consistently explored in American sports fiction are examinations of fundamental archetypal patterns in American experience. This study traces these patterns—from a definition of the athlete-hero to the oppositions of country and city, youth and age, masculinity and femininity, and finally to an examination of the use of history and myth in the sports fiction. The book attempts to be comprehensive but it does not focus primarily on the *history* of sports fiction in this country. The fact that each novel follows the previous ones is certainly important in the development of the genre, but there was no orderly progression among the writers of sports fiction—to claim so would be misleading, but to discuss 100-odd representative works as discrete units would be tedious. The focus here is on the themes of sports fiction, for all of the works display amazing unanimity in their major interests, and naturally so, because they portray issues fictionally that are essential to the nature of sport in America.

The history of sports fiction briefly sketched out earlier is, however, reflected in the arrangement of my chapters. Although my focus is primarily thematic rather than historical, the organization of my chapters is roughly chronological none-theless. The focus of Chapter 2 is on juvenile sports fiction and its early beginnings, for that is where the hero was initially defined. Juvenile sports fiction is the origin of the entire gen-re. When sports fictionists began writing for adults, much of their work dealt with country and city—the subject of the next chapter—for the loss of the frontier experience and the rise of the city were recent and not fully accommodated. Chapter 3 focuses primarily on the rubes and naturals of early writers such as Jack London, Ring Lardner, Zane Grey, and Charles E. Van Loan; and on the writers of boxing fiction who suc-ceeded them in the thirties and forties as the city became real-ity for most Americans and its impact was being deeply felt. (However, this chapter also includes basketball fiction, which is among the most recent contributions to the genre.)

Chapter 4 is dominated by writers at midcentury who, fol-lowing the second of two devastating world wars and realizing fully the complexity of modern civilization, wrote of lost inno-cence, of clinging to a youthful past, and of the pain of aging and maturity. This period was followed by one in which American sport was dominated by football, the most sexually charged of our major sports. The reemergence of a powerful women's movement occurred at this time also, to challenge traditional sexual roles and cause American males to cling even more tenaciously to their all-male sports. Chapter 5 on sexual roles deals with these matters. Finally, Chapter 6 on history and myth focuses on Bernard Malamud and his suc-cessors, the contemporary writers such as Robert Coover, Don DeLillo, and Philip Roth who realized the deeply mythic significance of American sports and applied this awareness to their fiction. Their novels represent the artistic pinnacle of sports fiction to date, and they may indicate the trend of fu-ture years as well. As sport is increasingly revealed to have a vital importance in American life, skilled writers will express this expanded sports consciousness in fiction. Thus, we can identify a roughly chronological development of the sports fic-tion genre by periods: a hero period, a country-and-city period, a youth-and-age period, a sexual-role period, and a mythic period. While all of these themes are treated throughout the history of sports fiction, they identify dominant tendencies in a chronological sequence as well.

In claiming that this study is comprehensive, I am not saying that it discusses every sports novel written in America nor that I have even read them all. What I am saying is that it discusses all of the first-rate sports novels and a large representative number of second- and third-rate ones. I am further claiming that any of the novels not included here could be and even that sports novels yet to be written (until our basic national myths undergo substantial revision) can also be discussed under these same topics, because the themes on which this study focuses define the importance of sports to Americans. Because of this importance, even the cruder, oversimplified novels are valuable. In defining patterns and polarities in American thought, they not only provide an important index to American culture, but also stand as the norm against which our serious fiction contends or the extreme positions which our more complex novels question or modify. The first-rate sports novels, of course, do challenge the stereotypes central to sport and view American culture with all the complexity of our best literature. In doing so, they establish a genre within American fiction that demands our serious attention.

two

Frank Merriwell's Sons:
The American
Athlete-Hero

Mens sana in corpore sano.
—Juvenal, *Satires*, X., 356.

E very sports novel begins with a hero. The sports world itself is the particular domain of heroes, and the fiction that
describes sports must focus on this essential fact. When fans
think about baseball, their first reflections are not likely to be
on the perfect balance between offense and defense or on the
pastoral space and timelessness of the game. Rather, they
will recall Babe Ruth, clouting a game-winning homerun, the
catch they saw Willie Mays make in a game in 1962, or some
more recent exploit by a star of a favorite team who might
win the current batting title. When those fans think about football, they probably do not consider the subtle intricacy of a
play dependent on the coordination of eleven individual athletes, but rather they remember Red Grange, the pass they
themselves caught to win a high school game in the last minute, or O. J. Simpson accelerating out of the grasp of the last
tackler between himself and the goal line. Sport exists, in a
sense, to create heroes, and sports fiction can be viewed from
one perspective as a genre that defines exactly who the representative American hero is. American fascination with sports
heroes consumes an enormous amount of psychic energy—

25

those heroes must embody something very close to our national identity.

The hero-making impulse is strong in this country for a number of reasons. In such a new nation, because genuine folk heroes have not had centuries in which to grow in the minds of the people, many of our heroes were created deliberately. George Washington needed Parson Weems's fictionalizing to become a living symbol in schoolchildren's imaginations; Paul Bunyan was the offspring of an advertising campaign for the Red River Lumber Company. As Americans developed a national consciousness during the nineteenth century, they thought of themselves in two contrasting ways that fed the creation of heroes. On the one hand, America itself had heroic dimensions—the first grand-scale experiment in democracy; a virgin land uncorrupted by decadent European aristocracies; a land of freedom, openhandedness, and unlimited aspiration. Legendary heroes such as Pecos Bill and John Henry and fictionalized real persons such as Davy Crockett, Buffalo Bill, and Kit Carson were invested by the public fancy with the superhuman powers of natural sons of the American landscape. On the other hand, many Americans, including some of our important writers, looked to the wealth of European traditions and culture and lamented the paucity of genius, beauty, and native material in their own country. To become truly educated and cultured, an American had to travel to Europe, usually to live for an extended period of time. American architecture, art, reading tastes, and fashion were all dictated by European models. If native pride led to the creation of distinctive national heroes, these feelings of inadequacy and mediocrity likewise necessitated such heroes for reassurance that, in breaking from Europe, we had not lost more than we gained. Perhaps a democracy, lacking an acknowledged elite, particularly needs heroes.

The athlete-hero is one product of this hero-making impulse and an especially prominent one in American society. In fact, today, in an age of disillusionment when contemporary heroes are anti-heroes—embodying negative virtues of withdrawal or refusal—the athlete-hero is remarkably similar to his earliest appearances on the American scene. The apolitical, asocial, amoral, even timeless, placeless quality of the athletic contest itself enables the heroes of those contests to remain unchanged after decades. A baseball game is essentially the same in Tallahassee as in Minneapolis, in 1980 as in 1880. An athlete who participates in such a contest can perform the same heroic deeds today that his forerunners performed in the first baseball and football games generations ago. While to much of the public formerly revered soldiers have become exploiters of oppressed peoples and politicians are seen as abettors of age-old wrongs, a baseball player can still hit a home run in the bottom of the ninth to win the game, and a halfback can still zigzag ninety yards for the winning touchdown in the last minute of play. Commercialism and especially television have reduced the imaginative possibilities in American sports, but heroics are still possible—at any moment of any game. Every contest has its hero or heroes; sport itself is an arena for imminent heroics.

This chapter will explore the precise nature of the American athlete-hero. The purest embodiment of this figure is the hero of juvenile sports fiction, who became the norm for all subsequent sports heroes. His importance will be discussed shortly, but first he must be clearly identified.

The athlete-hero was born on April 18, 1896, in Street and Smith's *Tip Top Library* (later *Tip Top Weekly*) when Frank Merriwell stepped from the train at Fardale Academy to begin a career that covered over sixteen years and eight hundred-fifty issues of the magazine and reached the larger part of the nation in some form. Sports fiction existed before Gilbert Patten, writing under the pseudonym "Burl L. Standish," created his all-American hero. The parent of all schoolboy fiction,[1] Thomas Hughes's *Tom Brown's School Days,* published in England in 1857, was Merriwell's remote ancestor; but the first known American novel devoted exclusively to sports was Noah Brook's *Our Baseball Club*, written in 1884. *Beadle's Half-Dime Library* included four novels about "pitcher-detectives,"[2] and a few other scattered novels preceded Merriwell, but none of these was particularly popular, and it was Patten who discovered the formula that made Frank Merriwell one of the most widely known heroes in all American fiction. Between 1896 and 1912, Patten produced a Merriwell "novel" every week, and even after Patten quit *Tip Top Weekly,* his hero was continued for three more years in 136 issues written by other hacks. Even then, Frank, his brother Dick, and his son Frank, Jr., were not laid to rest. In addition to publishing them in *Tip Top Weekly,* Street and Smith reprinted the stories in 217 book-length editions,[3] and in the thirties Frank was resurrected first on radio and then in a comic strip. Patten's estimate that as many as 500 million Merriwell titles were sold is undoubtedly exaggerated, but the number is certainly great, and it is impossible to estimate how many knew Frank through the other media.

The Merriwell Saga[4] saw Frank enter Fardale Academy, graduate to Yale, and move on from Yale to the world. He discovered his long-absent brother Dick in the American West and sent him through Fardale and Yale, too. The writers who succeeded Patten had Frank, Jr., enter Fardale after Dick graduated from Yale, but the magazine folded before the youngest Merriwell could finish his education. School days for both Frank and Dick revolved around loyal and often eccentric friends, thoroughly villainous enemies, adoring women, daring rescues, mysteries to be solved, and athletic triumph after athletic triumph—all in an atmosphere of joviality, boyish enthusiasm, and sterling virtue. The Merriwells spent their vacations in Europe, Africa, South America, and the American West, where they fought the native villains and indigenous beasts and discovered local treasures. While Frank was at both Fardale and Yale, his alma mater did not lose a single important athletic contest, as Frank starred in football, baseball, crew, cycling, boxing, and all events in track and field—the dashes, halfmile, mile, pole vault, broad jump, high jump, and hammerthrow. Frank also left school for a time, during which he worked for a railroad, settled a strike, wrote a hit play, and bought a horse that won the English Derby and broke the course record at St. Andrews. Dick's career was a recapitulation of Frank's, and Frank, Jr.'s, was well on its way to a second retelling when the demise of the magazine interrupted it.

Friends were colorful and varied, came in all sizes, spoke a wide range of comic dialects, but were above all loyal to their beloved Merriwell. Villains either came eventually to love the hero or met suitable punishments of disgrace, banishment, or even death. All of the girls were attracted to Merriwell first and then to his friends when the hero's attentions were seen to be reserved for his own true love. Frank had two serious paramours, fair Elsie and dark Inza. Elsie later married one of Frank's best friends, though continuing to love Frank with platonic passion after she lost out to her rival. Frank wooed Inza to the extent of two kisses over a period of several years, finally marrying her, and somehow begetting on her Frank, Jr. Dick had an equally chaste and drawnout love affair with June Arlington.

These are only the broadest outlines of the saga, and a wealth of detail, fascinating in its outrageous incredibility, could be mentioned, but the important point is that Frank Merriwell became the model for a tradition of juvenile sports literature that continues to the present. From Ralph Henry Barbour and William Heyliger to John R. Tunis and Wilfred McCormick, authors of juvenile literature have created characters modeled as somewhat more realistic Frank Merriwells. They are the purest embodiment of the athlete-hero in America and in American sports fiction.

This prototypical athlete-hero is easily recognizable in a sample of juvenile novels covering a seventy-five year period (1899-1974) and written by the major writers of juvenile sports fiction.[5] It is hardly possible, in defining the athlete-hero and the hero tale, to be as precise or as dogmatic as, for example, Vladimir Propp can be in his *Morphology of the Folktale* in which he claims to identify *every* element that can appear in a fairy tale and the order in which they must appear.[6] These juvenile novels are composed works; they do not follow the oral traditions of a folk and are consequently not so formulaic as fairy tales. They also span a period of American history that has seen enormous social changes and have responded occasionally to popular cultural trends. For example, several novels of recent years have become more self-conscious about social issues—racial and sexual equality particularly—than was the older "classical" juvenile sports fiction. There can be no rigid model for all such writing, but juvenile sports novels do follow at least a loose formula, and it is possible to describe the elements of that formula broadly. Juvenile sports authors who do not reproduce this general pattern in their novels are deliberately deviating from it, for the model presented here is the standard that has existed for as long as juvenile sports novels have been written.

This, then, is the athlete-hero and the hero tale:

The Hero

The athlete-hero is primarily a "prowess hero" as opposed to a "trickster" or an "ethical hero."[7] The more moralistic of the novels—for example, Owen Johnson's *Stover at Yale* (1912) and John R. Tunis's *Iron Duke* (1938)—may make him in part an ethical hero, but this is rare. He is always handsome, generally medium in size, and in all ways manly. He is a good student, although not a brilliant one, and never a "greasy grind" (horrors!) unless he has a pressing reason —to get off probation or to win a particular scholarship, for example. He is industrious, persistent, honest, brave, steady, generous, self-sacrificing, and serious to the point of humorlessness. He is fair, always modest, committed to his duty, and loyal to his friends, team, and school. He is democratic— he recognizes the worth of others and the importance of the team—plays fairly and with good sportsmanship and is a gentleman around females. He is no "squealer," maintaining silence even when he is wrongly accused, he endures pain uncomplainingly, and he will fight (always victoriously) only if seriously provoked, to defend someone else, or for honor. The publisher's preface to Harold M. Sherman's *Strike Him Out!* (1931) describes the model for all juvenile sports fiction when it says of the author, "His heroes are the finest examples of sturdy American youth, lovers of sport and sportsmanship without being, in any sense of the word, 'sissies.' "[8]

Origins

The hero's roots are almost exclusively in the middle class;

he might on rare occasions be from the lower class, but never from the wealthy or near wealthy. He is usually from a small town, sometimes from the country, rarely from the city.

Parentage

There is generally little or no mention of parents; the hero may even be an orphan. When they are mentioned, parents are usually kind, understanding, and helpful, but occasionally a boy will have a demanding father.

Initial Plot Movement

The hero almost always leaves a small, safe environment for a larger, more intimidating, more challenging one. The pattern can be from the country to the city, from a small town to a larger one, or from a small school and team to a larger, more prestigious school and team. The hero is almost always in some sense an underdog at the beginning of the novel.

Reputation

Occasionally the hero is introduced to the reader by rumor or by minor characters' discussion of him before we actually meet him. In other cases, the point is explicitly made that the hero either has an impressive reputation known to his peers before his arrival or is entirely unknown. In view of the fact that much of the juvenile novel is concerned with the hero's acquisition of fame, two possible patterns are indicated: the hero must reconfirm a reputation gained in his previous smaller world, or the unknown must make himself gloriously known to his new associates.

Attachment

Having psychologically left his parents, the hero usually becomes attached in his new environment either to a coach or hero-model as a father substitute or to a girl in a chaste, romantic love. If there is no attachment, then the parents have not been truly left, but this is rare, particularly in "classic" boys' sports fiction of the first half of the century.

Early Success

The hero nearly always has an early triumph that establishes him as a minor hero in his new environment. The achievement of full heroic status, however, usually comes later. The actions of the hero and his fellows, moreover, are important in their community, whether that community be a school or a town. The honor of the school is dependent on the hero's success, and in novels set in towns, the adult citizens are vitally concerned with the success of the boys' team. To feel he is a key member of his society is an important fantasy for a juvenile reader.

Meeting the Antagonist

Sometime early in the novel, the hero encounters his specific antagonist, usually triumphing over him in a small but convincing way so that enmity is established. In more socially conscious novels, the antagonist may be not an individual but a "system" or widely held prejudice, such as the society system in Johnson's *Stover at Yale* (1912). At times the hero meets an early defeat by his antagonist that is not rectified until the novel's climax.

The Antagonist

The antagonist is most often a "bully," a "poor sport," or a "stuffed-shirt." As Marshall Fishwick notes, heroes require villains, for no creed is successful unless someone is trying to violate it.[9] The antagonist appropriately embodies the constellation of vices antithetical to the hero's virtues. Occasionally the antagonist is a noble adversary, but never as noble as the hero.

Friends

Early in the story we are introduced to the hero's friends, a loyal and devoted bunch of good fellows. The cast of characters is consistent in most juvenile sports novels and often includes among the hero's friends an outsider whom the hero befriends and a little brother figure who looks to the hero for guidance.[10] Usually the hero has a single best friend and sidekick, rarely in the Sancho Panza tradition of the comic companion, most often a *reduced* mirror-image of the hero; that is, a figure of noble qualities who lacks the perfections of the hero. For this reason the hero's best friend is rarely an interesting person, unlike the famous companion figures of literature. The epitome of this type is Ronald Cooper in Sherman's *Strike Him Out!*—Ronald is Speed Durgan's double in appearance and a friend who is loyal to the point of self-annihilation, but a nondescript nonathlete.

Accolades

The hero throughout the story receives accolades to his prowess, often from foes as well as friends.

Humor

The juvenile novel conforms to the American insistence on the importance of humor, but the two great strains of American humor—the Down East and Southwestern traditions[11]—are reduced to boyish pranks, stereotypical dialects (usually horrendous), and simple word games. There are no shrewd Yankees or ringtailed roarers in this fiction.

Adversity

The hero, despite his prowess, is initially an underdog and the team he plays for is generally the underdog in a big game. In addition, the hero must undergo any number of personal adversities: failures in secondary goals (such as winning of scholarships), early setbacks in his primary goal (relegation to the second team, for example), injuries that must be overcome, attempts to discredit him, kidnappings that make him late or exhausted for the big game, failure to be recognized for his true worth, or problems with studies—sometimes resulting in probation. Some of these adversities grow out of the antagonist's plots, others do not. Also, because the hero's ability cannot be severely questioned, in the pursuit of the

primary goal (victory in the big game, fame on a large
scale) the hero experiences difficulties largely *through the
fault of others*: an early season loss despite the brilliant play
of the hero; runs scored against the pitcher-hero because of
teammates' errors, not poor pitching; the hero's failure due to
causes beyond his control—injury, exhaustion, poor umpiring, or opponents' cheating.

Mystery-Rescue

There is nearly always a mystery to be solved or a rescue
to be made by the hero during the course of the novel. Rescues
include such actions as saving a child or sweetheart from
drowning or from a runaway vehicle or animal, or saving the
hero's own father or a friend's or sweetheart's father from
financial loss. Mysteries include kidnappings, thefts, conspir-
acies, an identity to be discovered, a wrongful accusation to be
rectified. The rescue or solving of the mystery sometimes
thwarts the antagonist and often causes harm to the hero
which threatens to impair his athletic performance. The hero
is aware of this danger, but he is undeterred. One example of
this occurs in *Baseball Joe of the Silver Stars* (1912) by Lester
Chadwick. Joe is riding a streetcar that runs out of control,
threatening to trample a young boy. Knowing fully that it will
strain his pitching arm, Joe seizes the boy as he flies past. The
resultant injury jeopardizes his pitching performance (no
fault of Joe's), but, of course, he overcomes the handicap to
win gloriously. Some recent juvenile sports novels, responding to recent trends in children's literature, de-emphasize
mystery and adventure for the sake of pointed lessons directed at the young readers, but the more classic elements of
mystery and rescue have not disappeared altogether.

The Task

The greatest responsibility for the success of the team is
given to the hero. This is not just an accident of his position,
although heroes are usually pitchers, quarterbacks, half-
backs, or captains; the hero is explicitly entrusted with primary responsibility by the coach.

Triumph

Every juvenile sports novel concludes with a big game (traditional rivalry or championship game) or its equivalent in which the hero achieves his greatest triumph. Generally this big game is further reduced to an heroic moment; that is, triumph occurs by the hero striking out the last man in the ninth inning after his teammates' errors have placed the winning runs on base, or the hero scores the winning touchdown in the final minute of play. The antagonist occasionally meets his final defeat before the big game, but more often during it, sometimes in the heroic moment in direct confrontation with the hero. The antagonist can be a participant in the big game or a spectator who is somehow foiled by the events on the field. He can be reformed—won over to admiration of the hero—or simply defeated and punished. His punishment is usually loss of game, of money, of reputation, and/or of position in school or community. The hero's triumph makes him the premier citizen of his community—praised, admired, and immortalized.

Boons

The final triumph of the hero, as well as earlier triumphs, rescues, and solved mysteries, nearly always bring benefit to other individuals: victories and championships for school, town, or beloved coach; personal benefit, either physical or psychological, for a deserving friend; or financial benefit for members of one's own or friends' families.

This portrait of the athlete-hero, derived from juvenile fiction, is the popular image of the athlete-hero even today. This athlete-hero bears little resemblance to the actual heroes of the sports world; such writers as Jim Bouton in *Ball Four* (1971), Leonard Shecter in *The Jocks* (1970), and dozens of others have exposed athletes to be as corrupt as ordinary mortals, which they in fact are. The athlete-hero as presented here is more important as an ideal than as an actual person, but he is no less real and powerful for being an ideal. The ideal is occasionally embodied popularly in real athletes—Bart

Starr and Stan Musial are two recent examples, and Christy Matthewson almost out-Merriwelled Merriwell with his clean-cut image early in the century. More important, the ideal of the athlete-hero is the rationalization for such organizations as the National Collegiate Athletic Association and the Amateur Athletic Union, for the inclusion of athletics in school programs at all levels, and for the hiring of public relations specialists by professional and college athletic teams. Perhaps most significant, the athlete-hero is the dominant image in the mind of every father who encourages his son to play baseball or football.

This athlete-hero is a potent image in the American imagination within the context of American goals and aspirations, but his unique character is most apparent when he is compared to other, transnational heroes—in particular to mythical heroes.[12] It appears at first glance ludicrous to consider the hero of myth and the athlete-hero as analogous. When Joseph Campbell identifies myth as "the secret opening through which the inexhaustible energies of the cosmos pour into human cultural manifestation," and the mythic hero as "the incarnation of God . . . the navel of the world, the umbilical point through which the energies of eternity break into time,"[13] the puny efforts of the athlete-hero do not seem comparable. The action of the athlete-hero is preeminently physical while that of the heroes of religious myths is moral. In comparison to the accomplishments of great world heroes, the athlete-hero's triumphs seem provincial and trivial. Further, according to Campbell, the symbols of myth are spontaneous productions of the psyche, while the stories of the juvenile writers are composed according to a commercially tested formula. This difference seems to make any comparison between them invalid, but the comparison is justified on two grounds. First, the formulaic character of the athlete-hero and his enormous appeal to his juvenile audience and to the adult popular mind indicate that the sources of that formula may be the same sources that spontaneously produce mythic symbols. Granted that the myth is plebeian, there is nevertheless a mythic quality about the athlete-hero and his wide acceptance in American society. Second, the psychoanalytical approach to myth, adopted by Otto Rank, Joseph Campbell, and others, emphasizes that heroic myths are allegories of the process of maturation.[14] Juvenile fiction is fundamentally concerned with the same process.

Campbell's morphology of the heroic myth is encapsulated in seventeen precise stages,[15] about which he observes: "If one or more of the basic elements is omitted, it is bound to be somehow or other implied—and *the omission itself can speak volumes for the history and pathology of the example"* (emphasis added).[16] This last statement is the key to the relevance of making the comparison at all. The comparison itself is easily made with Campbell's description of the hero's career:

The mythological hero, setting forth from his commonday hut or castle, is lured, carried away, or else voluntarily proceeds, to the threshold of adventure. There he encounters a shadow presence that guards the passage. The hero may defeat or conciliate this power and go alive into the kingdom of the dark (brother-battle, dragon-battle; offering, charm), or be slain by the opponent and descend in death (dismemberment, crucifixion). Beyond the threshold, then, the hero journeys through a world of unfamiliar yet strangely intimate forces, some of which severely threaten him (tests), some of which give magical aid (helpers). When he arrives at the nadir of the mythological round, he undergoes a supreme ordeal and gains his reward. The triumph may be represented as the hero's sexual union with the goddess-mother of the world (sacred marriage), his recognition by the father-creator (father atonement), his own divinization (apotheosis), or again—if the powers have remained unfriendly to him—his theft of the boon he came to gain (bride-theft, fire-theft); intrinsically it is an expansion of consciousness and therewith of being (illumination, transfiguration, freedom). The final work is that of return. If the powers have blessed the hero, he now sets forth under their protection (emissary); if not, he flees and is pursued (transformation flight, obstacle flight). At the return threshold the transcendental powers must remain behind; the hero reemerges from the kingdom of dread (return, resurrection). The boon that he brings restores the world (elixir).[17]

A typical plot of a juvenile school novel will make the comparison as concrete as possible:

The hero leaves his home and parents to go off to a challenging prestigious school. He encounters a rival and overcomes him, gaining admittance not only to the school itself but to the elite circles within the school. The hero then undergoes a series of adventures and adversities, with the aid of loyal friends and the hindrance of rivals, until he achieves his final triumph, creating joy for all the deserving and particularly elevating himself to great fame. The story ends.

The correspondence of the two myths is broadly similar except in two important features—the nature of the triumph and the conclusion of the tale. The triumph of the hero of the monomyth, according to Campbell, consists of one of three achievements: union with the feminine, atonement with the father, or apotheosis; all three are always signified by an expansion of consciousness. The triumph of the athlete-hero is an apotheosis—he is in a sense divinized by his heroics—but he rarely achieves any expansion of consciousness. Rather, he simply glories in his new adulation with a sense of self-completeness from the task fulfilled. As an apotheosis, this is very mundane but Campbell's conception could accommodate it. However, as an allegory of the process of maturity, the juvenile tale should more appropriately conclude with a union with the feminine or atonement with the father, not the more self-centered (and thus still immature) apotheosis of the hero. These are the two great tasks of the preadult in order to achieve maturity, but neither is fulfilled by the athlete-hero. These tasks are tacitly understood in the juvenile novels in the separation of the hero from his parents, but the authors never come to grips with this vital issue which they implicitly raise. The earlier description of the athlete-hero noted that the hero, once separated from his parents, usually attaches himself to one of two substitutes: his coach or a girl. Otto Rank observes that in growing psychologically, the child severs himself from his parents, assumes the hostility of his father, and attaches himself to another "of a higher social rank."[18] This father substitution is only latent in the juvenile novel—in fact, when parents are specifically mentioned they are generally kind—but the virtual absence of any parent and the extremely strong attachment the hero often has to his coach are manifestations of this fantasy-need. However, the boy does not finally assert his independence from his father substitute, nor pass from attachment to his coach back to a union with his real father or to the principle of paternity. He remains a child. The other choice—attachment to a girl—is an alternate way to break out of parental constriction and to achieve personal integration in the Jungian sense of a marriage of the masculine and feminine principles. But the sexual attachments of the athlete-heroes are chaste and romanticized, without significance beyond the superficial rituals of masculine strutting and feminine hero-worship. As a moral center, the girl can be the hero's inspiration for a virtuous life, but she is never a genuine sexual person.

The second omission is even more telling. Campbell's monomyth is triadic, involving separation, initiation, and return. In the standard juvenile sports story, there is no return; the novel concludes with the apotheosis of the hero. The contribution to mankind by the hero of the monomyth occurs only when he returns to his people to bestow his hard-won knowledge or bounty upon them. As mentioned earlier, the athlete-hero bestows boons on his friends—joy of victory, financial gain—but these are clearly secondary to his own glory and not the primary purpose of his quest. They are, moreover, not the result of the hero's newfound wisdom, for we have just seen that he experiences no expansion of consciousness. The boons are explicitly contributory to the hero's glory and are important for that reason only. When the hero rescues a child, the child is immediately forgotten—the novel focuses entirely on the hero's courage. The honor of the school and the pleasure of the coach because of victory in the big game are merely accidental adjuncts to the hero's unreflective glory. The novel ends with the simple physical triumph.

What these two omissions tell us about the myth of the athlete-hero is extremely interesting. First, for all his benevolent virtues he is essentially a self-centered hero. Second, no real maturity is achieved in his allegory of maturity—the athlete-hero remains a child. The prototypical athlete-hero celebrates unlimited human achievement and potential, but at the point at which his virtues should transform him from a pedestrian "star" to a mythic godlike hero, he fails. His accomplishments are self-directed and not other-directed as are those of the heroes of myth. He thus represents both the potential of the athlete to be a genuine hero and his too-frequent failure to be one. One might be tempted to dismiss these conclusions as unimportant since they only concern juvenile heroes, but the athlete-hero is in fact a distinctively American hero, a version of the major hero for American adults as well as children. The shortcomings of such a hero are, therefore, more telling and significant than they might at first appear.

Within the Anglo-Saxon tradition of schoolboy fiction, the self-centered, immature American athlete-hero appears unique.[19] As stated earlier, the parent of all schoolboy fiction is Thomas Hughes's *Tom Brown's School Days,* but there are marked differences between that novel and the American juvenile sports novels considered here. Hughes's emphasis is on the development of his hero from a sturdy, feisty, reckless lad into a responsible, educated, independent, Christian Englishman. Athletics are important as a proving ground, not as their own end. Two superior American school novels—Owen Johnson's *Stover at Yale* (1912) and John R. Tunis's *Iron Duke* (1938)—share these concerns with moral development and thus satisfy more fully the requirements of Campbell's monomyth.

Stover is an acknowledged classic and *Duke* was the winner of a *New York Herald Tribune Prize* for the best book for older boys and girls in 1938. In *Stover at Yale,* Dink Stover undergoes the separation and initiation of other juvenile heroes but his adversity is moral rather than physical. While at Yale, he becomes radicalized and opposed to the society system and other forms of elitism; his triumph is accompanied by an increased awareness of his proper role in the revitalization of Yale's traditions. His attachment to Jean Story is as chaste and romanticized as the rest of the juvenile loves, but Jean does challenge him—first not to be smugly satisfied with his accomplishments, and then not to be a simpleminded iconoclast and cynic when he rejects them. Partly through her encouragement, Dink "becomes his own man," and after being tapped for the Skull and Bones honor fraternity, he will return to Yale for his senior year as a genuine leader and champion of democratic values. Johnson specifically states that Yale is the real beneficiary of the story.

Iron Duke is a tale of atonement with the father. Duke Wellington leaves a small town in Iowa to attend Harvard, his father's alma mater and personal dream for his son. The small-town hero becomes a big-school flop, but by hard work and gutty perseverance, he becomes a dean's list scholar and the NCAA two-mile champion. Throughout his college career, his primary concern has been guilt over failing his father's expectations, and at the end of the novel, when he rejects the school honor society as snobbishly elitist, he must return home to face his father's disappointment. Instead, he discovers his father is indifferent to Duke's supposed failures, but thrilled with his success. The author implies that Duke will now realize that those assumptions about his father's demands existed only in his own imagination, and thus atonement is achieved; at the end of the novel, father and son talk as equals. Furthermore, Duke will return to Harvard for his senior year as captain of the track team, a leader of the lost young men who, like himself earlier, need "somebody to get after them, pull them out of themselves and throw them into things, the way [Duke] was thrown in."[20] His new awareness will benefit many others.

Both *Stover at Yale* and *Iron Duke* share the primary moral concern of *Tom Brown's School Days*. But even these superior juvenile sports novels differ from Hughes's original. Tom Brown does not win his one fight in that novel, but sustains a draw that binds him ever after to Slogger Williams by mutual respect. Further, cricket is important to Hughes and to Tom for its promotion of discipline, reliance on one's teammates, and sportsmanship. Winning is unimportant—in fact, Tom's team loses the big Marylebone match at the end of the novel and does so without anguish.[21] Even Johnson and Tunis cannot divorce themselves sufficiently from the American sports ethic to allow their heroes to suffer such final defeat.

An even clearer difference between American and British schoolboy heroes is obvious in a comparison of boys' weeklies. George Orwell describes the most popular British weeklies, *Gem* and *Magnet*, that began in the early years of the twentieth century and are thus contemporary with Frank Merriwell and the *Tip Top Weekly*. In addition to many similarities, one pronounced difference is evident between the British and American magazines. *Gem* and *Magnet* are concerned with fifteen or twenty different characters, "all more or less on an equality."[22] Among these multiple heroes are a normal athletic highspirited boy, a slightly rowdier version of this type, a more aristocratic version, a quieter, more serious version, a stolid "bulldog" version, a reckless dare-devil type of boy, a clever studious boy, an eccentric boy not good at games but with a special talent, a scholarship boy, and several British regional types.[23] All these characters appear in *Tip Top Weekly* but subordinate to, and dwarfed by, the single all-important figure—Frank Merriwell.

A closer comparison of a single British boys' sports story to our American prototype reinforces this contrast. In "The Cricket Pro of Halethorpe" by Horace T. Andrews,[24] Jack Ford appears to be a typical Merriwellian hero—frank, open, and plucky; as the captain and star of the school cricket team he is a talented batsman and pitcher, performing the nearly miraculous "hat trick" (putting down three batters on consecutive pitches), and retiring the final opposing batter in each of the story's two great Halethorpe victories. But Jack shares the heroics with his teammates, a group reflective of Orwell's cast of characters in the boys' weeklies: Gus Lambton is an active, buoyant, daring youth who is also the school's best boxer; the Honourable Tommy Mainwaring is a "precious dude" whose aristocratic airs do not disguise the fact that he is a good chap; Bhundet Rao has an ethnic identity, but unlike his comic American counterparts he is completely equal to the other boys; Dick Welsby is a small, lively, and carefree lad; Tom Nelson is a victim of perpetual bad luck, and although slow-witted, he is finally dependable.

In cricket the responsibilities are more evenly divided than in baseball; pitchers alternate, for example, and Jack Ford shares both the successes and failures of his position with his teammates. The others make spectacular catches and clutch hits, and Jack himself is quite fallible. When exhorted to "do the hat trick, Ford, old sport!" on a second occasion, Jack tries his best but fails. "'Tis not in mortals to command success" is his response. Jack retires the final batter in the first big match, not because he overpowers his opponent, but because the other is overeager. The conclusion of the second match is likewise muted—Jack receives no great accolade for retiring the final batter. This big game, in fact, is not the climax of the story; the solving of a mystery fills this function, in which Jack's leadership is supported by "his three equally plucky companions." Everyone "regarded one and all of the six as heroes" when the matter is successfully concluded.

Other patterns of the story also vary in slight but significant ways from those in similar American fiction. Halethorpe wins the first match, which reduces the magnitude of the victory in the big game. Jack is injured on the day before this contest, but a healing remedy prevents any ill effects on his performance. And the conclusion of the story—the rescue and solved mystery—focuses on the boys' genuine service to others, placing more emphasis on those who benefit from the uncovering of the mystery than on the boys who do it. American schoolboy fiction seems more hero-oriented than its British counterpart. In a country with ancient monarchical and aristocratic traditions, British boys' sports books are actually more committed to the qualities of cooperation and conformity prized by a powerful middle class than is the more individualistic juvenile sports fiction of democratic America.[25]

Much evidence is available to support this conclusion in the major literature of both countries. From a broad perspective, British fiction, at least in the eighteenth and nineteenth centuries, has been most concerned with the individual's adaptation to society's demands. The value of society is a given; its excesses can be satirized, but it is rarely rejected in its entirety. On the other hand, representative heroes of American literature who have most struck the chord of the national consciousness—Natty Bumppo, Ahab, Huck Finn, Jay Gatsby, Nick Adams, Ralph Ellison's invisible man, Yossarian—have been *individualists* not primarily contributing to society but attempting to avoid corruption or absorption by society. The hero of the juvenile literature we have considered is obviously more starkly drawn and is meant to appeal to a juvenile, not an adult, audience, but he is really the quintessence of the national heroic type—egocentric rather than sociocentric. The heroes of serious sports novels from Ring Lardner's Jack Keefe to Bernard Malamud's Roy Hobbs, Mark Harris's Henry Wiggen, John Updike's Harry Angstrom, and

Peter Gent's Phil Elliott are always individuals in conflict
with society—the image of the team is consistently super-
seded by the image of the individual athlete.

The Athlete-Hero as a Representative American Hero

The American tradition that produced this indigenous athlete-hero has its sources deep in the nineteenth century and
before. The athlete-hero did not leap Venus-like from the
head of Gilbert Patten into that first issue of *Tip Top Library*.
His inception, rather, was an inevitable response to current
trends in popular literature, particularly in the dime novel
and the novels of Horatio Alger. The dime novel,[26] the first
great American experiment in the standardization of fiction,
flourished between 1860 with the establishment of the publishing firm of Beadle and Adams, and approximately 1890 when
the market for such fiction finally collapsed, giving place to
the weeklies and then the pulps. The emphasis of the dime
novel was on action, generally of an improbable nature. In a
classification of 1,531 dime novels, Philip Durham discovered
that fully two-thirds of the novels concerned the Western frontier in some form or other, while the remainder dealt with
such diverse topics as the American Revolution, city detec-
tives, and sea stories.[27] But whatever the setting the heroes
were

> self-reliant, resourceful, self-made men, whether frontier
> scouts, explorers, miners, pirates, detectives, or street ur-
> chins who rose to fame and fortune. They never whined and
> never gave up. They were plain, unsophisticated "natural"
> men (some even illiterate) but unanimously virtuous, gentle-
> manly, and ethical by nature—cowboys, hunters, artisans,
> miners, policemen—with not an aristocratic dandy among
> them.[28]

The similarity between this description and the portrait of the
juvenile athlete-hero is obvious, but the correspondence is
not exact because this description of the dime-novel hero is an
overview of a changing formula. As more and more rival publishers began marketing their dime novels, competition produced changes in the format. Beadle's original conception of

the dime novel had a distinctly genteel flavor—among the requirements he dictated to his writers he claimed:

> We prohibit all things offensive to good taste in expression and incident.
> We prohibit subjects of characters that carry an immoral taint.
> We require unquestioned originality.
> We require pronounced strength of plot and high dramatic interest of story.
> We require grace and precision of narrative, and correctness in composition.[29]

What in fact occurred, though, was that, in order to stay one-up on the competition, the criterion for distinction became "to kill another Indian." As the genre degenerated rapidly in the seventies and eighties, the action became more improbable and the gratuitous violence more frequent until dime novels could be read by juveniles only behind haystacks or under the bed covers at night. What parents objected to in the dime novels was not their morality, but their emphasis on sensationalism, violence, and overwrought emotionalism.[30] On the other hand, the child reader did not want the priggish books typical of pre-dime-novel juvenile literature.[31] The reading public was ripe for a fiction that could satisfy the child's desire for stirring adventure and the parent's insistence on propriety; the juvenile sports novel filled this need. In the preface to *With Mask and Mitt* (1906), Albertus True Dudley characterizes this intention perfectly:

> A good juvenile [novel] must be one approved by the parent, enjoyed by the boy, and read with profit by both. It should, of course, interest and amuse; it should also help the parent to understand the impulses and the mental attitude of the boy, and the boy to accept the ideals of the parent.[32]

The second major influence on this fiction was the juvenile literature best exemplified by that of Horatio Alger, one of the most prolific, widely known, and influential juvenile authors ever. His 118 novels shaped the aspirations of generations of Americans, including such men as Benjamin Fairless (once head of United States Steel), Governor Alfred E. Smith of New York, Francis Cardinal Spellman, Carl Sandburg, Joyce Kilmer, Ernest Hemingway, and Knute Rockne.[33] The Alger story, as everyone knows whether he has read one or not, is the rags-to-riches myth of the self-made man. The hero is a youth who rises from poverty to wealth by luck and pluck; he is full of vigor, handy with his fists, ambitious, competitive, and shrewd in business. He is also gentle with children and old folks, protective of the weak, scrupulously honest, and generous with his friends. A master detective, the hero solves mysteries and rescues unfortunates in every story.[34]

His correspondence to the athlete-hero is obvious; in fact, Edward Stratemeyer, the founder of the publishing syndicate that produced the fourteen Baseball Joe books—one of the earliest of such series—began his career by completing Alger's unfinished books. So wholesome was the Alger hero that, unlike the dime novel, he not only was not hidden in the hayloft, he was espoused from the nation's pulpits. By the time of Alger's death in 1899, however, the popularity of the Alger novel was dying out, for reasons that Russel B. Nye explains:

> The rags-to-riches billionaire was becoming scarce; it took money to make money in 1900 and the sudden stroke of luck that in 1870 might take a poor boy from nothing to a million now needed plenty of capital to take advantage of it. The legend of Alger persisted, but the opportunities for making great wealth were narrowing fast; a boy needed technological skill, education, scientific talent, and highly organized business know-how to struggle upward—not just energy, sobriety, and the rescue of the boss's daughter.[35]

Athletics defined the spirit of the new times, and Gilbert Patten's Frank Merriwell became the new hero:

> As Alger equated wealth and virtue, so the Merriwells equated virtue with the discipline of sport—the books were intended, Patten said, "to fire a boy's ambition, to become a good athlete in order that he may develop into a strong, vigorous, and right-thinking man." Using the athletic contest as his central device, Patten stressed success as self-improvement, self-realization, self-control, self-conquest.[36]

The juvenile sports novel combined the action of the dime novels with the middle-class morality of the Alger novel. It is important to note that a single strain runs consistently through all three literary types—the concept of the self-made man. It is within this tradition of the self-made man that the athlete-hero emerges as an important American ideal. The rags-to-riches formula of the Alger novel defines the purest embodiment of this American hero, but the athlete-hero's career follows a nearly identical pattern, with the single substitution of athletic triumphs for wealth as the success goal. Gilbert Patten himself implicitly recognized the connection between the Alger version of the Protestant work ethic and the new ideal of the young athlete. In one of his Merriwell stories, Patten observes: "Work is the greatest sport in the world, for it is a game at which one plays to win the prize of his life."[37] In comparing one typical Alger hero, Ragged Dick,[38] to the formula for the juvenile sports novel, one finds several similarities. Both boys are challenged to prove themselves in a situation more intimidating than any they have yet encountered. They experience early success but must overcome adversity at every step of their rise. They are opposed by antagonists who nearly thwart their aspirations. They solve a mystery, rescue a child, and are chastely enamored of a special young lady. They are virtually parentless, but they are surrounded by loyal friends who later receive their benefactions. And they achieve their final triumph through precisely the same constellation of virtues. Both figures epitomize the concept of the self-made man.

The correspondence of the dime novel hero and the athlete-hero is not as obvious but just as true. There are essentially two prototypes for the dime novel hero: the natural and the self-made man. The natural is the leatherstocking figure, "a benevolent hunter without a fixed place of abode, advanced in age, celibate, and of unequalled prowess in tracking, marksmanship, and Indian fighting."[39] The self-made man in the dime novels represents "the American faith in rugged individualism and in bold-spirited struggle against unfavorable circumstances."[40] Examples of the two types can be seen in Seth Jones and Deadwood Dick,[41] two of the most popular of the dime novel heroes. Both of these types are represented in the athlete-hero, but the self-made man is more evident.

The athlete-hero, then, is a self-made man whose immediate literary heritage is in the dime novel and the success novel of Horatio Alger. However, the roots of the athlete-hero as a self-made man go much deeper than these two immediate precedents. The self-made man is indeed the dominant American hero and has been so since the founding of the new land. Many writers have attempted to identify American heroic types: Richard M. Dorson has written of American folk heroes—ring-tailed roarers, comic-demigods, Münchausens, noble toilers, and outlaws.[42] Marshall Fishwick has identified American real and imaginary heroes by their life-styles: swashbucklers, squires, cavaliers, natural men, self-made men, jolly giants, smooth roughnecks, poor whites, cool ones, celebrities, anti-heroes, absurd heroes, and racial heroes.[43] And Orrin E. Klapp has defined five hero types: winners, splendid performers, independent spirits, heroes of social acceptability, and group servants.[44] Following the old injunction to simplify, I believe nearly all of these American heroes can be reduced to two basic types: the natural and the self-made man. The natural is the hero of the "virgin land," our greatest fantasy ideal, and most of our imaginary folk heroes are of this type: Paul Bunyan, Pecos Bill, Joe Magarac, to name a few. In addition, highly mythicized real persons such as Daniel Boone, Davy Crockett, and Kit Carson have been recreated to fit this mold. The self-made man, on the other hand, the hero of the "land of opportunity," is our supreme role model, a hero to be actually emulated. Americans have dreamed of being Davy Crockett, but they have tried to imitate, and encouraged their children to imitate, Henry Ford, Thomas Edison, Abraham Lincoln, and the rest of our self-made men.

Heroes are, in part, products of their times, and particular historical events have produced particular American heroes. Had there been no George Washington, the American Revolution and the birth of the nation would have created one; Teddy Roosevelt arrived when America desperately needed a trustbuster; Babe Ruth, Jack Dempsey, and Charles Lindbergh were required by the spirit of the twenties as symbols of Americans' glorious self-conception. But the self-made man and the natural have not depended on historical incident for their existence; they are fundamental to the American experience. The natural is the primary concern of the following chapter; the self-made man will be examined in some detail now.

John G. Cawelti has discussed the many guises under which the self-made man has appeared in America, defining three primary versions of this figure.[45] First, the *ethical self-made man* was promoted by the conservative tradition of the middle-class Protestant ethic, which stressed the virtues of piety, frugality, and diligence in one's calling as the way to a respectable competence in this world and eternal salvation in the world to come. Second, the *economic self-made man* stressed those qualities which enabled the individual to get ahead: initiative, aggressiveness, competitiveness, and forcefulness. Third, writers such as Franklin, Jefferson, and Emerson championed the *ideal of individual human development* through self-improvement, self-culture, and self-reliance.

The self-made man is as old as the European settlement of the American continent. The first intellectual force in the New World, Puritanism, made the self-made man the model for God-fearing Christians. Cotton Mather was one of many representatives for the equation of religion and activism,[46] the accumulation of wealth for the glory of God, and the rest of the virtues we now associate with the "Protestant work ethic." Benjamin Frankiln was a successor, not to Mather's religiosity, but to his ethics. The virtues Franklin espoused in his aphorisms and in his own life—frugality, industry, cleanliness, resolution, chastity—define the self-made man's road to fulfillment. The successes of Andrew Jackson and Abraham Lincoln made the self-made man so politically attractive that many statesmen who followed them in the nineteenth century felt the need to apologize if they had too much money and had not been born in a log cabin.

During the heyday of the self-made man—the middle of the nineteenth century—Horatio Alger was not alone in popularizing him. William McGuffey's readers, first published in 1836, were "a skillful synthesis of bourgeois virtues and capitalistic maxims"[47] and taught generations of Americans to read. Elbert Hubbard's "A Message to Garcia" (1899), William Thayer's *Tact, Push, and Principle* (1880), Russell Conwell's speech "Acres of Diamonds" (delivered over 6,000 times), and Orison S. Marden's *Success* magazine were among the most popular publications of the day, and made the Gospel of Wealth the American ideal.[48] Such men as Gould, Fiske, Vanderbilt, Hill, Carnegie, and Rockefeller were but the most successful of all those who served it religiously. Even in the twentieth century, when it seems no longer possible to get rich quickly, the self-made man remains the ideal, only now his tool has become psychology, not economics. From Dale Carnegie's *How to Win Friends and Influence People* in 1937 to Wayne W. Dyer's *Pulling Your Own Strings* in 1978, the self-made man has simply operated in new arenas with new goals.[49] Moreover, the economic self-made man did not die with the last of the robber barons, as evidenced by this preface to 100 stories of business success compiled in 1954 by the editors of *Fortune* magazine:

> What these enterprising citizens do seem to share are certain distinctive traits: abundant energy, considerable intuitive intelligence, and a frank desire to get rich as fast as possible. Many have a gift for selling both their projects and their produtcs. In sum, they are evidence that there are plenty of opportunities, in good times and bad, for those who have the wit to see them.[50]

Even the major intellectual forces in America—Calvinism in its insistence on industry, transcendentalism in its claim for the primacy of the individual, Social Darwinism in its espousal of the survival of the fittest, and pragmatism in its attributing of moral decision to the individual—all support the ideal of the self-made man. It is difficult to imagine Ralph Waldo Emerson and Horatio Alger in a meaningful dialogue, but Emerson's essays on "Heroism" and "Self-reliance"[51] are philosophical counterparts to the Gospel of Wealth in their insistence on the ability and right of the individual to thrive by self-dependence. Theodore Roosevelt, insofar as he can be termed an intellectual, represents a footnote in this litany of spokesmen for the self-made man and makes the connection with the athlete-hero obvious. Roose-

velt's concepts of the strenuous life and the ideal boy correspond precisely to the ethic of the juvenile athlete-hero. Moreover, he was the most persuasive American apologist for
sport as a preparation for adult life; his philosophy could
have been expressed by the great Merriwell himself: "In
short, in life as in a football game, the principle to follow is:
Hit the line hard; don't foul and don't shirk, but hit the line
hard!"[52]

The impact of the self-made man on American intellectual
thought is further evidenced by the examples of much of our
major fiction. Herman Melville's Ahab, Mark Twain's Hank
Morgan, Henry James's Christopher Newman, Theodore Drei-
ser's Frank Cowperwood, F. Scott Fitzgerald's Jay Gatsby,
and William Faulkner's Thomas Sutpen are but a few of the
fictional characters whose relationship to the model of the
self-made man is explored by our best writers. They never
represent this figure as an object for simple adulation, but
test the societal and personal dilemmas that inevitably arise
with such an ideal.

The athlete-hero is, therefore, but one manifestation of this
dominant American ideal, though an extremely attractive
one to the popular mind. He is also the most widely popular
self-made man in America today. The self-made man has
always been limited to certain fields of endeavor—primarily
business, politics, and, in the twentieth century, athletics.
We have never pretended that anyone who merely tries hard
in the arts and sciences can succeed. Today, business and
politics as well are becoming more closed to the self-made
man; to make money in business one needs money, as one
does to succeed in politics. In sports, however, it is still possible to a limited extent for the slum child to become the
greatest in his field. The athlete-hero is still so real to the
American mind that his popular conception remains what it
was when first formulated by Gilbert Patten, and we feel he
still actually exists. Our notions of other kinds of heroes (politicians, soldiers, and so on) have changed with the passing of
time, and rarely have we claimed that they were completely
fulfilled in living persons, but the athlete-hero remains one of
the few constants in modern America.

Although he is so widely approved, the athlete-hero is a

paradoxical figure, a fact which illuminates an essential con-
tradiction in the American sports ethic and perhaps in American democracy as well. As a democratic ideal, he stands for
the possibility of anyone's making himself into a hero by hard
work, perseverance, and a bit of luck, and he champions the
idea that everyone else is important too, whether he achieves
hero status or not. Frank Merriwell's frequent disclaimers that
he is no better than his friends, that he only does his duty as
anyone would do, that he is but one member of a team and the
team deserves the credit—these attitudes are applauded in the
athlete-hero and allow everyone to share in his glory.

Other facts seem to contradict these platitudes, however. It
is the athlete-hero and not anyone else who wins the big game,
rescues the child, and receives the glory. It is the athlete-hero
who is explicitly entrusted with responsibility for the team's
success, whose near failure occurs only through the faults of
his lesser teammates, never through any inadequacy of his own.
He in all ways is the center of the universe, and about him are
constellated the lesser mortals—friends, foes, females, and by-
standers. The conception of the athlete-hero is an attempt to
have it both ways: individualism and democratic leveling are
both espoused, the former by what the hero does, the latter by
what he says. In the world of athletics, the conflict can be stated
simply, the value of the individual star versus the importance
of teamwork.

American democracy is in essence a similar attempt to have
it both ways: opportunity for every individual to develop to his
fullest potential, but also insistence on the absolute equality of
all persons. This dialectic generates the dynamism of American
society, so difficult to maintain in equilibrium. The Gilded Age
of the nineteenth century, one example of the complete shift of
the pendulum in favor of the fortunate individual, is now ab-
horred by the majority of Americans, but a complete shift to
the other extreme at the expense of personal accomplishment
would be equally offensive to the American mind, for it would
raise mediocrity to the ideal. By its nature, American democracy cannot ever be entirely self-fulfilling, for both values cannot be served simultaneously and equally. In fact, this point of
equilibrium is only theoretically possible and the greater tendency in America has been to favor the successful individual.
Social Darwinism was just a sophisticated term and rationale

for a practice already long established. The athlete-hero is a graphic example in microcosm of this emphasis on the individual at the expense of the group. His self-centeredness became apparent in the comparison to Campbell's monomyth; it is now possible to recognize this egocentricity in the American sociopolitical context.

A second idea that the all-conquering athlete-hero particularly highlights is the distinctively American belief in the possibility of perfection. The 1976 Winter Olympics in Innsbruck, Austria, offered an example of this trait in a way that is significant for understanding the American psyche. Americans have traditionally not performed well in the Winter Olympics—sports such as skiing, skating, and bobsledding are largely restricted to the moneyed classes in this country and have not consistently attracted our best athletes. In the 1976 winter games, however, Americans produced some surprising performances. Two young Americans particularly, Dan Immerfall in the 500-meter speed skating and Cindy Nelson in the women's slalom, unexpectedly won bronze medals. Immerfall was virtually unknown, not ranked among the best skaters at all, and Nelson was coming off a terrible month of skiing—in her preparatory runs she had fallen more often than not and had been consistently unable to complete the course. Neither was among the favorites, but both won medals, and when interviewed by American television commentators afterwards, each athlete offered an excuse why he or she had not won the *gold* medal. Immerfall claimed he rolled on his ankle on the first turn, and Nelson explained she slipped similarly on one of the turns.

The Europeans, on the other hand, tended to react differently. Bernhard Russi, a Swiss downhill skier, when asked by the same American sportscasters if he was disappointed that his leading time had just been beaten by the Austrian, Franz Klammer, responded instead with perfectly understandable admiration for Klammer's incredible performance, and even with the admission that Klammer was the better skier. Later in the games, a West German, Rosi Mittermaier, failed to win her third gold medal in skiing—finishing second. Interviewed by that most American of television commentators, she appeared dumbfounded by the suggestion that she might be disappointed that she had not won her third gold. Her obvious feeling was, how could anyone be disappointed who had won two gold medals and a silver against the best skiers in the world?

The implications of the coverage of the Winter Olympics were clear. The two Americans felt they could win and were disappointed that they did not, despite the fact that they both won medals few others thought them capable of winning. In others words, both felt that perfection was possible for them. The two Europeans, on the other hand, were elated by their successes and seemingly indifferent to the fact that they did not win everything for which they competed. It would be foolish, of course, on the basis of these few examples, to claim absolute proof of national characteristics, but the belief in the possibility of perfection does seem to be an American trait. Americans' belief in perfection is as old as their presence on this continent. Since the discovery of the New World, the American landscape was believed to be a source of unlimited bounty and opportunity for all who sought it. The reluctance of Americans in recent years to truly believe in the scarcity of energy resources is but one more example of a widespread faith in the inexhaustible bounty of a new Eden. Perfection is vested in America herself.

America's greatest writers have long recognized the consequences of this mythic belief; Melville's Ahab and Faulkner's Thomas Sutpen are the greatest of many tragic American overreachers. Other fictional heroes, such as James's Christopher Newman and Fitzgerald's Jay Gatsby, are confused or troubled by the inability of the world to match their notions of perfection, to find something commensurate with their capacity for wonder. Another Fitzgerald creation, Dick Diver of *Tender Is the Night*, tells a fellow psychologist that his own ambition is "maybe to be the greatest one that ever lived."[53] His friend appropriately responds, "That's very good—and very American." The belief in perfection is a sign of America's greatness—by striving after perfection, we have extended man's capabilities enormously in many fields. It is also a sign of America's foolishness. It lay behind the frustration over our inability to triumph in Indochina and our reluctance, already cited, to acknowledge the limitation of the earth's resources. It is also, finally, America's tragedy. To believe in the possibility of perfection is to be constantly reminded of perfection unattained. America evokes a sense of unfulfilled destiny, of continually trying to regain a former innocence, an arcadian past, which may or may not have ever existed, but which is now certainly unattainable. From Cooper to Hemingway and beyond, this sense of lost opportunities has been powerfully and poignantly considered by our finest writers.

The athlete represents one case of the American belief in the possibility of perfection; sport, as it so often does, simply highlights an important cultural phenomenon and offers a handle by which to grasp it. The juvenile athlete-hero sustains this belief uncritically, and his image, as has been emphasized, continues to be potent today. Americans need heroes who represent the attainability of perfection, and they can find confirmation of their dreams in O. J. Simpson or Julius Erving. There are indications, however, that the reign of the athlete-hero as the premier popular American hero may be diminishing. The commercialization of sport has reached such extreme limits that the public is beginning to realize that professional sports are indeed work, not play. Television, by reducing the dimensions of the field to the size of a screen and by dissecting the once almost magical feats of athletic skill with stop-action, instant replay, and slow motion, is reducing sport to the explicable—and our heroes must have magic. Should the athlete-hero be eventually eclipsed, however, his model—the middle-class ideal of the self-made man—and his representation of the possibility of perfection will appear in some other guise. These values are so intrinsic to America's existence that nothing short of revolution could remove them permanently from the foremost position in the American hierarchy.

The Athlete-Hero in Sports Fiction for Adults

Thus far I have attempted to delineate the athlete-hero as he appears in his simplest, most pristine avatar—as the hero of juvenile fiction. He is, of course, also the hero of the other forms of sports fiction, among which are the pulps, the literary heirs of the dime novel. In an anthology of pulp stories Tony Goodstone identifies the very first of the type to be Frank Munsey's *The Argosy,* when it was changed in 1896 from a boys' magazine to an all-fiction adult magazine on rough wood-pulp pages. Goodstone places the end of the pulps in 1953 when a major distributor's embargo pushed their already dwindling circulation to the bottom.[54] Their heyday had actually ended much earlier; after the boom in the late twenties and early thirties, their popularity had been slipping for years. The pulps, then, ran concurrently with the flood of juvenile sports literature which Gilbert Patten unleashed, also in 1896. The pulps offered an "adult" alternative to juvenile sports, and the difference between the pulp hero and the juvenile athlete-hero is considerable. The juvenile stories are children's fantasies, while pulps portray adult dreams. The fresh, all-successful, handsome young hero of the juveniles has no place in the pulps. A man dragging himself home from the steel mills six nights a week could scarcely identify with the schoolboy rushing exuberantly off to Hilton Academy to test his mettle against new challenges. The juvenile athlete-hero was a consciously created image of socially approved conduct, not a fantasy hero who could move adult readers as well.

The pulp sports hero[55] is older, of course, but he is also flawed—he may drink or gamble or swear a little, be afraid or be a troublemaker, be simply too old or have limited ability. The plots concern underdogs overcoming handicaps to achieve limited, often temporary, success. The final triumph is not perfect and the hero struggles past his own shortcomings, not just his teammates' errors, to achieve it. A pulp magazine's typical description of a story is the one of Eric Rober's "Crucial Game for Pop" (1943-44): "All they could do was send Pop Dreber in and pray he wouldn't try to use his burned-out fireball against the victory-mad Moguls!" (*always* an exclamation point). The stories are about overcoming cowardice, overcoming old age, overcoming a bad reputation or abuse and lack of recognition.

In their particulars, too, the stories differ greatly from the pattern of the athlete-hero. There is little rah-rah exuberance, and more pain, violence, and hate. Coaches are often hardboiled martinets rather than benign father figures. There is rarely an actual villain, and never a woman. These differences can best be understood by considering again the typical worker-reader. Because he is acutely aware of his own limitations, his greatest fantasy would be to excel and achieve recognition despite them. In this fantasy, his triumph must take place in a world with which he is familiar, not a juvenile Camelot. His employer is no father figure to him, and his enemies are not specific individuals (this is a comfort available only to the young) but are his own handicaps and the confusing environment in which he works. The absence of women is the only surprising feature of the sports pulps. The sexless nature of the hardboiled world these magazines portray implies a need among pulp readers to escape the complications of sexual relationships. This exclusivity of the all-male athletic world will be explored fully in a later chapter.

These sports pulps were not very popular. Ron Goulart has observed that "the fictional sports hero was never as popular in the pulps as he had been in the more innocent years of Frank Merriwell and the *Tip Top Weekly*."[56] The most popular pulps were first the westerns and then the love pulps, the former for men and the latter for women. The detective and adventure pulps were also more popular than those dealing with sport. The relative unpopularity of the sports pulps demonstrates in miniature the reasons cited in the previous chapter for the lack of popularity of the entire sports fiction genre. Boys envision themselves as athletic heroes, men do not. An adult reader of sports pulps could not imagine himself ever scoring the winning touchdown for old Siwash, nor could such an accomplishment satisfy any of his most pressing needs. During the heyday of the pulps, reality in America was first a depression, then a war—the ivied walls of Yale were never more anachronistic. Pulp readers during this period could identify with the detective hero or the war ace, men who triumphed over grim reality. The athlete-hero merely triumphed over other boys playing games.

The pulps were one attempt to create sports heroes for an adult readership, but *every* sports novel is at least in part a story about the hero. The image of the athlete-hero created in boys' sports books is still powerful; in a sense it remains a frame of reference in all sports fiction. Since the author and reader share common knowledge of the model, the author can play his characters off against that norm without representing it in any particular figure. In an unpublished dissertation on "The Unheroic Hero," Robert Higgs identifies eight sport hero types: the dumb athlete, the brute, the bromide, the hubristic hero, the bum, the darling, the natural or folk hero, and the absurd athlete.[57] With the exception of the natural, none of the other seven could really be identified without the athlete-hero model. Each

is defined by his deviation from that norm, by a failure in goals
or character associated with the athlete-hero ideal. Each of the
novels to be considered in the rest of this study will be likewise
related to this primary model. Their heroes will be youths striving to achieve that heroic idea; veterans attempting to regain
it; ex-athletes still living in the past, in that moment in which
they briefly embodied the ideal; nonathletes hungry for the
fame of the ideal; ghetto boxers struggling for the ideal to give
them status in their community and an inroad into the genteel
world associated with it. Some of the novels will deal with the
disparity between the actual hero and his public image as the
ideal; others will be refutations of the ideal of the hero by
creating a victim-hero or anti-hero. These novels have other
primary concerns on which the discussions will focus, but their
relationship to the athlete-hero is implicit in all of them.

Before turning in the following chapters to the important
recurring themes of sports fiction, however, we must consider another dimension of the athlete-hero. Although the
heroes of all sports novels share similarities to the prototype
developed in this chapter and are essentially derived from
that one basic figure, each sport also consistently presents in
fiction a unique version of the athlete-hero. The nature of the
sports themselves determines these models, for each of the
major sports that has produced a body of literature has its
particular as well as generalized appeal to the American
imagination, embodied in its distinctive hero.

The boxer is the easiest to identify; he is *man the animal*—
virtually naked, in a stark environment, locked in elemental
combat with his foe. His literary portrait is nearly always as
the urban victim, the ghetto dweller whose ultimate confinement of body and spirit is symbolized by the squared ring
within which he struggles. The boxer represents a figure
that predates American experience; his origins are universal, not national. The boxer's appeal in America for this reason has never been as pervasive as the appeal of the other
sports hero types. He represents dominance and survival,
not soaring aspirations or quixotic quests for glittering ideals,
and these are the ideas that stir the imagination. Actual
American boxing heroes have been most clearly identified
in the public's mind with their class or ethnic origins. Box-

ing's appeal has always been primarily to the most disadvantaged groups in society; Poles have been able to look to Stanley Ketchel, Jews to Barney Ross, blacks to Jack Johnson for confirmation of their ability to survive with dignity in an inhospitable society. The heavyweight champions of the twentieth century in particular appear to have been a succession of white hopes and black messiahs: Jack Johnson and Jim Jeffries fought what everyone knew was a racial war; Jack Dempsey refused to fight his most worthy challenger, Harry Wills, because Wills was a black man; Joe Louis vindicated not just Americans against the German Max Schmeling, but blacks against all those who claimed racial superiority for the white races; and Muhammad Ali, as Eldridge Cleaver brilliantly observed, represents not only the black race, but a particular image of it—the first "free" black champion ever to confront white America. Among Ali's opponents, according to Cleaver, Liston was nonideological, and Floyd Patterson was the "subordinate Negro."[58]

Writers of boxing fiction have dealt very little with this fascinating dimension of the sport, and with another aspect of boxing that seems particularly conducive to literary treatment—the large question of the fan's response to the brutality of boxing and the degree to which some primitive bloodlust still enthralls members of sophisticated modern societies. Rather, novelists of boxing have invariably focused on the individual boxer as a victim of society struggling to overcome that society's repressive weight by a suicidal commitment to a boxing career. The form of these novels is naturalistic, and they share the limitations inherent in simplified literary naturalism. By focusing entirely on man as an environmentally controlled animal, the writers of boxing novels reduce the human dimension of their characters to such an extent that all but a few become uninteresting. The following chapter will discuss those novels that do rise above these limitations.

The hero of the second sport, baseball, is also a solitary figure, but of a quality far different from that of the boxer. He is the *individualist*, the self-sufficient but social man whose imaginative origin as the rugged individualist of the American frontier makes him in many ways the most distinctly American of sports heroes. The baseball player, like the boxer, is isolated from his fellows, visible to all the world —a man who must depend on his own resources. Unlike the boxer, he is also a member of a team, so his human interactions become more complicated. He is distinguished from players of other team sports by the fact that only a limited amount of coordination with his teammates is absolutely required of him. He is a member of a team but is not absorbed by it; as an image of the ideal American citizen he is the self-reliant individual who contributes to his society what it requires of him and receives from that society the support he needs, but who maintains his essential autonomy.

One recent baseball novel, *Runner Mack* (1972) by Barry Beckham, uses baseball appropriately as a representation of this American dream of the self-made man, and parodies it from a black perspective. Henry Adams, the novel's hero, attempts to make the New York Stars baseball team in a scene that brilliantly satirizes the endless but futile striving of black people for success in white America. Henry's efforts to catch a fly ball are typical:

> The first ball was a high, high accelerating fly, and Henry turned to go back, finally reaching the wall.... He knew if he leaped he would still be four or five feet too short, so he began furiously to scale the wall, sticking his cleats into the wood—his glove had been thrown away for the climb—and fingernails grabbing into the tiny cracks.... There was one possibility, he thought, and balanced himself on the railing, jumped in the air toward the arc of the ball's flight, and cap in hand, stabbed at the ball. He felt it break into the cap as he plummeted down to the grass.[59]

The lesson of the tryout is that Henry has amazing ability, exerts superhuman effort against overwhelming odds stacked against him, but is unfairly denied a job. Baseball, according to Beckham, is the ideal metaphor for the elusive and illusive ideal of white success.

The baseball player, as the descendent of American frontier heroes who lived close to the land, is also a "natural." He is dependent on nature—on climate, on wind direction and velocity, on even the smallest pebble that can turn a routine grounder into a base hit. The greatest players are considered to have skills no coach could teach, because of innate ability seemingly granted by the gods: Ted Williams' 20-10 vision made him the greatest hitter of his generation; Walter Johnson, Bob Feller, and Sandy Koufax had speed so awesome they were barely hittable; Willie Mays could judge a fly so accurately that his "basket catches" appeared effortless. Baseball folklore relates the tales of numerous ballplayers who arrived in the big leagues from tiny rural communities to become the greatest players the game has known; Ty Cobb, Rube Waddell, and "Shoeless Joe" Jackson are but three of this multitude of great naturals.

Writers of baseball fiction have responded to these images of the athlete much more successfully than have the writers of boxing fiction. The heroes of baseball novels tend most often to be young, innocent, and talented. Mark Harris, for example, wrote three novels about a youthful, gifted pitcher from a small town who discovers the world through his interactions with teammates and management. Roy Hobbs of Bernard Malamud's *The Natural* (1952) and Joe Kutner of Eliot Asinof's *Man on Spikes* (1955) are emotionally and psychologically young until they encounter the complex reality of big-time baseball. The vision of a baseball novel is often nostalgic—William Brashler's *The Bingo Long Traveling All-Stars and Motor Kings* (1973) recalls the era of the Negro baseball leagues with all its grimness but also with its legendary uniqueness and Lucy Kennedy recalls a different golden age in *The Sunlit Field* (1950), an historical novel about the origins of organized baseball in America. Nostalgia is even the dominant tone of the nonfiction works of the best sports writer on baseball, Roger Angell. In *The Summer Game* and *Five Seasons*, Angell's descriptions of recent games and heroes bathe them already in the glow of memory, making baseball a game of yesterdays stored in the mind of the devoted fan. The baseball player is perhaps, above all, innocent in his dominant image, with all the virtues and limitations that innocence entails.

Football offers two representative figures, the *cavalier* and the *corporate man*. The cavalier is the heroic figure who maintains grace and honor in the face of destruction and chaos. This is the quarterback, coolly ignoring the pass rush of 280-pound behemoths to release the ball only when the moment is right and his receiver is prepared. Or he is the receiver, leaping gracefully for that ball with outstretched fingers, disdainful of the crushing tackle to which he has made himself vulnerable. Such a figure, surviving courageously and continually making heroic gestures, is at the root of the appeal of football in the South, deprived now of blood sports and of antebellum and Civil War cavalier heroes. Southern writers such as Robert Penn Warren, William Styron, James Whitehead, James Dickey, and even William Faulkner have all written about football. This figure also defines an extreme ideal of masculinity—the football player more than any other kind of athlete popularly exemplifies manliness. Contemporary heroes such as Paul Hornung and Joe Namath are the epitome of this type, but the high school or college quarterback's dating the best-looking cheerleader is a familiar occurrence in the popular imagination if not in reality. The "stud" football player is indeed more a creation of the public imagination than of the game itself, as is evidenced by the shifting from the early years of the game in which all eleven positions were more or less equally honored, to the situation today in which a hierarchy or "pecking order" has been imposed by the public on the football team. The supreme sexual being is the figure at the top of this hierarchy—usually a quarterback or running back.

The football hero's second image is that of the corporate man. Teamwork, cooperation, and precise timing are essential to football more than to any other American sport. Formations and plays are intricately devised, endlessly practiced, and successfully executed only if every member of the team performs his portion of the overall design. Certain key performers appear to be more important than others, but in reality the beauty of a well-conceived and executed play is the creation of order out of seeming chaos by the precision teamwork of eleven men. In direct contrast to baseball players, football players are virtually anonymous, their shapes distorted by padding, their faces disguised by masked helmets, and their actions often obscured by the massing of other bodies.

Fictional treatments of the football hero have focused on these two images almost to the exclusion of any other concerns. The cavalier hero appeared first in a large number of college-football novels in the twenties, thirties, and forties, that portrayed the football player as "Big Man on Campus." This fiction was a response to the rise of college football from a mere clash of school loyalties to big business. In novels such as Percy Marks's *The Unwilling God* (1929), Charles Ferguson's *Pigskin* (1929), Millard Lampell's *The Hero* (1949), Howard Nemerov's *The Homecoming Game* (1957), William Manchester's *The Long Gainer* (1961), and Lloyd Pye's *That Prosser Kid* (1977), these writers explore the disparity between the ideals of the university and the glorification of the athlete at the university's expense. (This fiction also gave birth to the "dumb jock" image, most often attributed to football players, but his is a less important image than the two I have mentioned.) The college-football novels reveal some variety of approach: *The Unwilling God* examines the unfair burden hero-worship places on the athlete, but it ends by justifying it; *Pigskin* and *The Long Gainer* detail the self-destruction of an academic community and its leader that occurs when the university subordinates itself to the athlete-hero; *The Hero* observes the injury to the star athlete caused by the illusion of fame in a society motivated solely by economics; *The Homecoming Game* focuses on the professor caught between academic standards and athletic department pressures; and *That Prosser Kid* emphasizes the university's hypocrisy in using athletes as disposable property whose sole value is to promote the school's reputation. These variations on a standard plot are slight, and college-football novels are almost uniformly unexceptional. Only Joel Sayre's *Rackety Rax* (1932) appears at all inspired—the reductio ad absurdum of the whole subgenre, it describes satirically the creation of a hypothetical university by gangsters, in order to field a football team of ex-professional boxers and wrestlers. *Rackety Rax* contains much hyperbolic violence, but there is as much truth here as there was in Frank Merriwell who was playing strictly for loyalty and character building in 1903 when forty-four students in this country were killed playing football.[60]

More recent variations of the cavalier football hero are found in the glut of sex-and-violence professional football novels of the past few years. The extreme representation of the sexual athlete is Billy Clyde Puckett of Dan Jenkins's *Semi-Tough* (1972), but other novels such as Peter Gent's *North Dallas Forty* (1973) and Jack Olsen's *Alphabet Jackson* (1974) describe this figure more critically. Most impressively, Frederick Exley in *A Fan's Notes* (1968) poignantly considers the awful burden the sexual ideal of the football hero places on the nonathlete.

The corporate man also figures prominently in these professional football novels. The athlete, dehumanized not just by the violence of his sport but by owners' manipulations and coaches' treatment of him as mere property, has become a familiar fictional creation in the last decade. Heroes of these novels typically rebel against this corporate oppression, but they are most often crushed. A single representative example of this type of novel is *Only a Game* (1967) by Robert Daley, which explores the crippling consequences of a team's insistence on crushing the athlete's individuality. Duke Craig, the novel's embattled hero, expresses this depersonalization early in the novel:

> The hero on Sunday is number 6. The mob cheers me as a number, not as a man. They cheer the result of a run, they don't cheer the thought and experience and—and imagination I put into a run. They don't know who I really am, and they don't care. The touchdown is all that counts. The number is a hero to them, not me.[61]

The public's desire for images rather than men is fed by the team owner and coaches, who treat the players like children, fining them for every deviation from an essentially juvenile code of acceptable behavior. When Duke chooses to have an affair rather than remain loyal to an incompatible wife, the movement toward his inevitable banning from football is assured. Duke Craig is given two options—to conform, to submerge his own identity in the team's corporate structure, or to assert his rights as a man, by which choice he effectively bans himself from his profession. This dilemma is a recurring pattern in novels such as Gary Cartwright's *The Hundred-*

Yard War (1968) and Peter Gent's *North Dallas Forty*. The degree of personal loss varies in these novels, but not the basic conflict.

Finally, basketball offers a fourth image of the athlete-hero. Until very recently, basketball had not produced a substantial body of literature, but its current status as the most popular spectator sport in America and its impressive metaphorical possibilities virtually guarantee that its use in fiction will increase in the next several years. The basketball hero can be most readily defined not as the animal man, the frontier individualist, the cavalier, or the corporate man, but as the *artist*. Specifically, basketball and the basketball player are best explained by analogy to jazz music and dance. The game of basketball, more than other American sports, has a rhythm that is recognizable by most fans. The bouncing of the ball and the pounding of feet on the hardwood provide a continually changing metronomic tempo for each game. The tempo or rhythm is never steady or constant, as in a Bach fugue, but is ever shifting, like the improvisations of a jazz combo. The rhythm of individual players is syncopated, as they fake opponents by shifting speeds and changing the beat unexpectedly. The flow of the game often plays to a contrapuntal rhythm as, for example, when a running team plays a slow-down, patterned team. The tempo of baseball or football is much more regular and predictable. The basketball court is the player's restricting medium, like the musician's scale or keyboard, but within this basic constriction the player has great freedom to create or improvise. There are occasions for solo virtuosity, but success more often depends on all the members of the quintet creating harmony, not dissonance, by complementing each other. Each player improvises independently but must be aware of what the other four are doing so that his actions are in harmony with theirs.

The basketball player is freer than his baseball or football counterparts. He is less constrained by organization and discipline, less encumbered by his uniform. He even has another dimension in which to perform—vertical space is as important to him as horizontal space. The players' movements are often dancelike—not the formalized movements of a waltz or minuet, but the spontaneous, unpredictable movements of modern jazz dancing. At times these movements resemble classical ballet in the players' maintenance of grace and intricacy of movement within confined space and in the importance of vertical space in which sheer leaping ability is not as important as the players' ability to perform graceful maneuvers in the air. More than one sports fan has likened Julius Erving of the Philadelphia 76'ers to a ballet dancer, but "Doctor J" himself describes his art in the terminology of jazz: "When it's my turn to solo, I'm not about to play the same old riff."[62] The ability to be but *barely* in control, to exert to one's limits and still maintain control of the ball and of one's own body is the mark of the great basketball player, and of jazz performers as well.

Basketball is a less rationalized game than baseball or football. Accuracy in shooting is due not to careful aiming but to "touch"—an irrational, almost mystical quality. Like the musician who can learn chord theory but must have an irrational quality we call "genius" to be a great improvisational artist, a basketball player can learn and practice the basic skills of his sport, but must have this same genius to excel. The productions of all artists are a sum of their parts plus genius—and the basketball player is no exception. Ralph Ellison, in an essay on jazz, explains this relationship between skills and genius beautifully:

> For after the jazzman has learned the fundamentals of his instrument and the traditional techniques of jazz—the intonations, the mute work, manipulation of the timbre, the body of traditional styles—he must then "find himself," must be reborn, must find, as it were, his soul. All this through achieving that subtle identification between his instrument and his deepest drives which will allow him to express his own unique ideas and his own unique voice. He must achieve, in short, his self-determined identity.[63]

Basketball teams use patterns rather than plays; strategy lies in general principles rather than decisions made for each pitch or play. A football team practices a particular play repeatedly before a game, against every defense the opponent might possibly use. A baseball team practices double plays, throws to the cutoff man, responsibilities in covering the bases until actions in a game become automatic. In its earliest days basketball, too, was rigidly patterned and strategized, but in the modern game dominated by blacks, a team takes the court with little more than the players' skills and a few basic principles of play—loose patterns like the melody line of a musical score. The players improvise on these basic principles; they spontaneously create as they play. They must react to unforeseen accidents, adjust to abrupt shifts in the game's rhythm, improvise the best maneuver for each situation as it arises. The game is a fluid but erratic flow of great intricacy, and the players are independent but intimately related creative artists. They are not bound to regimented control; they freely and instinctively create.

If the basketball player is an artist, then, his position in relation to society is problematical. Society is a rational structure and the artist is an "irrational" being. Plato was perhaps the first to warn that the artist is dangerous to society, and many subsequent commentators have reiterated this opinion. Writers of basketball fiction implicitly endorse this judgment, for they tend most often to portray heroes who are fundamentally incompatible with their society. Mack Davis of Jay Neugeboren's *Big Man* (1966) is the superhuman "Plastic Man" on the basketball court where he finds his true identity, but a misfit off it in structured society. Hector Bloom in *Drive, He Said* (1964) by Jeremy Larner is also an instinctive basketball star, but a revolutionary who is either "deranged," or sane in an insane world. Elwood Baskins, hero of Lawrence Shainberg's *One on One* (1970), exists more often in the private world of his own psyche than in the public world of family, friends, and teammates. And Harry Angstrom, John Updike's creation in *Rabbit, Run* (1960), refuses to relinquish his star status despite the conclusion of his basketball career and finds in his own heart, not in social responsibilities, the absolute by which he lives his life. All of these novels are products of the 1960s and 1970s, of a time in which the heroes of most important American fiction are out of step with what is perceived to be an increasingly oppressive society. The basketball hero is an ideal subject for the fiction of this period.

Each of these four major sports, then, provides the writer of sports novels with a particular version of the athlete-hero

for his fictional uses. Of course, not all of the sports novels
define their heroes in precisely the ways suggested here, but
these are the dominant images of the boxer, and the baseball,
football, and basketball players. To repeat, however, these
are but four versions of the one basic image of the athlete-
hero, defined for all time by Gilbert Patten. Elements of this
basic type are present in *all* sports fiction; writers create
their own heroes in opposition to this prototype, but the model
is evoked at least faintly in every sports novel. The athlete-
hero is the embodiment of much that is both best and worst in
America. He celebrates soaring aspirations and opportunities for excellence. He is a symbol of youth and joy and the
love of play. His world is the best, even though imperfect,
arena of social mobility. Sport, our most egalitarian institution, is a constant reminder of the importance of the inter-
dependence and camaraderie of a group. In today's unstable
times, the athlete-hero is proof that permanence is possible.

On the other hand, the athlete-hero is also a disturbing reminder of American anti-intellectualism, self-centeredness,
immaturity, and failure to extend our supposed inalienable
rights to all people. For every sports hero, there are thou-
sands who have failed to achieve that plateau, who had to fail.
A hero, after all, can only be a hero by uniquely rising above
the mass of men. He is also an expression of the excessive
privileges and responsibilities we give to a few despite our insistence on the equality of all. The sports world is indeed a
microcosm of American society, and the athlete-hero in many
ways is its representative man.

three

The Sunlit Field:
Country and City in American Sports Fiction

In sunburnt parks where Sundays lie,
Or the wide wastes beyond the cities,
Teams in grey deploy through sunlight.
—Robert Fitzgerald,
"Cobb Would Have Caught It"

In 1866 Charles A. Peverelly published a book on baseball entitled *The National Game.*[1] Since that time, the presidents of the American and National Leagues and millions of baseball fans as well have insisted that baseball is "the national game." But that a man writing about a sport officially organized for barely two decades could so designate his subject is rather remarkable. Baseball had existed in various forms for centuries; in early America, boys played town ball, rounders, and four-old-cat as avidly as their great-great-grandchildren would play work-up or stick ball. Not until 1845, however, did Alexander Cartwright, a member of the aristocratic Knickerbocker Club of New York, codify the rules of baseball and organize the first baseball team in America. The game was immediately successful, and a host of challengers emerged to oppose the Knickerbockers' supremacy. By 1866 when Peverelly wrote his book, baseball had indeed earned its appellation, and it continued to grow in popularity throughout the century. In 1869 the Cincinnati Red Stockings became the first professional baseball team. In 1876 the pro clubs were organized into the National League, to be challenged by the American Association in 1882, the Brotherhood League in 1890, and the American League in 1900. By the turn of the century, baseball was not just a recreation, but a passion to millions of Americans.

Football also developed rapidly during this same period as the premier college game. The first intercollegiate contest in America was played in 1869 by Rutgers and Princeton. This game was based on English soccer, but in 1874 McGill University of Montreal introduced a rugby-type game to Harvard, and this became the basis for American football. The year 1875 saw the inaugural of the Harvard-Yale rivalry; 1876, the formation of the Intercollegiate Football Association; and 1889, the selection of the first All-American team by Walter Camp. By 1905 football had grown to such an extent that even so staunch a supporter of the "strenuous life" as President Theodore Roosevelt had to warn the colleges to modify the more violent phases of the game.

Historian John Rickards Betts has identified the years 1860-90 as "the athletic impulse," and the period 1890-1920 as "the triumph of athletics,"[2] for, in addition to baseball and football, numerous other sports emerged prominently during this period. Basketball was invented in the winter of 1891 by Dr. James Naismith. Boxing acquired its first organization and moderate respectability with the introduction of the Queensbury code and banning of bare-knuckle championships in 1889 and with the reigns of popular champions such as John L. Sullivan and Gentleman Jim Corbett. Between 1875 and 1900, lawn tennis was introduced into this country from England and ice hockey from Canada, and the United States Skating Association, the National Bowling League, the National Croquet Association, and the Amateur Athletic Union were all formed. The first country club, the first playground, the first sports page, and the first summer camp all contributed during this era to the growing interest in athletics in America.

Sports leaped obtrusively into the American scene during the last third of the nineteenth century, during the time of a more significant and more widely observed development, the rise of the city. In 1860 less than a quarter of the American population lived in a city or town, but by 1890 the figure had reached a third, and by 1910 nearly a half.[3] Immigrants, uprooted by the commercial transformation of traditional European agriculture, and Americans, driven to cities by the intense isolation and hardship of rural life, swelled the newly emerging industrial centers of the nation and drastically altered the quality of Amerian life. More important than the actual changes in the conditions of existence, however, the essential American myth of the New-World Eden was permanently disrupted. America has always been self-conscious about her relationship to nature. The New World appeared to Europeans as a "virgin land," an opportunity for the rebirth of Western civilization, but accounts of New England winters and other hardships were also sent across the Atlantic during the years of settlement. The early colonists reported a contradictory mixture of awe and terror before the wilderness confronting them. The "hidious and desolate wilderness" into which William Bradford stepped from the *Mayflower* bears little resemblance to the land described seventy-five years later in Robert Beverley's *History and Present State of Virginia* (1705): "In fine, if any one impartially considers all the Advantages of this Country, as Nature made it; he must allow it to be as Fine a Place, as any in the Universe."[4] These statements represent the two conflicting ways in which the first European settlers of the New World viewed the landscape, but the myth of the garden, that is, the agrarian ideal of nature improved by man, has prevailed as the dominant attitude towards nature in America. Leo Marx's *The Machine in the Garden* and Henry Nash Smith's *Virgin Land*[5] trace this attitude throughout America's history; Marx, for example, cites Richard Price, a leading British champion of American independence, as a representative of this ideal:

> The happiest state of man is the middle state between the *savage* and the *refined,* or between the wild and the luxurious state. Such is the state of society in CONNECTICUT and some others of the *American* provinces; where the inhabitants consist, if I am rightly informed, of an independent and hardy YEOMANRY, all nearly on a level—trained to arms ...clothed in homespun—of simple manners—stranger to luxury—drawing plenty from the ground and that plenty, gathered easily by the hand of industry.[6]

This definition of the agrarian ideal of the middle state was reconfirmed by J. Hector St. John de Crèvecoeur in *Letters from an American Farmer* (1782), Thomas Jefferson in *Notes on the State of Virginia* (1785), Alexis de Tocqueville in *Democracy in America* (1840), and many other champions of rural life.[7]

The failure of this agrarian ideal, the recession of the frontier, and the consequent rise of the city necessitated a radical transformation in Americans' perceptions of themselves as Adamic children of nature, but a belief so intrinsic to the nation's very existence could not be overturned easily. As Americans accommodated themselves to urban life, they continued to cling to fragmentary or vicarious experiences of nature. Boy Scouts, camping trips, and vacations to the mountains or the beaches became weekend wilderness tonic for urban Americans entering the twentieth century. In literature, the cowboy hero of the vanished Wild West was transformed into the detective prowling the urban asphalt jungle, or Tarzan swinging through the new frontiers of Africa. More important for our interests, in response to the rise of cities and the recession of the frontier, sport emerged as a new American obsession.

The concurrence of the rise of the city and the rise of sport is not coincidental, as simple observable facts can attest. In an article entitled "The Technological Revolution and the Rise of Sport, 1850-1900," historian Betts cites the major technological advancements that significantly increased the popularity of athletics; the railroad system, the Atlantic cable, the improvements in printing and the rise of newspapers, the electric light, the camera, the wireless, the rapid transit system, and the motion picture all brought news of athletic events more quickly to more people or enabled the teams themselves to play opponents over a wider geographical region.[8] The manufacture of standardized sporting goods created for the first time the possibility of sports played with comparable equipment in every part of the country. In the nineteenth century, sport itself became an integral part of the rise of big business—professional teams were owned and operated as businesses; the manufacturing of sporting goods became a major industry; players were hired, supposedly as industrial workers, but actually as ballplayers on factory teams.

Industrialization and urbanization also created a large working class for whom sports became a major leisure outlet. Prizefighting had long been of interest only to the lower (supposedly depraved) classes, but now baseball also became a sport of the worker. The first baseball club, the Knickerbockers, was really a social club in which the well-born or successful gentlemen of Manhattan could engage in dignified exercise. But the more rough-and-tumble Brooklyn and Jersey teams composed of factory workers soon proved their superiority. In fact, it was well into the twentieth century before baseball players regained respectability in the moralistic public eye. Football began as a game for the proper youths of the ivy league schools, but rivalry soon led to the recruitment of semi-professional athletes who were often not even students at the schools for which they played; thus football was radically democratized. The sport did not become highly organized on the professional level until 1920, however, and professional players did not achieve the respectability of their baseball counterparts until mid-century. Writing in 1908, Thorstein Veblen defined the sporting temperament as exploitative and predaceous, typical of the leisure class and of lower-class delinquents.[9] The earliest days of football and baseball may be described in this way, but lower- and middle-class emulation of the wealthy and increased opportunities for respectable lower-class individuals to play soon broadened the appeal of these sports.

Immigrants, too, became ready participants in the country's games, as a way of assimilating American life. They contributed their own sports and their relaxed European Sabbath introduced Sunday baseball to puritanical America. Professional sports in America have always drawn heavily from waves of current immigration and from internal migrations of previously oppressed peoples. Baseball appealed most to the Irish and the Germans before World War I and attracted large numbers of Poles and Italians as well as southern and southwestern rural Anglo-Americans between the wars. Since the late 1940s American blacks and Spanish-speakers from the Caribbean and Central America have become increasingly conspicuous among the outstanding players of the game. Boxing and football also offered opportunities for social mobility to those most desperately in need of it. Thus, the waves of immigrants in the last part of the nineteenth century that swelled American cities created a base for the rise of American sport.

The rise of sport was also indebted to more subtle causes. Historian Frederick L. Paxson in 1917 offered the hypothesis that sport provided a "safety valve" outlet for American city-dwellers that made urban existence bearable under the increasing pressure generated in industrial society. He wrote: "When the frontier closed in the eighties the habit of an open life was too strong to be changed offhand. The search for sport revealed a partial substitute for pioneer life."[10] Paxson was responding to Frederick Jackson Turner's claim that the frontier operated as a safety valve for Eastern urban centers. Turner's thesis has since been challenged by a number of historians,[11] but whether "safety valve" is the proper term for sport's relationship to the frontier or not, a clear correspondence is evident between the two, particularly in their impact on the American imagination. A special regard for nature and the natural is essential to the American experience, and nineteenth-century urbanization and industrialization necessitated significant changes in the conception of American life. Sport is representative of the way in which Americans accommodated themselves to urban existence while retaining at least a vestigial sense of their original closeness to nature.

On the simplest level, sports offered the urbanite an opportunity for physical exercise, for pushing oneself close to one's physical limitations, and for perfecting physical skills. To engage in sports was also to react against the depersonalization of cities by creating "communities" of individual athletes bound together for the common good—as homesteaders had done on the frontier. These communities in turn produced communities of spectators unified by their team loyalties.

The grass of the football or baseball field also creates a naturalistic setting within the concrete and asphalt city. The city imposes its order on these natural fields, limiting them to precisely demarcated sizes and shapes, yet within those boundaries empty space—the essential quality of nature or the frontier—is maintained, in contrast to the compression and compaction of bodies in the city. The relationship of baseball players within the space of the ball field is defined by the earth, grass, and air separating them, just as settlers of the sparsely populated frontier were so related; in football, the crowded cluster of bodies on one part of the field is compensated by the space around them. In this space, events can happen; a ball is hit between outfielders, who must converge on the point of impact, or at some particular point on a football field a thrown ball, a receiver, and a pass defender simultaneously converge to create the drama of the game. In these sports, events and their dramatic consequences occur by design in open space, not in the accidental collisions of overcrowded cities or in secret board meetings. The football or baseball team is challenged to defend its space against bad luck and the opponent's offensive thrusts by clever positioning of players and manipulation of the ball. This attempt to achieve maximum control of the environment where total human domination is impossible is analogous to the task of the pioneer who had to defend his homestead or claim against the encroachment of beasts, enemies, and nature.

Time, too, is an urban obsession and is regulated by clocks in the city. Urbanites wake up to an alarm clock, not with the sun; work from 9:00 A.M. to 5:00 P.M. rather than from sunrise to sundown; keep appointments, meet deadlines, and entertain themselves during specific hours not allotted to other activities. On the other hand, time in nature is the time of the seasons, of the rising and setting of the sun, and of the configuration of the stars at night. Time in sports combines this natural organic time of the country with mechanical urban time. In baseball, time is in a sense defeated, for the length of a game is nine potentially limitless innings not governed by clocks. There has never actually been an endless game, but contests have been terminated by loss of sunlight—the kind of time that functions in nature—and the possibility always exists that a game could last forever. In football, mechanical time imposes itself by the fact that the contest is limited to sixty minutes, but the game exerts pressure against this artificial restraint by allowing the clock to stop with incomplete passes, a player's stepping out of bounds, or simply by the desire of one of the teams for a "time out." A sixty-minute game usually lasts about three hours, but it can vary greatly in length; by clever manipulation of time, a team can run several plays in mere seconds at the end of a game to prevent defeat before the final gun. If time is not defeated here, it is at least expanded and contracted.

What conclusion, then, should we draw from the relationship between sport and nature? Sport is clearly one attempt to compensate for urban America's loss of contact with its wilderness origins, for a nation defined initially by its relationship to nature must maintain at least some contact with those roots. Sport clearly provides an outlet for rural nostalgia, but more complexly, sport is both a product of urbanization and an antidote to it. It is only appropriate, then, that sports literature reflect the myth of America's identification with nature and struggle to accommodate urban reality.

The *natural* is the purest embodiment of the wilderness ideal. In essence he is a figure born in nature, who maintains an intimate relationship to his natural environment, and who is blessed with inborn skills that enable him to exist happily in his natural state. The natural is the companion figure to the self-made man in the pantheon of American mythic heroes and is deeply rooted in American folklore. Since the New World was long perceived by Europe as a virgin land which offered men the opportunity for a return to a natural state, it was inevitable that Americans would embrace the natural, the quintessential inhabitant of the virgin land, as a major expression of the national character. As a mass conception, and one motivated by nationalistic pride, the idea of the natural in America is invariably simple and naive. Americans, with no native mythology, consciously created one, and such legendary figures as Paul Bunyan, Pecos Bill, Joe Magarac, and John Henry are all primitivistic incarnations of the natural. The careers of real Americans have also been so interpreted, giving us many of our "authentic" American heroes: Daniel Boone, Davy Crockett, Johnny Appleseed, Buffalo Bill, Kit Carson, Babe Ruth, and Sergeant York, to name a few. As R. W. B. Lewis points out, however, this impulse to identify

Americans with natural virtue was originally far from simple-minded:

> A century ago the image contrived to embody the most fruitful contemporary ideas was that of the authentic American as a figure of heroic innocence and vast potentialities, poised at the start of a new history.[12]

The writers Lewis examines who explored this Adamic theme include the major figures of the period: Holmes, Whitman, Henry James, Sr., Bushnell, Brown, Cooper, Bird, Hawthorne, and Melville. The original vitality of this idea soon eroded, however. As the country inevitably failed to fulfill its regenerative promise, the image of the American natural became increasingly simplified. In the popular mind, and in the minds of many great American writers as well, stereotyped images of "country" and "city" calcified. The country became a place of innocence, virtue, spontaneity, and fulfillment; the city of experience, corruption, scheming, and frustration. The country was life, the city death; if not quite good and evil, they at least suggested divine support for human endeavors and cosmic indifference to insignificant mankind. These ideas were already well entrenched by the beginning of the twentieth century and the introduction of sports fiction in America.

Rubes and Other Naturals

Athletes are perhaps the figures most consistently interpreted today as naturals. Certain individuals seem to be naturally coordinated and athletic, and "natural athlete" distinguishes those players from the ones who acquire competence by hard work and correction of normal weaknesses. In fiction the baseball player is the premier natural. Baseball is *the* country game; football compromises with urban limitations on time and space to a greater extent than does baseball, and boxing and basketball are our most urban sports. Other athletes are sometimes portrayed as naturals, but the majority are baseball players. The problem for the fictional natural athlete lies in the fact that the source of his power and virtue is undefiled nature, but he must come to the city to demonstrate his skills. Some writers of sports fiction have used this archetypal situation to embrace the stereotyped images of country and city, while others have used the convention of the natural to criticize the corruption of the urban sports establishment or of urban life in general; only a few have created complex visions of the relationship of country and city, the natural and the civilized, in American life.

The "rube" is a common figure in sports fiction, a descendent of the longest line of native American humor. His great grandfather was the shrewd Yankee peddler, identified by Constance Rourke as "a symbol of triumph, of adaptability, of irrepressible life—of many qualities needed to induce confidence and self-possession among a new and unamalgamated people."[13] The rural Yankee was repeatedly shown in plays and tales to be superior to the New Yorker; he was a trickster with distinctive American wit and cleverness. The rube combines this Yankee tradition with a naive version of the natural, or frontier roarer, and the result is not a comic figure who outwits his city cousin and is always in control of his destiny, but a blundering and simple but physically talented hick who succeeds almost miraculously at the expense of his sophisticated city brothers. The rube leads a charmed life —God seems to look after him as He looks after half-wits and other "naturals"—but the rube is never in complete control of any situation. His athletic skill is immense, and outside his native habitat he is most at home and most successful in the athletic contest. Yet, his untrained ability constantly threatens to break out of control, to explode to the detriment of himself and those around him. If he is a pitcher, he is extraordinarily fast, but also wild, and each pitch seems equally liable to hit the batter in the head, sail over the backstop, or cut the heart of the plate for an unhittable strike. The rube is a force as natural and as powerful as the elements, and as unpredictable. "Rube" Waddell, a great pitcher with the Philadelphia Athletics in the early years of the century, is the classic example of this type. He is reputed to have left games to chase fire engines, and he was found one day—while he was supposed to be pitching—under the grandstand playing marbles with some young boys. But as a pitcher of baseballs he was nearly incomparable.

George Fitch was one of many writers who created rubes in their fiction. In *The Big Strike at Siwash* (1909) and *At Good Old Siwash* (1911), one of the major characters is Ole Skjarsen, "a timid young Norwegian giant, with a rick of white hair and a reenforced concrete physique . . . as big as a carthorse, as graceful as a dray."[14] The football coach finds this rare specimen in a lumber camp, explains to him what a college is, and then drags him to Siwash:

> When Skjarsen landed he wore boots, stuffed with trousers, yarn socks and feet, and the rest of his clothes had come over in the steerage with him. Whether they had ever come off him was a little doubtful. He talked a little English, chiefly through his shoulder blades from the sound, and his education was what you might call sub-primary.[15]

The coach attempts to make Ole into a fullback, because he is "hard as flint and so fast on his feet that we couldn't tackle him any more than we could have tackled a jackrabbit,"[16] but Ole seems incapable of learning even the simplest fundamentals of the city game of football. His most serious handicap to learning is his persistent literalness—he runs exactly as far and in the direction the coach tells him. Such literalness is typical of the rube-natural whose rural life is instinctive and simple and unsuited for any of the complexities of the city.

Ole's first crisis occurs in his initial game against Muggledorfer. In practice during the week, after having trampled through the entire scrub team, he had repeatedly stopped running short of the goal line to obtain further instructions. When coach Bost finally explodes, "And when they give you the ball you take it, and don't you dare to stop with it. . . . If you dare to stop with that ball I'll ship you back to the lumber camp in a cattle car,"[17] Ole takes this command to heart. At his first opportunity, he thunders the length of the field through the Muggledorfer team and continues out of the stadium and down the highway, stopping only when Bost catches him in his automobile and apologizes profusely for the verbal abuse. Ole not only proves his physical superiority to all his city teammates and opponents, he also bests the cunning and vitriolic city coach.

Ole experiences other aspects of college life, most noticeably initiation into not one but three fraternities, and on every occasion his bumbling uncouth ways succeed. He never fails to get what he wants, is never hurt or embarrassed, and always triumphs over his sophisticated but helpless classmates. In fact, a pattern emerges in the stories: the more sophisticated a character is, the more foolish and helpless he appears. On an ascending scale, Englishmen, Easterners, Siwash faculty, Siwash students, and finally the rube become shrewder and more successful in achieving their ends. At the conclusion of *The Big Strike,* we are even told that Ole is now running for governor. This is an essay in primitivism that needs only a monkey as the supreme hero to be complete.

Other writers have also utilized the rube in their fiction. Zane Grey's *The Red-Headed Outfield and Other Baseball Stories* (1915), Franklin M. Reck's *Varsity Letter* (1942), and Charles E. Van Loan's *Taking the Count* (1915) all relate accounts of the rube. Zane Grey's rube is Whitaker Hurtle from Rickettsville, the hero of five of the stories in the volume. Interestingly, the five tales appear in a 1-4-3-2-5 order; the clock runs more or less backward—an appropriate metaphor for the past-oriented cult of the natural. The physical description of Whit is virtually interchangeable with the portrait of Ole Skjarsen:

> He was over six feet tall and as lean as a fence rail. He had a great shock of light hair, a sunburned, sharp featured face, wide sloping shoulders, and arms enormously long. He was about as graceful and had about as much of a baseball walk as a crippled cow.[18]

He is also an amazing pitcher: incredibly fast, occasionally wild, and absolutely certain of his ability—all typical rube traits. He whips all the city boys on the diamond, wins the Eastern League Pennant for his team, and breaks into the major leagues with the Chicago White Sox. In his first start with the Sox, he bests the world champion Philadelphia Athletics 1-0.

Grey does make a major shift from the rube portrayed by Fitch, however, when he also has Whit court and marry the most popular girl in town. In writing a love story with a rube as hero, the writer faces the same problems that plagued James Fenimore Cooper. The rube is no more appropriate as a mate for a proper heroine than Natty Bumppo is. Grey is, accordingly, forced to modify his portrait. Whit improves with civilizing: he doesn't "wallow in society" as Ole Skjarsen does but overcomes his awkwardness, dresses properly, and acquires the basic skills of social decorum. This is a return to the "middle ground" of improved nature, and the author sacrifices humor for the sake of the love affair. The stories become, as a result, much less interesting or enjoyable than the more naive Siwash stories.

Franklin Reck's Buck Weaver of "The Gawk," a story in *Varsity Letter*, is another figure whose rural greenness must be modified. His appearance again is typical of the rube, and his cockiness only makes him the butt of jokes when he demonstrates his swimming ability. His "double trudgeon" is no match for the more sophisticated Australian crawl of his opponent, and he loses the race convincingly. But after he learns "city" techniques, his own natural strength overcomes his rival in a contest pitting the "vast endurance and simple courage of a rawboned freshman against the oil-smooth form and competitive experience of Red Gardner."[19] Natural virtue with just a little refinement proves unstoppable.

Only Charles E. Van Loan, of these four writers, treats the rube with any real irony. In "Easy Picking" from *Taking the Count,* the city comes to the country where the city trickster is tricked. Old Bird, the "official stumbling block" in the lightweight division, feigns ignorance of boxing so that he can fight the local farmers' champ, Arthur Cullen, and make a killing by betting on himself. Arthur turns out to be a great natural fighter who can "slip a punch with his head" as only a handful of fighters can do, and who knocks Old Bird out with a single blow. (A one-punch knockout is the boxer's equivalent of the natural pitcher's unhittable fastball.) The rubes outsmart the city slickers, and Arthur uses one of Old Bird's own ruses to clobber him.

This sounds like standard rube fiction until the last paragraph when Old Bird says, "A feller told me once that all the wise guys in the cities came in from the small towns."[20] This statement places the rube in a new light. The boxing world is full of cheats and crooks, and in this story they meet their match in some simple farmers. But the farmers are not simple after all; Arthur kayoes Old Bird not with his natural skill but with the help of supposedly urban deceit. And one of the farmers tells Old Bird:

> We may be hayseeds up here in Parkerton, but we know a fighter when we see him. I've got this boy tied up for ten years, and as soon as the apple crop is in I'm going to take him down to San Francisco and get a chance to bet some money on the short end for a change.[21]

Van Loan is surprisingly subtle here. Since the farmers are somewhat corrupt already, the city will simply offer them opportunities to become more so. The farmers also have the fine young boxer "tied up" for ten years, and the reader immediately recalls other stories describing the manipulation of fighters by self-interested managers. We are left with the possibility that citizens of the country are no more virtuous than the worst corruptors of boxing, and that their seeming simplicity allows them to connive more effectively. This suggestion is barely implicit in the story, but it demonstrates how a writer can use the convention of the rube for its intrinsic possibilities of humor and surprise, but not yield totally to its potential for oversimplification.

The rube is one narrowly defined example of a comic natural, but the natural also appears in sports fiction in other more serious guises. Jack London was the first important American writer to use sport prominently in his fiction, and in *The Abysmal Brute* (1913), he created the classic stereotype of the natural in sports literature. The fact that the characterization of Pat Glendon is so totally stereotypical should not prejudice readers today entirely against London's accomplishment. London wrote this novel when sport was not widely recognized as a significant part of American culture; in recognizing that the archetypal opposition of country and city is fundamental to sport's appeal to Americans, London was actually ahead of his time.

Young Pat Glendon, London's titular hero, is a child of nature, the American Adam in his simplest guise. Our first glimpse of him defines for all time the physical appearance of the natural:

> ... a young giant walk[ed] into the clearing. In one hand was a rifle, across his shoulders a heavy deer under which he moved as if it were weightless. He was dressed roughly in blue overalls and woollen shirt open at the throat. Coat he had none, and on his feet, instead of brogans were moccasins. . . . His walk was smooth and catlike, without suggestion of his two hundred and twenty pounds of weight to which that of the deer was added. . . . He seemed a creature of the wild, more a night-roaming figure from some old fairy story or folk tale than a twentieth-century youth.[22]

No hint appears here of the gangliness of the comic rube, only sheer animal grace. His entire personality and his values further support this romanticized depiction. His father tells the manager, Sam Stubener, that Pat has "lived natural" in his wilderness abode. He has never drunk alcohol nor tasted tobacco; he loves nature, is afraid of cities, and is woman shy. And, as his father tells Sam, he is a perfect fighter: "He is a wiz. He knows a blow without the lookin', when it starts an' where, the speed an' space, an' niceness of it. An' 'tis nothing I ever showed him.'Tis inspiration. He was so born."[23] His fighting is play to him, and while occasionally a challenge, it is never brutal.

Sam has appeared at the request of Pat's father (a former boxer himself) who wishes his son to prove his ability to the world. Young Glendon abandons his mountain home to fight in San Francisco only to please his father; he knocks out every ranking heavyweight, including the world champion, exposes the corruption he has shockingly discovered, and returns to the wilderness with his chosen woman. This is an easily recognizable portrait of the romanticized natural, and London extends the stereotype to its romantic limits. In the city Pat is utterly innocent, yet he is naturally keen and shrewd. Although he becomes homesick for his mountains and hates the city, he is imperturbable and never lost. He is sexually inexperienced, but he reveals an intuitive response to the opposite sex that young animals naturally possess.

However, his natural qualities are most evident in the ring, where his boxing is effortless and instinctive. A succession of opponents fail to seriously challenge him, but pose only minor problems to which he easily finds solutions. He is at times like a mother bear playfully cuffing her cubs—he does not wish to hurt his ring partners, only to show them their proper place. In a practice bout with Sam Stubener, for example, we are told:

> Young Pat played with him, and in the clinches made him feel as powerful as a baby, landing on him seemingly at will, locking and blocking with masterly accuracy, and scarcely noticing or acknowledging his existence. Half the time young Pat seemed to spend in gazing off at the landscape in a dreamy sort of way. And right here Stubener made another mistake. He took it for a trick of old Pat's training, tried to sneak in a short-arm jolt, found his arm in a lightning lock, and had both his ears cuffed for his pains.[24]

In his professional bouts, too, he occasionally reacts to opponents' flurries with whimsy, to his own strength with curiosity; only unsportsmanship can anger him. In all his bouts he wins at will, usually with a single punch, outdoing even the young Muhammad Ali in his ability to predict the outcome: "Inside ten seconds.... Watch me."[25] The combined talents of all the greatest fighters are his, but none of their unscrupulous tactics.

Near the conclusion of the story, Pat even demonstrates that he is a natural orator, not an inarticulate hick. He prefaces his final fight with an address to the crowd denouncing the corruption of professional boxing and thereby incites a small riot. He then proceeds to knock out both his opponent and the heavyweight champion with one punch apiece and returns with Maud Sangster, his natural mate, to a life of arcadian bliss in his mountains. The simplicity of London's vision seems striking today; the natural appears to be used merely to establish the corruption of the city and the virtue of the country, while the natural himself is shown to be self-sufficient in either world but more at home in his natural environment. But historical perspective should enable us to appreciate London's conceptions. In 1913 when London wrote this story, athletes were not widely perceived as exemplars of natural virtue. Professionalism was still regarded by the cultured classes as a perversion of amateur sport, and prizefighters particularly were shunned by respectable society. It was not until the 1920s and Jack Dempsey, aided by the promotional genius of Tex Rickard, that the public fully embraced a boxing hero. Dempsey's conqueror, Gene Tunney, even more so in retrospect seems an example of life imitating London's art. Pat Glendon was an imaginative creation—as a fictional character he is not memorable, but as the embodiment of a popular myth he is important. London was able to see, before intellectuals made their judgments, that sport was becoming in the twentieth century a repository for American pastoral myths. His insight is impressive from this perspective, and he performed a specific service for future writers and students of sport; by defining the stereotype of the natural athlete in such rigid outline, he created an image subsequent generations could modify for their own uses.

In *Autumn Thunder* (1952), Robert Wilder virtually accepts London's stereotype but expands on the values implicit in the concept of the natural. Like Pat Glendon, Larry Summers leaves his mountain home to compete in the city, but he is overwhelmed by urban depersonalization and finally returns with his woman to the country. Wilder, perhaps influenced by Hemingway's metaphoric use of the mountain and the valley in *A Farewell to Arms*,[26] has Larry leave Gaynor's Notch to play football at the University and to "show those valley dudes a thing or two." He describes Larry in predictably natural terms through the perceptions of the boy's father:

> Latham used to watch the boy, unconsciously admiring the lithe, flowing grace which was characteristic of his movements. When he walked or ran or just stooped to pick up a rock for throwing, the actions flowed, one into the other. You had to notice this easy, natural rhythm. It was the way a cat moved. He'd been that way, it seemed to Latham, ever since he was a baby. There had never been anything awkward about him and he'd never run to ugly pimples the way most kids did. Studying him covertly now, Latham realized his son was probably what people called handsome: clear, dark features and the black hair and sort of gray-green eyes to go with it. . . . When he walked he toed in the same way, until it

didn't seem at all like a regular walk, but something sort of liquid, the way water ran.[27]

Such beauty, grace, and kinship with natural creatures and elements are standard fare in descriptions of the natural, but what Wilder adds to London's portrait is an expanded sense of the values this rural figure represents. Wilder has construc-ed the most complete version of idealized rural virtues and urban vices in all sports fiction. In the city, despite his mete-oric success on the football field, Larry feels as if he were on "some sort of mechanical conveyor belt moving down an as-sembly line."[28] In the city, clothes are important; fashion disguises the man as it cannot do in the country. Urban sexu-ality is unnatural—adultery and perverse fantasies stimulate Larry. The city is a sterile place—his own child is stillborn, and his mistress has never borne a child for her own husband.

Larry is a football star who plays for fun and for the *sensual* pleasures of the game—the sights, smells, sounds, and tactile sensations that define the natural aspects of the sport. In the city, however, football is business. In the country a direct re-lationship exists between work and rewards—one plows and one is able to harvest; in the city this correlation does not exist—Larry is given a job at which he is paid well for doing no work. In the city, too, fame comes easily to Larry as he be-comes an All-American and leads his team to victory in the Rose Bowl, but again a lack of correlation is seen between cause and effect. Fame makes Larry seem more than human and is not entirely warranted, but it is also transitory, and the loss of fame after his career ends deprives Larry of his iden-tity. In the country men are accepted at face value and cannot be traumatized either by fame or the lack of it. After his col-lege career ends, Larry works in a restaurant at a job he would enjoy were it not considered "low." In the idealized country, no such assignment of value is given to tasks; democ-racy rather than hierarchy prevails.

In the city, moreover, activities are compartmentalized; Larry must play football, keep up with his studies, and main-tain his personal relationships as separate activities. In the country one's activities together make an organic whole. Na-tural rural life is its own end, and it sustains no standards of success or advancement. In the city everyone looks out for himself—genuine neighborliness characterizes relationships in Gaynor's Notch—and the city with its many people is actually a much lonelier place. In the country a strong body and determination are all that are necessary in order to live; in the city these qualities often prove ineffectual.

Finally, women are confusingly liberated and unpredictable in the city; in the country they have prescribed roles. With his natural simplicity, Larry is no match for Doreen Stanton who uses her body and predatory instincts to achieve her own selfish ends. She is unnatural—when she returns to Larry after twenty years, she has apparently not aged. In contrast, love in the country is Edenic. When Larry returns to Gaynor's Notch at the end of the novel with Fern (note the name), they are reborn. Larry had been an old man in the city, where time is age; in the country, time is the cyclic rebirth of the seasons. In Gaynor's Notch, Larry and Fern are young again, productive at last, content in their simple life, and perfectly in love. Larry even returns to football—as coach of his old high school team—for no pay.

This idealization of the country is no more complex or subtle than London's vision, but Wilder has shifted the focus from that in *The Abysmal Brute*. London's natural is essentially an *Ubermensch* who draws his strength, the story implies, from his own resources—he was born that way. He is self-sufficient in either the country or the city, but the former is a more amenable habitat. Wilder has shifted the focus from the individual natural to the quality of life in the city and the country. Larry, too, is born with exceptional qualities, but they are insufficient to sustain him in the city; they need a natural environment in which to be constantly revitalized. Wilder thus has created polar metaphors of the country and the city, and although they fail on the realistic level through lack of complexity, they are effective as fully wrought symbols.

Wilder's novel is the most fully developed portrait of the country and city in American sports fiction, but somehow the central metaphor of *Autumn Thunder* does not seem quite right. Larry Summers should be a baseball player—trying to imagine him as an Adamic natural playing football in Gaynor's Notch causes a jumble in the reader's mind. Baseball is the preeminent country sport, not football, and if the country is to be idealized, it is most appropriately done so in the terms of the most rural of American games. The boxer in *The Abysmal Brute* actually works better, for although boxing is most insistently an urban sport, the boxer is ironically a natural, as will be discussed later in this chapter. He is a natural who struggles against urban conditions; the football player adapts to urban reality and acknowledges the corporate ideals of cooperation and selflessness. The natural is an autonomous individual, and the image of baseball supports this ideal more effectively.

The majority of naturals in sports fiction have indeed been baseball players; in fact, few baseball novels have failed to use this image to some degree. Ring Lardner was our first great writer of baseball fiction—in some ways he is still unsurpassed—and in collections such as *You Know Me Al* (1916) and *Lose with a Smile* (1933), as well as in his superb short stories, he portrays baseball players as rural naturals impossibly confused by their urban environments. He idealizes neither country nor city, but satirically comments on the most important sociological development of his time—the migration of Americans from small rural communities to the urban metropolis.

Lardner was born in 1885 in Niles, Michigan. In 1905 he left Niles for South Bend, Indiana, for his first newspaper job; in 1907 he moved to Chicago and a better job, and in 1919 to metropolitan New York—first to Greenwich, Connecticut, then to Great Neck, Long Island, in 1921, and finally to East Hampton, Long Island, in 1928. His career was thus a highly successful version of the larger trend in the country—the movement from small towns to the large urban centers in quest of fame and fortune. His migration from west to east represents an antimythic backlash to the supposed opportunities of the frontier West. The country moved west, in spirit and in fact, in the nineteenth century; in the twentieth, the hardships of rural life drove Americans back to the cities— psychologically eastward.

Lardner's representative participation in this movement lies at the heart of his life and work. He achieved the success that all Americans who moved to the cities dreamed of finding. Lardner's biographer Donald Elder claims that in 1926 Ring was among the ten most famous men in the United States, but Elder's book is a chronicle of Lardner's dissatisfactions and disillusionment with his life and career. His alcoholism and his long illnesses were a drawn-out suicide, a retreat from the condition that became characteristic of twentieth-century America. In commenting on Lardner's iconoclasm Elder observes:

> If in the end he became a greater iconoclast than any of the self-conscious rebels of his generation, it was not the images of Niles, home, family, or childhood that he shattered. He remained faithful all his life to the values of his early environment; it was the world he found outside it that was to repel him.[29]

Lardner moved to the city for opportunity, fame, and wealth, but when he achieved them, he discovered they were empty, because they were so alien from the simple, decent values of his small-town boyhood. Once deserted for the sophistication of the city, those values were lost forever. Americans discovered this by the millions; Lardner felt it acutely and wrote of small-town characters hopelessly lost in the city.

Among these characters are a variety of athletes, including the baseball players who are the heroes of his two longer works of sports fiction. Lardner's foremost fictional creation, Jack Keefe of *You Know Me Al* and four other volumes, as well as Danny Warner of *Lose with a Smile* and the heroes of most of his short stories are brash, cocky, ignorant, conceited, self-deluding, narrow minded and often insufferable. All are small-town stars attempting to make it in the big city. Although Lardner ridicules their provincial pretensions, he also directs much of his attack against the cities, which he indicates bring out the worst in these small-towners. In his first letter to his friend Al, immediately after being bought by the Chicago White Sox from Terre Haute of the Central League, Jack Keefe is candidly modest: "I will just give them what I got and if they don't like it they can send me back to the old Central and I will be perfectly satisfied."[30] Although we never see Al's replies, they imply that back in Bedford,

Jack is well liked and respected. Likewise, Jessie's responses to Danny Warner in *Lose with a Smile* imply that Danny is a proper citizen of tiny Centralia, but the pressures to succeed in the big city on a big league team and the distorted fame that accompanies even their smallest success reduce both these figures to conceited, thick-headed boobs.

Lardner does not give in to illusions of rural virtue and urban vice. The small town is sincere but also narrow (Jessie in *Lose with a Smile* is the perfect example). The city, and particularly its women, are exploitative, but the city also is the home of decent persons such as Casey Stengel and Kid Gleason. Lardner is not concerned with comparative evaluations, but with observation of a social change which made America seem ludicrous to his satiric eye. Lardner was the chronicler of a painfully changing America; his "busher" (bush-leaguer) is a representation of the town mentality attempting to assimilate cosmopolitan values. Lardner shared both the personal values of the small town (he even waged a campaign against the indecency of radio song lyrics in the thirties) and the attraction to the glitter of cities, for the theater was his first love throughout most of his life. These dual impulses kept his satire two sided.

The complexity of the interplay of town and city during the first part of this century is reflected in this fine analysis by historian Page Smith:

> The truth was these values were not the town's. They did not come out of the tradition of the noble farmer, nor out of the town's version of the Protestant ethic with its emphasis on "calling," on frugality, and self-denial. They came from the city, which discovered and promoted "rugged individualism," which developed the Gospel of Wealth according to which godliness and riches were in league and the Almighty had delivered into the hands of the financiers the destiny of the country. The town at last had come to accept the city's values, and the city, having triumphed, now claimed that the values it had imposed on the town were, in fact, the values of the town. And the city lauded the town and sentimentalized it, and driveled over it, and called it the heart of American democracy, the moulder of men, the ancient defender of American ideals.[31]

This is the situation to which Lardner was responding. Jack Keefe's obsession with money is but one example of the distorted values the town inherited from the city.

Jack Keefe is Lardner's finest fictional creation, the epitome of the busher in the big city. Jack is a genuinely talented pitcher, but his ability alone cannot sustain his self-esteem in Chicago. In Bedford or Terre Haute, he is secure in his talents, but in Chicago the constant threat of anonymity drives him to incredible excesses. Jack is modest at first, but begins to boast mildly, and quickly becomes outrageously conceited, comparing himself favorably to Ty Cobb, Sam Crawford, Walter Johnson, and Christy Mathewson, among others. He begins to excuse every failure—blaming it on poor fielding, no support, bad umpiring, a sore arm, or simply bad luck—even making excuses when he does not need them: alibiing for the single hit of a one-hit shutout, for example. At times he hilariously compounds his excuses:

> They batted all round in the fourth inning and scored four or five more. Crawford got the luckiest three-base hit I ever see. He popped one way up in the air and the wind blowed it against the fence. The wind is something fierce here Al. At that Collins ought to of got under it.[32]

Perhaps he realizes the first excuse is so implausible that he has to add the second to be convincing.

Jack's basic problem is his total misunderstanding of everything that happens to him. In his first letter to Al, he mentions the novelty of Chicago: "I never was really in a big city before. But I guess I seen enough of life not to be scared of the high buildings eh Al?"[33] The "high buildings" are the extent of Jack's comprehension of urban America. When criticized, he thinks he is kidded; when told he is great, he foolishly believes. He often criticizes others for faults that are glaringly his own; he reacts wrongly to praise, will not accept friendly advice, does not know when others exploit him, and unconsciously hurts his friends and takes advantage of them. He repeatedly does the opposite of what he has just said he will do, and then claims it was his original intention. A vague pattern emerges in the letters: the better he becomes as a pitcher and the more pressure he faces, the more conceited he becomes.

Strangely enough, he gains our sympathy, too. Lardner art-fully avoids sentimentality by having Jack undercut his every good deed by immediately contradicting it, but Lardner also offers glimpses of Jack's humanity. He understands a few ideas, occasionally performs the socially proper action, peri-odically makes a witty comeback to one of his tormentors, and proves himself a well-meaning, loving father. Jack gains our sympathy most of all by his utter helplessness; his wife Florrie is such an unscrupulous, exploitative shrew that Jack cannot help but look noble in comparison. He is simply a hick uncomfortably placed in the big city. He has lost his small-town values as he has lost his taste for beer, but he is left with nothing to sustain himself beyond the self-delusions that feed his ego.

As a representative of provincial America, Jack Keefe seems an extreme example. The only other small-towner in the book is Al, and the reader wonders in response to the re-frain, "you know me Al," what kind of person Al is and how much he really knows Jack. Because the reader identifies with Al as the recipient of the letters, Al seems superior to Jack, but the fact that he continues to respond to the letters, lends Jack money, and offers him hospitality imply that Al accepts Jack at his own valuation. Al is probably very much like Jack was before he went to Chicago. He seems steady and dependable, as Jack probably was in his more familiar Bedford. Jack's fate would perhaps have been Al's too, had Al been the pitcher.

Jack Keefe, the busher, is a typical Lardner character, but what justification is there for Maxwell Geismar's claim, "Thus the Busher becomes cosmic: we are all bushers and wise boobs"?[34] Lardner certainly pricked the bubble of Amer-ican hero-worship by deflating the premier hero of the twenties—the athlete. The twenties were sports mad: Babe Ruth was the darling of the age, the first million-dollar gates in boxing were promoted by Tex Rickard, and sports became big business. Lardner's bushers are parodies of the athlete-hero described in the previous chapter. They move from a narrow environment to a new challenge and meet early suc-cess, but their adversities are self-inflicted and are lamely excused away; they mistake abuse for accolades, their friends for tormentors, and their detractors for friends. Their only foe is their own thick-headedness, and their primary attachments are disastrous sexual relationships. They are the butt of the books' humor, and their triumphs are either severely undercut or are actually defeats. In debunking the athlete-hero, Lardner also ridiculed the millions of other Americans who idolized the jock. In an attack on the excesses of spectatorism and lack of participation in athletics, Lardner was emphatic:

> But hero-worship is the national disease that does most to keep the grandstands full and the playgrounds empty. To hell with those four extra years of life, if they are going to cut in on our afternoon at the Polo Grounds where, in blissful asininity, we feast our eyes on the swarthy Champion of Swat, shouting now and then in an excess of anile idolatry "Come on, you Babe. Come on, you Baby Doll![35]

Ironically, Lardner himself was a victim of this American brand of hero-worship. We demand our heroes be perfect and have no place to accommodate the talented minor artist or the skilled specialist. Critical opinion in this country early discovered Lardner to be a writer of great promise. He was compared to Mark Twain, but as Edmund Wilson did, most of the critics publicly wondered if Lardner would go on to write his own "Adventures of Huckleberry Finn," or would remain in his narrow world of baseball players and theatrical people. Lardner's close friend, F. Scott Fitzgerald, stated most clearly the position of those who found sport unsuitable as a topic for serious American fiction:

> Ring moved in the company of a few dozen illiterates playing a boy's game. A boy's game, with no more possibilities in it than a boy could master, a game bounded by walls which kept out novelty or danger, change or adventure. . . . However Ring might cut into it, his cake had exactly the diameter of Frank Chance's diamond.[36]

It is surprising that so insightful a critic of the failure of America's mythic promise did not recognize the paradoxical implications of this condition. Strange, too, that Fitzgerald particularly—a man who idolized Hobey Baker and other great athletes and fantasized fame for himself, who struggled to overcome his own shortcomings as a football player, who defined several of his fictional characters (Tom Buchanan, Jordan Baker, Dick Diver in part, Basil Duke Lee) by their involvement in athletics, and who avidly followed the Princeton football team till the moment of his death—strange that this man particularly could not appreciate the seriousness of adult athletic passions. The weaknesses Fitzgerald cites are, in fact, Lardner's strengths, as they are the strengths of the sports fiction genre. The fact that sports heroes often are "illiterates" makes them appropriate as *representative* figures—the interest in the story is often not in the character but in the character's interaction with society. The irony of men playing a boy's game provides the writer of sports fiction with an opportunity for examining the most fundamental issues in American life. Such contradictory values as simplicity and complexity, idealism and cynicism, lyricism and violence, freedom and responsibility, spontaneity and regimentation, playfulness and commercialism are implicit in this essential paradox in American sport. And finally the "walls" that signified to Fitzgerald the limited experience which a writer of sports fiction can explore actually represent the *necessary* narrowing of the focus to a central group representative of the entire society. Fitzgerald was wrong to claim that Lardner's subject matter necessarily limited his scope as an artist. Lardner did not go on to write another "Huck Finn," and as a result he is sadly neglected today, but what Lardner did he did exceptionally well and the fact that he may not be as great as Mark Twain is irrelevant to any consideration of his work.

If Lardner were attacking only heroes and hero-worship, his satire would still be parochial, but the baseball diamond became for him a convenient arena within which to examine the pretensions of an entire society. Virginia Woolf observed this fact in her essay on "American Fiction":

> It is no coincidence that the best of Mr. Lardner's stories
> are about games, for one may guess that Mr. Lardner's in-

terest in games has solved one of the most difficult problems of the American writer; it has given him a clue, a centre, a meeting place for the divers activities of people whom a vast continent isolates, whom no tradition controls. Games give him what society gives his English brother.[37]

Further, baseball is particularly appropriate for a writer dealing with the changing landscape of American towns and cities. Baseball in the early years of the twentieth century was a town game. The town was proud, and part of that pride centered on the baseball team which it supported. According to Page Smith, "The town prided itself on having *the best baseball team in the area*, the best band in the state, the winner of the district declamatory contest, and the fastest trotting horse to be found at any of the nearby county fairs" (emphasis mine).[38] But baseball players had to come to the city. Because the Major Leagues were founded in the big cities, they siphoned off all the best players from the small towns. On this more sophisticated level, baseball was played for money, not for civic pride; the Black Sox scandal of 1919 demonstrated the worst consequences of this urbanization of the sport. Lardner was crushed by it, but he revealed in 1916 in *You Know Me Al* that he understood the conditions that could produce such an outrage.

Baseball during the 1910s and 1920s is thus one of the best possible metaphors for focusing on the problems of the age. Baseball underwent in miniature the same convulsions that shook the larger society, but it must be emphasized again that Lardner did not naively attack only the town or only the city. Instead, he focuses on America's fondest self-image—the hero who is both a natural and a self-made man, the character from humble small-town origins who comes to the city with his ability, his humor, his deserved good luck, and his breezy confidence. In contrast, the busher limits his own ability by his stupid play, is the unconscious butt of the humor, attributes every failure to bad luck, and is offensively conceited. Lardner expresses the confusion of urbanism, and the falsity of belief either in pastoral simplicity—the busher's naivete is obnoxious, not winning, and certainly not virtuous—or in the progressive strides of civilzation. Baseball provided the ideal

arena for making this judgment. Lardner did not even have
to look beyond real life to find examples of mindless folly.
Eddie Cicotte, a fine White Sox pitcher whom Ring once
greatly admired, explained his involvement in the fixing of
the World Series in 1919: "I did it for the wife and kiddies."
Lardner could not have written it better himself.

Lardner's was not the last word on the baseball-playing natural in American sports fiction; writers as diverse as Bernard Malamud, Mark Harris, and Robert Coover portray this
figure in their novels. These writers will be considered in other
contexts, but one footnote to the discussion of the natural
must be offered by a Southerner, for the rural South is indeed
the origin of Ty Cobb, Shoeless Joe Jackson, and many of the
other actual heroes of baseball who became famous as "naturals." Robert Penn Warren was one of twelve southerners
who, in *I'll Take My Stand*,[39] presented themselves to the nation in 1930 as agrarians, but "Goodwood Comes Back"
(1947) is as distant from that tract as any story could be. The
longing for a return to the Jeffersonian ideals that characterize *I'll Take My Stand* makes the pastoral myth of country
virtue seem a potential reality. Urbanization dimished the
importance of certain values inherent in rural life, but the
rise of cities did not simply signal a second loss of Eden. In
"Goodwood Comes Back," Warren counters the pastoral
myth with evidence that rural America can be barbarous, too.

In his story, Luke Goodwood is a fine baseball player from
rural Alabama who pitches briefly but brilliantly for the
Philadelphia Athletics as "the Boy Wizard from Alabama,"
but whose weakness for alcohol ends any chance of a long and
distinguished career: "They say it was likker got Luke out of
the big league, and none of the Goodwoods could ever leave
the poison alone."[40] He returns home to Alabama, pitches a
little ball for the town team, demonstrates his natural ability
by throwing rocks at telephone poles and by hunting, and lies
around his farm "relaxed all over just like an animal."[41] The
natural is traditionally described by animal imagery—Warren indicates here that the difference between one of nature's
noblemen and a lazy hick is often just a difference in the observer's point of view. Luke eventually marries in order to

acquire a piece of land, but after a year his brother-in-law shoots him with Luke's own 12-gauge pump gun.

The reasons for Luke's failure to succeed in the city are hinted at in the story. He did not know how to spend money, could not get used to sleeping late, and drank continually. This is no view of a corrupt city, but of a severely limited individual who cannot cope with even the most trivial adjustments urban life requires. No judgment of the city is found in the story. Warren is not interested in broad, mythic generalizations—he creates a particular example that debunks the myth of the natural. He is no more saying that the country is corrupt, or even always so brutally limiting, than he is saying that the country is virtuous. He is merely observing that Luke Goodwood, a country boy acclaimed as a natural wonder by the Northern press, is simply white trash with a good pitching arm. By choosing the name "Goodwood," after Caspar Goodwood, Henry James's prototypical American in *The Portrait of a Lady,*[42] Warren might be suggesting that insofar as Luke represents a typically American heroic ideal, that ideal is false. The natural is essentially a creation of the urban mind responding to the complexity of cities with nostalgia or mythic longing. Warren, with his Southern sense of the reality of rural America, does not share this illusion.

Boxing and Basketball Fiction: Images of the City

As mentioned earlier, Lardner's bushers are an ironic combination of the natural and the self-made man, but it is paradoxical that the athlete can combine both traditions, for the two are antithetical. Although both have humble origins, the natural is innately gifted and provided for; the self-made man succeeds by striving and perseverance. The natural is essentially static, the self-made man dynamic. The natural is a denizen of the wilderness, the normal habitat of the self-made man is the city. No separation occurs between the natural and the objects of his environment—he is one with his surroundings; the self-made man imposes his ego between himself and his setting, masters his environment, and uses it for selfish ends. As Leo Marx observes, Americans have been able to embrace both the garden and the machine without awareness of their mutual exclusivity.[43] With no greater trouble, they can also embrace both types of heroes. Chapters 2 and 3 have considered them as separate figures, but this distortion is for the sake of analysis only. The self-made man and the natural represent the two primary characteristics of a single American heroic ideal which embodies the values of both figures. The ideal athlete contains both—he is a prototypical American hero—but in this combination he reveals the uneasy tension that two such incompatible ideals can create. The natural abhors structure and restriction; the self-made man checks his spontaneous, but unfocused inclinations, to direct them constructively toward future goals. Since the athlete must be both talented and disciplined, the excess of one attribute at the expense of the other is ultimately self-defeating.

American sport can thus embrace both the country and the city. To repeat once more, baseball is the country game. Football shares at least some of baseball's rural qualities, but Americans are also attracted to sports that seem to defy any connection with nature. Boxing and basketball, in particular, are city games. Although they celebrate different values, they both create images of urban existence and man's ability or inability to survive it. Baseball and football developed as rural America discovered the city but clung to the older way of life, while boxing and basketball emerged as important national sports after the city had become dominant.

Boxing is the most constricted of all sports. Its space is prescribed by a twenty-foot square bound by actual physical barriers; time is rigidly limited to a precise number of three-minute rounds. The Foreman-Ali fight in Zaire in 1974 even demonstrated that the time of day is irrelevant to boxing. The match was fought at the bizarre hour of 3:00 A.M. for the sake of closed-circuit television viewers in America; it was manipulated by men who made no concessions to the demands of nature. The boxing ring is also totally artificial and sterile—no grass vivifies the deadness, no bumpy places or sudden gusts of wind can affect the outcome of the match. Thus, for writers of literary naturalism, the ring became the ideal metaphor for urban existence.

The naturalistic method—treatment of the city as a laboratory, insistence on strict determinism, and attention to the sordid details of urban life—found a nearly perfect application in the boxing novel. Boxing offers writers a sufficiently narrow focus upon which to center their observations of the complex and expansive city. The world of the boxer gives a writer a ready-made cast of characters who act upon, or are acted upon by, the fighter: trainers, managers, promoters, girl friends, sportswriters, punch-drunk ex-fighters, and opponents. The history of boxing is a chronicle of early hopes, small successes, large failures, and final hopelessness—the classic pattern of urban experience promoted by most naturalists. Unfortunately, this drama is easily reducible to an uninspired formula. Thus a "typical" boxing novel has emerged: the minority youth living in an urban ghetto envisions his way to the American Dream through success in the ring, but crooked managers and promoters, as well as his own limitations, ensure his failure, and he is reduced to a battered, punch-drunk, mindless pug. This kind of simplification is a too-frequent weakness of the naturalistic novel. Naturalism's premise of an empirical method severely limits the novel's ability to surprise us or even to present any broad vision.

Examples from nearly four decades of formulaic boxing novels include *The Set-Up* (1928) by Joseph Moncure March, *Pug* (1941) by Albert Idell, *The Square Trap* (1953) by Irving Shulman, and *The Circle Home* (1960) by Edward Hoagland. The protagonists of *Pug* and *The Set-Up* are victims of corrupt managers and promoters; those of *The Circle Home* and *The Square Trap* are simply inadequately skilled fighters. The careers of all four spiral downward to despair or death. Each novel has a distinctive feature: *The Set-Up* is written entirely in verse; *Pug* emphasizes the physical world of the fighter; *The Square Trap* uses boxing as a metaphor for the entrapment of the Mexican community within Chavez Ravine; and *The Circle Home* examines the pattern of dependence-independence in the sexual relationships of a fighter skidding into oblivion. But neither these distinctive aspects nor the generally satisfactory quality of the writing are sufficient to raise these novels above the level of the tediously formulaic.

An especially skilled writer—Ernest Hemingway, for example—can use these stereotyped figures and situations to create something fresh, and in such stories as "The Killers," "The Battler," and particularly in "Fifty Grand," Hemingway is able to evoke the terror, brutality, and courage of boxers through subtle suggestion and understatement. "Fifty Grand" is Hemingway's most extensive treatment of the boxer and his best boxing tale. No illusions or myths are found in this story; boxing is simply a business and the boxer is a man who does what he has to do to survive. Jack Brennan, at the end of his career with one last chance to make his family financially stable, bets all his savings, $50,000, on his opponent in their upcoming championship fight. There is no sense in the story that this action is really crooked; Jack merely assesses his own and his opponent's chances and determines that Walcott will prevail. Had he thought he could win, he would have bet on himself. Throughout the fight, Brennan boxes to the best of his ability, but he knows that he cannot last long enough to win. The fix is not a fix—it is only smart business.

In the final round, however, Jack becomes a true Hemingway hero, not merely a businessman. When Walcott tries to disqualify himself by throwing a low blow, Jack withstands the searing pain of a severe rupture to deliver a low but harder blow of his own. Walcott is unable to rise, and Jack loses by the foul. This situation has obvious possibilities for farce or propaganda against the viciousness of boxing, but Hemingway is more subtle than that. Rather, he stresses the fact that Jack is simply a man who does what is necessary no matter how difficult. Jack is conscious of money, not greedily, but with an understanding of its inevitable importance. He accurately sizes up his opponent, the racial bias of the crowd, and his own limited ability. He uses dirty tricks in his bouts, calmly and professionally—doing what he has to do. And when he is fouled and must literally hold his guts in with one hand, he quickly appraises the situation and finds the necessary strength to complete his task. This is Hemingway's "grace under pressure." The story is no indictment of boxing; if anything it is an indictment of those who take boxing to be in any way romantic. When Jack says in the last line of the story, "It was nothing," he is not being falsely modest; he simply did what was necessary. It is not "nothing" to Hemingway or the reader, however. Hemingway, throughout his novels and stories, sees this particularly unheroic kind of courage as the necessary virtue for post-World War I man.

Hemingway was, of course, one of the finest American writers of the twentieth century, and his inspired use of standard boxing situations is far from typical. The vast majority of writers used the stereotyped ideas without originality. Still, the frequent weaknesses of the boxing novel do not mean that the typical fictional fighter is necessarily uninteresting. In the context of the opposition of country and city, the boxer represents one of the most telling indictments of urban life. He appears at first glance the ultimate urban victim. His world is brutal and corrupt, his genuine opportunities for improvement almost nonexistent, and his physical, spiritual, and psychic determination by his urban environment nearly complete. The fictional boxer is rarely a victim of misplaced aspiration. His vision of self-advancement through boxing is a delusion, but it is the only hope he has. The possibility of improvement through education or legitimate occupational channels is generally not considered. These pugilists do the only thing they can do, and with the failure of their careers they simply assume their predetermined positions at the bottom of society. The square ring is the symbol for this ultimate confinement of the human spirit brought about by urbanization. No escape is possible from this "square trap" —only victory or defeat, no postponement or regrouping or strategic withdrawals. Each weight division has only one champion; all the rest are defeated.

Nelson Algren's *Never Come Morning* (1942) portrays viscerally the effects of urban confinement on the human spirit. Insofar as man is an animal, he has a territorial instinct—the need for private space upon which others may not encroach. Such a need can be satisfied in the open country, but urban density stacks men on top of each other. The result, Algren implies in his story, is that men react more and more like animals as their animal needs are violated.

The boxer thus seems the most extreme portrait of the urban dehumanized man, but paradoxically he is also a manifestation of the natural. The boxer is pitted, nearly naked, in primal combat against his foe, with only the protection of his two fists and his wits. He must be totally self-sufficient and self-reliant, for once he enters the ring no one can assist him or fight his battle for him. He is the man standing alone, simple and unsophisticated, in the midst of the urban wilderness, pitting his natural instincts as a fighting animal against his foe. His natural world is a physical one to which he responds sensually; he takes obsessive care of his body and is responsive to the sights and sounds and smells of the gym— his only retreat from the myriad cacophonic stimuli of the city. The successful boxer often has his training camp in the mountains or some other natural environment, but he must return from such pastoral retreats to the ultimate test of his manhood in the city.

The boxer is an *ironic* natural, for urbanization has replaced his natural foes with another man like himself. The enemies of the classic natural are wild beasts and the threatening aspects of nature itself, but in the ring the boxer must bludgeon one like himself, another man as desperately alienated from his urban environment as he is. The fight becomes a symbolic suicide as the natural destroys his own image. The boxer is also a *grotesque* natural. The natural in his sylvan habitat is always graceful, at ease, at home. Transplanted to the city, the boxer is barely articulate, awkward in society, and brutish in appearance. Boxing is what makes him stumbling and ugly—when we see a fighter at the beginning of his career, he is invariably graceful and flawlessly handsome. The natural is reduced to a brutish state by the perverse activity the city forces on him. The hero of the boxing novel, as a natural, is defined by his environment and receives his strengths and weaknesses from his relationship to his environment, but what he receives from his urban surroundings is insufficient to enable him to live a fully human life.

The paradoxical quality of the fighter as both a natural and a quintessentially urban character enriches the boxing novel. It evokes the country by its conspicuous absence and creates a sense of the loss precipitated by urbanization. It also adds stature to the pathetic figure of the boxer. He does not belong in the city, is not there by choice, and is more naturally suited to the wilderness. In this light, the city becomes his fate, as incontrovertible as any of the pronouncements of the Delphic Oracle. In his inevitable downfall, the boxer is tragic, and in the hands of a skilled writer, his story can be profoundly moving.

Three novels—Budd Schulberg's *The Harder They Fall* (1947), W. C. Heinz's *The Professional* (1958), and Leonard Gardner's *Fat City* (1969)—are the best of the boxing novels. Although they use standard boxing material, they do so with shrewd and tough-minded insight and with carefully wrought prose. *The Harder They Fall* is a loosely fictionalized account of the meteoric rise and fall of Primo Carnera, world heavyweight champion in 1933 and has-been in 1934. In the novel, the giant Italian becomes an Argentine, Toro Molina, but the connection between the two figures is close enough to establish the novel as an indictment of the actual boxing establishment in America. The interest of the novel, however, is not in its relationship to real history, but in Schulberg's adroit handling of the material. The usual menagerie of ring characters appears: Nick Latka, the gangster with a stable of fighters, who hungers for that most urban of virtues—"class"; Danny McKeogh, the manager and trainer who is a skilled craftsman and who loves and respects his fighters, but who has fallen into bondage to Nick; Vince Vanneman, the weak-willed, slimy opportunist who will do anything to anyone for a buck; George Blount, the old black trial horse who never had a chance at the big time; plus an assortment of punchy ex-fighters, small-time chiselers, and gullible sportswriters. There is nothing exceptional about any of these, except that Schulberg sketches their portraits with fine skill and control. But, he also adds another character, Eddie Lewis, a narrator who has an ironic view of himself and his world. Eddie is the publicity agent for Toro Molina, the man paid to write the lies, and the disparity between what Eddie sees and knows and what he writes creates the tension that holds the novel together.

Eddie's ironic viewpoint raises Toro above the level of a mindless victim of urban corruption. Toro is a young giant, discovered in rural Argentina by the owner of a traveling circus who sells controlling interest in his fighter to Nick Latka. Toro is from a tiny village in a distant country and seems stu-

pidly bovine; he is 6'8" tall and weighs 285 pounds—a perfect
dupe to be promoted into the heavyweight championship by a
series of fixed fights and a clever publicity campaign. The
selling job will have to be brilliant because Toro's punch,
despite his size, is no more lethal than a bantamweight's. The
plan is executed perfectly. Toro becomes champion, but when
he learns his fights have been fixed, he is abandoned by Nick
—first to be butchered by a legitimate champion, and then to
be dragged around the country by Vince Vanneman to be clob-
bered in turn by each of the fighters he supposedly knocked
out on his rise to the top. Toro is the helpless victim of this
calculated slaughter.

Eddie alone discovers that Toro is no dumb brute. Over-
sized and unable to speak English, he seems no more intelligent than Nick supposes him to be. But Eddie sees him once
with his own countrymen, and the young giant is animated,
articulate, and bright. Innocent, sentimental, creative, and
loyal, he is a child in the positive sense of the word. Toro is
simply a victim of physical and ethnic stereotyping that is
totally false. He is a mindless puppet because he is treated
that way, susceptible to the city's ability to determine human destiny. He feels every betrayal and every head-ringing
punch from his opponents, but alone, in a strange country,
with no knowledge of the language, he is powerless to prevent them. Toro is believably human as few fictional fighters
have ever been.

Eddie thus invests Toro with pathos, but he also makes of
him an ironically tragic figure. Early in the novel Eddie
refers to boxing as

> an ancient sport already old in Roman times, a cruel and
> punishing enterprise rooted deep in the heart of man that be-
> gan with the first great prehistoric struggles and has come
> down through the Iron Age, the Bronze Age, the dawn of the
> Christian Era, medieval times, the eighteenth and nineteenth
> century renaissance of pugilism, until at last New York, heir
> to Athens, Rome and London, has made the game its own
> . . . a hundred-million-dollars-a-year industry that Daniel Men-
> doza, poor Old Peter Jackson or the blustering John L.
> would never recognize as their brave old game of winner take
> all.[44]

Toro participates in this timeless combat and Eddie specifically likens him to Samson, Atlas, Hercules, and Goliath—nearly a complete lineup of pre-Christian strong men. Toro is an "epic figure of a man"[45] who exerts "a Stone-age influence" on girls.[46] Toro is not simply an anachronism; by connecting him with the heroes of classical legends, Eddie makes Toro a mock tragic hero. Toro shares only the size and strength of his heroic predecessors, not their full triumphs and tragedies, although in another sense he is their equal—he is as lost in twentieth-century America as Samson or Hercules would have been. They were innocent naturals, too, and would be as cruelly abused as Toro is if they were suddenly reincarnated. These are not just unheroic times; they are times that reduce the authentically heroic to the grotesque. To the reader Toro is genuinely tragic—he does not fall from an undeserved championship to life as a pug; his fall is from Olympus to the Bowery.

If Toro is truly a tragic hero, he must, as Aristotle would tell us, have a tragic flaw, but his only contribution to his downfall is a perhaps excessive desire for money to build a home and marry his sweetheart. His guilt is small compared to that of most of the other characters, whose moral responsibility Schulberg minutely observes. Corrupt owners and managers are stock figures in boxing fiction, and Nick and Vince fill these roles, but Schulberg is too shrewd to suppose that an entire sport can be debased by a few outright criminals. Luis Acosta is also guilty—as Toro's first manager he planned to exploit him on a small scale, and to do so lovingly, but he was swallowed by a bigger fish. Danny is guilty—he goes along with the fake build-up because Nick owns him, too. The sportswriters are guilty because they allow their goodwill to be bought; they print stories about Toro's miraculous ability which they know are phony. And the fight fans are guilty because their blood-lust enables men like Vince to exploit Toro mercilessly. Eddie Lewis, however, is the most guilty of all. He is the only one with a moral sense, but he hides behind his cynicism. Not only does he let everything happen, he *makes* it happen. The focus of the novel finally becomes Eddie more than Toro—the fall in the title is Eddie's loss of self-respect. The final scene of the novel imagines the publicist as a beaten fighter stripped of his manhood. In the movie version, starring Humphrey Bogart, Eddie gives his own money to Toro and sends him back to Argentina, but the book is uncompromising. Eddie knows he is the "biggest heel of them all," but he does nothing.[47]

Schulberg's focus is primarily on the milieu of boxing; Heinz and Gardner, his successors, perceive the sport from alternative viewpoints. W. C. Heinz in *The Professional* (1958) is primarily interested in boxing as a sport, or, rather, as an art. His hero, Eddie Brown, has a name remarkably free of sociological or historical resonance. He has no ethnic background; he represents but one thing—the prizefighter—for the novel is about boxing itself, not about boxing as dehumanization or as a false means of social mobility. Boxing is what it is, the novel tells us, the most rudimentary confrontation of two men, at once brutal and fair.

> The basic law of man. The truth of life. It's a fight, man against man, and if you're going to defeat another man, defeat him completely. Don't starve him to death, like they try to do in the fine, clean competitive world of commerce. Leave him lying there, senseless, on the floor.[48]

These are the words of the novel's narrator, a sportswriter whose function is to speak for the author—himself, a sportswriter. Heinz is less interested in plot and character than in definitions; *The Professional* is an intellectual's primer on boxing.

Fighters, we are told, are the best-adjusted males in the world; proving their manhood every time they step into the ring, they do not have to assert it elsewhere. Fighters in the ring can achieve an integrated vision of their world, "like pieces of a jigsaw puzzle and everything fits into place," that is rarely possible for other men.[49] Eddie's manager, Doc Carroll, explains why fighting is no business except for the best: "Be a half-baked plumber, you won't get hurt. You'll make a living. You're a half-baked fighter you may get killed."[50] The narrator, Frank Hughes, explains that for the fighter it is particularly true that a man at any moment is the sum of all the previous moments of his life.

When a match is made what each man does with the same
moment is a part of it, just as every act a man has ever performed, every thought he has ever possessed and that made
him as he now stands becomes moves in it, for time has now
revealed that these two have been in combat forever.[51]

Later Eddie reveals the paradoxical love-hate fraternity of
boxers: "I mean for ten rounds I wanted to kill him and he
fought like he wanted to kill me, and then I wanted to kiss
him."[52] Men are seen as most alive when they perceive death
as possible or even imminent—a familiar theme among writers from Hemingway to Thomas McGuane. Boxing, and
other violent sports, offer this particular pleasure to participants. These insights are interesting in themselves, but the
main analytic focus of the novel is on the "art" of boxing.
Eddie's skill as a fighter and Doc's skills as a manager developing a fighter are associated throughout the novel with sculpture, painting, writing, music, and even oratory.[53] Eddie is
an artist; his hands are his tools, and he has mastered the
intricacies of pugilism to a degree not even suspected by the
fans or sportswriters.

He's even learned how to walk out there and make it look
tough. He makes it look like it's close, but it isn't. He's
just inside those punches or outside them. The one he's
taking he's taking where it doesn't matter. He's even kept the
secret. That's the great talent, because nobody knows this except the guys who've fought him. . . . They still aren't sure
what happened, but whatever it was they never thought anybody could do it to them.[54]

Unlike most other artists, Eddie has to perform in public,
which makes boxing among the most difficult arts of all. A
painter can hide his failures, but a boxer fails before the
world.

Doc, too, is an artist, a sculptor trying to create the absolutely perfect fighter—"In the boxing business, as in any business, there are hundreds of masons and three or four master
sculptors, and the best was Doc."[55] He trains Eddie in every
minute detail of his craft, has him defeat his opponents by

going at the other's strength rather than taking the easy way, and creates the master fighter. Doc resists the showmen and the "amateurs," the inexpert practitioners and followers of boxing, but he is alone with his "lonesome crusade against reality."[56] In Eddie Brown, Doc finds his perfect clay, and by the time the climactic championship fight occurs, the reader has become utterly convinced that Eddie cannot lose. But Eddie does lose. Just once he becomes overeager, loses his balance, and is knocked down. Although he should have been able to continue the fight and win, the fluke blow damages his eyes and he is unable to focus after he rises. He becomes an easy target for a knockout punch.

What appears at first a gimmicky reversal, a trick ending, is seen on second glance to be a necessary and inevitable conclusion to the novel. Doc has attempted, through Eddie, to justify his own forty-five years in boxing, his methods, and his ideas. Like Sam Dee in Brian Glanville's superb British novel, *The Olympian* (1969), Doc tries to build a monument to himself in his athlete. There is something disquieting, however, about a man who attempts to create with human material for his own benefit. Eddie is not a lump of unfinished marble, but a human being. Doc is attempting the impossible—to create permanent static art out of human material. He does not believe in breaks. He believes the fight is won in the gym and on the road, not in the ring. Doc wants to create perfection, which is by definition static, but a fighter is never static because he is human. Because boxing is an art of becoming, of process, never of completion, what Doc attempts is, in the final analysis, unnatural. Any criticism of Doc in the novel is implicit, because not only does he care deeply for his fighter, we also invariably agree with what he says about boxing and boxers. The excesses of his authoritarianism, however, require that Eddie lose his fight—had he won, the human mechanism by implication would be perfectible.

If Budd Schulberg is our best chronicler of the boxing world, and W. C. Heinz of the "art" of boxing, Leonard Gardner is the outstanding creator of the boxer himself. *Fat City* (1969) sketches the portraits of four prizefight personalities who collectively create the image of the boxer. Gardner flawlessly creates a sense of place in his novel—the action occurs in Stockton, California in the sleazy hotels, back-breaking produce farms, and run-down boxing rings of that Western town. Against this naturalistic backdrop, four figures enact a futile drama of groping and defeat that poignantly captures the desperation of the mass of boxers.

Billy Tully at age twenty-nine lives in the fantasies of the aging athlete. Once a competent fighter, he now glorifies his boxing past and longs to regain his wife and a sense of his own manhood. He shares the dream of immortality with the greatest boxers who ever lived, yet at twenty-nine he no longer has even the meager ability that once brought him local success. He lives in fruitless searching and unrealizable dreams, bouts of drinking and demeaning love affairs. The unbridgeable gulf between his hopes and his actual life are epitomized by the entertainment he finds at an "adult" theater near the end of the novel. The film offers Rama, a jungle maiden who lives on fresh air and sunshine in a world without dresses or tight shoes or any of civilization's restrictions. This fantasy movie is followed by live strippers whose "orange and platinum heads" and breasts "blue-white, bulbous, low, capped with sequined discs"[57] represent Billy Tully's own tawdry world.

Ernie Munger is a young Billy Tully—youth to Billy's age, virginal in every sense. He sees a way into the world of men through sexual conquests and through boxing, but his inability to achieve his desires is equal to Billy's. Sexual experience gains him only a marriage for which he is ill-prepared and increased sexual anxiety. A need to boast in the locker room about sexual conquests leads to his marriage, but, ironically, he then feels inadequate when he compares his marital sex life to the exploits others brag about. Boxing offers a similar double-bind experience. Without it, he has nothing to justify his "inconsiderate act of existing"; but with it, he will become another Billy Tully. Fired by the false hopes of early success, he returns at the end of the novel from a victory in Salt Lake City "feeling in himself the potent allegiance of fate."[58] The reader knows that Billy felt the same elation once. Only time—and not very much of it—stands between Ernie and an altogether different "fate" than he foresees.

Ruben Luna is the third part of Gardner's composite fighter

—an ex-boxer living vicariously as a manager. He is older than Billy, but younger in dreams than Ernie; his dream is for a champion, for immortality through another. His is a more difficult fantasy, because someone else has to do it for him, and he blames all his failures on his fighters. In fact, he is only as good a manager as his fighters are boxers—Ruben, Billy, and Ernie are conspicuous only for their mediocrity. In this constricted world, managers blame fighters and fighters blame managers—all have their illusions but no one realizes his dreams. Ruben's loss is as great as the others', but he does not believe it; his hopes are less threatened by age, but they are equally unattainable.

Arcadio Lucero completes the portrait. Appearing briefly as Billy Tully's opponent late in the novel, he is the most admirable boxer in the book. He represents the fighter who has been there, who has achieved a measure of the fame for which the other three long, but who is now on the way down (his age is twenty-nine, the same as Billy Tully's). He became a fighter as a slum kid fighting in the streets, fighting prejudice and poverty, but he is one who made it. When he fights Billy, we are at a loss to know who should win or why—this is not an ethical world. In fact, Lucero loses, and his loss truly matters. He fights for work, not for illusions; what he loses is real—the more he loses, the less money he will make and the fewer fights he will get. He achieved the common dream for a time, but his destiny is the same as the others'.

The boxing descriptions in *Fat City* are brilliantly done, terse, precise, neither sensationalistic nor sanitized—descriptions of violent action like those Hemingway strove so meticulously to achieve. Billy's fight with Lucero is typical.

The Mexican waited at the ropes. Tully's first lead drew no response. Wary, he stepped out of range, bounced on his toes, shuffled in, again pushed out his left, and Lucero, taking it on his high-arched nose, swayed back in the ropes. He leaned there, unflinching as Tully feinted, and in a single reflex Tully smashed his jab, cross and hook against that scarred and patient face. Then he was struck by a blow he had not even seen. Grasping for Lucero's arms, he was pounded over the heart. He retreated, bounced, breathed deeply, and as he stepped back in, Lucero catapulted off the ropes toward him, and Tully was stunned. At the end of the round he returned to two grave faces.[59]

There is nothing heroic in this description, no meeting of good and evil, although this is the emotional climax of the novel. This is a world without winners and losers, in which victory only delays ultimate defeat. Thoreau said that the mass of men lead "lives of quiet desperation"; Leonard Gardner's boxers dream of escape and believe in their illusions for a time, but they all return to aimless futility.

Boxing has inspired few recent novels. During the past decade or so interest in boxing has focused mainly on a single individual—Muhammad Ali—and a number of boxing movies, beginning with *Rocky*, have been quite successful. But boxing novels such as *Flesh and Blood* (1977) by Pete Hamill and *Sunday Punch* (1979) by Edwin Newman have not been particularly noteworthy. Hamill spices up a fairly routine story of an Irish heavyweight who almost wins the championship, with an incestuous relationship between the fighter and his mother. *Flesh and Blood* may be a most sensational boxing novel on the surface, but underneath it is the same chronicle of a tough ethnic kid with a loyal manager in a corrupt business. *Sunday Punch,* on the other hand, is a comic novel about an undermuscled British middleweight named Aubrey Philpott-Grimes, who spouts macroeconomic theory. Newman is more interested in the vagaries and abuses of the English language than in boxing.

Boxing no longer seizes the public's imagination as it once did; a new sport has emerged to capture the imaginative dimension of urban America—basketball. In fact, perhaps we should distinguish between boxing as an urban sport, and basketball as "the city game." Boxing inspires images of a condition of life dominated by the urban environment; basketball focuses on what men can do given that urban milieu. Whereas boxing is grim, basketball is playful. Boxing harks back. As already discussed, the boxer is an ironic and grotesque natural, and the absence of the "country" is felt in the boxing ring. Basketball, on the other hand, exists solely in the present. Besides being the most recently developed of our major sports, it has no connection to the mythic frontier or to any part of America's past. Played *now*, in gyms and on playgrounds, its meaning lies solely in the playing of the game. Boxing in fiction describes a condition; basketball invokes a mode of human action that resists that condition or even denies it.

Pete Axthelm, author of a very good book about basketball, identifies the sport specifically as "the city game":

> Basketball is the city game.
> Its battlegrounds are strips of asphalt between tattered wire fences or crumbling buildings; its rhythms grow from the uneven thump of a ball against hard surfaces. It demands no open spaces or lush backyards or elaborate equipment.
> ... Basketball is the game for young athletes without cars or allowances—the game whose drama and action are intensified by its confined spaces and chaotic surroundings.[60]

Axthelm writes about basketball in New York City, about the World Champion Knicks—Walt Frazier, Jim Barnett, Willis Reed, Bill Bradley, and Dave DeBusschere—but also about the playground heroes—Earl Manigault, Herman "Helicopter" Knowings, and Joe Hammond—for whom basketball is a way of "defining identity and manhood in an urban society that breeds invisibility."[61]

Basketball fiction confirms Axthelm's observations. Of five basketball novels of the past twenty years—*Drive, He Said* (1964) by Jeremy Larner, *Big Man* (1966) by Jay Neugeboren, *One on One* (1970) by Lawrence Shainberg, and *Have Jump Shot Will Travel* (1975) and *A Mile Above the Rim* (1976), by Charles Rosen—only the first does not deal explicitly with basketball as a city game. Wayne Smalley, coach of the New York Stars in Rosen's *A Mile Above the Rim*, reveals himself to be a man without poetry, but his recognition of the distinctive character of Madison Square Garden—the ultimate basketball court—could be found in any of the four novels: "Wayne loved the still lifelessness of the deserted Garden. He loved the ghastly glow of the artificial lighting. His world was basketball, which happened indoors. Wayne couldn't care less if he never saw the sun again."[62]

Even when basketball is played outdoors, the natural surroundings are irrelevant to the game; basketball is defined simply by a court—whether Garden hardwood or playground concrete—and a hoop at each end. In fact, basketball's essence is somehow more apparent in playground games, as most of the authors seem to recognize. Mack Davis of *Big Man* is a superbly gifted black basketball star whose involvement in fixing games in the 1950s has banned him from play in the NBA. Once king of New York's playgrounds, he is now washing cars at the Minit-Wash. However, he still finds his true identity when he becomes the superhuman "Plastic Man" in schoolyard games. Such reliance on basketball, of course, is potentially tragic, as he himself realizes.

> Oh yeah, you don't watch out, Mack, you gonna be dragging your body down to that schoolyard when you fifty, all these young kids running around you and through you and jumping over you, but they still gonna call you Plastic Man. Only you not gonna be stretching and sliding and leaping then, you gonna be wishing you could change yourself into a bench or a backcourt, your rate.[63]

The playground can offer an apprenticeship, but it is more often an end in itself, and something akin to desperation becomes a part of the game. Elwood Baskins, hero of *One on One*, is the most acclaimed player in the country before he even plays his first varsity game for NYU, a celebrity whom the entire country wants to love, but the players he observes on the New York playgrounds receive very different rewards:

> The players were seven Negroes, a Puerto Rican, two whites. They were bouncing off the fence, sliding on the concrete, throwing knees and elbows around like clubs. No laughter, no talk, no teamwork. Unlike college and professional players, they took the game down to its most essential problem: put the ball in the basket as quickly and as often as the other team allowed. *Playground basketball.* What you played for here wasn't fame, or money, or headlines, or trophies, but "winners"—the right to go on playing. One loss and you might sit out for the rest of the day.[64]

Even the winners, as Axthelm poignantly chronicled, too often lose to alcohol, drugs, and poverty.

Perhaps the epitome of the city-game novel is Charles Ro-

sen's *Have Jump Shot Will Travel*. The characters in this rau-
cous comedy fall midway between playground athletes and
NBA heroes; they are members of the Wellington Rifles of
the Atlantic Professional Basketball Association (APBA), a
league composed of six tiny coal towns in Pennsylvania and
two hamlets in New Jersey. The players perform for $150 per
game in contests more akin to professional wrestling than to
basketball. Referees fearful of maulings by the fans rarely
call fouls on the home team; players who are paid only if they
play purposely lose games to assure that the playoffs run the
full five games. Playoff scores such as 170-138, 163-140, 176-
149, and 149-138 (a tight defensive contest) confirm Bo Lassner's observation: "Our boxscores should be printed in 'Variety.' "[65]

Basketball in the APBA is definitely a city game. The bleak-
ness of the towns in which the Rifles play characterizes the
quality of their play itself and is starkly contrasted to basketball as played by the New York Knicks. Basketball in the city
of Wellington is different from basketball in the city of New
York. Failure, incompetence, and uneasy adjustments to
frustrated aspirations characterize both Wellington and the
Rifles. The fans who attend the games for relief from urban
existence reflect the diminution of human experience that
dominates the novel:

> There was, as usual, a full house of some 2500 kings and
> queens of the blast furnace. The fans around the league are
> interchangeable—bitter, tight-faced people who break out of
> their bleak lives by going totally berserk at APBA ballgames.[66]

For the players, as Pete Axthelm observed of the real playground athletes, basketball becomes a source of identity. The
high-school players Bo instructs as a substitute physical education teacher, find in basketball "the only means of defining themselves without stealing anything or killing anybody,"[67] and the league players as well have virtually the
same options. Bo, the novel's hero, as an adolescent was accepted by his peers only when his ability on the court became
noticeable, and he must continue trying to earn the respect of
his Rifle teammates in the same way. He is the team's back-

up center, valuable only because he's white; he's 6'8" and weighs 225 pounds, but as he says himself, he shoots, rebounds, and plays defense like a little man. Bo regards basketball as only a game, something certainly not worth risking bodily injury for, and he plays like it, running from physical contact whenever possible. He comes to realize, however, what Foothead Jones—"the Grand Old Fart of the league"— tells him: that "ev'rythin's a game." Bo has played neither basketball nor his life very well. Not only does he avoid confronting how good he might really be on the basketball court, he also avoids any real contact with other people: "I was also discovering that by isolating myself from the ballgame, I had likewise sequestered myself from the living."[68] Participating fully in the game may free Bo from hang-ups that block his full participation in life, but there are still obstacles to overcome. What really disturbs him about APBA basketball is that it bears so little relationship to the game of "beauty and precision and grace" that he truly loves, but he proves his toughness to his teammates by playing with a broken nose in the championship contest and playing as dirty as his opponents. He does win the acceptance of the other players, but Rosen violates his comic vision by making Bo lose his girl as a consequence. I have described the "serious" theme that runs through the novel, but the treatment of this theme is extravagantly and raunchily comic, and this somber conclusion is jarring. The "message" is that Bo, by responding to unbasketball-like roughness with a knee to his antagonist's groin, may have learned to play by APBA "rules," but he sacrificed his humanity in doing so. Such a view is not only simplistic, it ends a comic novel on a note of inappropriate seriousness.

Rosen's conclusion is unfortunately grim, as is the contemplated fate of playground superstars losing the battle with drugs. Basketball's primary image of the city, on the contrary, is not as bleak as boxing's. Boxing creates a vision of confinement, limitation, and ultimate failure; basketball, on the other hand, suggests the possibility of not just survival with dignity at best, but of creativity within urban limitation. Space and time are not as constricted as in boxing, although more so than in baseball or football. Within these restrictions, the basketball player discovers the infinite possibilities of motion and reflex. Limited in horizontal space, he utilizes a third dimension, vertical space, more fully than does any other athlete; the possibilities of performing with grace and style are perhaps greater than in any other of the sports we have mentioned. Basketball symbolically embraces the city and fully exploits the options for achievement that the city uniquely offers.

Chapter 2 identified the basketball player as the artist, a vision which is shared by basketball novels. Axthelm also agrees when he quotes Bob Spivey, a playground star who survived: "Cats from the street have their own rhythms when they play. It's not just a matter of somebody setting you up and you shooting. You *feel* the shot."[69] About the World Champion Knicks, Axthelm observes: "For all the success of the intricately planned, balanced offense, however, the plays that did the most to turn on the crowds were the bursts of inspired improvization."[70] Of Earl Monroe of the Baltimore Bullets, he says, "But at his best, The Pearl seems to defy time and space and noise and reality."[71] And on Earl Manigault, the greatest of the playground stars:

> He was a six-foot-two-inch forward who could outleap men eight inches taller, and his moves had a boldness and fluidity that transfixed opponents and spectators alike. Freewheeling, unbelievably high-jumping, and innovative, he was the image of the classic playground athlete.[72]

Here are images of the artist and his art, and the fiction creates them, too.

"Touch" is a nonrational quality that sets the basketball artist off from more earthbound mortals. Silky Sims, pure artist of the New York Stars, in *A Mile Above the Rim* observes, "It's tough to think and shoot at the same time."[73] The fingers of Hector Bloom, hero of Jeremy Larner's *Drive, He Said,* are said to have "a special something with the ball"[74] that Hector does not even control. Writers become most lyrical when they describe this mysterious phenomenon; Bo Lassner in *Have Jump Shot Will Travel* describes it this way:

> Most of the time, good shooters have their spots on the floor, their totally synchronized patches where ball, fingers and

basket are entirely congruous. But maybe once every ten
outings, the whole court seems to be covered with all your
little secret X's, and whatever you can get away will fall in.
You don't have to see the hoop, or follow through, or even
know where you are. All that is required of you by the
forces that temporarily control your body is that you throw
the ball high in the air. Then you silently tremble with the
Presence as you watch it descend in a perfect parabola.[75]

Even more penetratingly, Elwood Baskins of *One on One* explains:

Touch, we call it. If you have touch, the ball is part of your
hands. You shoot it, dribble it, pass it, but it never leaves
your hands.... The biggest part of touch is feeling—the feeling of *rightness*, almost of magic when you touch the ball and
start to shoot it.... Before the ball leaves your hands you
know the shot is good. You don't have to watch. The ball will
travel through an arc maybe forty feet long and land perfectly
in the center of a hoop twenty-four inches in diameter and
drop hardly touching the net, and you *know*. Not because
you've decided somewhere in your mind to shoot so hard, so
high, and give the ball just so much spin, but because suddenly you and the ball and the hoop are *together*, all of one
piece, and it is impossible to miss.... Touch is the center of
the game, the one thing about it that's impossible to learn.[76]

Basketball is played as much by instinct and intuition as by
pattern and rational control. Silky Sims's form is unorthodox,
but he plays with "pure unspoiled basketball instinct"[77] that
makes him the most exciting star in the league. Hector, too,
shoots "from instinct,"[78] and Elwood observes, "Every time
you think, you lose your space! And space is the name of
this game."[79] Often basketball novelists describe a conflict
between players whose instinctive mastery of their art conflicts with a coach's rigid insistence on mechanical patterns.
Wayne Smalley of *A Mile Above the Rim* distrusts his players, "who destroyed the beauty and precision of his immacu-
lately designed patterns with their incessant free-lancing,"[80]
but Wayne is a fool whose team wins despite him. Elwood
Baskins is similarly afflicted with a coach "who in no time at
all could bury you with fundamentals and kill your moves

with strategy."[81] The goal of the nonartist is winning; the goal of the artist is "peace and joy" and "magic." Jeremy Larner explores this conflict fully in *Drive, He Said*. There are two styles of basketball, according to Larner—"white boss" and "Negro." "White-boss" basketball, advocated by Coach Bullion, involves hustle, rough play, exhaustively practiced patterns, and the absolute necessity of winning. "Negro" basketball is loose, recklessly beautiful, joyful to watch and play; the best Negro players are "the artists of basketball, the ones every pro team needs two or three or six of if it is to stay beautiful and win."[82]

My specific analogy to jazz music is even repeated in the novels. Bo Lassner longs for the beauty of the game—"like a magic concert in the Filmore East."[83] Spencer Lavelle opens *A Mile Above the Rim* playing to a "discoboogie beat" and with "syncopation."[84] During one game, Hector Bloom "was hearing his own music, moving out & on to the most electric rhythm section ever convoluted together in a single brainpan."[85] And Elwood Baskins again makes the connection most specific: "Players move with the ball as if they are musicians and it is their conductor."[86]

One on One explores the basketball-player-as-artist theme more thoroughly and interestingly than any of the other novels. Shainberg's book is, in fact, a lengthy gloss on the idea found in John Dryden's "Absalom and Achitophel": "Great Wits are sure to Madness near ally'd; And thin Partitions do their Bounds divide."[87] Elwood Baskins is a "great wit" for certain; he is the artist par excellence of collegiate basketball —a 6'9", 244-pound athlete of extraordinary ability—but he is also certifiably crazy. No bounds divide his genius from his madness; they are one. As he says, "I'm too fucked up to be an athlete, too good an athlete to be a regular big man, too big to be a regular man."[88] He hears voices in his head, but he also hears himself hearing voices and hears the voices talking about his hearing them. He not only fantasizes about the people he knows, he fantasizes about their fantasies. Reality for Elwood is so buried in layers of fantasizing—he even imagines his fantasies played out on television, yet another layer of withdrawal from reality—that his ability simply to function in the world of objects is seriously impaired. The comic possibilities in the collisions of reality with his fantasies are exploited nicely, but Shainberg also pursues the implications of the athlete-as-artist to some intriguing conclusions. Elwood began playing as a child for fun, but watching the first of the great jump shooters on television opens up for him a realm of art and beauty he cannot resist. As he practices his jump shot he discovers that it is "like a gift," a "miracle." Jumping, you have no time to think, he learns; thinking ruins the shot. His pleasure in basketball lies in his complete absorption in playing; he finds through basketball a unity of mind and body—the shooter and the shot, the idea and its execution, are truly one—and this awareness transforms him: "There was almost no relationship between the person I was before the jump shot and the person I was after."[89] From this moment, he is incapacitated for action in the social world.

The artist lives in his own time and his own space; to Elwood his parents become intruders, enemies of the game, and he lapses into a silence that lasts from September 12 until November 2. Doubting his sanity, Elwood's father takes him to a psychiatrist, an act that proves to be the ultimate violation of the artist's being. Elwood as an artist is totally self-absorbed; the artist destroys barriers between himself and the objects around him. Even people are not real to Elwood until he incorporates them into his mind, and in all his doings as an artist he acts without reflection, without plan. A psychiatrist is the artist's natural antithesis—an ultra-rationalist—and Dr. Horton forces Elwood to move outside his mind to reflect on what is within. A psychiatrist wants to objectify, but the artist is a totally subjective being. This conflict between Elwood and Horton is similar to his basic disagreement with his pattern-minded coach.

> If things happened on the court the way coaches diagram them, every game would come to a standstill: a perfect offense and a perfect defense add up to a state of paralysis. Every move they make, we answer, every time we answer, they make another move, and we have the answer for that one too. It was the second time that day [Coach] Lavelle had reminded me of Horton, because that's the way I saw most of Horton's theories. Listen to him enough and you'd develop a perfect defense for all your hangups. You wouldn't get rid of

them, just learn to protect against them. Then you'd spend the
rest of your life in the lowest scoring game the world had ever
seen.[90]

Elwood is torn between his artist's self-contained vision of
the world, and the need forced upon him to be self-reflective.
Although the voices in his head run frequently out of control,
the salvation of his sanity lies not in exorcising them but in
truly believing in himself—"When I believed, I'd be inside
myself and then nothing else would matter."[91] In other
words, just as the shooter and the shot are one for the basket-
ball-playing artist, so Elwood needs to break down the barriers between his actions and his reflections on them. When
he realizes this, he expresses it appropriately with a basketball metaphor: "The form and the rhythm! The shot is gone
before you think it!"[92] His final fantasy sees himself sealed entirely in plaster as part of a life-sized sculpture of a basketball
game; he is an artist become art, the ideal of both his athletic artistry and his sense of himself in his world. He has rejected Horton and accepted his girlfriend Jeanie by allowing
her into his head to see the real Elwood. He walks into Madison Square Garden for the game with a smile of self-accept-
ance that signifies there are no barriers between himself and
reality: "The smile stayed with me as I walked toward the
locker room, spread through my body while I dressed, and
grew until it filled the Garden when I came out on the
court."[93] The smile fills the Garden because the Garden has
become part of himself, as has everything in his world.

The artist as an autonomous, totally subjective, nonrational
person is inimical to society; Elwood Baskins is at peace with
the world, but the world may not be at peace with Elwood.
Society is a rational structure that demands pattern and ob-
jectivity, and that requires citizens be aware of others as
separate persons. Social responsibility cannot exist for an
artist, however; the heroes of all the basketball novels considered in this chapter are somehow beyond the boundaries
of society—above it or outside it, but not quite part of it. The
extreme example of this dimension of the basketball artist is
Hector Bloom in Jeremy Larner's *Drive, He Said*. Hector is a
"half-hick, half-Jew, left-handed neurotic basketball player
from the green hills of California"[94] who is disturbed and dis-

illusioned by political reality. *Drive, He Said* is an exemplary novel of the 1960s, with a hero who is alienated from the "system" and who attempts to war against it.

Larner stresses the equation between competitive sport and war which became a particularly simplistic cliché during this period, but he also is able to distinguish between acceptable and unacceptable athletic temperaments. Hector is an athlete, but this fact does not automatically disqualify him for a meaningful contribution to a new social order. As a man of action and commitment, he is actually an ideal potential revolutionary. As an "artist," Hector is particularly opposed to rational structures; in a world turned corrupt, these need to be destroyed. For people to be "rational" is "to force whole sets of old learned vocabularies between themselves and the lives they were leading."[95] Such vocabularies are the outpouring of Western thought, irreverently symbolized in chapter 18 by the football coach, the biologist who developed nerve gas, and the university president. If the world these men created is intolerable, then a new one must be created on new foundations—rationality itself must be rejected.

Hector's roommate has scrawled on a wall of their room the novel's essential message:

SQUARE—SELF CONTROL
HIP—THE RIGHT REACTION

and this slogan epitomizes the relationship of the artist to rational society. "Square" connotes rules, discipline, order, and pattern—Coach Bullion and his "white-boss" basketball; "hip" means freedom, spontaneity, and instinct—the artist of "Negro" basketball such as Hector. Hector finds his identity in basketball, but the basketball he is forced to play by Coach Bullion is inimical to his sense of himself. Basketball as it is formally played only frustrates him; what he longs for is a victory he can enjoy that will exorcise his need for the sport. When he scores sixty-four points in the big game, he achieves his desire; he quits the team, commits himself to antiwar demonstrations, and ultimately to revolution. As an artist, he was never committed to society; now out of the game, he can be fully committed to overturning it.

The consistency with which writers of basketball fiction

describe basketball as a city game and basketball players as artists—with the values that the word entails—is truly remarkable. Basketball's popularity developed during the same decade in which confidence in traditional social structures was crumbling. Whether basketball appealed to spectators on some deep psychic level where it was perceived to represent an alternative lifestyle or whether writers simply discovered that in basketball could be found images for an increasingly insistent contemporary vision is impossible to assert with any certainty. But it is certainly true that the basketball novels of the sixties and seventies—including John Updike's *Rabbit, Run* which will be considered in another context—imagine their characters in surprisingly similar ways.

It is also certainly true that the emphasis on the city game is part of a long tradition in the attitudes of Americans toward sport. Country and city have meanings for Americans that they have for no other people, and these images are an important part of every American sport. Rubes and naturals, struggling boxers and playground artists are a major part of the myths of American sport—they are found abundantly in both its folklore and its fiction. If these figures did not pluck strings deep in our psyches that reverberate with our nation's history, they would not have received the consistent representation they have had throughout the years. Even basketball, a sport I claim has little tie to the past, participates in symbolic American history in its rejection of yesterday for today. Blacks dominate basketball for a number of reasons; one of those may be that a sport without links to the frontier—to the formative myth of *white* America—is the one sport that blacks can feel to be truly their own. They have created the game, not inherited it, and America's blacks do not look nostalgically to the past, but look to now, to the city game, for mythic identity. All four sports then—baseball, football, boxing, and basketball—probe sources of national identity deep within us. The fact that they profoundly move us offers the writer of sports fiction an opportunity to touch us deeply as well.

four

Intimations of Mortality:
Youth and Age in American Sports Fiction

This is a children's game. It's
played by men, but it's still a
children's game.
—Fred Shero, coach of the
Philadelphia Flyers

The opposition of country and city in American culture and sports fiction has an analogue in the polar relationship of youth and age. Qualities associated with youth—innocence, hope, naivete, exuberance, impulsiveness, health, beauty, and a sense of immorality—are the same virtues archetypally associated with the country. Experience, complexity, seriousness, worldliness, despair, and consciousness of death are among the attributes mythically assigned to both age and the city. The natural, the quintessential inhabitant of the country, is a child-like figure; the urban self-made man is defined, on the other hand, by the values of maturity and age. Although Americans have made at least partial peace with the reality of the city, they have stubbornly refused to accept the inevitability of aging. An obsession with youth is, in fact, one of the foremost characteristics of the American character.

A propensity for a youth cult can be seen in the very conditions of our nation's existence. As a part of the "New World," America until well into the twentieth century represented to Europeans the opportunity for a new start, a rejuvenation. America was a land of opportunity, and opportunity belongs to the youthful, accomplishment or failure to the mature.

123

Much of America's history can be (imaginatively) seen as an insistent preoccupation with youth. Democracy itself might be thought of as a "youthful" rejection of authoritarianism. Huck Finn lighting out for "the territory" is the fictional paradigm for a long history of American escapees from authority, from Roger Williams to the beats and hippies of recent years. More literally, a cult of youth developed in the nineteenth century, influenced by Rousseau's romantic primitivism and abetted by the liberalization of Puritan orthodoxy. The sentimental domestic novels that began to appear early in the century and that particularly flourished in the 1850s denied Calvinist notions of innate depravity, and made the child more angel than human. The image of age, of course, is not absent from this American history; Calvinism and its many descendant ideas suggest the antithesis of the youthful qualities I have mentioned and remain a potent influence. In fact, the simultaneous presence of Calvinism and the romantic American dream in the national consciousness define the tension between youth and age in America, but youth, not age, has dominated our conceptions of the ideal life at least from the middle of the nineteenth century. Ponce de Leon's search for the fountain of youth has become an obsession among Americans; a glorification of youth and consequent fear of aging are endemic in this country. According to Geoffrey Gorer, most Americans consider the years between adolescence and the birth of their first child the peak of life, after which there is a gradual but continuous decline.[1] There is very little cultural respect in America for the middle-aged and the elderly. The most flattering compliment one can pay most Americans is to tell them how young they look; "You're as young as you feel" is the pathetic cry of millions of Americans terrified of growing old, as any glance at American advertising or commercial television will demonstrate. There is no continuity in the cycle of generations in America. The old do not automatically receive respect for their years of experience and mature wisdom, but characteristically fear and envy the young and are obsessed with pleasing and imitating them. Americans generally approach death with horror and react to it with intense mourning. Any sign of age is a terrifying reminder of the imminence of death.

If youth is to be venerated, then the child as the epitome of youthfulness becomes nearly an object of worship. Max Lerner in *America as a Civilization* has described what he calls the "overrated American child":

> This conception of the child as a Noble Little Savage possessed of an artless innocence which is corrupted and distorted by civilization, and also the attitude that the child is always the victim, the adult always the guilty fumbler, bumbler, meddler, and destroyer, are part of the cult of the American child. The other strands in the cult are that the child must be "understood" instead of being allowed to become a functioning part of a functioning family and community; that he must be continually "adjusted"; . . . that the culture and future are founded on him; that he will have it better in a better future and will himself *make* the future better. Thus the American overvaluation of the child is compounded of equal parts of guilt, anxious concern and cultural hope.[2]

This cult of the child has also been recognized by numerous other writers, perhaps most perceptively by Leslie Fiedler whose identification of Good Good Girls and Good Bad Boys defines not just the peculiar American attitude towards childhood, but America's vision of itself.[3] Fiedler's point is the important one that youth obsession is a central fact in American life, one that clarifies a great deal about our attitude toward life itself. Youthfulness in itself is neither good nor evil, but Americans have invested it with such value that it becomes both good *and* evil. Our prevailing standard of *quantitative* achievement is immature, as is our need to determine "the best" in every field; the American dream promoted by mass advertising is childishly sensual and superficial. But youth is also spontaneous, energetic, fair, openhanded and openhearted; and these are among the most admirable qualities in the American character. Youthful idealism can be idealism without an object, but it can also be a fresh and innovative antidote to stale ideas and systems. Youth is always transitory, however, and it is in this context that the American preoccupation with youth is potentially tragic. Age is an inescapable fact of life, but Americans reserve no rewards for the aged; to grow old is to grow useless. Every person's life becomes a tragedy; the athlete, because his career is particularly short, has consequently become the object of some of our most poignant fiction.

As is the case in the consideration of the hero or the country and city in the American imagination, the polarity of youth and age is sharply focused in the sports world. The archetypal relationship of young and old in the Western world is defined by the killing of the aging king and replacement by a youthful aspirant; Sir James George Frazer's *The Golden Bough* observes this pattern in a number of cultures.[4] Some kings were killed when their strength failed, some were killed at the end of fixed terms, and some had continually to defend themselves against rivals. All these patterns appear in the sports world—a veteran who is replaced by a rookie because he has slowed a step and lost his reflexes; a veteran who is traded, although he has a few good years left, because the coach wishes to rebuild his team around younger players; and a veteran in the normal training camp situation who must defend his position every year against rookie hopefuls—all reenact ancient ritual deaths.

These patterns are structurally similar to Frazer's anthropological models, but the motivations behind the king-slayings differ significantly from their sport analogues. The king often had to be killed to protect his people, "For if the course of nature is dependent on the man-god's life, what catastrophes may not be expected from the gradual enfeeblement of his powers and their final extinction in death?"[5] Equally important, a king might also be killed before age debilitated him so that he could enter the afterlife as a vigorous hero and become a god. In all cases an old king was held in utmost respect and was worshipped after his death. In comparing this situation to the sport prototypes, we notice immediately that this esteem has been largely shifted from the veteran to the rookie. The aging veteran may be released to protect his heroic stature from degeneration, but more often he is simply regarded as a detriment to the team's success who must be cut adrift; the hopes of nearly every team reside in the younger players and their futures. When a veteran is released, he is not dispatched to glorious immortality, but to living out the remaining years of his life deprived of the fame he has grown to expect. We worship a chosen few in "halls of fame," but these are exceptions. Unlike ex-presidents who are retired with generous pensions to survive as revered elder statesmen till their deaths, most ex-athletes are quickly forgotten.

This shift in emphasis from the respect for age implicitly noted by Frazer to obsession with youth is symptomatic of the juvenile qualities of American sport. Although the veteran's experience, expertise, and knowledge are valued, they are deemed mere refinements of youthful strength and speed. When those more important physical qualities wane, an athlete's career is near its end. The growth and maturity of an athlete is thus very limited, and he looks continually backward towards youth. He is forced to remain physically youthful if he is to continue playing, and the fear of losing his physical vigor can induce him to cling to psychological and emotional immaturity as well. Jack Olsen's *Alphabet Jackson* (1974) describes this clinging to youth by an aging veteran very well:

> It's a funny thing about jocks. When you're young and strong you feel like a god, you're different than other men, nothing serious can ever happen to you, at least nothing that you can't heal with a whirlpool and some heat. And when you finally realize that you're wiped out, your first reaction is there's been a terrible mistake, they must mean somebody else, you're a god, don't they remember? And then you pass into a stage where you figure it's all a joke or a bad dream or a misunderstanding, and then when you get it straight, that it's no bullshit and you—are—*through*. ... Well, it's like they dropped you in the Sea of Antarctica, and you're just a punk little kid again with a snotty nose and screaming to your mama that the big kids aren't fair, and mama tells you she's busy. What can you do but bawl?[6]

Such pervasive juvenility is woven into the very fabric of American sport. When Thorstein Veblen denounced the exploitative hostility and chicanery at the foundation of sport, he associated those qualities with juvenility:

> It is perhaps truer, or at least more evident, as regards sports than as regards the other expressions of predatory emulation already spoken of, that the temperament which inclines men

to them is essentially a boyish temperament. The addiction to
sports, therefore, in a peculiar degree marks an arrested development of the man's moral nature.[7]

Veblen found an "element of make-believe" in all sporting activities. One need only think of a baseball or football game
to validate this claim: the wearing of gaudy but imposing uniforms, the secret language shared only by the participants,
and the highly ritualized preparations for and playing of the
contests all reflect the character of children's games.

Confirmation of this juvenility in sport is also apparent in
a glance at America's foremost athletic hero—*Babe* Ruth.
No other American athlete has enthralled so many to so
great an extent, and Ruth appealed to Americans in large
part as a perpetual child. He was impulsive, exuberant, given
to childish excesses, and he seemed to play baseball for the
joy of playing. He was an errant child, but Americans loved
him all the better for this frailty. When he once tearfully
apologized to Senator Jimmy Walker and the nation's youth
for his indiscretions, Americans adored him. He is the perfect
example of the Good Bad Boy who Leslie Fiedler describes as
America's self-image.

Ty Cobb was Ruth's only rival to baseball supremacy in the
public's estimation, but Cobb *worked* at baseball, *warred*
even, was humorless and "brainy"—in other words, excessively adult. His own words best describe his character:

> When I played ball, I didn't play for fun. To me it wasn't par-
> chesi played under parchesi rules. Baseball is a red-blooded
> sport for red-blooded men. It's no pink tea, and mollycoddles
> had better stay out. It's a contest and everything that implies
> a struggle for supremacy, a survival of the fittest. Every man
> in the game, from the minors up, is not only fighting against
> the other side, but he's trying to hold his own job against those
> on his own bench who'd love to take it away.[8]

Cobb was the finest hitter, the greatest base-runner, and a
perfectionist in all phases of baseball; yet, he was hated by
the fans, the opposition, and even his teammates. The Babe,
on the other hand, was universally loved. Ruth's childish
quality assumes strange forms because, in his titanic efforts,

his refusal to recognize any authority outside himself, and his ability to be so single-handedly effective, he represents a sort of autocratic ideal. But Cobb is an anarchic figure—the prototype of an opposite extreme of individualism—and, because of his seriousness, he is a less attractive hero.

The boyish quality of sport is further evidenced in the masculine camaraderie among players. Alphabet Jackson describes these pleasures with an almost pastoral dreaminess:

> When I'm old and weak and even balder than now, these are the times I'll remember best, these weird-ass hours of relaxation and ease, when there's no enemy line breathing in your face, no crucial play coming up, just a bunch of crazy assholes kidding and jacking around. If I was really honest with myself, I'd probably admit I never cared much about anything else in the world except the Goats—the Goats and my ex-son and Dorris Gene, but mostly the Goats. My ex-wife Cathy said I'd rather joke with the Goats than make love to her, and mostly she was right. Maybe that makes me a fruit on 1 level or another, I don't know, but I didn't want to fuck the Goats, I just wanted to be around them, hanging at the Dandy Don's or riding the plane or snapping towels or playing cards, abnormal things like that.[9]

As will be discussed fully in the next chapter, the all-masculine nature of the relationship is important, but it is also true that there is a clearly boyish, "no girls allowed in the treehouse" quality here that captures a distinctive pleasure of our games.

Many other attitudes toward sport are similarly juvenile. The total unacceptability of losing is childish; the lessons of defeat and failure are for the mature. America has always been unfortunately burdened with a need to be "the best" and with a naive insistence that we've never lost a war; this burden is merely amplified in the win-at-all-costs world of sport. On the other hand, some boyish qualities in sport are both attractive and admirable. The simplicity of sport is a relief from the complexity of modern life. The games are played according to universally accepted rules; the opponents are human, clearly perceived, and defined; and the unexpected can occur only within a known range of possibilities. Sport de-

fines a world of youth, for adults must cope daily with the unknown, the impersonal, and the inexplicable in the world of
commerce and politics. So also, a sporting contest has a beginning, a middle, and an end and concludes unambiguously
in either victory or defeat. The real adult world offers in-
completeness and usually uncertain, minimal success at best.
Only children and athletes can be free from such confusion,
but in fact, not even children are granted this convenience.
Child psychologist Erik H. Erikson and others have detailed
the uncertainties and ill-defined threats that children find
overwhelming at times. The youthfulness of sport celebrates,
therefore, a pseudoyouth, just as the pastoralism of sport is a
naive pastoralism. Neither have correspondents in the real
world. Sport is potentially regressive for the individual; it
offers escape from modern life, but no return passage.

This fact is nowhere more apparent than in the relationship of an athlete to his coach. Chapter 2 established the fact
that the juvenile athlete-hero often turns to his coach as a substitute for an absent father. The coach is an important authoritarian figure in America and, as such, would appear suited
to an extremely beneficial role. If the father frequently is
without sufficient status in the American family, then a coach
can assume the role of father in guiding the son to maturity.
However, an athlete does not necessarily turn to the coach as
a role model to define his own identity, finally breaking away
to assert his independence. Rather, an athlete may turn to
the coach as a strong male authority figure and passively
submit to him. The coach tells him when to go to bed, how
long to wear his hair, and where and when he may drink or
smoke. The actual playing of the game requires the strictest
discipline, conformity, and submission of the individual to the
common good, and these rules are determined for the players
by the coach. If an athlete never challenges his coach, he may
never acquire a genuine identity and comfortable independence, but those who do challenge coaches are too often dismissed from the team. Heroes of sports novels are often such
rebels; some succeed in breaking away from authoritarian
control, more are somehow crushed.

One recent novel, Philip F. O'Connor's *Stealing Home*
(1979),[10] focuses on the player-coach relationship on a Pee

Wee baseball team to explore the proper relationships between individuals. Benjamin Dunne is not just a manager, but
a husband, a father, a businessman, and a lover, and in all of
his personal relationships he discovers the truth that he
learns from his twelve- and thirteen-year-old players. Although he is the coach, he must allow them to play the game
their way as much as possible—choosing game strategy as
well as the proper response to opponents' dirty tricks, determining just what the game means to them. So too, if his wife's
pursuit of personal expression is impractical, she nevertheless has the right to continue as long as she believes in it. His
children cannot be forced to develop as he, Benjamin, desires, but as they choose; his business partner is entitled to
select a new career, however much Benjamin disapproves.
Benjamin himself may be uncertain where his own desires lie
—in Boise as the general manager of an independent Class C
baseball league, with his wife and three children, or with
Ellen Jennings, who fulfills all of his most passionate sexual
urges. But he realizes at the end of the novel that, whatever
his decision, he has the same power to choose that he allows
his ballplayers. This opting for individual freedom over submission to a collective goal is the answer Americans seemed
to increasingly make in the 1970s, and O'Connor finds in the
unconventional baseball coach his metaphor for the rejection
of traditional constraints.

O'Connor's vision runs counter to the dominant tendency
among sports novels to emphasize the regressive juvenility
that sport fosters. Sports are games after all, many writers
have insisted, and these novelists have debunked the seriousness with which we regard our games by writing frivolous
fantasies about them. Among the more extreme instances of
this reaction, H. Allen Smith tells the story in *Rhubarb* (1946)
of a cat who inherits a baseball team, Hal Higdon fantasizes
about *The Horse That Played Center Field* (1969), and Paul
Gallico makes a boxing kangaroo the hero of *Matilda* (1970).

Other writers have not found the juvenility of American
sport so humorous. John Alexander Graham, in *Babe Ruth
Caught in a Snowstorm* (1973), imagines a baseball team actually formed on the principles of the *game* as it is popularly
promoted: love of playing, joy of competition, unselfish de-

votion, and mutual respect. The realities of organized baseball intrude on this idyllic experiment, unfortunately, and
the Wichita Wraiths are wracked by dissension and final apo-
calypse. Even if athletes are, in a sense, children, Graham
implies that hanging onto childhood dreams is foolish, because living those dreams denies reality.

Two other recent novels, Alan S. Foster's *Goodbye, Bobby
Thomson! Goodbye, John Wayne!* (1973) and George Zuckerman's *Farewell, Frank Merriwell* (1973), are also concerned
with the serious consequences of the juvenility of American
sport. The hero of Zuckerman's novel wishes something
could "free me from the boy hiding within me."[11] The "boy"
in Forrest Devers is his youthful idealism and refusal to accept the death of things, and is named "Frank Merriwell,"
after the prototypical sports hero; sport and youth are explicitly made identical. Foster's hero, on the other hand, comes
to realize that the juvenile heroism which fired his high
school and college football careers has become a sick anachronism in the violent 1960s. The impulse to create heroes
that drives adults to transform a football game into a life-and-
death struggle is the same impulse that wages wars and as-
sassinates presidents, according to Foster. (It is fascinating
to note parenthetically the number of novels in which the as-
sassination of President Kennedy has a profound impact.
A partial list would include the two books just mentioned,
plus Peter Gent's *North Dallas Forty* (1974), James Whitehead's *Joiner* (1971), and Gary Cartwright's *The Hundred-
Yard War* (1968). The athlete and our former forty-three-
year-old president both represent youthful heroes to the American imagination; the death of one seemed to invalidate the
credibility of the other.) "The game is all right as long as you
remember that it's just a game—not a way of life"[12] is Pete's
conclusion at the end of Foster's novel. Herein lies the difference between positive youthfulness and regressive juvenility.

I have been stressing the latter because of its emphasis in
sports fiction, but, of course, the youthful vitality of sport is
also one of its primary virtues. In *Farewell, Frank Merriwell,*
when the "boy" in Forrest Devers, wounded by the assassi-
nation of President John Kennedy, is finally destroyed by the

murder of Robert Kennedy, Forrest Devers "dies" as well.
Human happiness needs the joys associated with youth, particularly the joy of play. When Johan Huizinga argues in *Homo
Ludens* that play predates culture, creates civilization, and
produces the fundamental forms of social life such as law,
war, poetry, philosophy, and art,[13] he implicitly makes a
powerful case for the value of sport in modern culture. Sport
with only the appearance of play becomes "puerile," to use
Huizinga's term, but sport suffused with the true play-element can be the purest expression of our humanity. Youthfulness—that ever-present partner of play—can represent both
the best and the worst aspects of American sport, and of the
American character as well.

The Novel of Youth

American sports fiction has long recognized the importance
of archetypal patterns of youth and age in sport. The displacement of the veteran by the rookie; the relative merits of
youth and experience; and the particular problems of the as-
piring youngster, the player at the end of his career, or the
frustrated ex-athlete are at least minor themes in almost
every sports novel. Few boxing novels have been written that
do not include a portrait of the punch-drunk ex-fighter as a
reminder of the condition toward which the protagonist is ad-
vancing. Time in the boxing world is measured in blows, not
seconds; a boxer can be "old" at twenty-nine or even nineteen. In a college football novel, the span between youth and
age is only a few years, but in a novel such as Owen Johnson's
Stover at Yale (1912) the difference in maturity and experience between a freshman and a senior is extensive. And baseball novels, such as Martin Quigley's *Today's Game* (1965),
invariably probe the insecurities felt by both the young and
the aging players striving to succeed.

For a prototype of the story of youth and age, one need only
look again to Jack London. Just as our first serious writer
of sports fiction provided the model for the country-city novel
in *The Abysmal Brute,* his widely anthologized short story,
"A Piece of Steak" (1909), creates the type for the novel of
youth and age. London's genius certainly was not his subtlety,

but rather his ability to see the underlying tensions and the broader philosophical implications of the sports world in universal, generalized terms. His stories have an archetypal quality that appears stereotypical in retrospect, for they have been retold numberless times by countless authors. "A Piece of Steak" is no exception.

The plot concerns a forty-year-old boxer fighting a young challenger in Australia for a winner-take-all prize of thirty quid. Tom King, once a brilliant fighter, desperately needs this money for the continued survival of his family. Prior to the fight, Tom muses on his own glorious past and now sees himself personified in the old fighters he has battered on his rise to the top:

> Those had been times! But he realized now, in his slow, ruminating way, that it was the old uns he had been putting away. He was Youth, rising; and they were Age, sinking.[14]

Tom is now Age and his opponent, Sandel, is Youth, and the stake for Tom is no longer glory, but survival. London leaves no doubt about the issues in his story, and he characterizes each of the polar categories thoroughly. Age is grotesquely ugly, fights for money not for glory, is smart, and clever.[15] Age must win by cunning, not by strength and speed:

> He occasionally feinted, shook his head when the weight of a punch landed, and moved stolidly about, never leaping or springing or wasting an ounce of strength. Sandel must foam the froth of Youth away before discrete Age could dare to retaliate. All King's movements were slow and methodical, and his heavy-lidded, slow-moving eyes gave him the appearance of being half asleep or dazed. Yet they were eyes that saw everything through all his twenty years and odd in the ring. They were eyes that did not blink or waver before an impending blow, but that coolly saw and measured distance.[16]

Youth, on the other hand, is beautiful, graceful, and "dazzling," is proudly defiant, fights for glory, and relies on stamina and endurance to compensate for mistakes.[17] The "way of Youth" is sharply contrasted to the way of Age:

> He was swift and clever. It was a dazzling exhibition. The

house yelled its approbation. But King was not dazzled. He had fought too many fights and too many youngsters. He knew the blows for what they were—too quick and too deft to be dangerous. Evidently Sandel was going to rush things from the start. It was to be expected. It was the way of Youth, expending its splendor and excellence in wild insurgence and furious onslaught, overwhelming opposition with its own unlimited glory of strength and desire.[18]

In this pitting of Youth against Age, Youth must triumph. King wins the early rounds easily, but he is unable to finish off his superbly conditioned opponent, and when his own endurance fails, he is knocked out. London makes the obvious claim that the ideal fighter is a sum of the wisdom of Age and the stamina of Youth, but in any confrontation of the two, Youth must prevail. Youth is myopic, however; only Age understands the cycle of youth and age, as King observes:

Yes, Youth was the Nemesis. It destroyed the old uns and recked not that, in so doing, it destroyed itself. It enlarged its arteries and smashed its knuckles and was in turn destroyed by Youth.[19]

The world belongs to the young, but the young suicidally ensure their own future destruction.

These are the extreme portraits of youth and age, which became the stereotypical standards for subsequent sports fiction. A most familiar situation in any sports novel finds the rookie attempting to make the team, as exemplified in Gary Cartwright's *The Hundred-Yard War* (1968). The forty-four rookies arriving at the Dallas Troopers' training camp are faceless bodies known to the coaches only as jottings on a scouting report:

For months now Bullocks, Cox, etc. were names, heights, weights, schools, and method acquired to office personnel of the Dallas Troopers. Many of them . . . would never be more than that. They arrive, mix with the crowd of unfamiliar faces wearing familiar uniforms, and then, with a perfunctory back spin, disappear forever.[20]

They submit to physical and psychological testing, and if

their times in the forty-yard dash are too slow, or their IQs too high, they are released. They are segregated from the veterans who ignore and resent them for attempting to steal their jobs, and who are trying to reaffirm a sense of their own youth by proving themselves better than the young studs. The "process of natural selection"[21] enables some of the rookies to make their presence felt if they perform on the field with reckless violence and enthusiasm, but in an ironic display of respect, the coaches ignore the rookies who are insufficiently talented and continually harass the promising ones, assuming that this treatment will motivate and drive them to self-improvement.

Against this impersonal treatment by coaches and veterans, the rookie struggles to satisfy his basic human needs. He knows his chances of making the team are small and his remaining in camp may jeopardize his opportunities in other careers. He becomes desperately lonely for his wife or girlfriend. Sexually and emotionally deprived, he desires to be released so that he may go home, but he wants at the same time to make the team. Even more fundamentally important, a feeling of anonymity creates in the rookie a desperate need simply to confirm his existence. The most trivial indication that *anyone* knows who he is becomes crucially important. One of the rookies in the novel, discovering his name has been mistakenly omitted from the dining hall checklist, is overwhelmed by anxiety.

For the rookie, the training camp becomes a state of limbo until he is released to rejoin his friends and family, or he makes the team and imagines he has achieved some kind of ultimate manhood. In the meantime, the rookies drift through training camp with "the thousand-mile stares":

> The bewilderment, the disorientation, the depression that visits explorers in a country where the land is the same shape and size and color as the sky, the endless quest, the devalued objective, all huddled like freezing pups suckling dry cactus.[22]

The ultimate degradation of human life occurs in the novel when one rookie, driven relentlessly by his coaches, dies from heat prostration.

The relationship of the rookie and the veteran player are

typically present in sports novels in such vignettes, but some sports fiction focuses on *either* youth or age as its primary concern. Novels of youth focus on the initiation of the young athlete into the adult reality of big-time professional sport; novels of age focus on the aging athlete struggling for survival; both are characteristically baseball novels. As was discussed in the previous chapter, an essential part of baseball's myth is its association with the frontier; innocence and the promise of immortality are consequently part of the image. As an innocent, the baseball player is the hero of the novel of youth tested by a more complex reality than he has yet encountered; as a believer in immortality, he is also the hero of the novel of age confronting the reality that immortality is not his.

The novel of youth, then, is a *bildungsroman,* or novel of a young man's education; Eliot Asinof's *Man on Spikes* (1955) is one such novel. Its hero, Mike Kutner, begins his career as a nineteen-year-old outfielder with a Class D team in Maldeen, Mississippi, and concludes it by striking out in his single at-bat in the majors as a thirty-five-year-old rookie. His debut is delayed for sixteen years by a number of unfortunate handicaps. Though an outstanding player, he is small, wears glasses, and plays aggressive, intelligent baseball in the manner of Ty Cobb at a time when the Babe Ruthian slugger is the big gate attraction. He is cheated by an unscrupulous minor league manager of money and a chance to play. He then loses three years in the army during World War II. He is victimized by shoddy sports reporting, bypassed by the big-league club in favor of a black competitor who is needed as a token symbol of tolerance, and eventually becomes too old to be given a real chance. But these sixteen years become Mike Kutner's education. Each of the first thirteen chapters focuses on a single individual who influences Mike in some way: the scout, the father, the manager, the old ballplayer, the clown, the sergeant, the reporter, the Negro, the sister, the commissioner, the wife, the junior executive, and the mother. From these people, Mike learns to fight, discovers human unscrupulousness, acquires respect for others and acceptance of responsibilities outside baseball, and learns the value of family peace and love.

Despite this accumulated knowledge of the world, Mike

must still fail in his one chance with Chicago before he can be liberated from an obsessive desire to be a major league ballplayer. In finally accepting his own failure as an athlete, he achieves maturity as a human being. His frantic quest had blinded him to the harm he was causing others. His insistence on playing the final game of one season in the hope of winning the batting crown causes him to arrive home after his father has already died, and thus denies his father the peace of reconciliation with his son. Further, the unfair burden his monomania imposes on his wife culminates in her desperately offering her body to a ball-club official as a bribe for her husband's promotion. By finally accepting his failure, he is reunited with his wife, and the novel ends with their ecstatic realization of a new beginning in life.

Acceptance of defeat in the sports world is particularly difficult, for final failure invalidates all previous success in the hero-worshipping public's estimation and lingers most insistently in the athlete's own memory. But premature resignation is no virtue because, as Mike says, "A man makes his choice. He has to take his chances."[23] *Man on Spikes* does not adequately pursue the serious implications it raises—the paradoxical virtue of failure and evil of success; rather, the novel merely claims that the athlete must abandon his total commitment to athletic success if he is truly to mature. As a result of this limitation, Asinof's novel is uninspired. Mark Harris, on the other hand, has created one of the most impressive achievements in American sports fiction in a trio of baseball novels. *The Southpaw* (1953), *Bang the Drum Slowly* (1956), and *A Ticket for a Seamstitch* (1957) were not conceived as a trilogy; they are rather three separate novels about a left-handed pitcher named Henry Wiggen, that are among the most entertaining yet "serious" novels in American sports fiction.

The Southpaw is Harris' "Adventures of Huckleberry Finn," from the introductory "Special Warning to All Readers!!!" reminiscent of Twain's prefatory "Notice" and "Explanatory," to the first-person dialectal narration, deft comedy, and major themes of the novel. Henry Wiggen is "Henry, the Navigator," on his own metaphorical raft of discovery—discovery of America and of himself. Henry's "raft trip" begins as a train ride from Perkinsville, New York, to the New York Mammoths' training camp in Aqua Clara, Florida, then carries him west to Queen City in the Four-State Mountain League AA, and finally back to New York and the Mammoths. He has many companions—one of whom is a black roommate—encounters much selfishness and hypocrisy as well as moments of pastoral serenity, and chooses, if not his "damnation," at least his estrangement from society rather than succumb to hypocrisy.

Writing in a post-Freudian age, Harris is naturally more explicitly concerned with youth and initiation, and the possibilities of maturity in the modern world than was Twain. Harris also writes in the tradition of Hemingway and Faulkner, whose youthful protagonists—Nick Adams in "Indian Camp" and Ike McCaslin in "The Bear," for example—are initiated through blood and violence into manhood. However, such blood rites belong to the wilderness; the disappearance of any meaningful rites of initiation in urban America necessitates a prolonged, uncertain process of maturation. *The Southpaw* is a recording of such a process.

This indefinite quality of contemporary maturity is reflected in the examples of aging that dominate the novel. The main action concerns a single baseball season which itself undergoes an aging process. A season begins in youthful exuberance and confidence, has "middle-aged" crises of purpose and courage in the long summer days of mid-season, and ends in either mature triumph or aged failure. So, too, the individual teams have a definable quality of age. Young teams such as Cleveland in the novel have their recognizable character:

> They was mostly a very young club, rough and ready, and they hustled, and they fought with the umps and they fought with the opposition and played a good brand of ball up through August or thereabouts until they began to go down in a heap and wound up fighting amongst themselves.[24]

Old teams, such as the Nine Old Men of a former Mammoth team, start the season strong and make few mistakes, but since they lack the stamina to last, they fade through the hot summer. The successful teams have a mature balance of youth and age—youth to carry the veteran players with strong arms, backs, legs, and enthusiasm; age to steady the team and teach the young players to avoid mistakes.

Within this framework of generalized youth and age, the particular youth of Henry Wiggen is the concern of the novel. "The way I first knowed for sure I was growing was I was out behind the house 1 day, throwing the rubber ball, and the clothes-line kept rubbing me along the top of my head."[25] Thus the theme is introduced on the most superficial level. Other simple signs of growth—learning the basic facts about sex, developing speed on his fast-ball, acquiring a little pitching savvy, being permitted new privileges and responsibilities— set the pattern for the rest of the novel. Henry's first sight of a big city, his first train ride, his introduction to professional baseball, his initial success and failures are all concrete experiences necessary for the growth of a young man—but they do not comprise true maturity.

Maturity has many false guises. Maturity as a pitcher has little connection with personal development. Henry arrives in Aqua Clara with all the brash confidence and egoism of a boy who has never been tested. Sent to the minor leagues for two seasons, he loses much of his greenness, learns patience, and becomes heroically successful. On his return to Aqua Clara, he feels smugly superior to the green recruits: "You can tell a ballplayer from a punk," Henry says, "by the cut of his clothes and the way he walks and the way he handles himself not only on the field but off."[26] Henry amuses himself by observing the "punks" until some of his peers arrive. Rushing up to welcome a veteran teammate, he is greeted, "Hello punk."

This put-down is echoed by the author who is more aware than Henry that physical skills and familiarity with one's surroundings do not make a man. Henry, at this point, perceives himself only in terms of success on the baseball diamond. A successful ballplayer's career rises to a peak and then declines; adulthood conversely is the attaining of genuine maturity, and not only maintaining that level but continuing to grow. Henry later comes to recognize his own limitations:

Give me a baseball in my hand and I know where I am at.

Give me a piece of machinery and I may be more or less in the dark. Give me a book and I am lost. Give me a map and I cannot make heads nor tails, nor I could no more learn another language then pitch with my nose.[27]

Although Henry explains these personal limitations in terms of skills, the reader also recognizes Henry's serious shortcomings in understanding himself and the world. Henry is brilliantly successful in his first year with the Mammoths, but he eventually realizes how little this success means:

Outside of Sam I was the only Mammoth in history that won 25. The nearest anyone else ever come was Egg Barnard in 1920, with 24 wins, and Peter Rosegrant in 1916, also 24, Peter now a turnstile turner in the grandstand section back of the plate.[28]

Henry's real growth does not occur within the framework of the baseball diamond, but in his personal relationships. His psychological position throughout most of the novel is as a son to a number of father figures, and it is by freeing himself from submission to such authority figures that he establishes at least a tentative independence. The opening six chapters deal primarily with Henry's relationship to his real father. "Pop says . . . " is a refrain throughout this section, as the boy Henry idolizes his father and absorbs his wisdom. To the boy's mind, his father is infallible on matters of baseball skill and lore, and the other men of Perkinsville too "looked on Pop as the final word."[29] Pop pitches for the local semi-pro nine and is a hero to his son, whose only desire is to emulate the older man: "I throwed slow and easy, and I felt in my mind like the sight of Pop out there on the same pitching hill."[30] Henry practices constantly and learns all he can from his father until a crucial moment occurs in his adolescent life. He has become a batting practice pitcher on his father's team, but one day when Pop is pitching poorly, Henry is sent in to relieve him:

A kind of fog settled down over me. It was like a dream, and I heard all the sounds that you will hear in any ball park of a Sunday afternoon, and men come up to hit against me,

7 I guess, for 1 man singled. As for the rest they come up and went down, and I seen Pop on the bench and it seemed like he was somewheres where he ought not to been and I looked for myself and could not find myself though I ought to been sitting on the bench and was not, and then the fog begun to lift, and things that was wrapped in the clouds come out in the open.[31]

This first necessary step to independence, the son's break from submission to the father, is wonderfully understated, because Henry cannot understand its significance. The moment of a reliever replacing the starting pitcher is an ideal image for this psychologically charged moment, and Harris exploits it perfectly.

Henry does not comprehend what has happened but his relationship to Pop is subtly changed. He comes to realize his father's limitations: that he is not infallible, is a "master" only on the pitching mound, and is as baffled as Henry by the statements of their erudite neighbor, Aaron Webster. Having been in the shadow of his father for so many years, Henry now begins to be the substance and Pop the shadow. This is a gradual process, developing in concrete stages over the course of the novel. Pop, who had represented to Henry the boy's fantasies of success, eventually receives his own vicarious fulfillment through the success of his son. As a boy Henry had been something of a celebrity as Pop's son; as Pop implies in a letter late in the novel, Henry's success with the Mammoths makes the reversal of roles complete:

I will hang up the glove and call it quits, youngsters coming in and teeing off on my stuff that a few years back they never could touch, but the club keeping me on I know because I was a sort of an attraction, being your old man and all or they would have let me go by now.[32]

To repeat, Henry does not understand the implications of such moments, and his supplanting of Pop is not a sudden traumatic thrust into manhood. He remains a boy and turns to a succession of father figures to fill the unconsciously felt void. Sad Sam Yale, the great Mammoth pitcher, was Henry's other boyhood hero and role model. Mike Mulroony, his coach at Queen City, assumes Pop's role as his baseball mentor: "Pop set me up and Mike put the finish on."[33] Aaron Webster, more a grandfather than a father figure, counsels Henry wisely. And Red Traphagen, Henry's experienced and learned catcher, becomes his "old redheaded papa" while Henry is on the mound.

Henry's supplanting of Pop in the Perkinsville baseball game becomes a paradigm for subsequent father replacements. His first appearance in a Mammoth uniform is again as a relief pitcher near the end of his second year with Queen City. The following year when Sad Sam Yale fails to pitch the opener for the first time in years, Henry not only starts the opener in Sam's place, but replaces Sam as the team's mainstay southpaw, and is obviously on his way to breaking most of Sam's records. Bub Castetter, another veteran pitcher, is released from the club to make room for Henry, whose inexplicable sadness can be attributed only to an unconscious recollection of guilt over surpassing his father.

The final, and most important, paternal figure in the novel is the Mammoth baseball club itself, which consciously assumes an in loco parentis role towards the players. The team owner, Mr. Moors, tells Henry during his first training camp, "You have got to start considering Mr. Mulrooney in place of your pop, for he is in charge of you from now on."[34] Later Pop reports to Henry a letter he has received from the club: "It said you done well and listened to what you was told and never spoke back and kept good hours and no monkeyplay. You keep that up."[35] Henry himself naively prepares for his first airplane flight by buying $50,000 of insurance from an airport machine, claiming the New York Mammoths rather than his father as beneficiary.

This corporate paternal figure is the hardest of all for Henry to reject, but only by doing so does he finally leave his adolescence behind. Manager Dutch Schnell is the team's representative authority figure, and Henry finally discovers at the end of the novel that Dutch is not a loving father but a self-serving manipulator of his players. As the workhorse of the staff and its most effective pitcher, Henry has felt so much pressure that he has developed excruciating back pains simply from the tension. In the final series of the season, with the pennant at stake, Dutch announces that he will pitch Henry with only one day of rest if necessary. Henry rebels at a team meeting, and, although obviously right, he is not supported by any of his teammates. He is left without illusions:

> There is nothing Dutch will not do for the sake of the ball game. If he thinks it will help win a ball game by eating you out he will eat you out. If sugar and honey will do the trick out comes the sugar and honey bottle. If it is money you need he will give you money. And if he has no further need for you he will sell you or trade you or simply cut you loose and forget you.[36]

In addition, his teammates, with whom Henry shared the dreamy pleasures of the successful days and desperate tension of long slumps, are now seen to be hypocritical puppets. Henry's rupture from the club is violent enough to be a final severing from youthful illusion.

Henry returns after the world series to Perkinsville and to Holly Webster, who has been from the beginning Henry's moral center. When he first left home, she told him:

> Henry, you must play ball like it does not matter, for it really does not matter. Nothing really matters. Play ball, do your best, have fun, but do not put the game nor the cash before your own personal pride.[37]

She has taught him that love must cope with bad days as well as good, that human worth is not measured in dollars and cents, that true friends do not care about fame, that manhood is not proven in bed, and that a man's heart must be soft even if his hand is hard. Her relationship to the motherless Henry is thus strikingly maternal. As his moral center, she is the woman in whose eyes he must make himself worthy: "For I loved her and believed she loved me, though what she seen in me I cannot say, for a stupider, thickheaded, stubborner smart-aleck never lived."[38] In addition, she maternally comforts him, soothes him with hot chocolate, and reads to him with his head in her lap. When Henry recognizes the team for what it is and separates himself from it, he's finally worthy of Holly. Commenting on Henry's statistics, she tells him:

What they do not show is that you growed to manhood over the summer. You will throw no more spitballs for the sake of something so stupid as a ball game. You will worship the feet of no more gods name of Sad Sam Yale nor ever be a true follower of Dutch Schnell. And you will know the Krazy Kresses of this world for the liars they are. You will never be an island in the empire of Moors, Henry, and that is the great victory that hardly anybody wins any more.[39]

Henry achieves the maturity of independence and self-identity, but Harris cannot resist an ironic touch or two at the end. Henry's new approach to baseball is that he will play "for the kicks and the cash only,"[40] perhaps the proper attitude under the circumstances, but obviously a self-centered one. He signifies his defiance of the baseball establishment by giving the finger to the crowd during the world series—a juvenile gesture. And his relationship to Holly remains faintly Oedipal in the final pages. But maturity is not simply a plateau that, once attained, is won forever. Henry has made a significant beginning; Harris pursues his education further in *Bang the Drum Slowly*.

Max Lerner is one of many observers of the American scene to note our striking unwillingness to face the fact or meaning of death.[41] *Bang the Drum Slowly* runs counter to this tendency, in the tradition of Hemingway's *A Farewell to Arms* and *For Whom the Bell Tolls* or contemporary novels such as Thomas McGuane's *Ninety-Two in the Shade*. Even these novels, Harris's included, do not deal with old age and death; rather they are the best examples of a sentimental fascination with dying young. Harris himself, in an interview nine years after the publication of *Bang the Drum Slowly,* criticizes his novel for its "sentimental ideas and notions."[42] In comparison to the maudlin treatments of terminal illness on television and in popular movies, however, Harris handles his theme with remarkable restraint.

The novel opens with Henry anticipating the start of his fourth season with the Mammoths. The vestiges of immaturity that lingered at the end of *The Southpaw* are confirmed by the opening pages of the subsequent novel. Henry had resolved to play for kicks and cash and now he is virtually obsessed with money. His simple philosophy is summed up: "First you think about money."[43] The world seems to be divided in Henry's mind between those expenses which are deductible and those which are not; he has even nicknamed his unborn child "600 Dollars." Likewise, Holly is still Henry's moral center, as this simple exchange implies:

> "All he says is I have got to go and see him," I said.
> "What did he do?" she said.
> "He is in the hospital," I said.
> "Then you have got to go," she said.
> "I will come," I said.[44]

The "he" in this case is Bruce Pearson, third-string catcher for the Mammoths and Henry's roommate. The reason he has called Henry is that he is dying of Hodgkin's Disease and does not know what to do. How Henry reacts to this awareness of imminent death is the principal concern of the novel.

Henry's understanding is a gradual awakening. He reacts to the news of his friend's illness with disbelieving shock, anger at the unfairness of death, and incomprehension of its arbitrariness. Afterwards he is offended by the casual way in which words like "death" and "dying" are bandied about by people with no awareness of the words' true significance. But soon he receives his first glimpse of the positive function of death in human life—that it makes life itself more intensely pleasurable. Bruce explains to him:

> "But the world is all rosy," he said. "It never looked better. The bad things never looked so big. Food tastes better. Things do not matter too much any more."[45]

Neither Bruce nor Henry can articulate the precise relationship between this knowledge of death's imminence and Bruce's intensified sensual pleasure, but Henry is on his way to understanding.

Out of friendship and pity, Henry remains with Bruce for the remainder of the off-season, teaches him the rules of the ruleless game TEGWAR so that Bruce can share in the team's private jokes, and refuses to sign his contract until a clause is added that binds him to Bruce in a package deal. He works to build up Bruce's confidence, encourages him to approach baseball more intelligently, and succeeds in radically improving Bruce's performance. He is committed to making Bruce's last days as enjoyable as possible, as any sentimentalist would do, but he also comes to recognize the broader significance of death. On one occasion, Bruce thinks he has had his final attack and is frightened:

> "Hold on to me," he said, and I took his shoulder and held it, and he reached up and took my hand, and I let him have it, though it felt crazy holding another man's hand. Yet after awhile it did not feel too crazy any more.[46]

Henry also makes the observation, "You all die soon enough, so why not be nice to each other?" In simple terms, Henry is beginning to formulate a sense of the sanctity of human life.

The effect of this embryonic insight is marked. Henry noticeably loses his obsession with money and deductions; he demonstrates a new respect for aged ex-ballplayers reliving their pasts with tedious reminiscences; and he is able to make the simple but profound declaration, "Life is good."[47] Death retains its sadness; he nearly bawls when his daughter is born, realizing even if he cannot verbalize the thought that the infant in his arms is yet another person who must die. But he is also beginning to comprehend that death is part of the normal cycle of life and death.

Henry also learns much from the reactions of others to their knowledge of Bruce's dying. Katie, Bruce's whore-girlfriend, agrees to marry Bruce in anticipation of benefitting from his $50,000 insurance policy. Goose and Horse, aging teammates on the Mammoths, are moved to sentimental self-loathing for their own shortcomings and show excessive kindness to Bruce. Dutch Schnell reacts to the imminent death only as an obstacle to be overcome—the fact that Bruce will die soon is important only insofar as it affects the pennant hopes of his ballclub. Mike Mulrooney responds with religious trust in a better afterlife; the skeptic Red Traphagen sees only death's black humor. Henry tacitly rejects all these displacements, evasions, and rationalizations and deals directly with death. Red's attitude towards life is to look back to his youth and lament its passing; Henry, by looking toward death, makes the present precious.

As the story approaches Bruce's climactic death, Harris expertly prevents it from slipping into sentimentality. The novel becomes a gentle dirge, like the song, "The Streets of Laredo," from which the title is taken. Bruce is almost wholly inarticulate and reacts to his fate with an uncomprehending and comic, "I am doomded."[48] Furthermore, the use of baseball settings and metaphors enables Harris to make potentially sentimental statements in a tearless manner. A subplot of the main story concerns Sid Goldman's assault on Babe Ruth's record of sixty home runs in a season. As the papers proclaim daily Sid's statistical relationship to the Babe at every stage of the season, the players react by seeing "records" everywhere they turn—in the number of times a player has switched off the radio, the number of times a player has hung his jock on a particular nail, and so on. Henry, too, sees records in Bruce's improved play. He comments, for example, on "the first time he hit for extra bases in 2 consecutive trips to the plate since September of 49."[49] Henry's point, unlike his teammates', is not to emphasize the absurdity of records, but to imply that Bruce's minor accomplishments are as significant as the exploits of the greatest superstar, because both are human beings who must die. Death is the great democratizer.

There is another side to this obsession with baseball history: statistics become the permanent record of a man's life, and, as history, they give to human endeavor a continuity transcending death. Sid's attempt on Babe Ruth's record not only brings Ruth back from the dead and puts him on the front of every sports page in the country, but also bridges the gap between 1927 and 1955 and even looks to the future, documenting the permanence of human achievement. Even the box scores and scorecards that appear periodically in the novel become permanent monuments to the existence of those athletes; immortality of sorts is available to a few. By utilizing these archetypal baseball situations in the context of the dying athlete, Harris is able to make such idealistic claims without cheapening them with banal statements.

The major way in which Harris uses the baseball setting is

to observe the effect on the team of Bruce's dying. The 1955 Mammoths are immensely talented, but dissension and lack of respect for each other cause them to struggle through the season. Owing to his ignorance and his plans to marry a whore, Bruce is a particular butt of their jokes, but when his teammates learn of his illness, they are suddenly united by their concern for him. Henry explains their feeling:

> It made me feel very sad. Yet I knew that some of the boys felt the same. Not being alone with it any more was a great help, knowing that other boys knew, even if only a few and you felt warm towards them, and you looked at them and them at you, and you were both alive, and you might as well said, "Ain't it really quite a great thing at that?" and if they would of been a girl you would of kissed them, though you never said such a thing out loud but only went on about your business.[50]

The team becomes nearly unbeatable and sweeps through the world series. The knowledge of the imminence of death makes the life of each player more precious to his teammates, and the men at last become a club.

Finally, Harris avoids sentimentality by using Henry Wiggen as his narrator. Henry's humor and semi-literate dialect keep the book above pathos. The novel focuses on Henry's growth rather than on the tragedy of Bruce's death, which finally occurs almost casually. By the end of the novel, Henry has lost his obsession with money, has decided independently of Holly (though he asks and receives her approval) to prevent Katie from unscrupulously acquiring Bruce's insurance benefits, and even undergoes mature critical self-examination. Having failed to send Bruce a scorecard from one of the series games, Henry says:

> Goddam it, anyhow, I am just like the rest. Wouldn't it been simple instead of writing a page on my book to shoved it in the mail? How long would it of took? Could I not afford the stamps?[51]

Despite his self-accusation, Henry is not like those who were momentarily united by pity but have learned nothing permanent. When Henry ends his narration with the words, "From

here on in I rag nobody," it is clear that he has learned the
lesson that men should live their lives as if they really knew
everyone was doomed to die, that every life is sacred because
tragically short. This is a mature vision that has brought him
far from the conclusion of *The Southpaw*. In that novel, Henry
established his independence; in *Bang the Drum Slowly,* he
turns back to the world of men with a sense of his own responsibilities.

A Ticket for a Seamstitch is little more than a slight footnote to *Bang the Drum Slowly*. It adds little to Harris's
achievement, but it does confirm that Henry has persisted in
his maturity and reasserts the sanctity of human life. The
plot concerns a seamstitch (seamstress) who works her way
across the country against numerous obstacles to see Piney
Woods, Henry's new roommate, and her other heroes on the
Mammoths. When she arrives and proves to be drably plain,
Piney immediately deserts her. Henry jeopardizes his own
chance to break one of baseball's greatest records by neglect-
ing his sleep and concentration in order to entertain the seamstitch. He loses the game, but recognizes that her happiness is
more important than a statistical record, and that his fame is
not something to be selfishly hoarded. As Red Traphagen
tells him, "It is not the privilege of many men to live longer
than their bones and their flesh live. You must expect people
to share with you in the struggle."[52] Just as Bruce's play
improved when he discovered he had friends, so the seamstitch responds to kindness and blossoms into a moderately
attractive girl:

> She looked better than she looked. A good sleep always done
> wonders for her, she said, or maybe she only looked better
> because once you hang with somebody awhile they look bet-
> ter, and everything she seen she admired.[53]

Henry forces Piney to take her out again and they have a
"pretty good" time.

This unpretentious third story is obviously unworthy of the
first two, but it does add a certain completeness to them.
Henry's education is successful, his continued maturity assured. He does not have great respect for collective human-

ity, for the "clucks" as he terms baseball fans, but he knows the value of an individual human life and lives accordingly. Joseph Campbell presented the myth of the hero as a tripartite quest: separation-initiation-return. Harris's three novels can be seen to fulfill these functions. In *The Southpaw*, Henry separates himself from his old world; in *Bang the Drum Slowly*, he overcomes obstacles to learn the secret of life. Unlike the popular athlete-hero whose career ends with his own initiation and triumph, however, in *A Ticket for a Seamstitch*, Henry returns to his people with his hard-won knowledge to become their moral leader. By teaching Piney the lesson he had struggled to learn, Henry becomes a legitimate hero.

The Novel of Age

Twenty-two years after *A Ticket for a Seamstitch*, Mark Harris published a fourth Henry Wiggen novel, *It Looked Like For Ever* (1979). The final installment of Henry's pitching career is of a kind with the previous three. Henry still tells his own story in the same semi-literate idiom; he is still an individualist who demands to do things his own way or be convinced that he should not. He opposes the Vietnam War as he had opposed the Korean conflict in 1952; he is no longer concerned about money only because he has so much of it now; he is still married to Holly, still lives in Perkinsville, still despises fans. But there is one all-important difference between this novel and the earlier three. Henry is now thirty-nine years old, and *It Looked Like For Ever* is not a novel of youth but of the aging athlete clinging to a career at its end. Henry is no longer a boy, but a man who wears contact lenses, has prostate trouble (or "prostrate," in Henry's inimitable style), has indulged in casual love affairs, and has four daughters, one of whom requires psychiatric care. The tone of the book is more subdued and the possibilities for heroism much reduced, for Henry's life is defined by his mortality now, not by his limitless hopes for the future.

Just as the opening chapters of *The Southpaw* contain numerous signs of Henry's emergence from childhood to manhood, so the first chapter of *It Looked Like For Ever* presents various images of death. Dutch Schnell, the manager of the

Mammoths, has just died at seventy-eight, but his is only the most literal death in the chapter. Dutch's departure marks "the end of an era"[54] in Mammoth baseball; Henry tells his daughter Hilary about hitting a homerun in the *old* St. Louis ball park that is now torn down; one of the mourners at Dutch's funeral is a team owner named Suicide Alexander. Most important, retirement from baseball is a kind of death. "Once you stop playing you are idle," says Henry, "you are nothing, you got nothing to do, you roam around feeling useless, you got nothing left to do but put your hands in your ass pockets and look alive if you can."[55] Perry Simpson, Henry's former roommate, attends the funeral—a man who played ten years before drifting out of baseball and out of the news. Henry recalls Perry's talents:

> He was a blessing to a pitcher. He fielded balls back hand on the other side of second base and threw out his runner going the opposite way. He was power and speed, he hit long, he hit short, he hit straight away or he pulled, he stole bases, he now had diabetes, heart trouble, arthritis, he was blind in 1 eye at the age of 40 and deaf in the other, and the time was here that he could not possibly rise from his chair without groaning.[56]

Forty is young in human years, but it is ancient in baseball time. The retired player faces the predicament of every human growing old, but at a much earlier period in his life. And Henry Wiggen must face this problem, too, for at the end of the chapter he learns that, after twenty-one years in the organization, he has been released by the Mammoths.

The remainder of the novel describes Henry's attempts to deal with the death of his career. "What am I going to do with the rest of my life?"[57] is the question that haunts him, and his first choice is to continue playing. But Henry won only three games in his last year with the Mammoths; rival owners are not overly anxious to sign a nearly-forty short-relief pitcher. He is a "younger older man," as Holly terms him, who is not as young as he feels but "as young as Nature says."[58] Although his fastball is gone, he can compensate with savvy to pitch perhaps two strong innings at a time, but he can never again be the overpowering force he once was. As a young man he felt invulnerable and immortal:

> When I first come it looked like for ever, I was confident, I was strong, I had enthusiasm, I had motivation, I drank nothing, I smoked nothing, and I could throw a baseball harder than almost any body.[59]

Now, his glory in the past, not the future, he realizes that he never appreciated his fame while it was his. "I was always looking ahead," he says, "and now the future is past."[60]

Henry repeatedly says that he wishes to continue playing only so that his daughter Hilary will have a chance to see him, but the desperation of his attempts belie such explanations. He falls lowest on Old Timers' Day, when he strikes out six old men on eighteen pitches in the two-inning exhibition, simply to advertise what good shape he is in. That same night Suicide Alexander calls to sign him for the California Angels, and his wish is fulfilled at last. With the Angels he saves the first six games he enters, pitching nine scoreless innings, allowing only one hit, and leading the team into first place. But he fails to recognize his slower reflexes and poor eyesight until in his seventh appearance he is hit in the head by a line drive which he never sees or reacts to. At last he admits what Nature has been telling him—his career has ended.

It Looked Like For Ever is a less interesting novel than either *The Southpaw* or *Bang the Drum Slowly,* but, by capturing Henry Wiggen in his transition from baseball to retirement, it does identify clearly the main interests of the sports novel of age. The novel of age has two possible heroes—the aging veteran or the ex-athlete. The former appears in a minor role in nearly every sports novel as the athlete trying to hang onto his job by savvy rather than physical prowess. Most often he is the pathetic older ballplayer replaced by a youthful competitor, but he can appear as a legitimate hero— an Odysseus-figure as opposed to the Achilles-types who are the typical athlete-heroes. Wiles, deception, and knowledge of the world and of men are the virtues of this athletic Odysseus. Stat Hunter of Charles Einstein's *The Only Game in Town* (1955) is such a figure, an aging but still capable centerfielder, now player-manager for the Class C Conway Bears. He has major-league ability but a throwing arm that is no longer capable of the daily strain of top-flight baseball. He copes with his diminished physical capability, however, through an abundance of baseball savvy, and by the end of the novel he has been promoted to the parent Philadelphia club where his playing and managing help the team to a successful third-place finish. The novel of age focuses on small achievements rather than on the glorious heroics that a young man's novel could appropriately celebrate. Stat Hunter is a man who *copes*—on the field and in his private life. He acquires the mature vision to reject an infantile commitment solely to the game; it is still the only game in town, but he can find a place in his life for a wife and daughter, too.

Einstein's novel is obviously a low-keyed realistic portrait of everyday baseball. Heroics are on a small scale, and failures are not ignored. Stat must respond to the numerous problems that beset a team during a long season: the antagonisms that develop from long days and nights of playing in miserable conditions; the politics of self-promotion; the injuries, slumps, and breaks that determine a season's outcome. The novel of age is not without its poignancy, however, as Michael Novak brilliantly suggests in *The Joy of Sports*:

> Each time one enters a contest, one's unseen antagonist is death. Not one's visible opponent, who is only the occasion for the struggle. But the Negative Spirit, the Denier. That is why the image of the aging athlete is so poignant: it begins to mix the ritual contest with the actual contest, ritual death with the coming of real death. In the aging athlete, the ultimate reality of sports breaks through the symbol, becomes explicit.[61]

Stat Hunter is a representative of us all, as we proceed toward death, too.

The novel of age most frequently deals with the ex-athlete, the former hero in his decline. Conditioned by public acclamation to regard himself as someone special, the retired ballplayer must deal not only with the universal problems of age, but also with the specific burdensome knowledge of his former greatness and present anonymity. In addition, because the athletic world can be a prolonged adolescence if the athlete passively accepts its values, retirement can be a sudden shocking thrust into adult reality. The former hero's problems, as John Barth's *Chimera* would have us believe, are as old as the lives of the world's first heroes. How does Perseus feel, growing stodgily old at home with Andromeda, his heroic adventures but memories of his past?

This universal condition is amplified in youth-oriented, success-addicted, hero-worshipping America. The problem of the athlete is exaggerated, of course, for he must usually retire altogether at an early age from the field in which he acquired fame. Not only must he then experience relative failure or anonymity, he must, in effect, create for himself a substantially new identity. Tom Buchanan of F. Scott Fitzgerald's *The Great Gatsby* is one prototype of this ex-athlete, the obnoxiously aggressive individual who treats his peers as if they are mere underlings, while he remains the star athlete. The other prototype is a pathetic figure who cannot adjust to his anonymity, but is trapped by a longing for return to his days of fame.

Two fine short stories—Irwin Shaw's "The Eighty-Yard Run" (1941) and John Cheever's, "O Youth and Beauty" (1958)—handle this second figure with touching pathos. Shaw's Christian Darling is a thirty-five-year-old salesman whose life peaked fifteen years before. As a sophomore second-string halfback, he had taken a swing pass in practice one day and raced eighty yards for a touchdown. It had been a perfect moment, a communion of mind, body, and earth, as he ran "without thought, his arms and legs working beautifully together."[62] That run had won him recognition and a starting position on the varsity team, but never again did he recapture the euphoria of that moment. He became a blocking back for a more talented teammate, married a campus beauty, and worked for her father. But the stock market crash wiped her father out, and Darling drifted in and out of menial jobs as his wife moved up in fashionable literary circles and became more and more intellectually estranged from her husband. Now (in the story's present) he has returned to his alma mater to sell custom-made suits to the students and to reflect on his past:

That was the high point, Darling thought, fifteen years ago, on an autumn afternoon, twenty years old and far from death, with the air coming easily into his lungs, and a deep feeling inside him that he could be anything, knock over anybody, outrun whatever had to be outrun. And the shower after and the three glasses of water and the cool night air on his damp head and Louise sitting hatless in the open car with a smile and the first kiss she ever really meant. The high-point, an eighty-yard run in the practice, and a girl's kiss and everything after that a decline.[63]

His moment of glory had fulfilled all his physical desires in the sensual world of the athlete. Afterwards he luxuriated in the sound of the smack of leather against the ball, the quarterback's voice, the pounding of cleats, the yells of coaches, the laughter of the players, the sensation of a hot shower and soft warm clothes after practice, the smell of oil of wintergreen and iodine, the sight of clean, white tape against his ruddy skin, and the taste of cold water. This world of physical sensation is a youthful one in its simplicity, and it is complemented by the adolescent satisfaction of his first sexual experience with Louise.

Darling earned this moment simply by training his instincts and developing his physical prowess. He did not prepare himself for responsibility, work, a depression, or intellectual development. The failure of his subsequent life is due to the reinforced juvenility of his athletic career. Stated simply, Louise continues to grow after graduation; Darling does not. His name is emblematic of his problem; he had once been a "darling" and cannot adjust to not being one now. He cannot accept Louise's new friends because he is at the periphery of her group, not at its center. On one occasion, after exploding, "Doesn't *anything* happen inside your head?" Louise apologizes, "as she might to a child."[64] She calls him "Baby" and treats him with "a kind of patient, kindly, remote boredom."[65] Like a child he is vindictively happy when he learns that his former star teammate has been walking around in a cast for seven years after a professional football injury. He even *looks* as youthful as ever.

Nevertheless, he is no longer twenty; he is thirty-five. When, overcome by nostalgia, Darling mimes his glorious run on the field on which it occurred, he is still well conditioned, but he appears foolish, not heroic, to two unexpected onlookers. The sweat he had delighted in as "warm moisture lubricating his skin like oil" fifteen years before is now unpleasantly "breaking out on his face and running down into his collar."[66] Christian Darling's wife and even his nation have matured while coping with a depression, but they have left him behind because he is doomed to be perpetually a twenty-year-old. Shaw's handling of his theme is exquisite, particularly in his refusal to cast blame. Darling is never belittled or made to appear arrogant or cruel; he truly loves his wife, even desperately needs her, but he is simply incapable of matching her intellectual growth. Nor is Louise merely an emasculating bitch as women in similar roles are so often portrayed in American literature. She adores and supports him early in their relationship, only reluctantly moves outside his world while always trying to include him in her interests, but must finally accept their inevitable incompatibility. If blame is to be assigned, it belongs to the unnamed people who make Christian Darling think of himself as an "important figure" in his football-playing youth and who fail to educate him "for 1929 and New York City and a girl who would turn into a woman."[67] But even such judgments misrepresent Shaw's intention. "The Eighty-Yard Run" offers a textbook definition of pathos—Christian Darling is crushed by his own virtues which are defined by American society in the thirties as weakness. Darling's human potential lies in his physicality, but American culture judges a man who knows Ernest Dowson to be superior to a man who is physically fit at age thirty-five. Sports are for the young, not the middle-aged, but Christian Darling is a man who never ceased being a boy.

Cash Bentley of Cheever's story suffers from similarly stunted development. He is five years older than Darling and has thinning hair, but he retains "a charming quality of stubborn youthfulness."[68] Though he and his wife have their occasional squabbles and his financial position is rarely stable, he is a "happily married"[69] typical suburbanite. He is like his neighbors with this one exception—he concludes every party he attends by running a "hurdle race" over furniture and other household obstacles to remind himself and others that he was once a track star. By clinging to this vestigial link to his early fame, Cash maintains his equilibrium, but when he breaks his leg during one such exhibition, this illusion is also shattered.

Unable to run his hurdles, he becomes overwhelmed by images of decay everywhere he turns: he discovers rank-smelling spoiled meat in the icebox, accidentally thrusts his face into a spider's web, encounters an old, sluttish whore on a New York side street, and is overcome by the putrid smell of earth from a bouquet of faded roses. Parties now seem interminable and stale, he is continually irritable with his wife (also named Louise, like Darling's), and he is suddenly jealous of the young:

> He does not understand what separates him from these children in the garden next door. He has been a young man. He has been a hero. He has been adored and happy and full of animal spirits, and now he stands in a dark kitchen, deprived of his athletic prowess, his impetuousness, his good looks—of everything that means anything to him.[70]

When his leg mends, he races again, but his ease and grace are gone. When he had hurdled before, "it was extraordinary to see this man of forty surmount so many obstacles so gracefully." But now when he runs: "His face was strained. His mouth hung open. The tendons of his neck protruded hideously. . . . His clothes were soaked with sweat and he gasped for breath."[71] The story concludes with a scene that recalls Hemingway's "The Short Happy Life of Francis Macomber." Cash returns home from a party and asks Louise to fire the starting gun so that he can run his hurdles race:

> He had forgotten to tell her about the safety, and when she pulled the trigger nothing happened. "It's that little lever,"

he said. "Press that little lever." Then in his impatience, he
hurdled the sofa anyhow. The pistol went off and Louise got
him in midair. She shot him dead.[72]

As in the Hemingway story, Louise's act is ambiguous. The
shooting could be an accident, a freeing of herself from a
helplessly childish husband, or an act of mercy. But the significance for Cash is clear. Francis Macomber died happily at
the peak of his self-esteem; Cash Bentley has been virtually
dead for months, and Louise's act simply frees him from the
illusion that he was alive.

Christian Darling played football, Cash Bentley ran track;
novels dealing with ex-athletes can include any of the major
sports. Baseball may be particularly suited to the novel of
youth and the novel of the aging athlete, but the burden of
coping with a loss of status and fame is common to players
who retire from any sport. Jay Neugeboren's *Big Man* (1966)
describes the efforts of Mack Davis to survive his banning
from NBA basketball because of his involvement in point-
fixing scandals in college. More interesting, James Whitehead's *Joiner* (1971) is the story of Eugene "Sonny" Joiner,
a six-foot-seven-inch, two-hundred-seventy-pound ex-football
star searching for a life of action that can equal the satisfaction he found in his playing career. Sonny is a man of immense size, charm, and intelligence, a man born to be a mov-
er of men. He is a romantic with a large need to be involved in
heroic action, to storm some fortress while his woman in satin
and lace awaits his triumphal return, but life in Bryan, Mississippi, offers few opportunities for such escapades.

Near the end of the novel, Joiner identifies his dilemma:
"The metaphysics of claustrophobia may finally be the sum
of what a large man's book is all about"[73]; his largeness is
spiritual as well as physical, but after football he has no
space into which his presence can expand. Football had been
an arena for heroic activism; it offered the opportunity for
uniting mind and body in ritual action. It is a romantic and
purposeful activity, yet at the same time earthy and practical. Had Sonny become an all-pro tackle in his rookie year, he
might have felt involved in the humanly expressive activism

for which history destined him. Instead he discovers that as a pro lineman he is only competent, and that football in "The League" is simply hard work.

For Sonny, events occur in large historical contexts, but nothing he does after his retirement seems significant. History is a vast panorama in the present—the novel's style reflects this in its achronological juxtaposition of events—but Joiner cannot find his proper position in this process. He is smothered by a feminine reality he cannot accommodate, redneck prejudice he cannot tolerate, and passions and needs he cannot consistently satisfy. What he chooses to do must involve activism and commitment to this world, but understanding what that course of action ought to be constantly eludes him. The knowledge of his failure in the National Football League, and the knowledge of his wife's and friends' awareness of his failure drive him to mindless violence in the cause of civil rights and a resultant exile from Bryan. At the end of the novel he contemplates his return, but because he has not yet been purged of his sense of destiny, his future ability to accept life there remains doubtful. Sonny Joiner—as well as Christian Darling, Cash Bentley, Mack Davis, and other incidental characters in dozens of sports novels—represents every individual whose sense of destiny is stimulated by early achievement but unfulfilled by the passing of years. Unconsummated early promise is a characteristically American burden but is not exclusively ours; A. E. Housman spoke for all men in his elegy "To An Athlete Dying Young"—for all "Runners whom renown outran/And the name died before the man."

The best of the novels dealing with the ex-athlete is *Rabbit, Run* (1960) by John Updike, whose stunning prose and complex vision raise this novel high above the others discussed. One indication of this complexity is the incredible range of critical opinions proposed to explicate the novel. One writer, summing up the previous criticism, observes: "Harry is either a completely insensitive, irresponsible cad, or a saint and the only man of integrity in the entire novel."[74] The truth seems to lie in a combination of these two extremes, and the key to this paradox lies in Rabbit Angstrom's youthfulness.

The conception of the ex-athlete interested Updike even be-

fore he wrote *Rabbit, Run*. "Ace in the Hole" is a short story
that appears now to be an outline for the later novel, and "Ex-
Basketball Player" expresses in verse the main theme to be
explored in *Rabbit, Run*.[75] Although these early attempts
add little to the portrait already conceived by Shaw and
Cheever, *Rabbit, Run* extends the treatment of the ex-athlete
to define an essential paradox in the American character.

Rabbit Angstrom is a twenty-six-year-old former basketball star who now demonstrates Magi-Peel Kitchen Peelers
for a living. Feeling trapped by his job and by his marriage,
he runs away from both:

> It just felt like the whole business was fetching and hauling,
> all the time trying to hold this mess together she was making
> all the time. I don't know, it seemed like I was glued in with
> a lot of busted toys and empty glasses and television going
> and meals late and no way of getting out. Then all of a sud-
> den it hit me how easy it was to get out, just walk out, and
> by damn it *was* easy.[76]

Like Christian Darling, Rabbit was once a star and nothing in
his present can compare to that past:

> I once played a game real well, I really did. And after you're
> first-rate at something, no matter what, it kind of takes the
> kick out of being second-rate. And that little thing Janice and
> I had going, boy, it was really second-rate.[77]

Rabbit's condition can thus be defined by the terms of the
novel of age. The opening chapter finds him intruding on a
schoolboy basketball game, "reaching down through the
years"[78] as he handles the ball. The perfect moment of his
youth that is now forever beyond his grasp was a practice
game against a tiny rural high school—Oriole High—in which
he achieved that feeling of unlimited power that haunted
Christian Darling: "And all of a sudden I know," Rabbit
reminisces, "you see, *I know* I can do anything."[79] But that
moment is past; it lingers only in Rabbit's memory and in his
metaphorical reconstruction of his present: taking a shortcut
reminds him of his coach teaching him to shoot fouls under-
hand; driving fatigue recalls the weariness of the last quarter

of a basketball game; the sky reminds him of the "blank scoreboard of a long game about to begin."[80]

Unlike Darling, Rabbit has found substitutes for his lost athletic career; he views life itself as essentially a performance, with himself as star.[81] Specifically, sex has become his arena for the exhibition of his prowess. After his high school games, when he parked with his girl friend, Mary Ann, he discovered the correspondence of athletic success and sexual satisfaction:

> He came to her as a winner and that was the feeling he missed since. . . . So that the two kinds of triumph were united in his mind. She married when he was in the Army; a P.S. in a letter from his mother shoved him out from shore. That day he was launched.[82]

He is "launched," that is, on a futile attempt to regain that lyrical simplicity of adolescent basketball glory and titillating exploratory sexuality.

Sex as performance does not equate with love, unfortunately, and it inevitably leaves Rabbit unfulfilled. He marries Janice Springer when she becomes pregnant, because he has known moments of perfect love with her. Moments must end, and Janice, pregnant again, is now no longer attractive to Rabbit and no longer makes him feel special. He runs from Janice to Ruth Leonard, whose companionship pleases his ego, and who becomes, to his mind, his possession: "His, she is his, he knows her as well as the water, like the water has been everywhere on her body."[83] Unfortunately, he cannot be satisfied by adult "love," which involves coping with problems as well as sharing ecstatic moments. He wants not just Ruth's body, but "whole women." "It is her heart he wants to grind into his own."[84] He refuses to let her use a diaphragm because it seems cold and mechanical to him, yet he will let her douche afterwards and clean up the mess, so long as he does not have to watch. With his wife his pleasure derives from an athlete's egocentric pride in his love-making abilities, afterwhich "he is filled with the joyful thought that he has brought her to this fullness. He is a good lover."[85]

Although he says, "I am a lover,"[86] and consciously seeks

perfect love, he is incapable of love because his ego always intrudes—he must be the "star." Genuine love obliterates the ego at least momentarily, but Rabbit is incapable of so forgetting himself. In his attempt to run away from Mt. Judge at the beginning of the novel, he finds himself on a sinister dead end, a "road of horror" which turns out to be a lovers' lane. This becomes a metaphor for Rabbit's love affairs in the novel. Rabbit cannot really love because he loves himself loving and does not truly love the other person. For Rabbit, sex is the moment of perfect union, but orgasm is brief and is followed by postcoital depression. Trying to extend that moment into a permanent reality is as futile as trying to regain permanent possession of a moment of basketball glory that occurred eight years earlier.

The ideal is indeed momentarily attainable in the world of sport. Even Rabbit, a golfing beginner, occasionally hits a perfect drive:

> It [the ball] recedes along a line straight as a ruler-edge. Striken; sphere, star, speck. It hesitates and Rabbit thinks it will die, but he's fooled, for the ball makes this hesitation the ground of a final leap: with a kind of visible sob takes a last bite of space before vanishing in falling. "That's *it!*" he cries.[87]

Life, however, rarely offers such moments, and even in sport they remain momentary. More often Rabbit's swing is faulty:

> Somehow Rabbit can't tear his attention from where the ball should have gone, the little ideal napkin of clipped green pinked with a pretty flag. His eyes can't keep with where it did go. "Here it is," Eccles says. "Behind a root."[88]

Rabbit's problem simply stated is that he is a child, as the athlete-hero is typically a child. He is the son of a domineering mother and a weak father—his mother calls him "Hassy" and justifies his evasion of responsibility by such attitudes as this about Janice: "She wasn't too shy to get herself pregnant so poor Hassy has to marry her when he could scarcely tuck his shirttail in"; his father is described as "the limp-faced old woman of a printer."[89] In Marty Tothero, his basketball coach, Rabbit finds the male authority figure he lacks at home, but high school graduation leaves him without that model and still immature. When he meets Tothero eight years later, Rabbit still thinks of their relationship as player-to-coach. He mentions that he does not drink and is "proud to be able to report to his old coach that he has not abused his body."[90]

With this background, then, Rabbit inevitably fails to grow emotionally or psychologically. His only sense of personal morality is the code of training rules; he doesn't drink or smoke and is compulsively neat and clean and respectful of his body. He is ruled by his natural impulses and feels happiness in cleanness, order, and light. He is even specifically associated, on several occasions, with his son, Nelson; he is envious of his son being cared for by his grandparents, he shares Nelson's jealousy of the new baby's exclusive right to Janice's breast, and like Nelson he is reluctant to leave mother-Janice even temporarily when he needs her affection. When he goes to bed at night, he offers a "God bless . . ." prayer, like a child taught by his parents.[91]

Rabbit also has a child's idealism, an unconscious belief in the perfectibility of life, and a child's inarticulate inability to define what it is he seeks: "Well I don't know all this about theology, but I'll tell you, I *do* feel, I guess, that somewhere behind all this . . . there's something that wants me to find it."[92] Edward Vargo terms this attempt to corroborate a vague feeling of immortality Rabbit's quest without guidance, but rather his quest is specifically *for* guidance. The absence of an authority figure in his home makes him turn to his coach. In Tothero's absence, Rabbit then turns to Rev. Eccles, the Springers' minister, who is himself an ineffectual child-man without answers. Ultimately, Rabbit wants direct revelation from God, "He wants to believe in the sky as the source of all things."[93] Ironically, the one person who could give Rabbit this certainty is Rev. Kruppenbach, the Angstroms' own minister, and the one genuine male authority figure in the novel. His advice is abhorrent to such Christian humanists as Eccles, but his thundering denunciation of good works rather than faith as a way to God—"Make no mistake. There is nothing but Christ for us. All the rest, all this decency and busyness, is nothing. It is Devil's work"[94]—is precisely the sort of absolute Rabbit is seeking.

In lieu of such certainty, Rabbit turns to the only other absolute available to him—his own heart: "Goodness lies inside, there is nothing outside,"[95] he tells himself at the end of the novel. Jimmy, the big mouseketeer on the children's television program, had earlier advised his audience, "Know thyself" and Coach Tothero had told Rabbit, "Do what the heart commands,"[96] but it is Mrs. Angstrom who finally frees her son from social accountability. When Janice accidentally drowns their newborn child, Rabbit accepts a full share of responsibility and receives almost total blame from the others. When his mother reacts, "Hassy, what have they done to you?" however, Rabbit recognizes "his liberation."[97] He renounces any personal liability in the death of the child and runs once more from his family. Unable to accept the responsibility of divorcing Janice in order to marry Ruth, he runs from her too, runs without destination, simply runs. "Ah: runs. Runs."[98]

Is Rabbit a hero, then, in his total commitment to the dictates of his own heart, or is he an irresponsible cad? Is he foolish or courageous to demand the ideal? The answer is, a little of both, for here lies the paradoxical combination of virtue and harm in the juvenility of sport and the athlete-hero. Early in the novel Rabbit claims, "If you have the guts to be yourself, other people'll pay your price."[99] This is a self-centered extreme, matched at the other pole by his quest for an external absolute. When he finds that absolute *in himself,* he appears committed solely to self-interest in the worst sense. "All I know is what feel right"[100] becomes his creed, but the reader recalls that forcing Ruth to perform fellatio on him seemed right to Rabbit at the time, but it is actually the lowest depth to which he plunges in the reader's esteem. Other values he rejects simply because they're difficult; for example:

> Harry has no taste for the dark, tangled, visceral aspect of Christianity, the *going through* quality of it, the passage *into* death and suffering that redeems and inverts these things, like an umbrella blowing inside out.[101]

But Rabbit is also a positive force. In his juvenile absolutism, he refuses to compromise with mediocrity; he is commited only to the affirmative, never the negative. Ruth tells him, "You're Mr. Death himself,"[102] and he indirectly shares the guilt for his daughter's death and nearly drives Ruth to an abortion. But he is also a life force—he makes Ruth bloom for a time, gives Rev. Eccles a special momentary zest, and prolongs the will to live of Mrs. Smith, for whom he was temporarily a gardener. As she tells him, "That's what you have, Harry: life. It's a strange gift and I don't know how we're supposed to use it but I know it's the only gift we get and it's a good one."[103]

The possibility that Rabbit is indeed some kind of secular saint in his allegiance to a self-oriented ideal is a radical conception not amenable to a developed social conscience. Rabbit is a star, not a team player—a "gunner" and a "show boat." We find this quality offensive—society by definition requires "team players" for its very existence—but the fact remains it is the "stars" who make life interesting for the rest of us, and who define the ideal towards which society as a whole theoretically strives. Whether we admire or revile them, they represent a quality in a pure state that fascinates nearly everyone. That quality is youth. For every George Blanda who captures the public's imagination with ageless heroics, there are dozens of Jimmy Connorses and Chris Everts whose dazzling youth thrills American spectators by recreating a timeless American myth. As they age, new youthful aspirants—John McEnroe and Tracy Austin, for example—take their place as the public's favorites. Rabbit Angstrom selfishly demands that he be treated as someone special, but he also makes life itself somehow special for others. The juvenility of sport retards the athlete's maturity and makes him, like Rabbit, often an irritating egotist, and severely hinders adjustment to a nonstarring role in the adult world after retirement. But that youthful quality is also the primary appeal of sport and the essential virtue of the athlete-hero. Rabbit Angstrom says that being mature is "the same thing as being dead."[104] Maturity *is* death, the death of youth, and is therefore, although *necessary*, also to be regretted. Rabbit is both a life force and a death force, and this is the paradox of the regressively infantile athlete. The childlike athlete exists against the grain of American society and against the course of necessary human maturity, but he embodies a wish-fulfillment deep in the psyche of the American public. In a country publicly committed to the equality of all, we privately long for uniqueness and distinction in ourselves and need their manifestation in our heroes.

The grudging admiration which readers feel for Rabbit, even while he is oblivious to the rights of those around him, derives from our acknowledgment that he represents something necessary, if perhaps to a less extreme degree, to both the individual and society. That recognition is confirmed by Updike's sequel, *Rabbit Redux* (1971) which finds Harry ten years later, deprived of his sense of his own specialness, a truly pathetic figure. Update defines "redux" on the title page to mean: "led back; specif., *Med.*, indicating return to health after disease." Rabbit has indeed returned—to ten years of labor as a linotyper and fidelity to Janice and Nelson—but his return is scarcely to health. Rather than life, Rabbit now radiates a "weakness verging on anonymity"[105]; his "spreading slack gut," tendency to drink, and inability to satisfy Janice sexually are the most overt signs of his decline from former athletic vigor. He has even lost his shooting touch, and he recognizes that basketball has changed—it is now dominated by blacks with their distinctive style so foreign to his own career.

Rabbit is still defined as the ex-athlete, but the rituals he clings to as a former player have lost almost all touch with the meaning and satisfaction they once gave him. Rules define the world's limits and the individual's course of action within those boundaries, but Rabbit's rules are dated. Janice tells Charlie Stavros, the man for whom she deserts Rabbit:

> Maybe he came back to me, to Nelson and me, for the old-fashioned reasons, and wants to live an old-fashioned life, but nobody does that anymore, and he feels it. He put his life into rules he feels wilting away now. I mean, I know he thinks he's missing something, he's always reading the paper and watching the news.[106]

The rules, he discovers, are more complicated now; there are "rules beneath the surface rules"[107] that also matter. He plays games; with Stavros, for example, whom he perceives to represent a type he never liked—"the type that sits on the bench doing the loudmouth bit until the coach sends them in with a play or with orders to foul"[108]—Rabbit competes, verbally duelling, winning and losing "tricks," exulting when he perceives "the game is on ice," but forfeiting his advantage after "Stavros has sneaked in for the lay-up and the game is in overtime."[109]

Rabbit acts by *instinct*, as basketball taught him to do, but his actions are mostly *reactions* because of this, as he implies when he confesses, "Janice had been doing some things out of the way, so I have to do things out of the way."[110] The sense of direction which the game ethic taught him is stripped to empty forms. Hemingway's characters find through rules and ritual the purpose and value in otherwise meaningless life; Rabbit only finds emptiness as the rules lose contact with values they formerly represented. As Jill tells him:

> We all agree, I think, that your problem is that you've never been given a chance to formulate your views. Because of the competitive American context, you've had to convert everything into action too rapidly. Your life has no reflective content; it's all instinct, and when your instincts let you down, you have nothing to trust. That's what makes you cynical.[111]

She is right; Rabbit reacts to Janice's affair by inviting Jill, a wealthy teenaged runaway, into his home. He passively allows events to dictate his subsequent actions; he lets Skeeter, a militant black bail-jumper and dope peddler, move in, share Jill sexually, and introduce her to heroin; and he fails to recognize the real threat in his neighbors' objections to these doings. The resultant arson fire not only destroys Jill and unfairly incriminates Skeeter, it alienates Nelson from his father—the child who could have been a focus for Rabbit's social responsibility—and who has been virtually ignored through all this.

Instinct could sustain Harry Angstrom's youth and his basketball career, but it cannot cope with the complexities of adult relationships. When Rabbit acknowledges that his touch is gone—"It's a funny feeling," he tells his son, "when you get old"[112]—he is speaking about more than his ability to shoot

baskets. By the end of the novel, Rabbit seems a childlike
figure in his dependence and his habits. Reconciliation with
Janice is a superficial return to normality, but her newly discovered strength and his weakness make their relationship
seem more that of a mother and son than a wife and husband.
It feels all right to him—he has always done what feels right—
but it does not feel right to the reader. In *Rabbit, Run,* Harry
indirectly contributed to his daughter's death, but he maintained a dignity and human integrity that redeemed him; in
Rabbit Redux, Harry indirectly contributes to Jill's death,
but readers are no longer able to admire him at all, only pity
him. Janice grows stronger with maturity, Rabbit grows
emptier; the life of Updike's ex-athlete has been cruelly symmetrical. At eighteen, he reached a peak of self-fulfillment; at
thirty-six, he has virtually returned to point zero.

five

Men Without Women:
Sexual Roles in
American Sports Fiction

There's no feeling like hitting a
home run to win the game. It's
even better than making love.
—Reggie Jackson, New
York Yankees' outfielder

When Christian Darling recalls the perfect moment of his
youth, the pleasures of his eighty-yard run are mingled in
his mind with the subsequent pleasure of his first sexual experience with Louise. For Christian Darling, as for Rabbit Angstrom, athletic prowess and sexual satisfaction are inextric-
ably entwined; writers such as Shaw and Updike have recognized that the athlete's sexual identity is often rooted fundamentally in his sport. Other fictional creations—Eddie
Brown of W. C. Heinz's *The Professional* and Jack Olsen's
Alphabet Jackson, for example—have described the almost
sexual nature of relationships among teammates and between opponents. In Eliot Asinof's *Man on Spikes* the sensu-
ality of the hero's play arouses the heroine, and the hero in a
batting slump becomes sexually impotent as well. In novel
after novel, writers of sports fiction have observed these aspects of sport and demonstrated in their books that the games
themselves are sexually charged.

A casual observer of any football game recognizes that the
ultra-feminine sexuality of cheerleaders complements the
ultra-masculinity of the players on the field; perhaps nowhere in our society are traditional sexual roles so clearly

171

stereotyped. While the players exhibit their strength, speed, courage, and ability to withstand pain, the cheerleaders encourage them, plead with them for protection against the enemy team, and applaud their every success, while titillating them and the other males in the stadium with glimpses of slender thighs and brightly colored panties—suggesting perhaps rewards for those who perform most heroically. Reversed roles in sport are almost unthinkable, because sport is, in fact, one of the firmest bastions of sexual stereotypes in our society. Sexual stereotypes did not originate in athletic contests, of course; the masculine nature of athletics is an outgrowth of preexistent roles, the components of which are common knowledge: men are supposedly logical, intelligent, unemotional, direct, aggressive, independent, and competent, while women are emotional, vain, nurturing, passive, dependent, and—God willing—beautiful. The sources of these stereotypes are too numerous to mention fully and too controversial to summarize simply. Whether biologically or culturally determined, however, distinct myths of sexual identity have dominated most of the Western world; men have been thought to be appropriately the hunters, protectors, and defenders and women the bearers and raisers of children. These stereotyped roles have been reinforced in America by the Judeo-Christian tradition with its patriarchal God, by the Calvinist inclinations of our founders who made work and self-sufficiency the *summum bonum*, and by the eighteenth- and nineteenth-century frontier experience which recreated the roles in an American context.

From the standpoint of the present study, the frontier experience may be particularly important, for in it lies the immediate origins of American sport. That the male role was clearly defined on the American frontier is clear; males were primarily the trappers, hunters, professional fighters, miners, and defenders of families and settlements. As the psychoanalyst Erik H. Erikson points out, many of the men who opened the American frontier had for one reason or other felt stifled in their countries of origin. Because they wanted to be free, the imposition of order, either external or internal, frightened them. "These men," Erikson claims, "insisted on keeping their new cultural identity tentative to a point where women had to become autocratic in their demands for some order."[1] Thus came the American counterpart to the Victorian ethic which made women the arbiters of culture and morality and men the entrepreneurs in industry and commerce. The relationship of the sexes is a complex and controversial issue, but we can safely say that from the middle of the nineteenth century to the present—the age of sports in America—American males have been dominant in the public sphere and women in the private sphere, and sport is a public institution.

Sports are not merely a reflection of preexisting sexual stereotypes, but they are some of the most influential reinforcements of them. The qualities necessary for success in athletics—strength, speed, agility, perfection of bodily form, endurance, perseverance, competitiveness, aggressiveness, self-discipline—are precisely those qualities that define the stereotyped masculine ideal. Winning is even popularly equated with masculinity; triumph in itself is seen as an expression of masculine superiority. Although the athlete may not possess "masculine" virtues to any great extent in his personal life, in the performance of his athletic speciality, the athlete represents those qualities to the public. Sport makes the stereotype real and preserves the illusion that it is an attainable ideal. As the credibility of the traditional masculine stereotype has diminished in the larger culture, men have increasingly found in sport a validation of "male" values.

One direct result of this masculine stereotype has been the exclusion of women from sports. If the athlete is perceived to embody a standard of masculinity, and that ideal is deemed desirable, then his arena must be kept free of feminine contamination. The sports world is a masculine world and has been so from its earliest beginnings in America. Through the years, tennis has had its Althea Gibsons and Billy Jean Kings, and golf its Babe Didricksons, but for every Billy Jean, there have been dozens of equally renowned male stars. Women have been largely restricted to the so-called minor sports (any sport, it seems, in which women can perform well would be considered "minor"), and until recent court decisions forced male sports organizations such as the Little League to admit female participants, the athletic interaction of the sexes was virtually nonexistent. Male physical superiority can account for this only in part; it is clear that the role of sports in sustaining certain values important to men has also caused them to maintain tenaciously its masculine character, and to consciously exclude women from their games.

An athletic contest creates a paradigm for the most ancient traditional roles of men and women in a society. The game becomes a symbolic defense of the home, as a character in Olsen's *Alphabet Jackson* observes:

> If we beat Dallas, then symbolically those big bastards from Dallas aren't gonna enslave our kids and rape our wives and kill our men. The spectators admire us because we've protected them from death and annihilation. The act is symbolic, but the feeling is real.[2]

In another context psychiatrist Arnold Beisser in *The Madness in Sports* calls attention to the Tchambuli tribe of New Guinea whose men traditionally performed the jobs of headhunting, war-making, and war preparation. When the British banned headhunting and imposed a peace on the people, the men continued their war preparations in ritual reenactment of their traditional role. Similarly, Beisser claims, Americans reenact their primal or frontier roles through sports, "For it is on the athletic field in those seasonal masculinity rites that males become the kind of men their grandfathers were and their mothers want them to be."[3] It is not only writers who see the parallels between the homefield and "territoriality," between games and sexual roles; those actually engaged in athletics implicitly support the idea that sport has a distinctly sexual nature. A high-school coach who warns his players against the distracting influence of girls and the professional-football coaches in the pre-Joe Namath years who demanded that their athletes remain continent the night before a game reflect a pervasive belief in a relationship between sport and sexuality. Medieval knights fasted and abstained from sex before a tournament or trial, and some of the sexual-religious motives behind such actions are retained in the more recent abstentions of athletes before football games, but biology is also invoked to justify such sacrifices. Most coaches believe a player must be "tight" before a game—nervous, tense, in need of an explosive release of adrenalin. They believe that pent-up sexual tensions contribute to this state and will result in furious, determined play. My own high-school football coach told us repeatedly that girls would make us "soft"—and we needed to be *hard* to win.

The masculine nature of sport has a number of complex consequences. Sports critics deplore the adverse effects on both men and women of sexual roles defined so narrowly and so unevenly, and they see in the exaggerated masculinity of sports one source of a macho fascism that makes violence so great a problem in society. The defenders, on the other hand, cite the need for unambiguous standards of masculinity that preserve necessary values threatened by the ideal of androgyny and see in sport not the fostering of violence but the celebration of beauty created out of the essential violence of human existence. Critics of sport see in the all-masculine nature of our games an infantile evasion of heterosexual maturity, but defenders feel that sport offers males one of the few genuine opportunities for necessary male bonding,[4] for all-male relationships not tainted by the suspicion of perversion. The writers of sports fiction deal with the many possibilities that both of these attitudes suggest. Sports novels movingly evoke the locker room camaraderie and close relationships between teammates that are uniquely a part of athletics,[5] but they also describe the physical and psychological abuse inflicted on wives and girlfriends excluded from the all-male *sanctum sanctorum*. They focus on the therapeutic effects of the nonathlete's identification with the masculinity of sports heroes, but they also deplore the emasculation that nonparticipants and even participants can face when confronted by their estrangement from the masculine ideal. Within these diverse treatments of the sexual themes in sports novels, one basic idea stands out, however: American sports fiction recognizes an irreconcilable incompatibility between the Woman and the Game.

Jack London again provides the paradigm for this basic theme of sports fiction. In *The Game* (1905), the first American "literary" treatment of sport and London's best boxing story, London describes in archetypal extremes of character and situation the basic issues of stereotyping and exclusivity that are explored by subsequent authors. *The Game* has a simple plot: a young fighter, preparing to marry, promises his fiancee to fight only once more; persuaded to watch this last bout, she is horrified to see her husband-to-be killed in the ring. Throughout this stark account, both characters are drawn with extraordinary narrowness. London begins his polarization of the sexes on the first page: "He was only a boy, as she was only a girl."[6] In a story ostensibly about young people in love, this statement emphasizes their youthfulness as they approach marriage, but it also makes explicit the sexual opposition central to the story. The stereotyping of "boy" and "girl" is exhaustive, beginning with the physical: "He matched her girl's beauty with his boy's beauty, her grace with his strength, her delicacy of line and figure with the harsher vigour and muscle of the male."[7] Even their names, Joe Fleming and Genevieve Pritchard, support the stereotypes—his abrupt, simple, direct, solid and hers elegant, exotic, refined, frilly.

The characters that emerge during the brief action of the story confirm the polarizations implicit in London's opening description. Joe is nonverbal: "He lacked speech-expression. He expressed himself with his hands, at his work, and with his body and the play of his muscles in the squared ring."[8] He enjoys feelings of dominance and finds his greatest fulfillment, his sense of power and achievement, in boxing. He appreciates the hardness and cleanness of his own body and is a tough and skillful boxer. Genevieve, on the other hand, feels her "instinctive monopoly of woman for her mate," envisions her future with Joe "through glowing vistas of reform," and is a suitably submissive female: "She shrank against him, clingingly and protectingly, and he laughed with surety."[9] This woman and this man are "pre-eminently mated," as male and female animals, for their union is biologically decreed:

> His masculinity, the masculinity of the fighting male, made its inevitable appeal to her, a female, moulded by her heredity to seek out the strong man for mate, and to lean against the wall of his strength.[10]

Having created, then, these archetypal opposites, London places them in a world bound on one side by the feminine frills of new home furnishings and on the other by the brutally masculine atmosphere of the prize ring. The major interest of the story lies in Genevieve's first steps beyond her feminine domain to encounter the masculine. Persuaded to witness Joe's final match, she attends the fight disguised as a boy (since women are formally banned from the ring) and views the bout through a peephole in the wall—London's reminder of a woman's narrow perspective upon such masculine events. She responds initially with intense pleasure at being admitted to the masculine mysteries: "And she felt other thrills. Her blood was touched, as by fire, with romance, adventure—the unknown, the mysterious, the terrible—as she penetrated this haunt of men where women came not."[11] As the fight commences, she is dazzled by Joe's semi-nude sensual beauty and repulsed by his brutal opponent, John Ponta:

> She knew terror as she looked at him. Here was the fighter—the beast with a streak for a forehead, with beady eyes under lowering and bushy brows, flat-nosed, thick-lipped, sullen mouthed. He was heavy jawed, bullnecked, and the straight hair of the head seemed to her frightened eyes the stiff bristles on a hog's back. Here was coarseness and brutishness—a thing savage, primordial, ferocious. He was swarthy to blackness, and his body was covered with a hairy growth that matted like a dog's on his chest and shoulders.[12]

This perception directly follows Genevieve's thrilled glimpse of Joe's physique, but his masculine beauty appears remarkably feminine to her: skin "fair as a woman's, far more satiny" with "no rudimentary hair growth"; face "like a cameo"; eyes "too mild"; body "too fragile." She does not recognize at all the fighter's qualities: "the depth of chest, the wide nostrils, the recuperative lungs, and the muscles under their satin sheaths." The story implies that it is simply her femininity that prevents her understanding these things.

This feminine viewpoint establishes the pattern for her observation of the bout. As the fight progresses and Ponta appears overpowering, she prays for Joe to wreak vengeance on the beast, exults as he begins to do so, but comes to fear Joe when she sees for the first time his "fighting face." Finally she even comes to pity Ponta as Joe begins to thrash him. The pattern that emerges here is that Genevieve fears whoever is dominant, which, according to the stereotypes established by London, means she fears the most masculine. As Joe begins to prevail, his boyish-womanish beauty changes in her eyes to a "face of steel, this mouth of steel, these eyes of steel flashing the light and glitter of steel."[13] The world of boxing is largely incomprehensible to her, but further, the totally masculine terrifies her; it does not appear able to accommodate her femininity.

Genevieve's initial judgment of Joe's boxing was to recognize it as her rival—something that drew Joe away from her, and which she was incapable of combatting. The fight so convinces her that this is the case, that she is not disturbed when Joe slips and is knocked out: "The Game had played him false, and he was more surely hers."[14] His subsequent death stuns her, of course, and ends her plans for a blissful marriage, but London informs us that these were merely feminine illusions anyway. In a concluding paragraph, he sums up the prospects for happiness of a young girl and a boxer:

> She was stunned by the awful fact of this Game she did not understand—the grip it laid on men's souls, its irony and faithlessness, its risks and hazards and fierce insurgence of the blood, making woman pitiful, not the be-all and end-all of man, but his toy and his pastime; to woman his mothering and caretaking, his moods and his moments, but to the Game his days and nights of striving, the tribute of his head and hand, his most patient toil and wildest effort, all the strain and stress of his being—to the Game, his heart's desire.[15]

Genevieve is not the only victim of this incompatibility. Joe, too, early in the story, perceives the conflict between woman and career, when he recognizes

> the antagonism between the concrete flesh-and-blood Genevieve and the great abstract, living Game. Each resented the other, each claimed him; he was torn with the strife, and yet drifted helpless on the currents of their contention.[16]

Although London paints this picture so starkly that it threatens to slip into bathos or even some kind of pseudo-allegory, he has nevertheless isolated in his extremes of character and situation the underlying assumptions of most sports fiction in America. There are many different treatments of the sexual theme, but all assume to some extent the stereotypes developed in London's story—there is an essential incompatibility between women and sports, and by extension, between women and the men who define themselves primarily by their involvement in sports.

Variations on the Sexual Theme

Subsequent sports literature responds to these issues with a variety of treatments. Early juvenile fiction accepts the masculine exclusivity of the sports world without reflection and without consideration of the consequences. Most often female characters are totally absent or represented only by an unimportant, seldom seen mother. In other cases, the hero has an admiring girlfriend, whose loyalty sometimes has to be reinforced by the hero's continued success. The third possibility, epitomized by Dink Stover's infatuation with Jean Story in Owen Johnson's *Stover at Yale*, gives the hero a girlfriend of stupendous grace and moral uprightness, who becomes a moralizing influence and constant reminder of the necessity of virtue for the hero. In no instance is the relationship of the hero and his girlfriend at all erotic, and the "proper" roles for each sex are strictly maintained. Juvenile heroes are always the doers, and the heroines, the watchers and admirers.

It is interesting to note that even the little juvenile sports fiction written by women maintains the genre's strict sexual code. Novels with girls as the main characters, such as Edith Bancroft's five Jane Allen stories (1917-22) and Amelia Elizabeth Walden's more recent novels, for the most part subordinate the girls' athletic talents to their love interests. The female authors who have written for boys frequently have taken masculine pen-names: Beth Bradford Gilchrist, Elsie Wright, and Constance H. Irwin wrote as John Prescott Earl, Jack Wright, and C. H. Frick respectively; B. J. Chute, M. G. Bonner, and H. D. Francis wrote under their own names, but

B. stands for Beatrice, M. for Mary, and H. for Helen. The boy heroes in these women's novels are more humanized than their mythically heroic counterparts created by male writers —they are more outwardly directed and family-oriented in most cases. But with few exceptions—H. D. Francis's *Double Reverse* (1958), for example—these novels embrace the same sexual code that characterizes the rest of the juvenile sports fiction. Boys do, girls watch.

The early comic sports fiction adds little to these images, simply recognizing the incompatibility of women and sport as a lightly mirthful dimension of the human comedy. The folklore of baseball in particular supplied plenty of material for such purposes: the story is told of Lefty Gomez's engagement to a beautiful musical comedy star, for example. After watching Lefty pitch a brilliant game only to lose 1-0 in fifteen innings, the bride-to-be tries to console him, "Don't worry, darling, you'll pitch and beat them tomorrow."[17] Another of the addle-brained-woman stories tells of the day that Joe Tinker of Tinker-to-Evers-to-Chance fame decided to impress his new bride. He stretches a pop-fly single into a double with a long, hard slide into second, then scores on the next hit with a headfirst dive into home plate. At the end of the inning, when he fondly asks his bride how she liked it, she beams back, "Oh wonderful, but I do wish you could be a little more graceful. You fell down twice going around the bases!"[18] Such stories are not particularly hilarious and they are most likely apocryphal, but they are part of the lore of the game, and sportswriters of the first quarter of the century found in such anecdotes the material for comic sports stories.

Charles E. Van Loan's *Score by Innings* (1919) and Heywood Broun's *The Sun Field* (1923) gently probe at the silliness of women who try to understand sport, and at the foolishness of athletes who range outside the narrow boundaries of their games to encounter the female of the species. Van Loan's "Excess Baggage" is the more interesting of two stories in *Score by Innings* whose theme is women's adverse effect on athletes. When the beautiful but flirtatious sister-in-law of a baseball player accompanies his team on a long western road trip, she flirts with nearly every player, instigates widespread rivalry and dissension, and causes the league-leading team to lose the pennant. To top it all, her admirers discover in the end that she was merely taking advantage of the players' trip to meet her fiance in San Francisco to be married. The mood of the story is humorous; the players appear as foolish children and the woman as a careless *femme fatale*. "Excess Baggage" assumes the incompatibility of woman and sport but adds a twist: The woman is superior to the simple boy-men and able to manipulate them. The story represents a child's wish to be let alone by his mother, so that he can play with his (boy) friends. The essential juvenility of sport was noted earlier, but here we can begin to recognize the sexual dimension of this fact.

Heywood Broun deals more fully with the incompatibility of women and sports, but the issues at stake in his novel are likewise inconsequential. He focuses on the relationship between a ballplayer, Tiny Tyler, and a romantic and intellectually chic girl, Judith Winthrop. Judith's feminine perceptions of baseball constantly clash with those of Tiny and of her friend George, the narrator. When George escorts her to her first game, Judith is initially repelled by the fact that baseball is "sillier than patriotism," and she despises the fans for living vicariously. To this George objects that they are simply "a whole lot of people having a good time." The Yankee left-fielder for the game is Tiny Tyler, a Babe Ruthian figure past his prime, whose spectacular catch to end the game triggers a wholly unexpected response in Judith:

> I think the man who caught that ball created the most beautiful thing I ever saw in my life. No sculptor ever achieved anything like that arm and shoulder of his when he reached out for the ball.[19]

When she also likens the catch to listening to music or reading Shelley, George responds typically, "He isn't a romantic symbol or anything like that. He's a person, a ballplayer and a good one. Not quite as good as he was a few seasons ago but still hanging on."[20] This initial situation establishes the conflict: Judith romantically admires "titanic efforts," such as Tiny's tremendous whiffs when he strikes out rather than take a "little poke" at the ball like the other "small rabbit-

headed man," the Ty Cobb type. George objects that such
grandiose failure is not competent baseball. He is not without
appreciation of the innate beauties of the game—he can enjoy
the "line of flight" of one of Tiny's homers as a "gorgeous
thing"—but his appreciation is rooted in the concrete. Judith
reacts to the same hit by telling George, "Don't use it against
me tomorrow, but now at this minute I believe there is a
God."[21]

It is one thing to differ with George on aesthetic grounds—
he considers the "sunfield" a position that requires extra pre-
cautions by the fielder, such as smoked glasses; to Judith it
means "looking straight at the sun and getting our light first
hand instead of having it reflected for us out of little cracked
mirrors that we call novels and poems and paintings"[22]—but
it is altogether different when such feminine distortions
threaten a personal relationship. Judith falls in love with
Tiny, or at least with her own romantic image of him, but
Tiny is not a Greek god or even a Greek sculpture; he is a
competent, uneducated baseball player, a "guess hitter,"
who becomes a conscientious husband. His attempts to culti-
vate himself are ludicrous and irritating to Judith, and the
effect of Judith's intrusion on his playing career is disastrous.
On a relay from the outfield in one game, he delays his release, unconsciously holding the pose which Judith had told
him is like Greek sculpture. The Yankees lose as the run
scores.

After several traumas including a separation the novel
ends happily with a marital reconciliation. The basis of their
renewed relationship is neither romance nor heroics, but simply good old-fashioned lust. Judith had earlier admitted to
George this was her reason for marrying Tiny, and she re-
discovers this strong physical attraction: "His baseball shirt,
where it showed through the V-necked sweater was black
with sweat. Judith tingled."[23] The point of all this is, of
course, the scarcely profound judgment that baseball is baseball and ballplayers are ballplayers and not poems or myths
or art. It is significant, however, that Judith, the woman, can
respond to Tiny only in two ways—by desiring him physically,
or by mythicizing him, making him into art. Neither response
deals with Tiny as a ballplayer, for his world is closed to her.

Even when he loves her loyally, and sheepishly tries to re-make himself to fit her image of him, he can still tell her after an important loss, "In the seventh inning I'd have traded you for a base hit."

Such gentle mockery is *not* the dominant attitude writers assume in discussing sexual roles in sport; in fact, most of the literature that focuses on this subject is excessively grim. Even the novels that deal with it in incidental ways character-istically find the relationships of athletes with women to be negative to some degree. Boxing novels, for example, typi-cally include a female character whose involvement with the fighter is always at the periphery, never at the center, of his career. In Idell's *Pug* and Van Loan's *Taking the Count* the woman is a hindrance to the boxer; in Gardner's *Fat City* she is a sexual conquest to feed the boxer's ego; in Heinz's *The Professional* she is simply a wife neglected and excluded by a husband more interested in his career than in his marriage.

One boxing novel in particular—*The Violent Wedding* (1953) by Robert Lowry—considers the relationship of the fighter and his woman as the central theme, and the sexual ethic of the sports world is seen to have brutal consequences. As a boxer, Paris "Baby" James has learned to depend only on himself—to do whatever is necessary, to *take* whatever he needs, to control as far as possible his own destiny. Such an attitude is essential in his profession, and its obstacles to a sexual relationship are immediately obvious. The novel on its simplest level concerns the love affair of a black middle-weight boxer and a white Greenwich Village radical chic artist. It ends in the girl's suicide while pregnant with Baby's child—a tragic conclusion that has complex causes. Laine Brendan, descended from a moneyed family and divorced from an effeminate husband, is a disillusioned dabbler in Greenwich Village bohemia. She is also a dabbler in Baby's life: she thrills to his blackness, to visiting "forbidden" Harlem bars, and to being seen in public with a black man, for "she was the whitest woman that ever lived—and he was the blackest man."[24] Baby's response to this surface attraction is a conscious detach-ment. He is a proud black man who wants to be "cool and alone" and who avoids mistakes. He initially reacts to her ad-vances by desiring to escape from the "crazy girl," because "whatever she might mean to him was probably not enough to compensate him for the awkwardness of knowing her."[25]

Their relationship develops in strange and complex ways, however. Laine is a disillusioned romantic, and in this paradox lies her equally paradoxical need for Baby. The black fighter represents life to her, a "vision of courage and beauty." In his bouts he seems to fight "with a savage grace that seemed cool and intellectual beside his opponent's frenzied feints and attacks and retreats"; he seems a "vision of courage in the face of death."[26] But Baby also represents death and destruction to her. His blackness and his animal passion arouse her: while making love she pants, "I want to be your nigger, your nigger, your nigger, to be your black nigger."[27] She calls her love for Baby "an annihilating thing," and sums up the paradox of this affirmation-annihilation in these words: "I want to throw myself away on you."[28] Baby reacts to this strange passion with bafflement, but something within him also likes the fact that it does not make sense. The normally cool, controlled, imperturbable boxer responds to her image of him as well as to her animal passion, and he is pleased to think he might truly be a vision of beauty and courage.

Such complex passions can only result in tragedy. Laine "had always given up the real, the present, what existed, for any passing dream that would lead her away from it."[29] Such dreams are indeed passing, and when she sees Baby's second fight, he seems inhuman in his skill and competence, and she opts for pity over power. Baby, the athlete, however, is no dabbler. He is a man committed, who plays for keeps, who takes what he needs. To him, boxing has no romance but is a sport played for blood, and this is the only kind of playing, in life or in boxing, that is clean and justified. When Laine refuses him, he rapes her and unknowingly impregnates her, but he is as much victim as victimizer. Baby had boxed for most of his life only for money and the world championship, but her love changes him. It somehow empowers him to rape her—and to kill an opponent in the ring:

> The only excuse he could live with was the special way she'd seen him and the special thing she'd made of him—some kind of hero fighting the odds for his life; fighting not something human but something big and bad.[30]

Feminine romanticism has no place in the prize ring nor in a prize fighter; its intrusion is calamitous.

Their tragic love results in a rape, a ring death, and, at last, Laine's suicide, and Baby is blamed for it all:

> [Laine] saw a futile round robin of masculine meaninglessness that reproduced itself endlessly by violence, by brute strength, by dumb relentlessness. Reproducing itself as Paris had reproduced himself in her. Relating to no dream she'd ever had.[31]

Baby also blames himself, but only with partial justice. He is not responsible for not relating finally to her "dream." Both lovers are victims of the forces that formed them—Baby by the necessities of his boxing career, Laine by her romanticism. For Baby a genuine relationship with a woman may not be possible; Lowry envisions his championship fight as a "wedding," perhaps the only wedding possible for such a man.

After Laine dies, Baby is left alienated from all he has believed in. When he fights for the middleweight championship of the world, he enters the ring "a hero of split-second shrewdness and a dedicated manhood that had honed his talents endlessly and aimed them all at this June night."[32] But the death of his previous opponent and the violence he brought to Laine Brendan have shown him his and boxing's brutality; he wins the fight as bloodlessly as possible and retires from boxing. What can a man do, however, who has trained himself in the necessities of boxing for nearly thirty years? Baby's only choice is to box or not to exist, to live or to die. He returns to the ring, choosing to live—a heroic decision, for he now carries within himself the burden of self-knowledge.

Baby survives, but necessarily *alone*; Lowry's novel does not even consider the possibility that love between Baby and Laine could have worked, that love can even exist in the world of the prizefighter. Lamar Herrin, in a recent novel titled *The Rio Loja Ringmaster* (1977), makes a similar statement, although less grimly and absolutely, about the world of the baseball player. Dick Dixon is a thirty-year-old relief pitcher who must quit baseball at the pinnacle of his career, because he has come to realize that his profession is a game of ego-inflation that makes him incapable of truly loving. Unlike the bullfighter in Spain or Mexico who represents his people when he faces the bull and whose enemy is not the bull but shame—his people's shame—the baseball player lives by a different code: "The fans' shame," Dick confesses, "is something they can take home and soak their heads in because the pitcher is all frozen self-glitter and shame is another game."[33] This awareness that baseball has made him cruel and unloving is long in coming; the novel relates how Dick reaches his self-knowledge and how he adjusts his life accordingly.

Dick Dixon's ambition as a baseball pitcher is to throw a perfect no-hitter, to become like the "ringmaster" of the Aztec ball game *tlachtli*. When a player in that ancient game performed the nearly impossible feat that earned him the name "ringmaster," he was entitled to the homage and even the portable property of the spectators—he became a godlike figure and lord of his domain. Such is Dick's ambition, but unfortunately it interferes with his marriage. He and Lorraine are competitors, not partners; "envy, pride, and gamesmanship"[34] define their relationship, not love and concern and mutual caring. When their marriage breaks up, Dick's egocentricity continues to obstruct his sexual encounters, making him a user rather than a lover of women, and until he can give up baseball, he will continue to be incapable of loving. As a friend tells him, "What you're really thinking is that you gave it all up—wife included—to be a lifetime lobber and you've been had."[35]

The heart of the novel occurs in chapters 12 and 14 which recount the Cincinnati Brewmasters' pennant drive and world series triumph, led by Dick's nearly flawless relief pitching. He motivates himself to pitch brilliantly by thinking about his wife and friend making love in his own living room—each pitch becomes an act of bitter anger, but it is also an exorcism. *I'm throwing this pitch,"* he says, *"at the walls that surround me, I'm dedicating it to my life outside."*[36] Baseball has been his life; it is the "curse of the House of Dixon handed on and on"[37] from a father who played third base well but marriage poorly. Dick plays because, as he says, "He had a rhythm in his arm, and apparently in his life, that corresponded to nothing else,"[38] but the life he really wants, he discovers, must be outside base-ball. Pitching in the series becomes an act of purgation.

These two chapters also include some of the best descrip-tions of baseball action in all sports fiction. In the world series, the "stumbling-cousin" Brewmasters from the midwest encoun-ter the seemingly invincible Yankees, who play like the aristo-crats of baseball:

> The Yankees, finally, had to amuse themselves. They'd wait till two-out, two-strike pitches before casually loading the bases, then lofting a home run; or they'd walk a Brewmaster on, then, skeet shooting, pick him off; or for no reason at all they'd gather at the mound, exchange knowing smiles, before taking urbane strolls back to their positions. Ten to nothing was the score.[39]

The writing is dense, economical, and evocative—and is far too rare in a genre plagued by the clichés of sports jargon. Another example demonstrates that Herrin is able to alter his pace drastically and achieve equally fine effects. The series has now moved to New York where the inept Brew-masters suddenly discover they can play:

> In the House that Ruth built, their eyes opened, their minds emptied, their piddling smarts poured out. They played on instinct. Running through signals they scored. Double-daring themselves they hit. Chasing the cows they caught fly balls. Digging in cow pies they fielded bad hops. Supper-bell ring-ing they rallied. And with LaurieLou, WilmaMae, and Betty-Ann McCorngrown winking their tits they pitched, pitched stomp-'n'-holler baseball—all except Dick, who pitched a lovely, nasty, wizardly four innings and picked up the wins.[40]

The high quality of this writing—its originality and verbal ex-citement—is not maintained throughout the entire novel, but for these two chapters at the focal center of the novel, Herrin is unsurpassed as a writer of sports fiction.

The series eventually goes the full seven games, as Dick carries the team with his brilliant relieving. In the final in-ning of the final game, he faces the power of the Yankee bat-ting order and decides to forget everything he had ever learned about pitching savvy and just throw hard fastballs right at their strength—for himself, to rid himself of baseball forever, to "quit hiding out in a baseball uniform before thousand [sic] of fans."[41] As he strikes out the side, with each of the last three pitches, he symbolically throws away ten years of his life. The final fastball completes his exorcism:

> The Last Great Pitch was nothing Dick had to reach back for. It stormed up through him as if the blood had left his legs, flooded his chest, then poured in a torrent into his arm. In a crimson flash his life with Lorraine and the Brewmasters rushed by. Oh, yes, he wanted it out, all of it out! Make him a vessel fit to live in again![42]

With this "Last Great Pitch" he is reborn outside baseball.

Returning to Mexico, Dick finds in Consuelo the replacement for baseball in his life. He learns that love is more important than mere conquest, that it is difficult but possible. The final chapter of the novel is a fantasy involving all of the characters in the drama that come to Mexico to see Dick and Consuelo wed in a religious baseball ceremony. Dick is a pitcher in this fantasy, but his role is to serve rather than oppose, to enable the batters to hit rather than strike them out. When he takes his turn at bat, he swings for all of his friends, not for himself; rather than try to score, he steps off the bag at third base to coach the others around. He has become the "Ringmaster," but not the "Ringmaster" who lords over the people by virtue of his unmatchable prowess. Rather he is like the matador now, who represents and serves his people. Baseball has become a game rather than a test of his manhood, something to be indulged in for pleasure, not pride. His last reminder to himself as he casts off his past defines the new perspective: "And Dick, one more thing, baseball's a game, play a little." Finally baseball *can* be play.

Sex and the Football Novel

Baseball and boxing novels such as Herrin's and Lowry's that focus primarily on the sexual nature of sport or the relationship between the woman and the athlete are actually rare, for *football* is the sport in which the sexual identity of the hero is most prominent. Eldridge Cleaver, in a brilliant essay in *Soul on Ice,* identifies the *boxing ring* as "the ulti-mate focus of masculinity in America."[43] In a Darwinian world of survival of the fittest, the heavyweight champion, according to Cleaver, is the fittest of all and the rightful claimant to his title "the real Mr. America." The heavy-weight champion may indeed have once had this appeal to the public's imagination, but today the athlete most identified with masculinity is the football player. If we wish to borrow Cleaver's analogy of sport to Darwinian biology, we can see in football the paradigm for sexual selection. Little imagi-nation is needed to see dominance hierarchies, or "pecking orders," on football teams (from the starting quarterback down to the reserve linemen); a sort of sexual selection oc-curs when the hero of the game "gets a piece" off the best-looking cheerleader on Saturday night—a familiar idea in the popular imagination if not in reality. Aside from such superfi-cial correspondences, football's image itself is sexually charged. Uniforms exaggerate physical features that denote male animal sexuality—broad shoulders, narrow hips, bulging thighs; the uniformed football player is a visual parody of masculine physi-cality. Appropriately the male sex symbols from the world of sport in the past two decades have been Paul Hornung and Joe Namath, both football players.

Football was not always the most sexually charged of Am-erican sports; this part of its myth is a recent trend since the rise of professional football to prominence in the late fifties. The dominant image of the college football hero early in the century was Frank Merriwell. When writers wrote college football novels to deride the abuses of the game, they por-trayed the athlete negatively by emphasizing his *arrogance* —the antithesis of Frank Merriwell's modesty—not his licen-tiousness. Compare, for example, Charles Ferguson's *Pig-skin,* written in 1929, to William Manchester's *The Long Gainer,* written in 1961. Sphinx Harmon of *Pigskin* is a con-ceited, selfish "jock"; the depravity of Red Stacy of *The Long Gainer,* on the other hand, is expressed in terms of his sexual involvement with Daffy Dix, a cheerleader. Other more recent college football novels—*That Prosser Kid* (1977) by Lloyd Pye and *Fall Guy* (1978) by Jay Cronley, for exam-ple—are more erotic yet. Increased permissiveness in Amer-

ican popular literature can partly account for this difference,
but *The Long Gainer* is actually an extremely priggish novel.
The major reason for the shift in focus is the altered image of
the football player. The most extreme image of the football
player today is the sexual "stud." Innocence is an essential
quality of the baseball player's image—in fiction his innocence is corrupted by the women he encounters. The football
player is not the *Naïf* but his opposite, the excessively sexed
male such as Billy Clyde Puckett of Dan Jenkins's *Semi-
Tough* (1972). This comic novel, with its outlandishly raunchy
humor, offers the most complete portrait of the stud football
player in American fiction.

Billy Clyde is a contemporary prototype of an American
"Good Bad Boy," who Leslie Fiedler states:

> is America's vision of itself, is authentic America, crude and
> unruly in its beginnings but endowed by his creator with an
> instinctive sense of what is right; sexually as pure as any milky
> maiden, he is a roughneck all the same, at once potent and
> submissive.[44]

Billy Clyde, of course, is far from being sexually pure, because, as Fiedler claims, sex is now allowed to the American
juvenile, replacing the violence that was his right in earlier
times. In fact, sex is the foundation of Billy Clyde's ideal
world—everyone enjoys it and nobody is hurt. *Semi-Tough* is
the ultimate male fantasy; it's a return to the raft with Huck
and Jim and also a return to an orgiastic Eden that exists
only in male minds.

Billy Clyde's world is a juvenile never-never land, peopled
only by perfect individuals. Shake Tiller, his best friend, is
also the premier pass receiver in the NFL; Barbara Jane
Bookman and Cissy Walford are the most voluptuous heroines this side of Dogpatch; even Dreamer Tatum is a superbly talented opponent and a sportsmanlike loser besides. All
have assembled in Los Angeles for the Super Bowl between
the New York Giants and the "Dog-ass Jets." This is no Los
Angeles of race riots and smog, but a child's version of the
city. Everything offensive or anxiety producing is reduced
through humor to an object of amusement. T. J. Lambert, the

huge offensive tackle, is renowned for his philharmonic farts, but their effect is comic—we giggle together with Billy Clyde. Racism is impossible in a world in which blacks and whites laugh together at each other in the perfect equality of humor. Big Ed Bookman, Barbara Jane's wealthy industrialist father, is a bigot, but his prejudice appears only in the hilariously ignorant things he says at the dinner table. Even religion and the Vietnam War, two of our most pressing concerns at the beginning of the 1970s, intrude only as decorative motifs in a restaurant and a nightclub. Watching a rock band from a camouflaged "bunker" is harmless fun and has no relation to the brutality five thousand miles away.

The essence of this juvenile world lies in the nature of its sexuality. Everyone experiences perfect sexual union, and no one is hurt, anxious, or threatened in any sexual encounter. Billy Clyde and Shake are nearly smothered by beautiful willing females; although they term all females "wools" after the pubic hair that identifies for them a woman's importance, Cissy and Barbara Jane do not feel demeaned but are as erotically motivated as their jock lovers. Perversion does not exist in this dream world; everyone has a mate—the beautiful stewardess who wants to lie naked in a bathtub while six men urinate on her finds at least one perfect partner in T. J. Lambert. The "Eastern Regional Eat-Off" and Billy Clyde's pulling "Cissy Walford's wool down over his ears like a helmet" are but boyish rowdy fun. Billy Clyde and his teammates live out the male fantasy of abundant and perfect sex.

Each child's world implies, however, another adult world into which the child must someday be initiated. *Semi-Tough* provides occasional glimpses of racism, elitism, managerial callousness, and global unrest, but Billy Clyde stubbornly and successfully refuses to meet that reality on its own terms. Shake, however, cannot continue to ignore it, and early in the novel he tells Billy Clyde:

> See I've known the all-time girl and I've loved her and she's loved me. I've had the all-time pal, which is you. And I've played a game as good as anybody ever played it. Now I think I want to do something else.[45]

Billy Clyde knows *nothing* else, and in this limitation lies the latent seriousness behind Jenkins' humor. Football is the institution that makes his arrested maturity possible. Shake observes that the key to success in pro football is for team members to "get drunk together, and get fucked together,"[46] but, as the previous chapter stresses, careers in football are brief and such activities cannot sustain one indefinitely. Although Billy Clyde and Barbara Jane settle down at the end of the novel to a life of perfect love-making, the reader knows that Billy Clyde must one day retire and that he and Barbara Jane will grow old—the real world will somehow intrude.

Such forebodings are only faintly heard in the novel, of course. Jenkins has, in fact, quite skillfully had his cake and eaten it, too. Male readers can enjoy the sexual fantasy of the athletic "superstud," and critics can look deeper and find in the hyperbolic sex and humor a parody of this sexual ideal. The first group made the novel a best seller, and the second established Jenkins's reputation as a writer by reviewing the novel favorably in a number of periodicals. The stud athlete as represented by Billy Clyde Puckett is an infantile figure, but Jenkins has made him a harmlessly comic one. Other more somber writers have not found him so innocuous.

Jenkins's is certainly not the only novel that focuses on the football superstud. In some way the figure is present in virtually every professional-football novel of the past two decades, from Robert Daley's *Only a Game* and Gary Cartwright's *The Hundred-Yard War* of the sixties, to Noel B. Gerson's *The Sunday Heroes,* Eliot Berry's *Four Quarters Make a Season,* Jack Olsen's *Alphabet Jackson,* and Nicole Warfield's *Superball* (a frankly pornographic novel) of the seventies. With the exception of *Alphabet Jackson,* however, the humor of Jenkins's novel is largely absent from these pro-football novels. Peter Gent's *North Dallas Forty* (1974) offers the most extreme portrait; the companion to sex in the professional-football novel is violence, and Gent portrays the violence of football with hyperbolic intensity. In its exaggerated definition, the masculine stereotype implies that certain forms of violence are permissible to men. Gent claims in his novel that football reinforces and intensifies this male violence until athletes become nearly incapable of action on any other level.

North Dallas Forty recounts eight days in the life of Phillip Elliott, wide receiver of the Dallas Cowboys. The milieu of professional football, Gent constantly reminds us, is a world of violence. This judgment is, of course, a cliché, but Gent pursues his theme with such relentlessness that the cliché achieves real power. The most overt form of violence, obvious to every follower of football, is the occasional brutality of actual games, vividly detailed in the novel: "His nose was smashed flat and split open as if someone had sliced the length of it with a razor. The white cartilage shone brightly from the red-black maw that had been his nose"; or

> The blow forced the bones the wrong way; ligaments and muscles stretched and tore. The two primary bones rode grinding over each other. For an instant the elbow dislocated, leaving a huge hole where the elbow point used to be. Somehow the remnants of the muscles and ligaments held and the bones popped back into place with a resounding snap.[47]

But there is another source of violence in pro football, more subtle and more destructive—the "violence" of management's manipulation of the players. Rather than physical violence to bodies, this is psychological violence to individuality, integrity, and self-worth. On the simplest level, it involves the lies and broken promises during contract negotiations, the fines for non-conformity to team rules, and the unofficial blackballing of rebels. The mishandling of players' bodies—treating them as pieces of equipment to be discarded and replaced when damaged—is the extreme example of owners' exploiting their ownership in the full sense of the word. Phil Elliott speaks with humor when he says, "It was terrifying to be owned by a fifty-year-old, devout Roman Catholic millionaire, whose only pleasure was hanging out in locker rooms,"[48] but humor is a feeble protection against the very real terror of being owned but not *known,* of feeling like a piece of property after constantly being treated like one. Football as a game has a strong appeal for Phil; it offers simplicity within the complexity of life, natural "highs" of playing before an enormous crowd, team-spirit, and pleasures of excellence:

> There is a basic reality where it is just me and the job to be

done, the game and all its skills. And the reward wasn't what
other people thought or how much they paid me but how I
felt at the moment I was exhibiting my special skill. How I
felt about me. That's what's true.[49]

The abuses of ownership intrude on that simplicity, beauty,
and self-knowledge, however, and foster the fear and hatred
that generate an endless chain of violence.

Gent emphasizes that the brutality of professional football
does not end with the sidelines and the final gun, but goes
on to create personal violence in the players. In the novel's
opening scene, Phil, Seth Maxwell, Jo Bob Williams, and O.
W. Meadows are relaxing on a hunting trip, but for Jo Bob
and O. W. pleasure requires brutality:

> He reached and picked up the first bird, which was still flop-
> ping, its wing shattered. Jo Bob caught the bird's head be-
> tween his thumb and forefinger and jerked it off. The wings
> flapped spasmodically and then the beheaded dove went limp.[50]

They also shoot a stray cat and laugh raucously as it tries to
drag its shattered hindquarters off the road. It follows naturally that such personal violence is extended to interper-
sonal relationships with both females and other males, but
ironically, the violence that football breeds can also be turned
inward against the essential values of football itself. The game
is predicated on the importance of the team rather than the
individual, but as Phil notes:

> When an athlete, no matter what jersey he wears, finally
> realizes that opponents and teammates alike are his adver-
> saries, and he must dispense with them all, he is on his way
> to understanding the spirit that underlies the business of com-
> petitive sport. There is no team, no loyalty, no camaraderie;
> there is only him, alone.[51]

Phil's best "friend" in the novel is Seth Maxwell, but their
friendship is based on their "brotherhood of mutilation,"
mutual envy, and manipulation of each other. Their sole
common interest is a liking for marijuana, but Seth even
betrays him to the owners for the dope-taking they had done
together. When a genuine relationship does appear, such as

the interracial friendship of Delma Huddle and Alan Claridge, the distrust of their teammates labels Claridge "queer for the nigger."

The violence done to heterosexual relationships is even more pervasive than such failed friendships. Marriages are described as sometimes physically violent struggles based on mutual disaffection and the absolute segregation of male and female activities:

> There was a curious homosexual bond that united the wives in their battles against the husbands and vice versa. The men shared the dark secrets of locker rooms, training camps, and road games. No matter the cost, these secrets were never to be shared with the wives. The women used baby showers and bridge games as strategy sessions for counterattack against this chauvinistic secret society.[52]

The incompatibility of women and sports is seen here as something consciously enforced by the men—like that promoted in fraternities through secret passwords and handshakes. Sport in its extreme actually offers an alternative to heterosexual bonds; by submerging himself in the simpler, less threatening world of sport the athlete can be unconsciously avoiding the responsibilities and complexities of sexual relationships. Phil is wrong, however, when he sees divorce as some kind of cure. Gent demonstrates that the players are as incapable of forming relationships with other women as they are with their wives. The players abuse and assault their girlfriends as well as everyone else they encounter, because the essential problem, as Gent reminds us, is that football players aren't people who leave home to play football; they are football players who come home to try to play people.[53]

Phil Elliott differs from his teammates in his recognition of these conditions, not his freedom from them. He is divorced from a wife who attempted suicide four times while he worried about missed pass receptions. His life is a continual high on some drug or other—a means to combat the continual pain which is football's legacy to him, but also to escape the futile morass of his existence as a football player. The power of violence to mold his inclinations even against his will can be

seen in his sexual arousal while watching Jo Bob grind his
naked pelvis into the "cute little bottom" of an outraged and
startled Miss Texas. He is repulsed by the action but notices
every erotic detail.

Charlotte Caulder offers Phil a way out of this viciousness
through love. Their affair develops in a pastoral setting outside the city, amidst the rustling and snorting of animals, the
flickering of stars, and the warmth of the hearth. The essential fact about this paradise is that it is beyond the reach of
the pro-football establishment. Charlotte considers football
players boring egomaniacs and tells Phil, "I don't like what
football makes you. You're a very mean man."[54] To experience love, Phil must come to her not as a football player but
as a man. As a football player, he has learned that survival is
the reason for life and that fear and hatred are a person's necessary emotions. As a man, he discovers that Charlotte is
neither frightening nor hateful, but a genuine loving partner.
She even demonstrates to him the source of self-worth:

> Football had been my refuge from the fear of loneliness and
> worthlessness. But now I was beginning to see what Char-
> lotte meant. I must have a value to myself and that has to
> come from inside, not from achievements in the world.[55]

Through Charlotte, Gent seemingly indicates an alternative
to the brutality of sexual relationships that sport fosters.
Satisfactory sexual relationships are not possible as long as
the male maintains identification with the athletic masculine
stereotype, but Gent rejects the idea that football is "the only
game in town"; Phil *can* leave it permanently. Or so it
seems. After he is barred from football for using drugs no
more potent than the ones the trainers inject in players'
bodies, he joyfully races off to join Charlotte—only to find
her murdered by a bigoted former boyfriend who found her in
bed with her black ranch hand. Another kind of brutality runs
concurrently with football's violence throughout the book.
The novel is set in the Dallas where John Kennedy was assas-
sinated and it constantly alludes to the pervasive violence
that is simply part of the American scene: drug pushers are
given the death penalty; a property owner is acquitted of kil-

ling a sixteen-year-old who was stealing tools from his garage; a man receives a 700-year prison sentence for possession of marijuana while a narcotics agent receives a seven-year probation for the kidnapping, sodomy assault, and murder of his girlfriend. When the sheriff who is investigating the murder of Charlotte with her black friend asks Phil, how could *she* do it? we know that the pattern of violence and corresponding violence of injustice will be repeated. Phil is left at the end of the novel "listening for sounds of life in the distance," for there are obviously none in his immediate world. Early in the novel, he voices the platitude, "Life is choice," and attempts to live by choosing Charlotte over football. But there is finally no choice; violence intrudes even into pastoral idylls, and all choices lead to death.

Although this apocalyptic ending seems overly contrived, Gent has effectively drawn an equation—football = life = violence = death—that epitomizes one aspect of American sport and American society. Gent's truth is not literal but metaphorical; he writes in the American romantic-gothic tradition identified by Richard Chase[56] in which characters are subordinated to representative ideas and the action takes place on the extreme periphery of realism. Throughout the novel, football is associated with big business, technology, religion, patriotism, and the essentially violent nature of urban society—that is, with the most important foundations of American life. The career of the athlete becomes a useful metaphor for representing the impact of these forces on the individual.

Gent's equation of football with violence and war has become a familiar cliché during the past decade or so, in the books of sports fictionists and social critics of sport as well. The implication in such writing that football epitomizes the fascist, militarist tendencies of a corrupt political system are not entirely convincing, however. The appeal of football is varied—its images of the corporate man and the cavalier have already been cited; it is also in many ways the most intellectual of American sports, and it is the sport most dominated by public spectacle. Rather than representing the violence of American imperialism, it can celebrate the ability of men to create beauty out of the essential violence of human existence. The danger for novelists such as Gent is that by so overstating their case they may detract from the credibility of the *portion* of the truth that they do express. More convincing examinations of the destructive consequences of the sexual stereotypes of sport are found in those novels that focus on the burdens of single individuals, not entire societies, in dealing with such images.

Footsteps (1961) by Hamilton "Tex" Maule is such a novel —it examines the human misery the athlete (or coach in this case) can actually cause himself by too great reliance on the athletic sexual ethic. *Footsteps* is the portrait of Paddy O'Connor, a football coach and ex-player who brings big-school football to tiny Peabody University. He defines his own character at the beginning of the novel when he asserts, "You can do anything if you push hard enough."[57] By athletic standards, he is an admirable man—the stereotypical poor kid from a small mining town who became a great player and coach through hard work and determination. This is the athletic version of the American self-made man in its most traditional form. But this myth contains the seed of its own destruction, for the self-made star who has defined his worth and his manhood by the yardstick of success must continue to succeed or he will become somehow less a man. The ex-athlete, in addition to the problems of identity epitomized in Shaw's portrait of Christian Darling, has a further basic problem of sexual identity if his manliness and athletic prominence are equated. Such is Paddy O'Connor's dilemma. Banned from a big southeastern football power for violations of NCAA regulations, he must rebuild his reputation at Peabody if he is to receive another prestigious coaching job. His methods are unscrupulous—illegal preseason practices, psychological manipulations of his players and coaches, even risking the life of his star running back by playing him against the orders of the boy's doctor and mother—but ultimately *he* is his own victim.

Paddy represents the paradigm of the win-at-all-costs football coach; the interest in the novel lies in the interaction of this type of man with women. Paddy has defined himself exclusively in terms of football success and the code of manhood it entails. He feels himself a man only as long as he can feel superior to, or more powerful than, everyone around him. Women become for him simply conquests to be as unscrupulously manipulated as his ballplayers, but his pleasure when he seduces his secretary, Martha, is strangely asexual. He feels excitement at Martha's fear before sex, exults in his triumph afterwards, and enjoys the "feeling of power" that conquest gives him. Such a person as Paddy is incapable of loving a woman, but his greater tragedy is that he cannot love himself either. For a man's identity—his self-concept, masculinity, sense of purpose—to be dependent on a tenuous feeling of manipulative power ensures catastrophe.

The catastrophe occurs through the agency of Tim Crowther, a wealthy alumnus who finances Peabody's rise to athletic prominence. Paddy enlists Crowther's aid to serve his own ends but he soon discovers his utter dependence on Crowther's goodwill, and the result is Paddy's emasculation. His loss of a sense of personal power makes him sexually impotent as well, because he can be potent only when he feels dominant. In Martha's words:

> When he slapped me again, I didn't mind. If Paddy wanted it that way I did too. When he took off his clothes and came to me, he was all right. I mean he was all right that way. He was ready to make love. But when I went to him and held him and wanted him then it was no good for Paddy. He couldn't do it then.[58]

After failing sexually with Martha, he regains a temporary feeling of domination by embarrassing a party of strangers at a bar, but this cannot give him any lasting potency. At the end of the novel, when he has lost the big game, his job at Peabody, and his chances of a job anywhere else, his loss of sexual capability is also permanent: "He knew the weakness was back and would stay."[59]

Paddy's tragedy is that such an ending is inevitable. The ideal of the masculine athlete is a two-edged sword; it victimizes women, but also threatens the male with emasculation. The footsteps Paddy has heard all his life are his own fears of failure. Martha recognizes this fear in his face while he sleeps, and Punchy, the ex-boxer whom Paddy provokes into a fight, sees the fear behind Paddy's toughness. In his limited world of football, Paddy is secure—in diagramming the Xs and Os of new plays, he can forget that a more complex reality exists—but when he leaves that world, he is vulnerable. In the world of sports, success or failure can be measured concretely in wins and losses; in the real world, success is much more uncertain. A man who depends on that concrete measurement of superiority for even his self-definition can only be destroyed. It is a cruel irony that the values which define athletics as a masculine ideal are potentially emasculating.

The Nonathlete and the Sexual Ideal

Tex Maule is not alone in focusing on the athlete or coach as a victim of his own sexual ethic, but a number of writers have been concerned with another consequence of sexual stereotyping: the plight of the nonathlete confronted by the athletic ideal. The nonathlete in an athletic context has received his own treatment in sports fiction and is, in fact, the subject of some of the most sensitive writing. His problem is not his inability to relate to the feminine because of athletic conditioning, or his victimization by a system that has served him once but destroys him now, but rather the more fundamental problem of the self-adjustment of the outsider in a society that holds the masculine stereotype before him as an ideal. Sports fiction is often concerned with this individual who does not fit his own perception of what a man should be—who defines himself by the standard of the athletic stereotype but who lacks the athletic ability to satisfy his needs by participation.

Many of these fictional nonathletes are scathingly drawn minor characters whose sole function is to illustrate the annoying demands the public makes on its heroes. Among these characters are the businessmen giggling like school girls when they meet a football star in a bar, or Beaudreau in *North Dallas Forty* who uses his money as an invitation to team parties and other social functions. Such "jock sniffers" are generally not developed psychologically and they appear in the novels only as fools or minor irritants to the hero, but many writers deal with the genuinely pathetic character of the frustrated nonathlete. As early as 1945, William Maxwell described this figure in an obtrusively psychoanalytical novel titled *The Folded Leaf.*[60] More recently, Jay Neugeboren has crafted subtly poignant stories about this alienated outsider. One of the finest stories in *Corky's Brother* (1964), "Something Is Rotten in the Borough of Brooklyn," deals touchingly but unsentimentally with this figure. The story, like the others in the volume, recreates an ethnically mixed Brooklyn neighborhood of two decades ago and pays loving attention to the forces that shape the young boys as they struggle to manhood.

"Something Is Rotten in the Borough of Brooklyn" is set against the backdrop of the basketball scandals of the early fifties. Howie, the narrator, tells the story of his best friend in grade-school, Izzy Cohen, who was the top basketball player in the school. In the seventh grade, basketball means everything to the two boys, and they share their dreams of playing for Erasmus High, but when Howie goes away to basketball camp that summer, Izzy has to remain in the city. At camp Howie grows five inches and vastly improves his basketball ability; Izzy does not grow at all. This situation is repeated the following summer and when the boys enter Erasmus High, Howie is over six feet tall and plays on the basketball team; Izzy is 5'1" and becomes a poet and radical.

Their friendship continues, but it is lessened in intensity because it is based only on their past shared experiences. Izzy becomes "weird," and when new point-fixing scandals break in the papers, he uncovers a mini-scandal at Erasmus. He distributes pamphlets throughout the school proving that Mr. Goldstein, a teacher and beloved ex-basketball coach, has profited by kickbacks from a sporting goods company. Goldstein suffers a new heart attack, and, despite Howie's attempts to prevent it, Izzy is beaten up by a dozen high school "jocks" in retaliation. Even when the beating becomes unbearably brutal, Izzy adopts the martyr's role, crying to Howie, "I can fight my own battles. Let me alone! Let these boors tear me apart for telling them the truth. Let me alone."[61] A year later when Howie returns from his first year at college with some of his teammates, he sees Izzy, having dropped out of Columbia, playing basketball with a group of little kids, some of whom are already taller than Izzy. While his teammates laugh, Howie looks away.

Neugeboren has created a muted tension here. Although

basketball can be regressively juvenile—some of the athletes are indeed childishly cruel—Izzy's rejection of athletics is no more mature. His forays into the world of ideas and adult truth are in part a compensation for his inability to play basketball. He sees through the hypocrisy and professionalism of even high school athletics, but he also compensates for his own athletic frustration by turning his aggression against those he most envies, and finally against himself. The story is not meant to be didactic; never does the author utter a cry of outrage, but only sighs for things that cannot be changed, for loved friends who have been hurt but will survive. The story is an elegy for childhood, for boys who must grow up to be men, and for men who can no longer be boys, and it laments the fate of the physically deprived individuals of a community in which sport is the acknowledged arena for achievement. The Izzy Cohens in American sports fiction are unfairly victimized for no other fault than their common humanity.

If Americans are to be divided into the Izzy Cohens and the Howies—the nonathletes and the athletes—the former obviously outnumber the latter by a large majority. The *fan* is a particular type of nonathlete, one that television has made a national phenomenon. I will not repeat the statistics about spectatorism cited at the beginning of this book but will simply recall that up to a third of the nation's population has viewed a single sporting event such as the super bowl. America has become a nation of spectators for a number of reasons. The softness of our lifestyle due to automobiles and electrical conveniences, our increased leisure time and earning power, and perhaps most important, the omnipresence of television have all contributed to our inactivity. Perhaps Americans are so obsessed with excellence that we would rather see it demonstrated by others than risk embarrassment and failure trying to achieve such levels of perfection. Sports fans define but one aspect of this phenomenon, and they seek through athletics particular solutions to particular needs. As Arnold Beisser has pointed out, the American city is a fluid centerless mass, and its citizens respond to a sports team as something concrete around which to rally, something familiar yet unique, to provide unity.[62] In a country which is highly success-conscious, failure to satisfy society's standards of achievement are inevitable; fandom can thus be sought as a compensation for disappointments in vocation, marriage, even in earlier athletic careers. To be a fan does not preclude personal success, of course; many great American writers have themselves been sports fans—Crane, Frost, Fitzgerald, Farrell, Hemingway, and Faulkner are but a few of the many who found great pleasures in sport all their lives. Americans obviously become fans for many reasons, and the varieties of their experiences are nearly limitless.[63] A fan can identify with individual athletes: by identifying with a hero he can vicariously share his glory, with an average player he can reassure himself that even in sports the common man is important, with the unsung hero he can share his frustrations over his own lack of appreciation by his employer. The fan can "be" a rugged linebacker or a graceful wide receiver, a slugger, an overpowering pitcher, or the flawless half of a double-play combination—whatever his mood requires can be found on the field.

The fan can also identify with values as well as players—with the exuberant youth of a rookie or the determined clinging to youth of a veteran playing a young man's game, and with the order, beauty, and excellence on the field which become the collective property of mankind. A fan can become part of something ritualistic and symbolic in a country with few traditions to create these experiences, or he can share in the immortality of a sport—baseball, for example, has long-dead heroes, successes, and failures, but the game goes on largely unchanged; it is indestructible. Sport for the fan can even be equated with the experience of Greek theatre; athletic contests are dramas with familiar heroes in familiar situations.[64] Sports vindicate the fan's longings for immaturity, for they are games played very seriously, and they also satisfy his need to participate in something that ends in a clear-cut decision—success or failure, win or loss. Finally, the fan can view the game intellectually, identifying himself with various perspectives during the game, or determining the proper strategy in each situation.

The bonds among fans are also important. As Beisser notes, in today's complex society in which family ties have become attenuated and clan ties have all but disappeared, fans form a

clan in which the individual is anonymous and therefore un-
threatened, yet in which he also belongs to a group—by de-
claring his loyalty he links himself to everyone else who
chooses his side.[65] William Heuman's short story, "Brooklyns Lose," offers a fine example of such instant communities; loyal Dodger fans in the story have a bond that unites
them against the nonfans and second-guessers:

> This is my neighborhood; this is where I was born, not on
> this block, but a few blocks away. This is a nice block, nice
> people, all good Brooklyn rooters. You feel bad and every-
> body feels bad with you. That's neighbors.[66]

The old Dodgers were, in fact, the center of the Brooklyn community; when Walter O'Malley moved the team to Los Angeles, his act affected more than the organization's finances.

A final value of spectatorism is that it can facilitate a ca-
thartic release of aggression and provide models of the masculine stereotype with which the fan who considers such a masculine ideal important can identify. Our considerations of
novels such as Robert Lowry's *The Violent Wedding* and
Peter Gent's *North Dallas Forty* demonstrated that these
stereotypes can be destructive to the athlete and those around
him. The possible therapeutic value of the stereotyped athlete
for the fan represents an opposite result of the same phenomenon. If the masculine ideal remains an oppressive aspect
of the individual's environment, he at least can vicariously
share with his heroes the communal qualities of manliness
which the star athlete represents. One of the finest of all
sports novels, Frederick Exley's *A Fan's Notes* (1968), deals
with this paradoxical destructive-constructive athletic ideal
in a painful, funny, autobiographical story of a man who
wishes he were Frank Gifford of the New York Giants.

Exley, the fictionalized narrator, attempts in his story to
understand himself through his past, a past that has left him
alienated from modern American society. The America he
perceives is drunk on physical comeliness, believes enough
money can solve any problem, and is obsessed with wrong-
headed and grotesque standards of success. The heroes of
American novels seem to him so unimpeachably virile that a
man cannot possibly live up to their image of masculinity.

On the other hand, American television presents the male as so emasculated and impotent that it threatens his sense of dignity. Exley perceives the American male to be inferior to the female, who must surely view a man's enthusiasms as "trivial, even contemptible things." In Exley's mind, America is a nation of insipid children with "rosy cheeks and untroubled azure eyes," "toothy smiles without warmth," incapable of a censorious scowl or even of perplexity, on a planet that in its entirety is assuredly mad.[67]

Existence in such a world, in such a country, is precarious at best, but for Exley the difficulty is compounded by his own past. The ghost of his father haunts his present—a father who was a superb athlete, admired and loved by his community, but a man who thirsted for fame so greedily that he left his son psychically scarred. The elder Exley played to the crowd in everything he did, and the crowd became a wedge between father and son. The incredible extreme of his father's egotism is reflected in the basketball game between Exley's Jayvees and his father's oldtimers' team, when Exley, Sr. humiliates his freshman son for the jubilant hilarity of the spectators. From his father, Exley inherits the need to have his name "whispered in reverential tones," but this lust for fame is an impossible burden for a man who lacks the ability to obtain it. One of the epigraphs to the novel is from Hawthorne's *Fanshawe*: "If his inmost heart could have been laid open, there would have been discovered that dream of undying fame; which, dream as it is, is more powerful than a thousand realities." This dream is in fact paralyzing, as the novel demonstrates.

Living in this world, then, Exley is no part of it: he is alienated from his past (his father), his present family (he is divorced), his career, his society's values, and, most cruelly, from himself. Burdened with the necessity of fame, fameless he is nothing. He feels a need to impose his personality, his ego, his dreams on New York City, but New York stonily refuses to esteem him. Rather, he discovers the ultimate reality of urban anonymity:

> I had wanted nothing less than to impose myself deep into the mentality of my countrymen, and now quite suddenly it

occurred to me that it was possible to live not only without fame but without self, to live and die without ever having had one's fellows conscious of the microscopic space one occupies upon this planet.[68]

Exley attempts various compensations for his lack of identity. He drinks "heroically," developing stomach hemorrhages and the d.t.s. He adopts the role of "The Cool Man," a feigned figure of self-sufficiency who is easily beaten down by the realities of society. He retreats for periods of up to six months to his aunt's or mother's or best friend's couches, between visits to Avalon Valley State Mental Hospital. The symptoms of Exley's mental illness correspond precisely to the consequences which psychologists claim result from the inability to express one's aggressions—depression, schizophrenia, paranoia, and psychosis.[69] These are the qualities of Exley's mental state as he vegetates on the couch, "holding onto his tired penis for dear life."[70]

His most consistent compensation for powerlessness lies in his fantasies and his allegiance to Frank Gifford and the New York Giants. Exley's response to the Giants encompasses nearly the entire spectrum of fan identification. On the superficial level, he vicariously stunts with Sam Huff, catches touchdown passes with Del Shofner, and sacks quarterbacks with Andy Robustelli. But football also reaches something much deeper in his soul:

Why did football bring me so to life? I can't say precisely. Part of it was my feeling that football was an island of directness in a world of circumspection. In football a man was asked to do a difficult and brutal job, and he either did it or got out. There was nothing rhetorical or vague about it; I chose to believe that it was not unlike the jobs which all men, in some sunnier past, had been called upon to do. It smacked of something old, something traditional, something unclouded by legerdemain and subterfuge. It had that kind of power over me, drawing me back with the force of something known, scarcely remembered, elusive as integrity—perhaps it was no more than the force of a forgotten childhood. Whatever it was, I gave myself up to the Giants utterly. The recompense I gained was the feeling of being alive.[71]

The Sunday Giant games are for him an escape from the world, a ritualistic, almost religious experience. Specifically Exley identifies with Frank Gifford. The superb Giant running back represents the realization of life's large promises; he sustains the illusion that fame is possible and that the bleak anonymity of life can be escaped; and he may be, Exley realizes, the only fame he (Exley) will ever have.[72] Gifford's every success and failure become Exley's own, and the Giant halfback enables Exley to transcend much of the petty oppression of his life. Exley cannot control his own sense of identity in this way, however, because obviously it is dependent on another man's fortunes.

In addition to being a fan, Exley lives in his fantasies, and the close bond of the two worlds is not a semantic accident. He consciously uses fantasies to forget his powerlessness—fantasies of great wealth in which he buys the Giants, fantasies of writing the "Big Book," fantasies of romping with erotic dream girls. Such dreams can be temporary expedients for combatting a lack of personal identity, but they can also incapacitate the individual. When Exley meets Bunny Sue Allorgee, he discovers his dream girl in the flesh, yet he is impotent in her presence:

> I had waited too long for her, lived with the dream of her for always, and the thought of actually grasping it struck me cruelly and ironically, impotent, in words to say, in motions to make, in every possible way.[73]

Here is demonstrated the paradox of the fan—identification with dreams and heroes enables him to cope with sometimes unbearable helplessness, yet the resulting sense of self and power is only vicarious, not real. Exley glimpses this danger in his devotion to the Giants: "I saw myself some years hence, drunk, waiting 'for the game,' without self-denial, without perseverance, without hope."[74] Exley is a fan, a nonparticipant, a spectator in his allegiance to the Giants, in his fantasies of wealth and women, and in his long sessions on couches where he watches TV, voyeuristically examines other people, and merely observes life. Exley himself eventually discovers this truth about himself:

> I understood, and could not bear to understand, that it was
> my destiny—unlike that of my father, whose fate it was to
> hear the roar of the crowd—to sit in the stands with most men
> and acclaim others. It was my fate, my destiny, my end, to
> be a fan.[75]

This is a powerful and poignant moment, the self-revelation
of what it is to be an "ordinary man." How one can respond to
such knowledge is fittingly ambiguous in the novel, but the
author gives us certain keys. The novel ends with the description of a recurring nightmare in which Exley is overwhelmed
by an image of America, and although he is always beaten
down by it, he continues to run *toward* it. This vision is an
affirmation of Exley's resolve to live the contributive and
passionate life, not to remain just a fan. There is nothing
romantic in this resolution; it is a confirmation of an earlier
judgment that admitting one's insanity may be the only redemption in America.[76] It is out of his insanity, his weakness,
his fan-ness, that Exley finds his little strength. Gifford was
his hero who sustained for him the illusion of fame's possibility, but Gifford also taught him how to live with scars, how
to come back after crippling injury so that he can walk out on
his own feet. Gifford has been both his weakness and his
strength. By recognizing that he is fated to be a fan, Exley accepts his oddness and his deviations from society's values—
accepts those qualities that make him Frederick Exley. For a
man not to become a neurotic weakling, he must exercise his
responsibility of choice, and implicit in Exley's acceptance of
the fact that he will not be a hero and not fulfill America's
masculine ideal is his choice to live his life as best he can. His
steps in this direction are tentative—he lists his name in the
phone book for the first time, and he begins a program of
physical exercise—but these minimal actions are the first
steps toward self-affirmation and self-assertion.

Exley's is not a heroic solution, but few men are able to be
heroes. For the rest, there must be compromise with the necessities of reality. Exley, the author, has presented in his
novel the definitive portrait of the fan, linking fandom with
both mental health and neurosis, with failure and fate. In its
emphasis on the complexity of the relationship between sport
and sexual stereotyping, *A Fan's Notes* represents a pinnacle

in sport fiction. Better than anyone else, Exley has recognized the paradox in sport's relationship to masculine identity. Sport is a product of prevailing sexual stereotypes and also a reinforcement of them. Because the stereotypes do exist, sport is a vital source of therapeutic identification for the beleaguered male, but sport also contributes to the societal and sexual pressures which threaten him. Sport is one of the few remaining outlets for all-male achievement; it assuages man's alienation from his traditional roles and possibly even satisfies an instinctual need for male bonding and aggressive action. Yet, for the man who by choice or inclination is not aggressive, sport is a constant reminder of what America expects a man to be, and what he is not. Sport is either a regressive enforcer of destructive sexual stereotyping or the last bastion of essential masculine identity—or both. The ability of *A Fan's Notes* to sustain the paradox of this "or both" without oversimplification is what places the book among the very best American sports novels.

six

In Extra Innings:
History and Myth in American Sports Fiction

Time is of the essence. The crowd and players
Are the same age always, but the man in the crowd
Is older every season. Come on, play ball!
—Rolfe Humphries, "Polo Grounds"

The year 1952 marks a turning point in this history of American sports fiction. All the themes discussed in the previous four chapters reached a sort of culmination in that year in a first novel by Bernard Malamud called *The Natural*. Malamud's vision was not necessarily more penetrating than any previous writer's; rather, what distinguishes *The Natural* from earlier sports novels is the context in which Malamud examines the archetypal themes of sport. Ring Lardner was our first writer to see convincingly in sport a microcosm of American life, and he spawned a half-century of realistic sports novels. Malamud was our first writer to clearly see that the character of the hero, and the relationship of country and city, youth and age, masculinity and femininity in American sport are explicitly mythic concerns. I have been talking about myths throughout this study, but the writers discussed so far did not explicitly describe their themes as myth. It was not until *The Natural* that any American novelist recognized that the major concerns of sport do, in fact, define the essential myths of the American people and related them to the timeless myths of Western civilization. Sport, in fact, as Malamud has taught us so well that we now take his insights

211

for granted, is the most important and quite possibly the sole repository for myth in American society today.

That Malamud deals with baseball in *The Natural* in a consciously mythic way is clear in a number of remarkable feature of his novel. The most obvious, yet most brilliantly original, of his insights into baseball is his recognition that the rich folklore of the sport is not only a compendium of amusing stories about eccentric athletes but is, in fact, a vital source of myth in a nearly mythless country. Professional baseball is now over 110 years old; in 1952, it was barely 83. Yet, in those few decades, history has dissolved into legend and the heroes of the early years of baseball are perceived by later generations as godlike creatures. In our fallible and disillusioning world surely "Iron Man" McGinnity could pitch endlessly without tiring; no ground ball could ever penetrate the defense of Tinker and Evers and Chance; Babe Ruth could stroke a home run at will—he missed occasionally only to maintain the drama when he did choose to connect. These and the other stars of the early decades of baseball created the only authentic American folk history with any potency today.

Malamud recognized this fact and structured his novel around specific incidents and characters from this rich folklore past.[1] Babe Ruth's orphan background, career as a pitcher and then a slugger, home run for a man's hospitalized son, and great bellyache that jeopardized the pennant are all reenacted by Roy Hobbs. Shoeless Joe Jackson, the greatest "natural" of all time and a guilty member of the Chicago Black Sox; Eddie Waitkus, mysteriously shot by a woman in a hotel room in 1949; Casey Stengel catching a canary in his baseball glove; Dazzy Vance doing magic tricks; Bob Feller striking out the most feared hitters in baseball at age nineteen; Rube Waddell, Babe Herman, and other former stars are all recalled by certain of Roy's exploits. Other characters, too, evoke legendary ballplayers. Pop Fisher duplicates Wilbert Robinson's attempt to catch a grapefruit dropped out of an airplane and shares the ignominy of Chuck Hoestetler who performed "Fisher's Flop" at a crucial moment in the sixth game of the 1945 World Series. Bump's death recalls Pete Reiser who continually ran into outfield walls and so ruined his career. The "window walker" is a reincarnation of Rabbit Maranville, and several of the Knights' fans are reminiscent of Hilda Chester and other eccentric Dodger rooters at Ebbets Field. The Knights themselves duplicate the exploits of past teams: the 1914 Boston Braves who came back from last place to win the pennant, and the 1945 St. Louis Browns who had a team psychologist much like Dr. Knopp. Even Sam's dream of a baseball team of bearded giants has its antecedent in a team of bearded ballplayers called the House of David during baseball's barnstorming days. These characterizations and incidents contribute realistically to the novel's plot and can be accepted at face value, but they are not always essential to Malamud's story; they are more important as a source of myth.

Besides recalling specific episodes of baseball folklore, these incidents conflate all time into a mythic timeless present. By recalling the Boston Braves of 1914, Babe Ruth of the 1920s, and Bobby Thomson of 1951 (Roy, of course, *fails* to hit the home run), *The Natural* transcends time and history as myth does. Baseball is the most timeless American sport; the duration of a single game is potentially infinite; and the game itself is virtually unchanged after more than a century of organized play. Malamud's descriptions of baseball action have little quality of particularity; when pitched balls become meteors and when Roy literally hits the cover off the ball, it becomes clear that Malamud is not describing individual games but the timeless "Game" by generalizing and mythicizing individual actions. In one game, in fact, Roy's home run bashes into the clock on the right field wall; the clock, the narrator informs us, "spattered minutes all over the place, and after that the Dodgers never knew what time it was."[2] Furthermore, by recreating Arthurian legends, Homeric myths, and fertility rituals of ancient peoples, Malamud extends the present into the remote past, making of his baseball story a paradigm of the essential myths of Western man. Because identification of these mythic understructures has been expertly done by other critics,[3] I will summarize their findings as briefly as possible. Roy can be seen as a modern Achilles, or as an Odysseus among Circean temptresses and the one-eyed cyclopic Gus Sands. More important, he is the Grail questor of Arthurian legend, reintroduced in the twentieth century by T. S. Eliot, by way of Jessie Weston and Sir James George Frazer. With his sword Excalibur (Wonderboy), Roy is tested by Harriet, hindered by Gus-Merlin, enticed by Memo-Morgan le Fay away from Iris, the Lady of the Lake. He attempts to cure Pop, the strangely afflicted Fisher King, the ruler of a parched and plagued Waste Land. Roy initially brings fertility into this barren land but fails finally to secure the Grail—the National League pennant—because he violates the symbol of his potency, Wonderboy.

These particulars of the Grail and Waste Land myths are built into the broader structure of the novel around the fertility cycle of the seasons. Ancient fertility rituals were based on these cycles—the vegetation gods remained in the underworld for half of the year and then were reborn bringing the crops to fruition. *The Natural* is likewise structured on the seasonal cycle; the book begins in spring in the "Pre-game" section, moves to summer in the heart of the baseball season, then to autumn and the impending World Series, and finally to a metaphorical winter as Roy fails: "It felt like winter. He wished for fire to warm his frozen fingers."[4] The second section of the novel is an expanded recapitulation of the first, mirroring the succession of years in the cycle of existence. This structure is further reinforced by the fact that Roy buries Wonderboy as the ancients buried images of their fertility gods, and by the fact that there is also a cycle of Grail heroes in the novel. Roy achieves superiority over the Whammer and Bump, the current heroes, and is then himself supplanted by Youngberry, the new natural, who has a "lifelong ambition to be a farmer," and who, while pitching, sees a "field of golden wheat gleaming in the sun."[5] Roy (the king) is dead, and next season will see a new king and fertility god.

This myth is constantly supported by the novel's other central mythic pattern, the Jungian myth of psychic integration. By explicitly incorporating this fundamental psychoanalytic myth into his story, Malamud extends his central myth not only into the remote past, but also widely in the present. By reenacting the primary conflict with the father and the mother, Roy becomes the prototypical Western man. Again, because this material has been handled expertly by others,[6] I will summarize briefly. Roy's constantly dominant characteristic throughout the novel is his infantilism. He plays a boys' game and is related to Sam Simpson and to Pop Fisher as a son to father figures. The king-must-die motif of Roy's displacement of the Whammer and Bump is essentially a father-replacement. Roy's relationships to the women in the novel as mother figures is the major source of the psycho-analytic theme, however. Roy rejects his own mother as a "whore"[7] and is torn between Memo, the "terrible" mother, and Iris, the life-giving mother. As one critic, Earl Wasserman, has written:

> The libido, in Jung's formulation, naturally yearns to retreat from harsh reality into the fantasy indolence of maternal pro-tection; but because this incest tendency is checked by so-ciety's prohibition, the consequent repression drives the psy-chic energy backwards into infancy and locks it inertly in the mother image. The mother so defined is the "terrible" mother of death, the destroyer who drowns man in his own source. This retrogressive mother must be renounced; yet, creative strength must derive from the mother, and hence, paradoxi-cally, renunciation of Mater Saeva is access to Mater Magna, the life-giving mother.[8]

Memo is the emasculating mother; like Harriet Bird she in-capacitates Roy with a psychic wound (a belly ache), and with a Mercedes Benz, supreme symbol of modern technol-ogy, she kills the boy that is Roy's pastoral image of himself. Conversely, with Iris Roy plunges into Lake Michigan, into the murky depths of the Jungian feminine, wherein lies his true selfhood. Iris offers him the possibility of mature mutual love and responsibility; Roy initially rejects her, rejects her extreme motherness (she is a grandmother) because he can-not accept his own paternity (or grandfatherhood), but at the conclusion of the novel he finally does embrace these respon-sibilities.

Malamud's purpose in relating the folklore of baseball to classical myth and psychoanalytic myth is to recreate the basic Western myth of the hero in a contemporary setting, and he rightly saw that baseball provides an appropriate con-text for such a purpose. The archetypal themes of sports fic-tion examined in this study have implicitly identified the components of the myth to which Malamud responded explicitly. The relationship of the sexes explored in the previous chapter is identified in *The Natural* in concrete psychoanalytic terms. Roy's infantile obsession with the acquisition of fame also suggests forcefully the juvenility of the athlete-hero discussed earlier. The relationship of youth and age, which was related to the king-must-die motif in chapter 4, is done so explicitly by Malamud, whose hero replaces the Whammer and Bump, the old kings, flourishes for his one season of potency, and is himself replaced by Youngberry, the new hero. Finally, the primary focus of the relationship between country and city is the natural, and this figure provides both the title and the particular American myth to which Malamud relates the communal myths of Western man.

Malamud's primary purpose in recapitulating all these mythic elements is to test his twentieth-century American derivative of the Western hero in a contemporary context, and he finds him incapable of survival. As was mentioned, this distinctly American hero is the natural. The first time we see Roy he is using the natural timepiece of the stars: "He appraised the night and decided it was moving toward dawn."[9] He thinks in the broad categories of natural time—night and dawn—not the mechanical division of a day into hours. In the outfield during his first game with the Knights, "He romped in it like a happy calf in its pasture." And later we are told, "He stood firm and strong upon the earth." Even his skill as a ballplayer is derived from an intimate knowledge of mother earth:

> He seemed to know the soft, hard and bumpy places in the field and just how high a ball would bounce on them. From the flags on the stadium roof he noted the way the wind would blow the ball, and he was quick at fishing it out of tricky undercurrents on the ground.[10]

Roy even has his talismanic natural weapon, his bat Wonderboy, made by hand from one of nature's trees, forged in nature's fire, and used by Roy with preternatural skill.

Malamud takes this mythic natural and places him in a twentieth-century American city. In the persons of Gus,

Memo, and Judge Goodwill Banner, Roy encounters urban corruption and surrenders momentarily to the temptation to throw the most important game of the year. At the end of the novel, he is to be banned from baseball, his records are to be destroyed, and he must live with bitter self-loathing. Such a fall is inevitable because the natural and the city are incompatible—Roy succumbs to the urban necessity of creating a secure future by making money quickly. In the country, careers are long and stable but in the city, brief, as age forces early retirement or competitors drive one from the marketplace. Because the athlete's career is particularly short, he must make it as financially productive as possible. Roy is not a mere victim, however; he gives in to the corrupting influences of sex and money willingly. The city does not simply fail the natural; the natural fails in the city.

A tragic dimension is injected into Malamud's novel as the reader realizes that it is not even possible for Roy to prevail. In order to succeed, he must maintain his natural virtue and innocence, and his connection with the landscape, for those are the sources of his power and are absolute. But the natural is by definition too naive and infantile to survive in the modern city. Roy's failure is inevitable, is fated, is posited in the definition of his character. The natural *must* come to the city; he cannot simply remain contentedly in Arcadia. Roy Hobbs is a great natural baseball player, but in order to exhibit his ability, to achieve his potential, he must play in the urban major leagues.

Roy, then, fails to fulfill the role of the hero as Joseph Campbell explained it, and, as we have seen, the original archetypal sports hero—the juvenile athlete-hero—fails. The hero's career is tripartite, involving separation, initiation, and return. Roy's quest is simply for his own glorification— he recognizes no obligation to "return" to his people; that is, to make them, not himself, the real beneficiaries of his success. When he tells Iris, "I had a lot to give this game," she responds, "Life?" But Roy cannot envision so selfless a goal; he answers instead, "Baseball. If I had started out fifteen years ago like I tried to, I'da been the king of them all by now."[11] Roy is a hero out of step with mythical heroes; life in the twentieth century is too accelerated for him. He possesses the powers of the hero abundantly, but not the ability to take control and direct the course of his own life, let alone the lives of others, as the hero is supposed to do. Rather he is always out of synchronization, trying to catch up, to make up for lost opportunities. At every crucial moment in the novel Roy is late; he arrives in the Major Leagues at age thirty-four, a time when most athletes must retire, not begin their careers; he acknowledges his love for, and acceptance of, Iris Lemon *after* he has already jeopardized her life and the life of his unborn child by his willfully erratic batting; he resolves not to throw the game *after* he has already violated the source of his power, leaving himself impotent without his Wonderboy.

This disjunction between the hero's expected actions and Roy's inadequate attempts to perform them is reinforced throughout the novel by a stylistic tension between myth and reality. The elaborate patterns of imagery in the novel—of dark and light, water, trains, forests, flowers, and birds[12]— often violate the requirements of a realistic baseball novel. When baseballs turn into birds or meteors, clearly realism is being sacrificed, as in this typical example when Roy strikes out the Whammer:

> The ball appeared to the batter to be a slow spinning planet looming toward the earth. For a long light-year he waited for this globe to whirl into the orbit of his swing so he could bust it to smithereens that would settle with dust and dead leaves into some distant cosmos. At last the unseeing eye, maybe a fortuneteller's lit crystal ball—drifted within range of his weapon, or so he thought, because he lunged at it ferociously, twisting round like a top. He landed on both knees as the world floated by over his head and hit with a *whup* into the cave of Sam's glove.[13]

The cosmic allusions in this passage are effective on the mythic level, but clearly they interfere with the reader's simple apprehension of a pitched ball. In addition, Malamud's baseball idiom is often stylized and stilted, as if Marshall McLuhan were substituting for Joe Garagiola on the "Game of the Week." As Max F. Schulz observes, "Rarely do the symbols seem to emerge naturally out of the exigencies of plot and character; rather plot and character appear to exist primarily as vehicles for the symbolism."[14]

Malamud obviously intended this tension, for his vision of the hero is essentially ironic—Roy's actions as a man are out of step with the hero's necessary accomplishments. Roy's failure is not a personal human failure—in fact, on a personal level he succeeds. At the end of the novel, although not by choice, he buries Wonderboy, the symbol of his selfish quest for immortality, and presumably will take up the responsibilities of paternity and marriage. His failure, rather, is the failure of the hero to be a permanent source of strength in modern society. The paradigms Roy represents finally are failed heroes—Casey at the Bat and Shoeless Joe Jackson, not Babe Ruth. Malamud clearly recognizes that even Ruth and other "gods" enshrined in Cooperstown had no permanent regenerative effect on their world. The athlete-hero must age and retire—his skills are clearly diminished at the end of his career, as Malamud would have observed in the final seasons of Joe DiMaggio and other aging heroes of the early fifties, and as we more recently have recognized in the last seasons of Willie Mays, Hank Aaron, and others. Sport provides heroes who *temporarily* infuse spirit into their world, and as such it performs an invaluable service for contemporary society. Roy's presence on the Knights' team inspires the other players to unaccustomed excellence, and Iris risks her self-respect for Roy because, as she says: "I hate to see a hero fail. There are so few of them. . . . Without heroes we're all plain people and don't know how far we can go."[15] But heroes do fail; it is the game finally, not the individual hero, which is the permanent source of psychic regeneration. The institutionalizing and commercializing of the game (as represented by Judge Banner) operate counter to its mythic function, but the game continually renews itself—raises up heroes who temporarily reign and are then replaced. There are two possible sequels to *The Natural*: one is the story of Roy Hobbs, the man, as he adjusts to the responsibilities of marriage and mundane employment; the other is the story of Herman Youngberry, whose reign as king is inaugurated at the end of this novel but will be terminated by a new young godlike slugger after Youngberry's season on earth. The vitality that such heroes as Roy Hobbs and Babe Ruth can impart to twentieth-century American society is temporary at best, but without them we might be without heroes entirely. The star athlete may be a diminished hero, but he is our only link to the Adonises and Galahads of the past.

History and Religion

The Natural can, then, be rightfully seen to embody a culmination of the major themes of American sports fiction from its earliest beginnings in the *Tip Top Library*. Malamud did not have the final word, however, and all subsequent sports fiction is not merely a series of footnotes to *The Natural*. Rather, by explicitly recognizing the mythic qualities of American sport, Malamud liberated sports fiction from earthbound repetitions of a limited number of familiar themes. Writers of sports fiction, particularly in the last dozen years, have used the mythic qualities of sport to explore some of the most basic issues in man's relationship to the cosmos. Before turning, however, to the novels of Robert Coover, Don DeLillo, and Philip Roth, which represent the spectacular flowering of sports fiction during the last decade, we should first observe more concretely this idea that sport is a major source of myth.

The mythic dimension of sport derives from two essential qualities; sport is both historical and religious. The function of history in sport is so important and so pervasive that it can be easily ignored. History separates competitive sport from simple recreation; it establishes the standards, precedents, and feats of excellence against which all athletes test themselves, and which become the frame of reference by which athletes are judged by others. There is perhaps no human activity other than sport which can compact as much history into so little linear time. Each season, progressing from pre-season youthful expectation, through mid-season crises of commitment, to end-of-season success or failure, is a lifetime. "Generations" within sport are foreshortened—a difference of five years' experience can establish a large gap between two players; sport "dynasties" often last only a few years; athletic careers are brief and teams are constantly rejuvenated with new blood as they move quickly through season after season. In sport time, Babe Ruth seems to have been a figure of the distant past—yet his record of sixty home runs in a season stood supreme for little more than three decades, during which time he became as much legend as man.

The accelerated slipping away of time, however, does not obscure the past from the present. There is certainly no other human activity in which the past is permanently recorded so precisely or completely. Events are instantaneous, but they are reclaimed forever in the mind as images, and in the record books as statistics. Certain timeless moments never change; the receiver stretching for a long pass floating over his shoulder, the boxer countering with his left and driving a hard right to his opponent's jaw, a second baseman suspended in midair as he pivots to complete a double play—all these images are permanently embossed on the fan's mind as if on Keats's Grecian urn. But in addition to these endlessly repeated movements of sport, certain singular events attain the permanence of immortality. Babe Ruth pointing to the outfield fence in the 1932 World Series against the Chicago Cubs, or Bobby Thomson exploding a home run into the left field stands to beat the Dodgers in the 1951 playoffs for the National League pennant created the kind of events that all sports fans feel they have witnessed; they are part of our collective past. Such timeless moments cannot be consciously contrived, as was obvious when Henry Aaron began the 1974 baseball season one home run shy of Babe Ruth's record. The media and the baseball establishment attempted to make Aaron's seven-hundred-fifteenth a mythic event, but in fact the home run was anticlimactic.

Spectacular moments are not the sum of sports history by any means. Record books retain specific details of every game ever played. The box score, as Roger Angell claims, is one of the most remarkable features of baseball:

It represents happenstance and physical flight exactly translated into figures and history. Its totals—batter's credit vs. pitcher's debit—balance as exactly as those in an accountant's ledger. And a box score is more than a capsule archive. It is a precisely etched miniature of the sport itself, for baseball, in spite of its grassy spaciousness and apparent unpredictability, is the most intensely and satisfyingly mathematical of all our outdoor sports. Every player in every game is subjected to a cold and ceaseless accounting; no ball is thrown and no base is gained without an instant responding of judgment—ball or strike, hit or error, yea or nay—and an ensuing statistic.[16]

Robert Coover's *The Universal Baseball Association* creates with dice and a record book the entire history of an imaginary fifty-six-year-old baseball league, and it is no accident that his protagonist is an accountant. Although other sports are not recorded with so compact or symmetrical an instrument as the box score, they are also permanently retained by records and statistics.

The most important function of history in sport is its creation of the possibility of "immortality." As was mentioned in an earlier chapter, the record book establishes a continuity to human achievement that is shared by all mankind, but an individual can also win permanent fame through his exploits during a brief career. Sport has become for the twentieth-century American what the frontier was for the nineteenth—an arena for heroic action in which the individual can achieve historical existence beyond his lifetime. The Daniel Boones and Kit Carsons of an earlier age have become the Babe Ruths and Jack Dempseys of the twentieth century. Any achievement or startling occurrence in sport today is automatically compared to similar events in the past. An appropriate analogue lies in the culture of the Greeks in their golden age. In their drama, the heroic past was constantly evoked in the present and was a daily frame of reference for their actions. Sport is also built on this historical structure but in such a way that the history is ongoing. Today's players become tomorrow's heroes and the next decade's legends. The acceleration of history in sport can even make some athletes "legends in their own time." One passage in Frederick Exley's *A Fan's Notes* finds Frank Gifford performing exceptionally well in a game at the end of his career. In so doing, the author tells us, he is becoming some legendary hero of the past, but *his own past*: "In the same way that Shaw threw to some memory of him, he became that memory."[17]

All sports novels rely on sports history for the source of their material—how, for example, could a character be made a hero if standards did not exist to which he could be compared —but sports fiction also includes a few explicitly historical novels. Lucy Kennedy's *The Sunlit Field* (1950) is an historical romance against a background of club baseball in the 1850s.[18] This saga of the earliest days of the "American pastime" chronicles the dethroning of the elitist Knickerbockers, the country's first baseball club, by the Brooklyn Excelsiors, a team of Irish factory workers who played for the joy of playing and not for the elegant banquets after the games. The natural spontaneity of the Excelsiors is soon partially sacrificed to the demands of business practice, as baseball becomes increasingly professionalized. Thus, in microcosm we see the aristocratic origins of baseball, the sport's usurpation by the immigrant working class, and the emergence of that group into a new American middle class. The events of the novel recreate and encapsulate the entire macrohistory of baseball.

A more interesting historical novel is William Brashler's *The Bingo Long Traveling All-Stars and Motor Kings* (1973), an account of a black barnstorming baseball team in 1939. Recognizable figures from the black baseball leagues appear—Satchel Paige, Josh Gibson, Cool Papa Bell, among others—in this story of black survival in a white world. Bingo's All-Stars have to contend with the strong-arm tactics of their former owner in the Southern Colored League, with uneven white justice in small Midwestern communities, with grueling travel through countless towns in one or two automobiles, with playing twenty games a week against twenty different opponents. As Leon tells Bingo, "Barnstorming is hungry ball more than anything else,"[19] but in these hungry Depression times, the players survive with dignity and without compromise. They often must feign subservience to the white power structure, but they never violate their self-respect among themselves, and they laugh at whitey behind his back. They are able to maintain their dignity partly because their main task is to play baseball, and no matter how much bias is directed against them, the game itself is fair. They can be banned from the major leagues, an umpire can call balls and strikes and the close ones at the bases unfairly, but for the most part a ball is either caught or dropped, a batter either hits or misses—and the unmatchable talent of Bingo's All-Stars cannot be denied.

The black baseball leagues were not subjected to the comprehensive recording of statistics that has accompanied the major leagues from their beginnings. Because the exploits of the great players were often witnessed only by the actual spectators and passed on orally, the history of the black leagues is part history and part folklore.[20] It is appropriate that many of the encounters of white and black in the novel appear as "Marster and John" stories of the old South; tricking the trickster became a way of survival, exploited by the players with enormous zest. Perhaps the novel makes the situation of black players less grim than it actually was, but nostalgia has become a popular American response to the Depression and to the rest of our past as well.

The history these novels fictionalize is itself a source of myth in sport, but it is the "religious" attitude that such folklore generates that makes sport truly mythic. As early as 1919, a comment by Morris R. Cohen appeared in *The Dial* that identified baseball as the national religion:

> The essence of religious experience, so we are told, is the redemption from the limitations of our petty individual lives and the mystic unity with a larger life of which we are a part.[21]

Baseball, according to Cohen, serves this function in American culture. More recently, theologian Michael Novak has brilliantly and thoroughly described the religious quality of sport. "Sports," according to Novak,

> are religious in the sense that they are organized institutions, disciplines, and liturgies; and also in the sense that they teach religious qualities of heart and soul. In particular, they recreate symbols of cosmic struggle, in which human survival and moral courage are not assured.[22]

Sports "flow outward into action" from "an impulse of freedom, respect for natural limits, a zest for symbolic meaning, and a longing for perfection"; "they feed a deep human hunger, place humans in touch with certain dimly perceived features of human life within this cosmos, and provide an experience of at least a pagan sense of godliness."[23] Novak goes on to describe the elements of religion, each of which is present in sport as well: religions are organized and structured; they are built upon *ascesis* (the development of character through patterns of self-denial, repetition, and experiment); they channel the feelings most humans have of fate; they make explicit the almost nameless dreads of daily human life (aging, dying, failure, cowardice, betrayal, guilt); they respect rootedness, particularity, and local belonging; they consecrate certain days and hours; they require heroic forms to live up to and patterns of symbols to grow old with; they offer ways to exhilarate the human body, desire, and will; and they create a sense of beauty and of oneness with the universe and other humans.[24] Novak is careful to note that sports *ideally* serve these functions, that the actual participants, owners, and fans often reduce sport to more mundane levels—but it remains true that they do operate in this religious sense for a great number of Americans. The intensity with which sports fans follow their favorite teams, the awe with which they regard the consecrated ground of the stadium where feats of unsurpassed excellence were performed in the past, the degree to which they are elevated outside themselves to unity with their fellow spectators and with the symbolic human drama enacted on the field testify to this religious quality.

A more concrete look at specific sports can further demonstrate this religious potential. The function of ritual is important in all sports, for they are defined by their rules and rules themselves have a ritual quality. Rules, like ritual, impose order and meaning on seemingly purposeless action, as Howard S. Slusher, in an existential treatment of sport, observes:

> The evolution of man has demonstrated a constant and prevailing need for ritual. . . . With the reduction of ritual in religion, it is not surprising man turns to other "rites" to again see some form of quasi-order in his life. For many, sport fulfills this function.[25]

Football and baseball are certainly the most ritualistic and mythic American sports. Baseball is the most visible of all sports and the easiest to retain in memory, as Roger Angell observes:

> Because of its pace, and thus the perfectly observed balance, both physical and psychological, between opposing forces, its clean lines can be restored in retrospect.[26]

Baseball has regularity and symmetry; the positioning of the players in the baseball space is as orderly as the Ptolemaic universe. The numerological substructure of the game seems almost mystical, with a predominance of threes, fours, sevens, and nines: three strikes with four balls equals seven chances to hit; three outfielders plus four infielders equals seven fielders; there are three outs per inning, four bases, and nine men on a side; it is ninety feet between bases; there are nine innings, and the fans stretch during the seventh. The players too have their private rituals; their actions at the plate as they prepare to hit, the fielders' refusal to step on the bases when they run in from the field or their insistence on doing so, and even the taping of ankles and dressing for the games can have a ceremonial quality.

Football players also have these private rituals, but to move from baseball to football is to pass from mystical to militaristic ritual. Football is militaristic in many of its team nicknames (Vikings and Raiders rather than Twins and Athletics, for example); in its codified secret language with terms such as *sweep, blitz, blast, dive*; in its rigid nonfluid formations; and especially in its tactics (the object is to utilize the field in such a way as to spread out the enemy's forces and attack its weakness by flanking maneuvers, massed assaults, subterfuge, and aerial bombardments). Football uniforms are more militaristic than those of other sports. The padding and helmets make the players appear ferocious and larger than life. Football uniforms conceal more of an individual's appearance than baseball uniforms, and like the uniforms of policemen and soldiers they have the power to transform the men within. Players are able to perform acts of violence, with impunity and without guilt, which they would not even consider off the field.

However, football also has strong elements of religious ritual, but of a different quality than baseball's. Baseball ritual seems mystical and private, while the spectacle of football is similar to mass religious and political celebrations. In the satiric piece, "Freud, Football and the Marching Virgins," Thomas Hornsby Ferril observes:

> The ceremony begins with colorful processions of musicians and semi-nude virgins who move in and out of ritualized patterns. This excites the thousands of worshippers to rise from their seats, shout frenzied poetry in unison and chant ecstatic anthems.[27]

Though parodic, this description is not far from accurate. The bands, the pageant, the cheerleaders and card sections are as much a part of football as the games themselves. The Super Bowl and Orange Bowl extravaganzas are but the reductio ad absurdum of these familiar spectacles.

It is significant how many national holidays are honored by sporting events. The baseball doubleheader is a traditional part of the Fourth of July celebration, Labor Day is observed with a baseball game, and Memorial Day by the Indianapolis 500. More ostentatiously, football games are often preceded by parades and supplemented by pregame and half-time spectacles. The college bowl games honor various crops (roses, cotton, oranges, sugar, peaches, tangerines), and one even celebrates the sun. John Steinbeck observed several years ago: "Nearly all sports as we know them seem to be memories and in a way ceremonial reenactments of situations that were once of paramount importance to our survival."[28] In the absence of public religiosity in America, these football festivals have become our fertility rituals and religious pageants, as well as reenactments of our frontier experience and our primal need for defense of the home against outside threats. As Howard S. Slusher observes, "Sport becomes both what it is and a declaration of the culture."[29]

The ideas that a stadium is sacred ground and that sport can serve as a cultural religion for displaced Americans are beautifully expressed in Irwin Shaw's *Voices of a Summer Day* (1965). Benjamin Federov, while watching his son play baseball, recalls his past life—his childhood, his love affairs, his war experiences, and his family relationships. Baseball provides the frame for these recollections; it is the game itself that triggers his memory:

> The sounds were the same through the years—the American sounds of summer, the tap of bat against ball, the cries of the infielders, the wooden plump of the ball into catchers' mitts, the umpires calling "Strike three and you're out." The generations circled the bases, the dust rose for forty years as runners slid in from third, dead boys hit doubles, famous men made errors at shortstop, forgotten friends tapped the clay from their spikes with their bats as they stepped into the batter's box, coaches' voices warned, across the decades, "Tag up, tag up!" on fly balls. The distant mortal innings of boyhood and youth. . . .[30]

Then follow memories of his immigrant father, who "was made into an American catching behind the plate barehanded in the years between 1895 and 1910,"[31] of his father taking him to see the Giants at the Polo Grounds, and of himself taking his son to see those same (but different) Giants at the same Polo Grounds:

> There was no ancestral keep to bring the male heir to; no hallowed family ceremonies into which to initiate a son; no church or synagogue or cult you believe in so that your son and his son after that could attach themselves automatically to three millenia of myth, no broad acres that had been lovingly tended for hundreds of years by people of the same blood and name to walk across with a six-year-old boy. . . . So, bereft of other tribal paraphernalia, he took his son to the Polo Grounds, because, when *he* was six *his* father had taken him to the Polo Grounds.[32]

Moses did not walk on the turf of the Polo Grounds, nor Christ, nor Muhammad; but Mel Ott did, and John McGraw and Christy Matthewson. This is as close to religious awe as we can come in a country unconsecrated by the blood of martyrs or the footprints of gods.

Baseball's pastoralism and historicism hark back to the past as Benjamin harks back in his own mind. The green grass and soothing warmth of the sun provide the mood for remembrance. Baseball is also the one truly stable aspect of Benjamin Federov's world. It establishes continuity between events in his own life, because many of his strongest loving memories of his father and brother, as well as important political events such as the execution of Sacco and Vanzetti, are linked in his mind with athletic contests. Baseball has been permanent through all this, binding together the generations in his family, and binding them to their new country. As a religion, baseball evokes little piety or fanatical commitment to dogma, but it serves the more humane functions of providing standards and connections through which order emerges in the midst of purposeless chaos. This is a religious function, and the particular importance of sport for many Americans.

The Mythic Novels

Sport *is* mythic in America, not only in its significance to individuals, but in its recreation of specific mythic episodes in Western culture. The mythic patterns of the hero's career and the king-must-die motif have been cited in previous chapters. But, in addtion to these, the great quest myths of diverse cultures have easily recognizable analogues in a team's pursuit of the pennant or an individual athlete's quest for a world championship. Indeed, in some sports a clearer symbol —a cup or a jeweled belt—is the prize, as it was for mythic heroes. The Homeric odyssey is likewise paralleled in novels such as Eliot Asinof's *Man on Spikes* (1955) in which the hero wanders from obstacle to obstacle in pursuit of his dream. The ugly duckling or Cinderella motif is reenacted every time a substitute or unknown player becomes a temporary hero. Even the Cid, riding forth to lead his people although he is dead, is recalled by emotional appeals to "win one for the Gipper." Jack Olsen's *Alphabet Jackson* (1974) concludes with a parody of this motif.

Malamud's *The Natural* was the first American sports novel to explicitly recognize that an athlete's career does, in fact, imitate these specific myths, but it did not so much spawn imitations as broaden the possible scope of sports fic-

tion by introducing an entirely new way of using sport for
literary purposes. For example, Babs Deal's *The Grail*
(1963) written more than a decade after *The Natural,* is a
translation of the Arthurian love triangle onto a college football team. The coach's name is Arthur Hill, his wife is Jennie,
his star quarterback is Lance Hebert, and his chief assistant
is Mel (Merlin) Grant. The novel is about order and chaos and
fate; order is possible in football, in

> the complex play and interplay of bodies in motion, the shift
> and countershift, the gap stopped, the hole opened, the intri-
> cate beautiful mechanics of a perfect connection between man
> and object in space.[33]

But order is temporary and must disintegrate; the only lasting pattern is a repetition of this degeneration.

To see ancient myth reenacted in contemporary life is to
recognize the possibility of order, so Deal's mythic method is
highly appropriate in this novel. The Arthurian legend finds
its proper reenactment in college football; teams are structured like Arthur's court and the king-coach must have the
total devotion of his knight-players who battle for his glory.
Although Arthurian material is not used subtly in *The Grail,*
it never draws attention to itself at the expense of the novel;
the characters are believable and sympathetic in themselves.

The Grail is thus a skillful, if not overly imaginative translation of myth onto a modern setting. The author's accomplishment lies in her recognition of the appropriateness of the
translation, not in any complex manipulation of the mythic
materials. The mere fact that direct translation seemed possible to her dates the book for readers in the seventies. *The
Grail* was written during America's "Camelot years," before
the murder of John Kennedy. Philip Roth sees that assassin-
ation as the first act of demythologizing committed in the
sixties, the "demythologizing decade." Roth describes this
term:

> I mean by this that much that had previously been considered
> in my own brief lifetime to be disgraceful and disgusting
> forced itself upon the national consciousness, loathesome or
> not; what was assumed to be beyond reproach became the

target for blasphemous assault; what was imagined to be indestructible, impermeable, in the very nature of American things, yielded and collapsed overnight.[34]

No longer does simple translation of myth seem possible to many writers, for permanence, order, and continuity no longer seem congruent with reality. Hans Meyerhoff identifies two literary uses for myth: "To suggest, within a secular setting, a timeless perspective of looking upon the human situation; and to convey a sense of continuity and identification with mankind in general."[35] In the wake of assassinations, political terrorism, racial violence, and genocidal wars, such a perspective appears an illusion. The post-Kennedy writers who adopt Malamud's mythic consciousness in their difficult and complex sports novels—Robert Coover, Don DeLillo, and Philip Roth—use myth in very unconventional ways, but ones reflective of the time in which they write.

Robert Coover is interested in much more than baseball, but he deeply understands the sport about which he writes. In *The Universal Baseball Association, Inc., J. Henry Waugh, Prop.* (1968), the foreshortened generations of baseball are even more foreshortened to produce a rich mythic history that becomes the material for his novel. Coover understands how players become legends, heroes, and gods through their existence in men's minds long after their careers have ended. He clearly knows that Ty Cobb, Babe Ruth, and Walter Johnson and Jim Thorpe, Red Grange, and the Four Horsemen are heroes of vital importance to a people with so little legendary history. He is the first writer to explicitly recognize that the *names* of ballplayers actually create folklore and myth. Coover's wildly inventive names for his characters—Scat Batkin, McAllister Weeks, Biff Baldwin, for example—simply capture the essence of real players' names: Wee Willie Keeler, Goose Goslin, Enos Slaughter, Gabby Hartnett, Whitlow Wyatt, Spurgeon Chandler, and hundreds more. Coover has also recognized that *numbers* are essential to baseball; three, four, seven, and nine have had mystical importance for numerologists for centuries, and define the underlying mathematical structure of the game.

Coover's fascination with sport is not a passing interest by any means. In two short pieces of fiction—"McDuff on the

Mound" and "Whatever Happened to Gloomy Gus of the Chicago Bears?"—he depends on the mythic quality of baseball
and football to make his points. Coover's interest in history is
apparent in all of his fiction; in "Gloomy Gus" he rewrites
the personal history of Richard Nixon, imagining the man
playing football rather than politics. In "McDuff" he retells
the story of "Casey at the Bat" from the perspective of the
pitcher who struck out the mighty slugger, creating myth
from the few details of a popular song. But Coover's great
contribution to sports fiction is, of course, his novel—not just
a fine baseball novel, but one of the important works of fiction
of recent years.

On the level of character and action, *The Universal Baseball Association* concerns a fifty-six-year-old accountant,
Henry Waugh, who has contrived an elaborate baseball game
played with dice and controlled by statistical probabilities.
The game is not mere amusement to Henry; it is his passion,
and during the course of the novel it becomes his obsession.
The central action of the novel occurs early, when Damon
Rutherford, a rookie pitcher dearer to Henry than any player
should be, is killed by the extraordinary roll of three consecutive triple ones on the dice. Henry's efforts and final failure
to cope with his grief at Damon's death describe the course of
the novel.

Henry is the quintessential *player*. His life is a succession
of roles dictated by his own moods and by external necessity
If he feels cynical, he is Rags Rooney; if philosophical, he is
Barney Bancroft; when rakish with a waitress, he becomes
Willie O'Leary. With Hettie Irden, the local B-girl, his sexual
moods are explicitly related to playing baseball: when exuberant and particularly potent, he is Damon Rutherford after
pitching a perfect game; when solemn, slightly desperate and
searching, he is Swanee Law, veteran pitcher. Coover's prose
is astonishingly erotic as well as comic when he describes
Henry trying for a "double-header" with Hettie:

> Oh, come on, come on, Henry, here, come on *home!* Yes,
> and they're pulling for him, Hettie, and he rounds second,
> he's trying to stretch it to third, but I don't know, it's still a
> long ways to the plate, no, he just can't make it, not this time,
> and the second baseman, he's got the ball, and he's gonna—

No, no, *I* got it, Henry, *I* got it! come on! come on! Keep it
up! Behind his butt, she clapped her cold soles to cheer him
on. Yes, he's pushing toward third now, yes! and he's picking up, yes, that's it! he's hard to stop now, he's churning, he's
pouring it on, and he's around third! on his way home! but
they've got him in a hotbox! wow! third to catch! back to
third! hah! to catch! to pitch! catch! pitch! catch! pitch!
Home, Henry, *home!* And here he comes, Hettie! He's past
'em! past 'em! he's bolting for home, spurting past, sliding
in—*POW!* Oh, *pow*, Henry! pow pow pow pow *POW!* They
laughed softly, hysterically, flowing together. She let go her
grip on the ball. He slipped off, unmingling their sweat. Oh,
that's a game, Henry! *That's* really a *great* old *game!*[36]

Not only the phallic bat and the sexual implications of pitching, catching, and batting, but also the rhythm, tensions, and
releases of baseball action become the ideal metaphor for
sexual intercourse, and for life itself. For Henry, who plays at
life, baseball is the perfect game in its balance between offense and defense and its "accountability—the beauty of the
records system which found a place to keep forever each least
action."[37] It is not the mere game that interests Henry, but
rather the records and statistics—"the peculiar balances between individual and team, offense and defense, strategy and
luck, accident and pattern, power and intelligence."[38] Only
baseball could be the sport for this novel, not football or basketball. In baseball the balance between opposing forces and
between skill and chance is most delicate. There are no lop-
sided confrontations, no two-on-one overpowerings or exploi-
tations of gross advantages. Each individual battle is one-on-
one: pitcher vs. hitter, pitcher vs. runner, fielder vs. runner.
Each confrontation is decided by inches or fractions of seconds: a swing that is slightly off results in a pop-up; to miss
by two inches is to miss entirely. The distance between bases
is just great enough so that ball and runner often arrive almost simultaneously; it is in the nature of the game that the
individual who executes only slightly better will prevail. Because of this delicate equilibrium, chance has a nearly equal
role with skill—a gust of wind, a pebble, a glare of sunlight
can tip the scale. Baseball is thus the appropriate metaphor
for Coover's vision of life as a precarious balance of forces
which, upset by an external agent, becomes chaos. Henry

must maintain this balance in his own life, and his inability to do so marks his ultimate insanity.

Henry plays his game alone and denies himself the fellowship of real baseball. His attempts to introduce first Hettie and then his colleague Lou Engel to the game prove disastrous. The death of Damon and Henry's inability to rectify this outrage make him feel like "an adolescent caught masturbating."[39] Henry thus metaphorically recognizes his own increasing solipsism. Playing must be done with others; baseball is a ritual activity that binds people together—to play with oneself is to deny the reality of the world and the necessity of community. As Henry submits himself ever more deeply to his game, he progressively loses contact with the external world. The novel is framed on the poles of illusion and reality, which gradually become not opposite, but identical. Henry plays a game of a game which is itself a reenactment of life's conflicts. He slips so easily in and out of these worlds that the distinction between illusion and reality is easily blurred. The players who Henry becomes are as "real" as Henry himself, or Lou or Hettie. The novel itself is a fiction of a fiction (Henry's game) of a fiction (baseball) of life—but who is to say with certainty that life is any less a fiction than these others? For Henry, at least, the distinction disappears.

His job in the real world is as an accountant for Mr. Zifferblatt, "a militant clock-watcher."[40] Henry accepts this job as a necessary counterweight to his "Association"—a subordinate activity, and occasionally a nuisance,

> but over the long haul he needed that balance, that rhythmic shift from house to house, and he knew that total onesided participation in the league would soon grow even more oppressive than his job at Dinkelmann, Zauber, & Zifferblatt.[41]

This precarious balance between illusion and reality, as fragile as the UBA itself, which a fire, a theft, even a hard wind could destroy, also places Henry on the brink between time and timelessness. A year of Association time can be compressed into a couple of months, or even into days if necessary. The major portion of the novel takes place in a year in which Association time (year LVI) and chronological time (Henry is fifty-six) intersect, but Henry's climactic action plunges him entirely into Association time. Although the proprietor of the Universal Baseball Association, Henry is subject to its rules, to the pattern of the charts, and to the randomness of the dice. However, when he tries to save the Association and revenge himself on Jock Casey, the pitcher who killed Damon Rutherford, by manipulating the dice so that Jock is killed by a line drive, he loses control of the Association and becomes its slave. He relinquishes his sanity, surrenders totally to the reality of the Association, and disappears from the last chapter of the novel. The time in this chapter is one hundred years later and the Association players are the only reality there is.

On this level of action, the novel is a compelling story of a man's disintegration into schizophrenia. It concerns an individual suspended on the narrow line between illusion and reality, who maintains his equilibrium with only momentary lapses, but who tumbles finally into insanity, solipsism, and complete loss of contact with physical reality. But Coover also weights his characters and events with obvious allegorical resonance. He is one of the few American writers of recent years to deal with ultimate questions of the cosmos. As the critic Leo J. Hertzel observes: "American novelists of the past forty years have been chary of the sweep of history, Big Questions, GOD."[42] Coover's readiness to pursue these topics relentlessly places him squarely in the older American tradition of Melville and Hawthorne. He chooses baseball as the proper metaphor for religion because, as Henry observes, ball stadiums and not European churches are the real American holy places.[43]

The initials of Henry's name, JHW, identify him as Jahweh, the Old Testament God of the Judeo-Christian tradition. Among the roughly seven dozen names of players who populate the UBA are included such Old Testament figures as Mose Stanford (Moses), Jonathan Noon, Gabe Burdette (Gabriel), Jake Bradley (Jacob), Abe Flint (Abraham), Mickey Halifax (Michael), Fancy Dan Casey (Daniel), Jumpin' Joe Gallagher (Joseph), and Seemly Sam Tucker (Samuel). To these are added the younger "New Testament" players: Goodman James, Hard John Horvath, Virgin Donovan, Uncle Joe Shannon (Joseph), Matt Garrison (Mathew), and Paul

Trench. Although these characters do not have important functions in the novel, they provide the biblical background against which the action takes place.

They also define Henry's essential god-function. Henry creates the participants in the UBA by *naming* them. As God's work, or like Adam's in the Garden, Henry's naming of a person gives him life and identity, and he chooses names "that could bear the whole weight of perpetuity." According to the name, a player "shrinks or grows, stretches or puts on muscle."

> But name a man and you make him what he is. Of course, he can develop. And in ways you don't expect. Or something can go wrong. Lot of nicknames invented as a result of Rookie-year surprises. But the basic stuff is already there. In the name. Or rather: in the naming.[44]

As names create the people, numbers create the world in which Henry places them. The years of the Association are designated by Roman numerals, which connote something ancient, rich with tradition. Numbers define the odds, identify the import of each dice roll and the total number of possible actions that can occur, comprise the statistics that become the history of the Association, and even have mystical significance. Henry as accountant is the appropriate numbers-god for the story.

The symbolic level of the novel thus begins with Henry as God, creator of the universe, who rules it by the laws of mathematical probability and chance. He is a God who maintains a balance between pattern and accident, as baseball also combines the two, and finally as life combines them. As one critic points out:

> The fact that baseball can comprehend the opposites on the one hand, of strategy and pattern, and on the other of luck and accident—suggesting that man is in control of events and yet at the mercy of whim or chance—makes the game fascinating and an ambiguous image of human life.[45]

Coover invites the reader to go beyond these general theological implications to read the novel also as specific allegory. The concentration on rules, averages, and figures suggests the Christian version of an orderly meaningful cosmos.[46] Damon Rutherford is an obvious Christ figure, who "saves" the Association with his perfect game from "that piled-up mid-autumn feeling, pregnant with the vague threat of confusion and emptiness—but this boy had cut clean through it, let light and health in."[47] Damon is termed "a self-enclosed yet participating mystery,"[48] doing his father's (Brock Rutherford's) business. Damon's "oneness with the UBA" and his excellence create both the past (by suggesting that the XXs ought to be termed the Brock Rutherford Era), and the future of the Association.[49] His death is memorialized by subsequent generations on Damonsday in ritual reenactment of the fatal beanball incident. His followers, the Damonites, grow from a small secret sect to become the established religion, combining ritual and the preeminence of law as the foundations of their belief.

Coover invites the reader to make these allegorical correspondences, then demonstrates the foolishness of doing so. He undercuts the allegory at every turn, for his parodist's intention is not to write an allegory of the rise of Christianity, but an antiallegory. Coover identifies his own apparent purpose in the prologue to "Seven Exemplary Fictions" appearing in his collection of stories, *Pricksongs & Descants*. Addressing Cervantes, he praises the writing of the master which

> struggled against the unconscious mythic residue in human life and sought to synthesize the unsynthesizable, sallied forth against adolescent thought-modes and exhausted art forms, and returned home with new complexities.[50]

Furthermore, he states:

> The novelist uses familiar mythic or historical forms to combat the content of these forms and to conduct the reader . . . to the real, away from mystification to clarification, away from magic to maturity, away from mystery to revelation.[51]

In *The Universal Baseball Association,* Coover uses the historical forms of the Judeo-Christian tradition and the adolescent thought-mode of Christian allegory and turns them on themselves. As Henry's Association is a game of a game of a game, so the novel is an allegory of an allegory of Christianity, which is itself in a sense an allegorical rendering of ancient events. Coover uses allegory in a unique way, not for traditional dogmatic moralizing, but for rejection of such moralizing. Rather than indicate a narrow path to salvation, the novel represents the diffusion and chaos and impossibility of certainty today.

The events in year LVI that become the cornerstones of religious belief in year CLVII are simple enough. Damon Rutherford is killed by a ball pitched by Jock Casey, an act demanded by a chance roll of the dice. Henry retaliates by manipulating the dice so that Jock is himself killed by a line drive. One hundred years later, Damonites and Caseyites, as well as nihilists, existentialists, determinists, and mythicists cannot even agree on these facts. They have conflated the two actions into a single Parable of the Duel and have interpreted the lives of their heroes in ways bearing no relationship to the originals. Henry is God and Damon is Christ in a Christian allegory, but Damon is also a Greek hero and a *daemon*—and therefore represents a pagan, even diabolic principle. He is a pagan fertility god when Henry contemplates how to interpret his coupling with Hettie: "What about Damon's consecratory romp in the sack afterwards? Sure, why not? Somebody's virgin daughter."[52] His slayer is Jock Casey, whose initials are Jesus Christs's, who is "lean, serious, melancholy even," as Christ appears in his popular image, and who glances up at Henry (God)—"only a glance, split-second pain, a pleading"[53]—before he dies, as Christ cried out on cross, "My God, why hast thou forsaken me?"

It is thus impossible to determine who is the Messiah; of the two candidates one dies by random chance, and the other by the vengeful whim of God. Damon's crucifixion is meaningless in its true context; Jock's is a parody of Christ's crucifixion, for he is killed *by* God, and the biblical thunder, storms, and tearing of temple curtains are reduced to Henry's vomiting on the playing table. The sacred book of the Damonites in the year CLVII is Barney Bancroft's *The UBA in the Balance,* which is a rewriting of Henry's *Book.* That original work had been forty volumes of statistics, journalistic dispatches, seasonal analyses, and general baseball theory,[54] but the new book discovers the pattern in this official history, the *process* that becomes transformation.[55] The parallels with the roughly forty books of the Old Testament coupled with the New Testament are unmistakable here, as is the implication that the New Testament is a fictitious pattern imposed on the random events of the Old Testament. Henry's *Book* is a recording of the results of the random throws of the dice; Barney's imposes an artificial order.

The characterization of God further parodies the Christian religion. Henry creates the Association but is subject to its rules and to the laws of chance. When he manipulates the dice in order to kill Casey, he violates his own rules, and thus ceases to be God; he becomes a slave to his game, not its proprietor. His absence from the final chapter implies a Godless world in which men are left with only the rituals of meaningless slayings which they no longer understand. Their rituals are grotesquely pagan as well, like the heathen sacrifices of the best young men of primitive tribes; the parody of the Eucharistic rite is even erotically cannibalistic.[56] As in his previous novel, *The Origin of the Brunists* (1966), Coover explores the nature of religion and sees its orgins in "desperate, pitiful, self-justifying and sometimes heroic but stupid efforts to make sense out of death and chance."[57] Henry, in the personae of the various players, reacts to Damon's death in ways paradigmatic of the several ways men try to fit misfortune into a coherent universal schema.[58] Rooney is cynical, Barney Bancroft is philosophical, Fennimore McCaffree is coldly practical, Sycamore Flynn is guilt-ridden; Sandy Shaw the balladeer, turns the death into folklore. But the following generations transform the death into myth, giving ultimate meaning to meaninglessness. The Christian myth, by implication, is a passionately held lie.

Coover also questions the meaning, or rather lack of meaning, of history. He does not say that history is unimportant, but that it cannot be known and is never passed on with its essential truth intact. With the passage of time, history becomes myth, then becomes open to interpretation—and thus becomes untruth. As a persuasive doctrine, it therefore can be dangerous. The past is no more knowable than the future; the present is the only truth, the only reality. Two of the performers of the ritual Parable of the Duel come to this realization at the conclusion of the novel:

And he [Paul] doesn't know any more whether he's a Da-
monite or a Caseyite or something else again, a New Heretic
or an unregenerate Golden Ager, doesn't even know if he's
Paul Trench or Royce Ingram or Pappy Rooney or Long Lew
Lydell, it's all irrelevant, it doesn't even matter that he's going
to die, all that counts is that he is *here* and here's the Man
and here's the boys and there's the crowd, the sun, the noise.
"It's not a trial," says Damon . . . "it's not even a lesson.
It's just what it is." Damon holds the baseball up between
them. It is hard and white and alive in the sun.[59]

Coover makes this judgment a statement of belief in his prologue to Cervantes when he comments on the philosophical
milieu in which the Spaniard wrote:

No longer was the City of Man a pale image of the City of
God, a microcosmic reflection of the macrocosm, but *rather
it was all there was,* neither micro- nor macrocosm.[60] (Emphasis mine)

Myths that distort reality must be rejected; life is its own
meaning and should be perceived unfiltered.

The ending of the novel thus ties all "levels" of narration
into a single conclusion. Coover constantly compounds and in-
verts the allegory to demonstrate the insanity of interpreting
history in a systematic way. The religious interests of the
book are the most important, but the reader can also identify
bits of political allegory—UBA as USA, a glut of political parties, political assassinations, a Big-Brother society dominated by the beast Dame Society. But all the various allegorical bits are parts of the overriding anti-allegory. The allegory and the action reinforce each other, as is too often not
the case with traditional allegory. Henry's insanity results
from his inability to maintain contact with concrete reality,
his need to create an illusory world governed by order and
rationality. For Henry history is a construction of numbers
and measurements,[61] but this constructed history is a false
one. Organized religion is "insane" for the same reasons.
Coover's anti-allegory questions the mythicizing of events
and ultimately challenges the "reality" of history, which is a
fiction whose relationship to truth is not a constant knowable
thing. Life is not process, but a series of random incidents.

One should not try to make sense of it, but play the game with love for the game, and for the reality of the shining white ball.

An equally complex but altogether different kind of sports novel is Don DeLillo's *End Zone* (1972). Its physical and metaphysical setting is described early in the book:

> We were in the middle of the middle of nowhere, that terrain so flat and bare, suggestive of the end of recorded time, a splendid sense of remoteness firing my soul. It was easy to feel that back up there, where men spoke the name of civilization in wistful tones I was wanted for some terrible crime.
>
> Exile in a real place, a place of few bodies and many stones, is just an extension (a packaging) of the other exile, the state of being separated from whatever is left of the center of one's history. I found comfort in west Texas. There was even pleasure in the daily punishment on the field. I felt that I was better for it, reduced in complexity, a warrior.[62]

So speaks Gary Harkness, the protagonist of the novel. The "end zone" of the title is the setting: the goal of the running back in a football game, but also a setting in time and space on the outer extremity of existence—a world on the verge of disintegration. The characters of the novel *End Zone* play football—that game performed at the limits of human capability within the bounds of barely contained violence—but they also live their daily existence at the extreme limit of human experience, psychologically and intellectually as well as physically. In this end zone of the mind, life is simplified; the characters confront the basic determinants of their existence in an effort to prevent their own fall into chaos.

DeLillo is concerned in all his novels with basic questions of language, violence, game-playing, and the need for order, but *End Zone* is his most successful book. DeLillo is less concerned in his novels with creating verisimilitude than with allowing his characters' deepest beings to speak directly to the reader. His writing is characterized by wacky offbeat humor, by verbal virtuosity that startles and delights and often puzzles, and by multiple digressions into realms of quirky erudition or profound wisdom. The novels are difficult—intentionally so—but in *End Zone*, DeLillo provides his readers with a stable center, a frame of reference from which to observe the rush of existence. Football functions extraordinarily well as the controlling center of *End Zone*. For one thing, an understanding of football is accessible to a far larger number of readers than, say, pure mathematics or theoretical science, the subject of *Ratner's Star*. More important, football embodies a view of life that can be contrasted to the chaos of reality. Football is ordered and meaningful. It is played on a field of specified size according to precise and clearly understood rules, against a single opposing team subject to the same restrictions, and it results most often in a clearly acknowledged outcome—one team wins and another loses, for every point the offense of one team scores, the defense of the other team gives up a point. The significance of the contest for the individual athlete is equally unambiguous; each player has a specific responsibility on every play which he either does or does not do—at the end of the game he knows exactly how well he played. The comfort of such certainty is not available to the citizens of the outside world who clearly see neither their purpose in life nor the obstacles to achieving it, who are individually subject to forces over which they have no control in a society that is moved toward unknown ends by unknown agents of power. The conflict between this world and the artificial ordered world of football is at the center of *End Zone,* and the reader can view the one from the ordered perspective of the other.

The novel takes place, then, against a landscape more metaphysical than physical, in "an obscure part of the world," in an environment of "simplicity, repetition, solitude, starkness, discipline upon discipline."[63] Gary Harkness is "one of the exiles" in that "remote and unfed place,"[64] having come to play football at Logos College after failing at four previous schools. Gary depends on football because it is primitive, it harks back to "ancient warriorship," it is built on pain and discipline, and it epitomizes simplicity: "Existence without anxiety. Happiness. Know your body. Understanding the real needs of man."[65] Football means "living close to your own skin," getting "right down to the bottom of it."[66] Football is thus the ideal metaphor for a confrontation with the essential principles of existence. The name of the school—Logos—obviously stands for both "word" and "reason." Football is a rigidly patterned activity, highly structured, ritualized and disciplined, which possesses its own intricately organized language. It has frequently been used by authors as a metaphor for war, but DeLillo explicitly rejects this equivalence: "Warfare is warfare. We don't need substitutes because we've got the real thing."[67] Rather, what most interests DeLillo in the sport is the fact that football "is the one sport guided by language, by the word signal, the snap number, the color code, the play name."[68] *End Zone* is, above all else, a novel about *language*.

That the novel is explicitly about language is hinted on the very first page when DeLillo playfully warns the reader, "double metaphor coming up." He belongs with contemporary writers such as William Gass, Vladimir Nabokov, and John Barth, among others, who have been termed "metafictionists."[69] This term designates those who are strongly aware of the nature of language, who make language itself and the process of using language their themes. DeLillo's consciousness of the reality of words as things is obvious at every stage in the novel. On one occasion Gary marvels at the words of a cliché:

> The sentiment of course had small appeal but it seemed that beauty flew from the words themselves, the letters, consonants swallowing vowels, aggression and tenderness, a semi-self-recreation from line to line, word to word, letter to letter.[70]

Later he comments on a conversation with his roommate in which their "words floated in the dimness, in the room's mild moonlight, weightless phrases polished by the cool confident knowledge of centuries."[71] And later yet, a conversation between Gary and a teammate is prefaced by the teammate's announcement of what will follow: "The dialogue. The exchange of words. The phrases and sentences."[72] Words can even have an erotic content in their substantiveness: "The words were ways of touching and made us want to speak with hands,"[73] Gary says of a talk with Myna Corbett.

A distinct play element is evident in DeLillo's use of language. Many words are spoken for their own sake, for their feel in the mouth of the speaker, for the harmony of their sounds, and for their originality. The book is filled with wildly inventive vulgarity: one of the players explodes, "That ass-belly sixty-two got his fist in. That magnolia candy-ass cunt"[74]; one of the coaches lambastes an errant player, telling him, "He looked like something that had just come inching out of a buffalo's ass."[75] DeLillo also revitalizes dead language and ideas, as for instance, in his description of a father driving his son to satisfy his own need for vicarious fulfillment: "This is the custom among men who have failed to be heroes; their sons must prove that the seed was not impoverished."[76] Such inventiveness and originality is often remarkable.

But playfulness and the imaginative pleasures of language are not its only function in the novel. Words often bear great power in and of themselves. The name of the football team at Logos College is changed from Cactus Wrens to Screaming Eagles—to the obvious improvement of its hostile image. Players have their "private sounds," their "huh huh huh" or "awright, awright, awright," or "we hit, we hit" that become magic incantations producing high emotional intensity. Words such as "queer," "relationship," and all "i-z-e words" are weighted with great significance for the characters, even when not specifically associated with any object or event. Even the names of persons can have potent connotations: Vera Chalk hates her name and tells her twin sister, "She should have named you Vera, You're the damn Vera. I'm not that damn person. I'm just me. You're the Vera. You're more her than I am."[77] And Anatole Bloomberg, Gary's three-hundred-pound Jewish roommate, finds his name as compelling as fate:

> I used to think of Anatole Bloomberg as the essence of European Jewry. I used to think I had to live up to my name. I thought I had to become Anatole Bloomberg, an importer-exporter from Rotterdam with a hook nose and flat feet, or an Antwerp diamond merchant wearing a skullcap, or a hunchbacked Talmudic scholar in a woolly black coat and shoes without shoelaces. Those are just three of the autobiographical projections I had to contend with. It was my name that caused the trouble, the Europeness of my name. Its Europicity.[78]

DeLillo's primary intention, however, moves beyond this

assertion of the creative power of the "word" to a judgment of language as an inadequate basis for our relationship to the objective world. Philosophers of language have taken two approaches to the limitations of language. Some feel that language itself is inadequate by reason of its vagueness, ambiguity, and context-dependence; others hold that ordinary language is perfectly suitable, and that the mischief lies in deviating from ordinary language without providing any way of attaching sense to the deviation.[79] DeLillo shares both skepticisms. The failure of ordinary language is manifested by the numerous clichés, which the author exposes as meaningless, contrasts to vital and significant language, revitalizes with a skillful twist, or satirizes by demonstrating how they cheapen experience and can lead to fraudulent action. The world of football is wonderfully appropriate as an arena for dissecting clichés, for no language is so fraught with them as sports jargon. DeLillo proves that even in sports reporting such overused terminology can be avoided by a sufficiently fertile imagination. Part two of the novel, for instance, contains the most inventive and vital description of a football game in American literature or journalism. In details throughout the rest of the novel the author is equally original. For example, when Gary says of one of his teammates, "He's the defensive captain. He captains the defense,"[80] he turns an innocuous but essentially unresonant phrase into a metaphor of the defensive team as ship or military unit. He does not change the connotations of "defensive captain" but rather restores its original meaning. DeLillo's comic touch is nearly perfect in his undercutting of clichés. When Gary, for example, complains of the "ambiguity of the whole business,"[81] he could not possibly be more ambiguous himself.

But if language is desensitized by overuse, it is likewise true that attempts to recreate language are often equally inadequate. The primary examples DeLillo uses for this abuse of language are the various jargons that dominate a technological society. The terminologies of business, electrical engineering, games theory, abstract philosophy, militarization, and space technology[82] are no more intelligible to the mass of mankind than is the complex jargon of football—"Blue turk right, double-slot zero snag delay." Billy Mast's course in the "untellable" is the reductio ad absurdum of language's loss of contact with reality, particularly in academic fields. One of the novel's characters includes in his list of barriers to communication "that of multiple definitions" and "that of terminologies which are untranslatable."[83] Both of these failures are demonstrated on the football field where the players themselves sometimes do not understand the jargon, and where one coach talks of "a planning procedures approach whereby we neutralize the defense," and another only screams, "I want you to bust ass out there today."[84] Neither coach communicates to his players how the job is actually to be done.

In view of these dual failures of language, DeLillo identifies the primary necessity for modern men:

> What we must know must be learned from blanked-out pages. To begin to reword the overflowing world. To subtract and disjoin. To re-recite the alphabet. To make elemental lists. To call something by its name and need no other sound.[85]

In other words, "A new way of life requires a new language."[86] Football becomes a metaphor for this necessary elemental revolution, because, in its simplest form, it is the most elemental and primitive of American team sports. When the season ends, the members of the team assemble one day for a game of football in the snow. It begins in playfulness but is continually simplified until the only tactics allowed are straight ahead dive plays, in which the players collide in "primal impact." The snow is so heavy that the players almost become part of the elements. This is a stunning metaphor for the primal healing effect and creative potential of violence. It is reinforced by Bloomberg's observation:

> We all know that life, happiness, fulfillment come surging out of particular forms of destructiveness. The moral system is enriched by violence put to positive use. But as the capacity for violence grows in the world, the regenerative effects of specific violent episodes becomes less significant.[87]

And Gary had observed earlier: "The universe was born in violence. Stars die violently. Elements are created out of cosmic violence."[88] Many writers have emphasized the destructive violence of football; DeLillo has more insightfully recognized the truer meaning of the sport. Football celebrates the ability of men to transcend the essential violence of existence, to create beauty and order where none seem possible.

Football in *End Zone* is the metaphor for positive violence, the kind of "violence" needed to recreate language and alter our perception of life. Such a regeneration is to be achieved by simplifying existence and harking back to primitive origins in order to recover the primal uses of language. The metaphor for the negative violence that overwhelms this possibility is war.

De Lillo does not see the excess of violence in modern America to be typified by football's likeness to war, as do such writers as Peter Gent in *North Dallas Forty*. Rather, the problem is the reverse, that war is treated too much like football. Major Staley, AFROTC professor at Logos College, speaks of "humane wars" as a solution to world problems: wars regulated by rules and limitations of megatonnage— "You'd practically have a referee and a timekeeper."[89] Such equation of war with games is an abomination—rather than limit wars, this approach makes war more possible because less apocalyptically terrifying. Staley approaches war as a game theorist,[90] sees Nagasaki as an "embarrassment to the art of war," and Hiroshima as supporting a "formula."[91] Such cold blindness to the human misery of combat is an inevitable outgrowth of the treatment of war as a game. When Staley plays a "war game" with Gary, the Major is terrified not by the imagined killing, but by the intrusion of reality in the sudden ringing of the telephone.

The language of warfare both contributes to this climate of violence and becomes the most striking example DeLillo uses for the inadequacy of language. Gary is fascinated by descriptions of global holocaust, as is Taft Robinson, whose particular obsession is reading about human atrocities such as those the Nazis perpetrated on the Jews. Neither of these men is sadistic or insensitive; rather, the language that describes these horrors is incapable of conveying any real misery. Instead, as Gary says, it becomes a cushion, a protective shield, between the individual and reality:

Major, there's no way to express thirty million dead. No
words. So certain men are recruited to reinvent the language.
... They [the words] don't explain, they don't clarify, they
don't express. They're pain killers. Everything becomes abstract. I admit it's fascinating in a way. I also admit the problem goes deeper than just saying some crypto-Goebbels in the
Pentagon is distorting the language.[92]

The problem goes deeper because language is distorted
everywhere. Language has become not a representation of
reality, but a buffer against it: a comfort like the clichés in
funeral eulogies[93] or a conscious evasion of communication
through words—" 'Don't use words,' Esther said. 'Either you
like her this way or you don't. You can't get out of it with
words.' "[94]

Words can either describe reality or camouflage it. The
world exists without language—"that other world, unsylla-
bled"[95] is objective reality not observed by men. But language
gives meaning to reality and patterns it; language produces
history. Linguists have observed that "the forms of a person's
thought are controlled by inexorable laws of pattern of which
he is unconscious,"[96] and these patterns, by extension, dictate action. Gary observes early in the novel: "Words move
the body into position. In time the position itself dictates
events."[97] On the metaphorical level of the novel, the calling
of a football play leads to the performance of the play; without such naming, the play cannot be run. Language thus
moves history and also becomes the only record of it; the
falsification of language, therefore, leads to "the lovely folly
of history," makes history "no more accurate than proph-
ecy."[98] Words can become traps: Myna Corbett is obsessed
with defining herself against some arbitrary standard of
"beauty"; Anatole Bloomberg cannot escape the burdens of
the word "jew." And anesthetized by the lies of language,
the whole world is moving toward global holocaust.

Language is based on pattern and order, as Edward Sapir
has observed: "At some point or other order asserts itself in
every language as the most fundamental of relation principles."[99] Football, "the one sport guided by language,"[100] is
likewise based on pattern and order, but objective reality
does not reflect these qualities. Football is an "illusion that

order is possible,"[101] and language has sustained the same illusion; to change history and correct the illusion, one must first change language. DeLillo attempts to do this on a small scale in his novel, but writers conscious of the need for a new language face a paradoxical problem. If language patterns inherited at birth dictate the patterns of a man's actions, how can a writer change those patterns through the medium of his inherited language? As Tony Tanner observes in *City of Words*:

> Any writer has to struggle with existing language which is perpetually tending to rigidify in old formulations and he must constantly assert his own patterning powers without at the same time becoming imprisoned in *them*.[102]

That DeLillo is conscious of this problem is clear in the novel's ambiguous conclusion. The final paragraph is this:

> In my room at five o'clock the next morning I drank half a cup of lukewarm water. It was the last of food or drink I would take for many days. High fevers burned a thin straight channel through my brain. In the end they had to carry me to the infirmary and feed me through plastic tubes.[103]

This ending can be viewed as a vision of defeat—admission that it is impossible to alter the course of history because the course of language is too firmly imbedded in our beings. We are doomed to remain "a nation devoted to human zerography."[104] But this concluding incident can also be seen as a retreat into the most extreme simplicity of existence, to a complete voiding of old forms, to an asceticism from which Gary can begin to generate something new. It can be a phoenix image of positive regenerative violence.

DeLillo does not attempt to solve this paradox with an easy answer. Myna Corbett earlier in the novel related a science fiction story that is an obvious allegory for the origin of language and its loss of contact with reality.[105] When Myna does not finish, the reader is left at the moment when language proves to be an inadequate basis for perfect order. DeLillo's similar failure to finish *his* story perhaps indicates his own lack of clear solutions, but he has made the reader aware throughout the novel of the primacy of language and the need for using it in an original manner. His novel itself is at least a tentative step toward reconstructing language into a truer description of reality; the author's "permanent duty," according to DeLillo, is "to unbox the lexicon for all eyes to see —a cyptic ticking mechanism in search of a revolution."[106]

The demythologizing trend in Coover's and DeLillo's novels appears to reach its ultimate expression in *The Great American Novel* (1973). Philip Roth has written of sport in earlier novels—the Patimkins of *Goodbye, Columbus* (1963) are defined for the readers as strangely sympathetic fools by their obsession with sports, and Alexander Portnoy finds in center field one of the few places of security, self-assurance, and simple "ease" in the midst of his anguished *Portnoy's Complaint* (1969)—but *The Great American Novel* is Roth's first full-length use of the sport of which he has been a fan for years. Roth's book is a comic extravaganza, a series of brilliant and hilarious set pieces, but an overlong novel unsustained by a sense of the author's control and direction. Roth's own avowed purpose in the novel was simply to allow his freewheeling imagination total liberty:

> The comedy here is not softened or mitigated by the familiar human presence it flows through and defines, nor does the book try to justify whatever is reckless about it by claiming some redeeming social or political value. It follows its own comic logic—the logic of farce, of burlesque, of slapstick— rather than the logic or demands of a political satire, or of an individual, "integrated" psychology.[107]

The comedy is indeed "reckless"—Roth is outrageously funny about such unfunny matters as racist stereotypes, physical handicaps, and mental illness—but the recklessness serves the underlying purpose of demythologizing America's sacred beliefs and thus making a serious statement about contemporary American life. His method is similar to Coover's though more explicitly comic. He tantalizes the reader with an overabundance of allusions and allegorical clues, inviting him to explain the book by identifying the underlying myth. By the end of the novel, the reader discovers there is no such myth to identify, and that all attempts end in dead ends, contradictions, or diffusion. The book is truly a demythologizing one, written for a demythologizing age.

The plot of the novel concerns the 1943 and 1944 seasons of the now defunct Patriot League, a third major league in addition to the more widely known American and National Leagues. The Rupert Mundys must play all their games on the road because their home park has been leased to the U.S. Government for use as an embarkation camp. The Mundys, with a fourteen-year-old second baseman, a fifty-two-year-old third sacker, a one-legged catcher, and a one-armed outfielder among other misfits and outcasts, stumble miserably through two seasons of road games and eventually to expulsion from baseball by the House Un-American Activities Committee. All records of the Mundys and the fifty-year history of the Patriot League are expunged from official chronicles. Only Word Smith, an eighty-seven-year-old former syndicated sports columnist, persists in combatting the official lies that deny the former existence of the Patriot League. As one reviewer observes, Roth is "trying to work conspiracy theories against myths, explode them both, and all the energy of paranoia is devoted to doing the job."[108]

The theme of the novel is not nearly as important as the fun of getting there. The book is in one sense a parodic history of American baseball. The characters are named after heathen gods and heroes from an incredible number of cultures: Hindu, Greek, Norse, Semitic, Canaanite, Sumerian, Celtic, Iranian, Aztec, Icelandic, Slavic, Japanese, and even Easter Island. The naming of characters is not simply haphazard, as at least one reviewer has claimed,[109] but often betrays a comic purpose. Agni is the Hindu god of self-perfection, and Roland Agni is plagued by the world's refusal to admit his excellence. Baal was the chief Canaanite god, and John Baal was known as the "Babe Ruth of the Big House" when he played prison baseball; but Baal was also Lord of Rain and Dew, and John's father, Spit Baal, was a hilariously raunchy practitioner of his special art. The name of the Sumerian deity, Damu, means "the Child," and Nickname Damur is a fourteen-year-old second baseman. Rama is the Hindu god of reason, right action, and virtue—the opposite qualities of Mike Rama who repeatedly runs into outfield fences while chasing fly balls. Many others, too, are appropriately titled.[110]

In addition, figures familiar to all baseball fans appear in slightly altered guises. The ghosts of Bonehead Fred Merkle and Shoeless Joe Jackson are prominent in the novel. The Gas House Gang of the St. Louis Cardinals of the thirties becomes the Whore House Gang in Roth's novel. Mike Rama's collisions with the outfield fence recall Pete Reiser, the former Dodger. Bud Parusha is one of three ballplaying brothers, like the DiMaggios; but also, like Pete Gray of the old St. Louis Browns, he has only one arm. His severest handicap arises when, attempting to get the ball from his glove to his hand to throw it to the infield, the ball becomes caught between his teeth for an "inside-the-mouth-home run." Parusha also mimics the famous incident in which Babe Ruth hit a home run for a hospitalized youngster. With his limitations, however, Bud can only hope

> to get a base hit for him the next time they threw him anything good . . . every six or seven times at bat, he managed to smack a single, and then from the loud speaker there would be the announcement that Bud's hit had been "for" so-and-so in such-and-such a hospital, and the fans would smile and clap.[111]

Such irreverence is typical of the tone throughout the novel. The black baseball leagues are represented by teams nicknamed the Boll Weevils, the Rastuses, and the Shiftless Nine, and by their owner, Aunt Jemima. The Latin winter baseball leagues are reduced to the Mosquito Coast League of Nicaragua. The most outrageous character of all is Frank Mazuma—club owner, entrepreneur, and con man, who combines elements of Branch Rickey and particularly Bill Veeck. His exploits include hiring a midget as a pinchhitter, trading another midget pitcher for a one-legged outfielder, pitting a player against a horse in a race around the base paths, and having his mother—herself a parody of Ty Cobb honing his spikes—attempt to steal second base on Hothead Ptah, who reputedly "couldn't throw out his own mother." These incidents are scarcely more spectacular than Veeck's actual career. He too hired a midget, Eddie Gaedel, to pinchhit for the St. Louis Browns in 1951; he sold Hal Peck, a three-toed outfielder (called a "one-legged outfielder" by his purchaser) to another club; he had a pitcher, Early Wynn, who claimed he would dust off his own mother if she were digging in too much; and he introduced clowns, fireworks, and circus acts to the game of baseball. It is said of Frank Mazuma that he "could out-bizarre you any day of the week,"[112] and his commercial approach to baseball is burlesqued by the names of his children—Jack, Buck, Gelt, Dinero, and Doubloon. Bill Veeck's similar philosophy is summed up in a chapter of his autobiography, *Veeck—As in Wreck* (1962), entitled "Every Day Was Mardi Gras . . .":

> We have never operated on the theory that a city owes anything to the owner of a baseball franchise, out of civic pride, patriotic fervor or compelling national interest. Baseball has sold itself as a civic monument for so long that it has come to believe its own propaganda. *There is nothing owed to you.* A baseball team is a commercial venture, operating for a profit. The idea that you don't have to package your product as attractively as General Motors packages its product and hustle your product the way General Motors hustles its product, is baseball's most pernicious enemy.[113]

Roth would agree wholeheartedly.

Although this rewriting of baseball history is farcical, baseball is not the primary object of Roth's satire, but only the central metaphor for broader satirical interests. As he states:

> It was not a matter of demythologizing baseball—there was nothing in that to get fired up about—but of discovering in baseball the means to dramatize *the struggle* between the benign national myth of itself that a great power prefers to perpetuate, and the relentlessly insidious, very nearly demonic reality . . . that simply will not give an inch in behalf of that idealized mythology.[114]

Baseball provides one example of such a benign national myth. The Patriot League, like America, claims to be sustained by 100 percent Americanism (General Oakhart), piety (Mister Fairsmith), and puritanical integrity (Mike the Mouth Masterson), but these forces are at variance with the capitalistic greed of the Mundy brothers, the cheap publicity methods of Frank Mazuma, and the corruption of such players as the Whore House Gang. Baseball mythology reinforces the illusion that such negatives do not exist. Referring to the memories of old timers, Smitty observes:

> Ninety-nine per cent of their baseball "memories," ninety-nine per cent of the anecdotes and stories they recollect and repeat are pure hogwash, tiny morsels of truth so coated over with discredited legend and senile malarkey, so impacted, you might say, in the turds of time, as to rival the tales of ancient mythology. What the aged can do with the past is enough to make your hairs stand on end. But then look at the delusions that ordinary people have about the day before yesterday.[115]

Baseball thus provides the model for the other forms of myth-making debunked in the novel.

As a nation, America is plagued by an obsessive need to mythologize. Lacking an inherited national mythology which grew during centuries of semi-literacy, we have consistently tried to create one. American writers have shared this need to define their country once and for all. The title of Roth's book recalls the quest by American writers of the past century-and-a-quarter to write the great American novel, and Roth has filled his with a cornucopia of literary put-downs. The satires on Hawthorne, who wrote about a "tough cunt," Melville and his "book about blubber," Twain, who described the "Great American Daydream," as well as James, Hemingway, Anderson, Wolfe, and others have little organic function beyond the farcical. But they do fit into Roth's underlying purpose; he attacks these conscious attempts to mythologize, and thus attacks that obsession with writing "great books" that often ruins good books.[116] *Moby Dick* provides the primary model of a Great American Novel—Roth's novel opens with the parodic line, "Call me Smitty"; baseball is associated with whaling as the subject for a Great American Novel; the players are introduced individually as Melville introduces the mates of the *Pequod*; the bats are harpoons; the technology of the ball mirrors Melville's cetology chapters; summaries precede each chapter as in *Moby Dick*; Smitty virtually disappears as a narrator as Ishmael does; and like Ishmael he is the sole survivor of the Patriot League. Melville's other books are even burlesqued; the Mundys' tour of opponents' emblematic cities is reminiscent of *Mardi,* and the African natives to whom Mister Fairsmith tries to introduce American baseball, cry at various times, "Omoo" and "Typee." But there is little method to this madness. The Melvillean elements are scattered haphazardly through the book. Gil Gamesh is termed the novel's Ahab, yet he is a minor character until the last chapter and is the hero of his own parodied epic; it is Frank Mazuma, not Gil, whose daughter is "Doubloon." Roth explains, "Smitty's book, like those of his illustrious forebears, attempts to imagine a myth of an ailing America,"[117] but the reading of his literary parodies offers no sense of this; they are merely playfully funny. In addition to ridiculing specific American writers, Roth sprinkles the novel with hyperbolic alliteration, commentary on the alphabet (the Big Twenty-Six), baseball idioms in common use, deathbed speeches popular in sentimental fiction, and references to Homer (Sy Clops, the one-eyed pitcher), the Chanson de Roland, Chaucer, Shakespeare, and Russian novelists—without any attempt to incorporate the literary material into the basic baseball story, or even to establish a pattern in the references.

The myth of an ailing America *is* central to *The Great American Novel,* however; the religious and political implications of Roth's satire are obvious. Religious mythology is deflated just as much as literary pretension is. Baseball as the country's religion, with its ballparks as American holy places, and Cooperstown as the goal for American pilgrimages in the Holy Baseball Empire,[118] provides the material for Roth's religious satire, just as it did for Coover's. Parodies of biblical passages; of religious platitudes and proselytizing; of the crucifixion, the Eucharist, the temptation of Christ in the desert, the prodigal son—even of Billy Graham—are scattered throughout the novel. Christianity, Judaism, African pagan rites, the ancient religions represented by the names of their chief gods and heroes such as Gilgamesh, and even patriotism as a religion are satirized through baseball metaphors. The most hilarious mixture of baseball, religion, and politics occurs when Mister Fairsmith, a "zealous Christian-imperialist-missionary-cum-salesman,"[119] attempts to convert African tribesmen to the American baseball religion. The ritual qualities of baseball apparently appeal to the Africans, whose children hunt for boiled baseballs as at an Easter Egg hunt, whose virgin daughters are ceremoniously deflowered with baseball bats, and whose old crones have their own "old-timers day" with the discarded clubs. The villagers eat boiled baseball gloves, spitting out only the metal eyelets; and the men prove to be typical Little League fathers brow-beating their sons for failure to hit the enemy skulls pitched to them.

Other American sacred cows receive similar treatment. American Moms are ridiculed in scenes of the "Mundy Mommys" (Jewish mothers), of Frank Mazuma's mother who steals second with her spikes high and smells like "a shrimp boat docking" when she raises her leg, and particularly of the "pink and blue" district of Kakoola, Wisconsin, which simultaneously parodies the American male's mother-fixation and the low respect for motherhood in radical feminism. Psychoanalysis, the Wild West, sentimental underdogism, and the American dream of success are similarly mocked.

The final chapter brings political satire into the foreground for the first time. American political ideology has been pilloried beside the other butts of Roth's jokes throughout the novel. American heroes have been seen to be "petty, grudging, vengeful, gloating, selfish, narrow, and mean." The national anthem is merely a pacifier for irate baseball fans.[120] But the final chapter is devoted solely to politics. Politics, Roth seems to say, is the largest source of mythmaking in America, and political myths about "the enemies of America" and such matters are singularly destructive. When Gil Gamesh returns from exile to expose a communist plot to infiltrate the Patriot League, political paranoia becomes a major theme. The House Un-American Activities Committee finds "evidence" of communist infiltration everywhere in the league and immediately disbands it. The identity of Gil himself is never certain—he might be an agent or even a double or triple agent, but perhaps he is just an individual seeking personal revenge for his earlier banishment.

Thus, although the satire is more focused in this chapter, the "truth" is as obscured as ever. By finally anchoring the chaotic narration in the HUAC, Roth attempts, as he himself says:

> to establish at the conclusion of the book a kind of passage-way from the imaginary that seems real to the real that seems imaginary, a continuum between the credible incredible and the incredible credible.[121]

Even though Roth's explanation sounds plausible, the novel does not work in that way. This final section is unconvincing and even boring, and it violates the logic of comic reckless-ness that governs the rest of the novel. *The Great American Novel* is perhaps the most telling instance of the fact that sports fiction by its very nature demands recognition of cer-tain formal requirements. The course of a single season, as has been observed before, is a "lifetime" with its beginning, middle, and end. To include two such lifetimes or seasons in a baseball novel, as Roth does, risks violating the readers' natural expectations to a degree that makes the second sea-son appear simply an anti-climactic appendage. Such is, in fact, the case with *The Great American Novel*. Roth should have been content with one Patriot League season; he tried to do too much with too little control and the first part of the book does not require this last chapter for completion. A shorter *Great American Novel* could have been a highly successful burlesque of American mythmaking.

Smitty's statement, "Truth is stranger than fiction, but stranger still are lies,"[122] recognizes the difference between the harmless fictions of comic writers and the destructive lies of national myths. A myth that inhibits corrective action for American ills or which initiates greater ills becomes far more destructive than any act of violence. Roth's purpose is to demythologize such myths and to demonstrate the ab-sence in America in the seventies of any myth that is self-sustaining and consistent with reality. He even undercuts his own novel, which is itself a myth. Attributing the novel to Smitty calls into question its truthfulness—his incredible sto-ry does appear believable within the framework of its comic logic, but Smitty could be simply a paranoid fantasist. Unlike the writers of other great American novels, Roth does not claim to know what America is really like—not knowing is a condition of being an American. As Roth observes, Smitty's book attempts to imagine a myth of an ailing America; "my own is to some extent an attempt to imagine a book about imagining that American myth."[123]

Roth's novel seems to be a dead end for the mythical treatment of sport, for he not only debunks specific myths, but deflates myth as myth. He also may have written the only sports novel without a hero—one cause for the shapelessness of the book at its center, but also a symptom of an age that seems devoid of heroes. The reader is left at the end of the novel wondering if the possibilities for sports fiction opened up by Malamud in 1952 have become closed again by an age that cannot sustain myths. Such is not the case, however. Malamud, Coover, DeLillo, and Roth did not exhaust the mythic possibilities in sports fiction, but rather have made writers much more self-conscious about their handling of myth. Jerome Charyn's *The Seventh Babe* (1979), for example, weds *The Natural* to Gabriel Garcia Marquez's *One Hundred Years of Solitude*, creating a mythic baseball fantasy in which the sport is recognizable but everything about it is enchanted, in which historical facts are embroidered with fantastic trappings. It is the story of Babe Ragland, who appears as a left-handed third baseman with the hapless Boston Red Sox in 1932 and who happens to be the seventh player in the big leagues named Babe. Rags claims to be an orphan from the same reform school that kept Babe Ruth; only later do we discover that he is Cedric Tannehill, heir of a copper and ranching millionaire, who will sacrifice everything for the chance to play baseball. The seventh Babe is a magician in the field, charging bunts, trapping every ball between himself and second base, and chasing flies all the way to the left field fence. When he is banned from baseball on trumped-up charges, he joins the Cincinnati Colored Giants, the true world champions of baseball, a barnstorming team of black desperadoes who are also the finest players in the land. Rags' constant companion is Scarborough, a hunchbacked bat boy and first baseman; he and his teammates live in seven Buick and Hudson roadsters, touring the country, building their own ball fields wherever they stop, then whipping the opposition whether local yokels or major league all-stars. The Giants survive the Depression, World War II, and raids by major league owners to sign black ballplayers, always finding enough opponents to supply themselves with sardines to eat, apparently the minimum necessary for life. In the novel's final chapter, Rags' team defeats an Amherst summer-school pickup nine, with Rags still playing third base at age 72. He has become a true magician, conjuring with his voodoo root inherited from the Giants' previous witch-doctor to keep away bad weather and local sheriffs and to keep intact his gnarled hands and legs so that he can continue to do the one thing that matters in his life—play baseball. He has become "an old wizard in kneepants, defying nature with a root."[124] Charyn appropriates baseball's actual history—both the official record of the major leagues for the past six decades and the less official saga of black barnstorming teams—and transforms it into a folkloristic fantasy in which the only restraint is the limit of the author's imagination. Ghosts, dwarfs, naked fat-lady boxers, and titanic ballplayers share the scenes with historical figures such as Babe Ruth and Judge Kenesaw Mountain Landis. Baseball provides the likeliest setting for such excursions into fantasy and fairy tale by an American writer, for its actual history, as Malamud was the first to show, often seems itself enchanted. Charyn makes no comments on America's formative myths, but simply "tells a story," as stories were once told by wandering bards. *The Seventh Babe* seems the sort of oral tale that might have been recited in a great hall a dozen centuries ago to a preliterate audience who still believed that magic was part of life.

The possibilities for American sports fiction have not been blighted, then, despite our recent history. The vagaries of the marketplace, of course, affect sports fiction as much as any other kind of literature, as is clear from a glance at the sports novels that have appeared in the past half-dozen years. Publishers attempt to capitalize on popular trends, however they may arise. The emergence in the seventies of tennis as a major spectator and participatory sport among the relatively affluent led, not unexpectedly, to the appearance of numerous uninspired tennis novels intended to capture the spirit of

jet-setting international stars' glamorous lives. Novels such
as *World Class* (1975) by Jane and Burt Boyar, *The Players*
(1975) by Gary Brandner, and *Break Point* (1978) by William Brinkley did not attain the popularity for which their publishers undoubtedly hoped, however. As terrorists became the
newest stars in crime and mystery fiction, several writers
incorporated terrorist melodrama into their sports novels.
Snipers at Wimbledon (Russell Braddon's *The Finalists* [1977])
and at the Super Bowl (George LaFountaine's *Two-Minute
Warning* [1975]) and bombers at the Super Bowl (Thomas Harris's *Black Sunday* [1975]) were intended to reach au-
diences not hitherto attracted to sports fiction. The one true
bestseller of the seventies—Dan Jenkins' *Semi-Tough* (1972)
—spawned numerous clones in comic, erotic novels such as
Alphabet Jackson (1974) by Jack Olsen, *Fall Guy* (1978) by
Jay Cronley, and *Breaking Balls* (1979) by Marty Bell.

Such attempts to capture a mass readership comprise the
bulk of the sports fiction—or of any kind of fiction—in any period, but the post-Roth era has also seen the appearance of
more satisfying sports literature. John Sayles' *Pride of the
Bimbos* (1975) and Lamar Herrin's *The Rio Loja Ringmaster*
(1977) are two first novels that reveal originality. Sayles' novel has little to do with sport, but it uses a midget shortstop
and his five-man carnival softball team playing exhibitions
in drag to explore the characters' sense of manhood and attempts to prove they have "balls." In the past two years alone
(1979-80), the number of sports novels published, many of
them quite good, is a clear indication that the genre is alive
and well. Al Young's *Ask Me Now* (1980) is a fine novel of a
black basketball player's adjustment to retirement and to
his wife and children, one of whom is a jazz musician. Young
works the analogy between basketball and jazz very well.
Mark Harris's fourth Henry Wiggin novel, *It Looked Like
For Ever,* plus Philip O'Connor's *Stealing Home,* Paul Hemphill's *Long Gone,* and Jerome Charyn's *The Seventh Babe,*
make 1979 a particularly fruitful year for baseball fiction.
Among other sports novels that appeared in 1979-80, the
sports mystery continued its recent vogue with John Redgate's *The Last Decathlon,* Charles Brady's *Seven Games in
October,* and Shannon O'Cork's *Sports Freak;* a noted television newsman, Edwin Newman, wrote a comic boxing novel,

Sunday Punch; and two sports hitherto graced by little fictional treatment—handball and high-school wrestling—produced *Kill Shot* by Tom Alibrandi and *Vision Quest* by Terry Davis. The quality of these books is not uniformly high, but a number of them are quite good. The appearance of two favorably reviewed first novels, one by a university professor (O'Connor) and the other by a journalist (Hemphill), is particularly noteworthy, but so, too, is the fact that two long-established writers, Jerome Charyn and Al Young, made baseball and basketball the subjects of their thirteenth and fourth novels, respectively. Prejudice clearly no longer exists against sport as a topic for "serious" fiction.

These novels published between 1974 and 1980 reveal the range of interests among writers of sports fiction. Currently fashionable sports, as well as the latest vogues in popular fiction, have their expected impact on sports novels, while the more ambitious writers attempt more originality in subject or treatment. But the weight of the tradition created by Jack London, Ring Lardner, Bernard Malamud, Mark Harris, and hundreds of others also sends the most recent writers back to the timeless themes that are the essence of sport's meaning in America. Of the recent novels, *Long Gone* particularly reveals the endurance of the sports-fiction tradition that this study has examined. The novel is virtually a compendium of traditional motifs plus currently popular elements blended into the raunchy-comic mold so successful in Jenkins' *Semi-Tough*—a combination that makes the story pleasantly predictable. The subject is Class D baseball in the Alabama-Florida League in the 1950s, in particular the Graceville Oilers, a woebegone collection of "skittering unwanted rookies earning a hundred fifty dollars a month and a scattering of scaly old pros . . . waiting for the other shoe to drop."[125] The Oilers are sort of redneck Rupert Mundys, transformed into pennant contenders but going nowhere nonetheless. The aging veteran with "a great future behind [him]"[126] and the innocent rookie initiated into debauchery as well as baseball are portrayed by thirty-nine-year-old Stud Cantrell and eighteen-year-old Jamie Weeks; the country towns of the Florida Panhandle and rural Alabama provide both the setting and the style of play. The evocation of 1950s baseball in the lower minor leagues nostalgically renders one period of the game's history. Stud, the player-manager who drinks, swears, and chases women, but is a lovable sentimentalist deep down inside, is a baseball-playing Billy Clyde Puckett, as well as a good ol' boy of the style popularized by Burt Reynolds in numerous recent movies. A run-in with the Ku Klux Klan over a slugging black catcher passing as a Venezuelan recalls William Brashler's *Bingo Long;* Q. Talmadge Raney and the other arrogant team owners forcing Stud to throw the pennant resurrect Malamud's *The Natural* and ultimately the Black Sox of 1919. The nostalgia for baseball of a "long gone" era when eccentricity seems to have been the norm rather than the exception suggests several baseball novels, particularly *Bingo Long.*

Long Gone reveals the appeal of successful formulas rather than the possibilities of invention in the genre, but other novels such as Herrin's *The Rio Loja Ringmaster* and Charyn's *The Seventh Babe* announce that more ambitious sports fiction is alive and well, too. But however outlandish the superficial setting of the sports novels of the past half-decade, the underlying themes inevitably focus on the hero, country and city, youth and age, sexual roles and relationships, and history and myth in ways that recall the many sports novels written over nearly a century. The tradition that began with Gilbert Patten continues with new heirs and awaits more to come. Despite seemingly drastic alterations in the major organized sports in the past decade, brought about by increased commercialization and technological "advancements," sport continues to play a prominent role in American culture. Sport has the capacity to move us as few things can. It transcends class lines and race lines to pinpoint a commonality shared by a large number of Americans— a bond not just of shared pleasures but of national identity. The fact that writers in increasing numbers are recognizing the essential American-ness of our sports culture, and that among those numbers are several of our best young novelists, virtually guarantees the continued appearance of superior sports literature for years to come. After more than eighty years of sports novels, the prospects for the genre today are more promising than ever.

Appendix:
A Checklist of
American Sports Fiction

The following is primarily a list of sports novels published in America through 1980. Short stories are not included, with the exception of collections of stories by a single author. Stories appearing in nineteenth-century dime novels and juvenile magazines, often termed "novels" in the periodicals, are included because they comprise almost all of the sports fiction before 1896. The book-length reprint editions of the Frank Merriwell series by Gilbert Patten ("Burt L. Standish") are included, rather than the original magazine titles. No attempt is made to differentiate between juvenile and adult fiction. In most cases the intended audience is obvious, but novels written for adolescents and novels meant for an adult readership are not always clearly distinguishable.

Alexander, Holmes. *Dust in the Afternoon.* New York: Harper, 1940.

Algren, Nelson. *Never Come Morning.* New York: Harper, 1942.

Alibrandi, Tom. *Kill Shot.* Los Angeles: Pinnacle, 1979.

Allen, Alex B.
  Basketball Toss Up. Chicago: Whitman, 1973.
  No Place for Baseball. Chicago: Whitman, 1973.
  Fifth Down. Chicago: Whitman, 1974.
  The Tennis Menace. Chicago: Whitman, 1975.
Allen, Merritt Parmalee. *Tied in the Ninth.* New York: Century, 1930.
Allison, Bob and Frank E. Hill. *The Kid Who Batted 1,000.* Garden City, N.Y.: Doubleday, 1953.
Alton, Everett. *Gridiron Courage.* Chicago: Wilcox & Follett, 1949.
Ames, Joseph B. *Torrance from Texas.* New York: Century, 1921.
Archer, Jay. Joint author, see Joseph Olgin.
Archibald, Joe.
  Rebel Halfback. Philadelphia: Westminster, 1947.
  Touchdown Glory. Philadelphia: Westminster, 1949.
  Hold that Line! Philadelphia: Macrae-Smith, 1950.
  Inside Tackle. Philadelphia: Macrae-Smith, 1951.
  Block that Kick. Philadelphia: Macrae-Smith, 1953.
  Fighting Coach. Philadelphia: Macrae-Smith, 1954.
  Double Play Rookie. Philadelphia: Macrae-Smith, 1955.
  Fullback Fury. Philadelphia: Macrae-Smith, 1955.
  Full Count. Philadelphia: Macrae-Smith, 1955.
  Go, Navy, Go. Philadelphia: Macrae-Smith, 1956.
  Circus Catch. Philadelphia: Macrae-Smith, 1957.
  Mr. Slingshot. Philadelphia: Macrae-Smith, 1957.
  Catcher's Choice. Philadelphia: Macrae-Smith, 1958.
  Fight, Team, Fight. Philadelphia: Macrae-Smith, 1958.
  Bonus Kid. Philadelphia: Macrae-Smith, 1959.
  Falcons to the Fight. Philadelphia: Macrae-Smith, 1959.
  First Base Hustler. Philadelphia: Macrae-Smith, 1960.
  Crazy Legs McBain. Philadelphia: Macrae-Smith, 1961.
  Outfield Orphan. Philadelphia: Macrae-Smith, 1961.
  Red-Dog Center. Philadelphia: Macrae-Smith, 1962.
  Shortstop on Wheels. Philadelphia: Macrae-Smith, 1962.
  Backfield Twins. Philadelphia: Macrae-Smith, 1963.
  Big League Busher. Philadelphia: Macrae-Smith, 1963.
  Hard Nosed Halfback. Philadelphia: Macrae-Smith, 1963.
  Old Iron Glove. Philadelphia: Macrae-Smith, 1964.

Quarterback and Son. Philadelphia: Macrae-Smith, 1964.

The Easy Out. Philadelphia: Macrae-Smith, 1965.

Southpaw Speed. Philadelphia: Macrae-Smith, 1965.

West Point Wingback. Philadelphia: Macrae-Smith, 1965.

The Long Pass. Philadelphia: Macrae-Smith; 1966.

Right Field Rookie. Philadelphia: Macrae-Smith, 1967.

The Scrambler. Philadelphia: Macrae-Smith, 1967.

Fast Break Fury. Philadelphia: Macrae-Smith, 1968.

Mitt Maverick. Philadelphia: Macrae-Smith, 1968.

Pro Coach. Philadelphia: Macrae-Smith, 1969.

Two Time Rookie. Philadelphia: Macrae-Smith, 1969.

Backcourt Commando. Philadelphia: Macrae-Smith, 1970.

Powerback. Philadelphia: Macrae-Smith, 1970.

Payoff Pitch. Philadelphia: Macrae-Smith, 1971.

Phantom Blitz. Philadelphia: Macrae-Smith, 1972.

Right Field Runt. Philadelphia: Macrae-Smith, 1972.

The Fifth Base. Philadelphia: Macrae-Smith, 1973.

Three-Point Hero. Philadelphia: Macrae-Smith, 1973.

Centerfield Rival. Philadelphia: Macrae-Smith, 1974.

Asinof, Eliot.

Man on Spikes. New York: McGraw-Hill, 1955.

Say It Ain't So, Gordon Littlefield. New York: Dutton, 1977.

Austin, Howard. "The Flyers of the Gridiron; or, Half-Back Harry, the Football Champion." *Luck and Pluck* No. 651 (23 November 1910).

Baldwin, Thomas. *Kickoff!* Chicago: Goldsmith, 1932.

Balliol, Anne. Joint author; see Dr. Ralph E. Hopton.

Bancroft, Edith.

Jane Allen of the Scrub Team. New York: Cupples & Leon, 1917.

Jane Allen: Right Guard. New York: Cupples & Leon, 1918.

Jane Allen: Center. New York: Cupples & Leon, 1920.

Jane Allen: Junior. New York: Cupples & Leon, 1921.

Jane Allen: Senior. New York: Cupples & Leon, 1922.

Barbour, Ralph Henry.

The Half-Back. New York: Appleton, 1899.

For the Honor of the School. New York: Appleton, 1900.
Behind the Line. New York: Appleton, 1902.
Weatherby's Inning. New York: Appleton, 1903.
On Your Mark. New York: Appleton, 1904.
The Crimson Sweater. New York: Appleton, 1906.
The Spirit of the School. New York: Appleton, 1907.
Forward Pass. New York: Appleton, 1908.
Double Play. New York: Appleton, 1909.
Kingsford, Quarter. New York: Appleton, 1910.
The New Boy at Hilltop, and Other Stories. New York: Appleton, 1910.
Winning His "Y." New York: Appleton, 1910.
Finkler's Field. New York: Appleton, 1911.
For Yardley. New York: Appleton, 1911.
Team-Mates. New York: Century, 1911.
Change Signals. New York: Appleton, 1912.
Crofton Chums. New York: Century, 1912.
Around the End. New York: Appleton, 1913.
The Junior Trophy. New York: Appleton, 1913.
The Brother of a Hero. New York: Appleton, 1914.
Left End Edwards. New York: Dodd, Mead, 1914.
Danforth Plays the Game. New York: Appleton, 1915.
Left Tackle Thayer. New York: Dodd, Mead, 1915.
The Lucky Seventh. New York: Appleton, 1915.
Left Guard Gilbert. New York: Dodd, Mead, 1916.
The Purple Pennant. New York: Appleton, 1916.
Rivals for the Team. New York: Appleton, 1916.
The Secret Play. New York: Appleton, 1916.
Center Rush Rowland. New York: Dodd, Mead, 1917.
Hitting the Line. New York: Appleton, 1917.
Winning His Game. New York: Appleton, 1917.
Keeping His Course. New York: Appleton, 1918.
Fullback Foster. New York: Dodd, Mead, 1919.
Guarding His Goal. New York: Appleton, 1919.
The Play that Won. New York: Appleton, 1919.
Quarter-Back Bates. New York: Dodd, Mead, 1920.
Kick Formation. New York: Appleton, 1921.
Left Half Harmon. New York: Dodd, Mead, 1921.
Three-Base Benson. New York: Appleton, 1921.
Tod Hale on the Nine. New York: Dodd, Mead, 1921.

Right End Emerson. New York: Dodd, Mead, 1922.

The Turner Twins. New York: Century, 1922.

For the Good of the Team. New York: Appleton, 1923.

Nid and Nod. New York: Appleton, 1923.

Right Guard Grant. New York: Dodd, Mead, 1923.

The Fighting Scrub. New York: Appleton, 1924.

Follow the Ball. New York: Appleton, 1924.

Infield Rivals. New York: Appleton, 1924.

Right Tackle Todd. New York: Dodd, Mead, 1924.

Barry Locke, Halfback. New York: Century, 1925.

Bases Full. New York: Appleton, 1925.

Hold 'em Wyndham! New York: Appleton, 1925.

Right Half Hollins. New York: Dodd, Mead, 1925.

The Last Play. New York: Appleton, 1926.

The Winning Year. New York: Appleton, 1926.

The Long Pass. New York: Appleton, 1927.

The Relief Pitcher. Boston: Little, Brown, 1927.

The Fortunes of the Team. Boston: Houghton Mifflin, 1928.

Hunt Holds the Center. New York: Appleton, 1928.

Lovell Leads Off. New York: Appleton, 1928.

Substitute Jimmy. New York: Century, 1928.

Tod Hale on the Scrub. New York: Dodd, Mead, 1928.

Grantham Gets On. New York: Appleton, 1929.

Candidate for the Line. New York: Appleton, 1930.

Danby's Error. New York: Cosmopolitan Book Corporation, 1931.

Fourth Down! New York: Appleton, 1931.

The Fumbled Pass. New York: Appleton, 1931.

Squeeze Play. New York: Appleton, 1931.

The Cub Battery. New York: Appleton, 1932.

Skate, Glendale! New York: Farrar & Rinehart, 1932.

Beaton Runs the Mile. New York: Appleton, 1933.

Goal to Go. New York: Appleton-Century, 1933.

The Scoring Play. New York: Appleton-Century, 1934.

Southworth Scores. New York: Appleton-Century, 1934.

The Glendale Five. New York: Farrar & Rinehart, 1935.

Merritt Leads the Nine. New York: Appleton-Century, 1936.

Watch That Pass! New York: Appleton-Century, 1936.

The School That Didn't Care. New York: Appleton-Century, 1937.

The Score Is Tied. New York: Appleton-Century, 1937.

Fighting Guard. New York: Appleton-Century, 1938.

Ninth Inning Rally. New York: Appleton-Century, 1940.

The Infield Twins. New York: Appleton-Century, 1941.

The Target Pass. New York: Appleton-Century, 1941.

Barclay Back. New York: Appleton, 1942.

Barker, Robert. *Love Forty.* New York: Lippincott, 1975.

Barnes, Sam G. *Ready, Wrestle!* New York: Ariel Books, 1965.

Barrett, Richmond. *Truant.* New York: Dutton, 1944.

Barton, George.

The Bell Haven Nine. Philadelphia: Winston, 1914.

The Bell Haven Eleven. Philadelphia: Winston, 1915.

The Bell Haven Five. Philadelphia: Winston, 1915.

Beaumont, Gerald. *Hearts and the Diamond.* New York: Dodd, Mead, 1921.

Beckham, Barry. *Runner Mack.* New York: Morrow, 1972.

Bee, Clair.

Championship Ball. New York: Grosset & Dunlap, 1948.

Touchdown Pass. New York: Grosset & Dunlap, 1948.

Clutch Hitter! New York: Grosset & Dunlap, 1949.

Strike Three! New York: Grosset & Dunlap, 1949.

Hoop Crazy. New York: Grosset & Dunlap, 1950.

Pitchers' Duel. New York: Grosset & Dunlap, 1950.

A Pass and a Prayer. New York: Grosset & Dunlap, 1951.

Dugout Jinx. New York: Grosset & Dunlap, 1952.

Freshman Quarterback. New York: Grosset & Dunlap, 1952.

Backboard Fever. New York: Grosset & Dunlap, 1953.

Fence Busters. New York: Grosset & Dunlap, 1953.

Ten Seconds to Play! New York: Grosset & Dunlap, 1955.

Fourth Down Showdown. New York: Grosset & Dunlap, 1956.

Tournament Crisis. New York: Grosset & Dunlap, 1957.

Hardcourt Upset. New York: Grosset & Dunlap, 1958.

Pay-Off Pitch. New York: Grosset & Dunlap, 1958.

No-Hitter. New York: Grosset & Dunlap, 1959.

Triple-Threat Trouble. New York: Grosset & Dunlap, 1960.

Backcourt Ace. New York: Grosset & Dunlap, 1961.

Buzzer Basket. New York: Grosset & Dunlap, 1962.

Comeback Cagers. New York: Grosset & Dunlap, 1963.

Home Run Feud. New York: Grosset & Dunlap, 1964.

Hungry Hurler. New York: Grosset & Dunlap, 1966.

Bell, Marty. *Breaking Balls.* New York: New American Library, 1979.

Berra, Yogi and Til Ferndenzi. *Behind the Plate.* Larchmont, N.Y.: Argonaut, 1962.

Berry, Eliot. *Four Quarters Make a Season.* New York: Brown, 1973.

Bethell, Jean. *Barney Beagle Plays Baseball.* New York: Grosset & Dunlap, 1963.

Bierman, Bernie. *Brick Barton and His Winning Eleven.* New York: Dutton, 1938.

Bishop, Curtis K.

Teamwork. Austin, Tex.: Steck, 1942.

Banjo Hitter. Austin, Tex.: Steck, 1951.

Saturday Heroes. Austin, Tex.: Steck, 1951.

Football Fever. Austin, Tex.: Steck, 1952.

Hero at Halfback. Austin, Tex.: Steck, 1953.

Larry of the Little League. Philadelphia: Lippincott, 1953.

Fighting Quarterback. Austin, Tex.: Steck, 1954.

Larry Leads Off. Austin, Tex.: Steck, 1955.

Goal to Go. Austin, Tex.: Steck, 1955.

Larry Comes Home. Austin, Tex.: Steck, 1955.

Dribble Up. Austin, Tex.: Steck, 1956.

Half-Time Hero. Austin, Tex.: Steck, 1956.

Little Leaguer. Austin, Tex.: Steck, 1956.

The Little League Way. Austin,Tex.: Steck, 1957.

Lank of the Little League. Philadelphia: Lippincott, 1958.

Little League Heroes. Philadelphia: Lippincott, 1960.

The Lost Eleven. Austin, Tex.: Steck, 1960.

The Playmaker. Austin, Tex.: Steck, 1960.

Sideline Pass. Philadelphia: Lippincott, 1960.

Sideline Quarterback. Philadelphia: Lippincott, 1960.

Little League Double Play. Philadelphia: Lippincott, 1962.

Rebound. Philadelphia: Lippincott, 1962.

The Big Game. Austin, Tex.: Steck, 1963.

Field Goal. Philadelphia: Lippincott, 1964.

Little League Amigo. Philadelphia: Lippincott, 1964.

Lonesome End. Philadelphia: Lippincott, 1964.

Little League Stepson. Philadelphia: Lippincott, 1965.

Gridiron Glory. Philadelphia: Lippincott, 1966.

Little League Visitor. Philadelphia: Lippincott, 1966.

Fast Break. Philadelphia: Lippincott, 1967.

Little League Victory. Philadelphia: Lippincott, 1967.

Hackberry Jones, Split End. Philadelphia: Lippincott, 1968.

Little League Little Brother. Philadelphia: Lippincott, 1968.

Bishop, Leonard. *The Butchers.* New York: Dial, 1956.

Blackburn, Casper. *Annapolis, Ahoy.* Philadelphia: Macrae-Smith, 1945.

Blatty, William Peter. *John Goldfarb, Please Come Home.* Garden City, N.Y.: Doubleday, 1963.

Bonehill, Captain Ralph. Pseudonym, see Edward Stratemeyer.

Bonner, Mary G.

Out to Win. New York: Knopf, 1947.

The Base Stealer. New York: Knopf, 1951.

The Dugout Mystery. New York: Knopf, 1953.

Two-Way Pitcher. New York: Lantern, 1958.

Spray Hitter. New York: Lantern, 1959.

Bowen, Robert S. (also, pseudonym J. R. Richards).

The Winning Pitch. New York: Lothrop, Lee & Shepard, 1948.

Fourth Down. New York: Lothrop, Lee, & Shepard, 1949.

Player-Manager. New York: Lothrop, Lee & Shepard, 1949.

Ball Hawk. New York: Lothrop, Lee & Shepard, 1950.

Blocking Back. New York: Lothrop, Lee & Shepard, 1950.

Hot Corner. New York: Lothrop, Lee & Shepard, 1951.

Touchdown Kid. New York: Lothrop, Lee & Shepard, 1951.

Behind the Bat. New York: Lothrop, Lee & Shepard, 1953.

Infield Spark. New York: Lothrop, Lee & Shepard, 1954.

Million-Dollar Fumble. New York: Lothrop, Lee & Shepard, 1954.

The Big Inning. New York: Lothrop, Lee & Shepard, 1955.

The Last White Line. New York: Lothrop, Lee & Shepard, 1955.

The Big Hit. New York: Lothrop, Lee & Shepard, 1958.

Triple Play. New York: Lothrop, Lee & Shepard, 1959.

Pennant Fever. New York: Lothrop, Lee & Shepard, 1961.

No Hitter. New York: Lothrop, Lee & Shepard, 1961.

Bat Boy. New York: Lothrop, Lee & Shepard, 1962.

Perfect Game. New York: Lothrop, Lee & Shepard, 1963.

Hot Corner Blues. New York: Lothrop, Lee & Shepard, 1964.

Rebel Rookie. New York: Lothrop, Lee & Shepard, 1965.

Lightning Southpaw. New York: Lothrop, Lee & Shepard, 1967.

Infield Flash. New York: Lothrop, Lee & Shepard, 1969.

Written by "J. R. Richards."

The Club Team. New York: Lothrop, Lee & Shepard, 1950.

The Fighting Halfback. New York: Lothrop, Lee & Shepard, 1952.

Quarterback, All-American. New York: Lothrop, Lee & Shepard, 1953.

"Boxer, Billy."

"King Kelly, the Famous Catcher; or, the Life Adventures of the $10,000 Ball-Player." *New York Five Cent Library* No. 85 (16 June 1894).

"Captain Billy Nash; or, the Doings of the Famous Third Baseman." *New York Five Cent Library* No. 86 (23 June 1894).

"Yale Murphy, the Great Short-Stop; or, the little Midget of the Giant New York Team." *New York Five Cent Library* No. 87 (30 June 1894).

Boyar, Jane and Boyar, Burt. *World Class.* New York: Random House, 1975.

Braddock, Gordon. Pseudonym, see Gilbert Patten.

Braddon, Russell. *The Finalists.* New York: Atheneum, 1977.

Brady, Charles. *Seven Games in October.* Boston: Little, Brown, 1979.

Brainerd, Norman. Pseudonym, see Samuel R. Fuller.

Brandner, Gary. *The Players.* New York: Pyramid, 1975.

Brashler, William. *The Bingo Long Traveling All-Stars and Motor Kings.* New York: Harper & Row, 1973.

Brennan, Peter. *Sudden Death.* New York: Atheneum, 1978.

Brier, Howard.

    Phantom Backfield. New York: Random House, 1948.

    Backboard Magic. New York: Random House, 1949.

    Shortstop Shadow, New York: Random House, 1950.

    Cinder Cyclone, New York: Random House, 1952.

Brinkley, William. *Breakpoint.* New York: Morrow, 1978.

Brooks, Jonathan. Pseudonym; see John C. Mellett.

Brooks, Lilian. Joint author; see Walter Camp.

Brooks, Noah.

    "The Fairport Nine." *St. Nicholas* 7 (May-October 1880).

    Our Baseball Club and How It Won the Championship. New York: Dutton, 1884.

Brooks, Walter R.

    Freddy Plays Football. New York: Knopf, 1949.

    Freddy and the Baseball Team from Mars. New York: Knopf, 1955.

Broun, Heywood. *The Sun Field.* New York: Putnam, 1923.

Brown, Kenneth. *Putter Perkins.* Boston: Houghton Mifflin, 1923.

Bruce, George. *Navy Blue and Gold.* New York: Grosset & Dunlap, 1936.

Brunner, Bernard. *Six Days to Sunday.* New York: McGraw-Hill, 1975.

Bunting, A. E. *Pitcher to Center Field.* Chicago: Childrens Press, 1974.

Burgoyne, Leon.

    Jack Davis, Forward. Philadelphia: Winston, 1951.

State Champs. Philadelphia: Winston, 1951.

Burleigh, C. B.

The Kenton Pines; or, Raymond Benson in College. Boston: Lothrop, Lee & Shepard, 1907.

Raymond Benson at Krampton. Boston: Lothrop, Lee & Shepard, 1907.

Burnett, W. R. *Iron Man.* New York: Dial, 1930.

Butterworth, William (pseudonym Edmund O. Scholefield).

Tiger Rookie. Cleveland, Ohio: World, 1966.

Li'l Wildcat. Cleveland, Ohio: World, 1967.

Maverick on the Mound. Cleveland, Ohio: World, 1968.

Byers, Herbert. *To the Victor.* Garden City, N.Y.: Doubleday, Doran, 1936.

Cabot, Carolyn S.

Football Madness. Boston: Small, Maynard, 1914.

Football Grandma. Boston: Small, Maynard, 1915.

Camerer, Dave. *Nine Saturdays Make a Year.* Garden City, N.Y.: Doubleday, 1962.

Camp, Walter.

Drives and Putts. Boston: L. C. Page, 1899 (with Lilian Brooks).

The Substitute. New York: Appleton, 1908.

Jack Hall at Yale. New York: Appleton, 1909.

Old Ryerson. New York: Appleton, 1911.

Danny Fists. New York: Appleton, 1913.

Captain Danny. New York: Appleton, 1914.

Danny the Freshman. New York: Appleton, 1921.

Cannon, Ralph.

Grid Star. Chicago: Reilly & Lee, 1933.

Out of Bounds. Chicago: Reilly & Lee, 1937.

Carol, Bill J. Pseudonym; see Bill Knott.

Carson, John F.

Floorburns. New York: Ariel, 1957.

The Twenty-Third Street Crusaders. New York: Ariel, 1958.

The Coach Nobody Liked. New York: Ariel, 1960.

Hotshot. New York: Ariel, 1961.

Court Clown. New York: Ariel, 1963.

Cartwright, Gary,

>*The Hundred-Yard War.* Garden City, N.Y.: Doubleday, 1968.

>*Thin Ice.* Greenwich, Conn.: Fawcett-World, 1975.

Cary, Lucian.

>*The Duke Steps Out.* Garden City, N.Y.: Doubleday, 1929.

>*The Duke Comes Back.* Garden City, N.Y.: Doubleday, 1933.

Chadwick, George B. *Chuck Blue of Sterling.* New York: Century, 1926.

Chadwick, Lester. Pseudonym; see Edward Stratemeyer.

Chance, Frank. *The Bride and the Pennant.* Chicago: Laird & Lee, 1910.

Chapman, Allen.

>*The Heroes of the School.* Cleveland: Goldsmith, 1908.

>*Fred Fenton in the Line.* New York: Cupples & Leon, 1910.

>*Fred Fenton the Pitcher.* New York: Cupples & Leon, 1911.

>*Fred Fenton on the Track.* New York: Cupples & Leon, 1913.

Charyn, Jerome. *The Seventh Babe.* New York: Arbor House, 1979.

Christopher, Matthew F.

>*The Lucky Baseball Bat.* Boston: Little, Brown, 1954.
>*Baseball Pals.* Boston: Little, Brown, 1956.
>*Slide, Danny, Slide.* Boston: Little, Brown, 1958.
>*Two Strikes on Johnny.* Boston: Little, Brown, 1958.
>*Little Lefty.* Boston: Little, Brown, 1959.
>*Shadow over the Back Court.* New York: Franklin Watts, 1959.
>*Touchdown for Tommy.* Boston: Little Brown, 1959.
>*Basketball Sparkplug.* Boston: Little, Brown, 1960.
>*Long Stretch at First Base.* Boston: Little, Brown, 1960.
>*Wing T Fullback.* New York: Watts, 1960.
>*Tall Man in the Pivot.* Boston: Little, Brown, 1961.
>*Challenge at Second Base.* Boston: Little, Brown, 1962.
>*Crackerjack Halfback.* Boston: Little, Brown, 1962.
>*Baseball Flyhawk.* Boston: Little, Brown, 1963.

Sink It, Rusty. Boston: Little, Brown, 1963.

Catcher with a Glass Arm. Boston: Little, Brown, 1964.

Wingman on Ice. Boston: Little, Brown, 1964.

The Counterfeit Tackle. Boston: Little, Brown, 1965.

Too Hot to Handle. Boston: Little, Brown, 1965.

Long Shot for Paul. Boston: Little, Brown, 1966.

The Reluctant Pitcher. Boston: Little, Brown, 1966.

Miracle at the Plate. Boston: Little, Brown, 1967.

The Team That Couldn't Lose. Boston: Little, Brown, 1967.

The Basket Counts. Boston: Little, Brown, 1968.

The Year Mom Won the Pennant. Boston: Little, Brown, 1968.

Catch That Pass! Boston: Little, Brown, 1969.

Hard Drive to Short. Boston: Little, Brown, 1969.

Johnny Long Legs. Boston: Little, Brown, 1970.

Lucky Seven. Boston: Little, Brown, 1970.

Shortstop from Tokyo. Boston: Little, Brown, 1970.

Look Who's Playing First Base. Boston: Little, Brown, 1971.

Tough to Tackle. Boston: Little, Brown, 1971.

Face-Off. Boston: Little, Brown, 1972.

The Kid Who Only Hit Homers. Boston: Little, Brown, 1972.

Ice Magic. Boston: Little, Brown, 1973.

Mystery Coach. Boston: Little, Brown, 1973.

Front Court Hex. Boston: Little, Brown, 1974.

Jinx Glove. Boston: Little, Brown, 1974.

No Arm in Left Field. Boston: Little, Brown, 1975.

Glue Fingers. Boston: Little, Brown, 1975.

The Pigeon with the Tennis Elbow. Boston: Little, Brown, 1975.

The Team That Stopped Moving. Boston: Little, Brown, 1975.

Football Fugitive. Boston: Little, Brown, 1976.

Power Play. Boston: Little, Brown, 1976.

The Submarine Pitch. Boston: Little, Brown, 1976.

Championship Team. Boston: Little, Brown, 1977.

The Diamond Champs. Boston: Little, Brown, 1977.

Johnny No Hit. Boston: Little, Brown, 1977.

Soccer Halfback. Boston: Little, Brown, 1978.

The 21-mile Swim. Boston: Little Brown, 1979.

Chute, B. J.

Blocking Back. New York: Macmillan, 1938.

Shift to the Right. New York: Macmillan, 1945.

Teen-Age Sports Parade. New York: Dodd, Mead, 1950.

Clymer, Eleanor. *Treasure at First Base*. New York: Dodd, Mead, 1950.

Coe, Charles Francis. *Knockout*. Philadelphia: Lippincott, 1936.

Cohen, Barney. *Coliseum*. New York: Dell, 1975.

Cohen, Octavus Roy. *Kid Tinsel*. New York: Appleton-Century, 1941.

Cohler, David Keith. *Gamemaker*. Garden City, N.Y.: Doubleday, 1980.

Colton, Matthew.

Frank Armstrong, Drop Kicker. New York: Hurst, 1912.

Frank Armstrong, Captain of the Nine. New York: Hurst, 1913.

Frank Armstrong at College. New York: Hurst, 1913.

Frank Armstrong's Second Team. New York: Hurst, 1915.

Cooke, David C. *While the Crowd Cheers,* New York: Dutton, 1953.

Coombs, Charles.

Young Infield Rookie. New York: Lantern Press, 1954.

Sleuth at Shortstop. New York: Lantern Press, 1955.

Cooper, John R.

The Mystery at the Ball Park. New York: Cupples & Leon, 1947.

The Southpaw's Secret. New York: Cupples & Leon, 1947.

First Base Jinx. Garden City, N.Y.: Garden City Books, 1952.

The Phantom Homer. Garden City, N.Y.: Garden City Books, 1952.

The College League Mystery. Garden City, N.Y.: Garden City Books, 1953.

The Fighting Shortstop. Garden City, N.Y.: Garden City Books, 1953.

Coover, Robert. *The Universal Baseball Association, Inc., J. Henry Waugh, Prop.* New York: Random House, 1968.

Corbert, Mack. *Play the Game.* New York: Stokes, 1940.

Corbett, Scott.

The Baseball Trick. Boston: Little, Brown, 1965.

The Baseball Bargain. Boston: Little, Brown, 1970.

The Home Run Trick. Boston: Little, Brown, 1974.

The Hockey Trick. Boston: Little, Brown, 1974.

The Hockey Girls. Boston: Little, Brown, 1976.

Cox, William R.

Five Were Chosen. New York: Dodd, Mead, 1956.

Gridiron Duel. New York: Dodd, Mead, 1959.

The Wild Pitch. New York: Dodd, Mead, 1963.

Tall on the Court. New York: Dodd, Mead, 1964.

Third and Eight to Go. New York: Dodd, Mead, 1964.

Big League Rookie. New York: Dodd, Mead, 1965.

Trouble at Second Base. New York: Dodd, Mead, 1966.

Goal Ahead! New York: Dodd, Mead, 1967.

The Valley Eleven. New York: Dodd, Mead, 1967.

Jump Shot Joe. New York: Dodd, Mead, 1968.

Rookie in the Backcourt. New York: Dodd, Mead, 1970.

Big League Sandlotters. New York: Dodd, Mead, 1971.

Third and Goal. New York: Dodd, Mead, 1971.

Gunner on the Court. New York: Dodd, Mead, 1972.

Playoff. New York: Bantam, 1972.

The Unbeatable Five. New York: Dodd, Mead, 1974.

Game, Set and Match. New York: Dodd, Mead, 1977.

Craig, John.

Power Play. New York: Dodd, Mead, 1974.

Superdude. New York: Warner Books, 1974.

All G.O.D.'s Children. New York: Morrow, 1975.

Chappie and Me. New York: Dodd, Mead, 1979.

Creighton, Don.

Little League Giant. Austin, Tex.: Steck-Vaughn, 1965.

The Secret Little Leaguer. Austin, Tex.: Steck, 1966.

Little League Old-Timer. Austin, Tex., Steck, 1967.

Little League Ball Hawk. Austin, Tex.: Steck-Vaughn, 1968.

Cronley, Jay.

Fall Guy. Garden City, N.Y.: Doubleday, 1978.

Screwballs. Garden City, N.Y.: Doubleday, 1980.

Daley, Robert. *Only a Game.* New York: New American Library, 1967.

Davenport, Spencer. *The Rushton Boys at Rally Hall.* Racine, Wis.: Whitman, 1916.

Davies, Valentine. *It Happens Every Spring.* New York: Farrar, Straus, 1949.

Davis, Terry. *Vision Quest.* New York: Viking, 1979.

Dawson, Elmer.

> *Garry Grayson's Hill Street Eleven.* New York: Grosset & Dunlap, 1926.
>
> *Garry Grayson at Lennox High.* New York: Grosset & Dunlap, 1926.
>
> *Garry Grayson's Football Rivals.* New York: Grosset & Dunlap, 1926.
>
> *Garry Grayson at Stanley Prep.* New York: Grosset & Dunlap, 1927.
>
> *Garry Grayson Showing His Speed.* New York: Grosset & Dunlap, 1927.
>
> *Garry Grayson's Winning Kick.* New York: Grosset & Dunlap, 1928.
>
> *Garry Grayson Hitting the Line.* New York: Grosset & Dunlap, 1928.
>
> *Buck's Winning Hit.* New York: Grosset & Dunlap, 1930.
>
> *Garry Grayson's Winning Touchdown.* New York: Grosset & Dunlap, 1930.
>
> *Larry's Fadeaway.* New York: Grosset & Dunlap, 1930.
>
> *The Pickup Nine.* New York: Grosset & Dunlap, 1930.
>
> *Buck's Home Run Drive.* New York: Grosset & Dunlap, 1931.
>
> *Garry Grayson's Double Signals.* New York: Grosset & Dunlap, 1931.
>
> *Garry Grayson's Forward Pass.* New York: Grosset & Dunlap, 1932.
>
> *Larry's Speed Ball.* New York: Grosset & Dunlap, 1932.

Dawson, Fielding. *A Great Day for a Ballgame.* Indianapolis, Ind.: Bobbs Merrill, 1973.

Deal, Babs H. *The Grail.* New York: McKay, 1963.

Dean, Graham.

Herb Kent, West Point Cadet. Chicago: Goldsmith, 1936.
Herb Kent, West Point Fullback. Chicago: Goldsmith, 1936.

Decker, Duane (also, pseudonym Richard Wayne).
Good Field, No Hit. New York: Mill, 1947.
Starting Pitcher. New York: Mill and Morrow, 1948.
Hit and Run. New York: Mill and Morrow, 1949.
The Catcher from Double-A. New York: Morrow, 1950.
Fast Man on a Pivot. New York: Morrow, 1951.
The Big Stretch. New York: Morrow, 1952.
Wrong-Way Rookie. New York: Mill, 1952.
Switch Hitter. New York: Morrow, 1953.
Mister Shortstop. New York: Morrow, 1954.
Long Ball to Left Field. New York: Morrow, 1958.
Third-Base Rookie. New York: Morrow, 1959.
Showboat Southpaw. New York: Morrow, 1960.
Rebel in Right Field. New York: Morrow, 1961.
The Grand Slam Kid. New York: Morrow, 1964.
Written by "Richard Wayne."
Clutch Hitter. Philadelphia: Macrae-Smith, 1951.

Deford, Frank.
Cut 'n Run. New York: Viking, 1972.
The Owner. New York: Viking, 1976.

DeForest, Barry. Pseudonym; see Albert Quandt.

DeLillo, Don. *End Zone*. Boston: Houghton Mifflin, 1972.

Dender, Jay. *Tom Harmon and the Great Gridiron Plot*. Racine, Wis.: Whitman, 1946.

Denker, Henry. *I'll Be Right Home, Ma*. New York: Crowell, 1949.

Devries, Julian. *The Strikeout King*. Cleveland, Ohio: World, 1940.

Dietzel, Paul and Everett Houghton. *Go, Shorty, Go*. Indianapolis, Ind.: Bobbs-Merrill, 1965.

Dix, Beulah Marie. Joint author; see Bertram Millhauser.

Doliner, Roy. *The Orange Air*. New York: Scribner, 1961.

Donohue, James F. *Spitballs & Holy Water*. New York: Avon, 1977.

Dooley, Eddie. *Under the Goal Posts*. New York: Pratt, 1933.

Douglas, Gilbert.
Hard to Tackle. New York: Crowell, 1956.

The Bulldog Attitude. New York: Crowell, 1957.

Hard Nose. New York: Crowell, 1957.

Drady, Alan.

Red Morton, Waterboy. New York: Appleton, 1932.

That Cathedral Team. New York: Dodd, Mead, 1935.

Drdek, Richard.

The Game. Garden City, N.Y.: Doubleday, 1968.

Lefty's Boy. Garden City, N.Y.: Doubleday, 1969.

Drury, Maxine. *Glory for Gil.* New York: McKay, 1964.

Dudley, Albertus True.

Following the Ball. Boston: Lothrop, Lee & Shepard, 1903.

Making the Nine. Boston: Lothrop, Lee & Shepard, 1904.

In the Line. Boston: Lothrop, Lee & Shepard, 1905.

With Mask and Mitt. Boston: Lothrop, Lee & Shepard, 1906.

The Great Year. Boston: Lothrop, Lee & Shepard, 1907.

A Full-Back Afloat. Boston: Lothrop, Lee & Shepard, 1908.

The Yale Cup. Boston: Lothrop, Lee & Shepard, 1908.

The School Four. Boston: Lothrop, Lee & Shepard, 1909.

At the Home Plate. Boston: Lothrop, Lee & Shepard, 1910.

Stories of the Triangular League. Boston: Lothrop, Lee & Shepard, 1910.

The Half-Miler. Boston: Lothrop, Lee & Shepard, 1913.

Unofficial Prefect. Boston: Lothrop, Lee & Shepard, 1915.

Duffield, J. W.

Bert Wilson, Marathon Winner. New York: Sully, 1913.

Bert Wilson's Fadeaway Ball. New York: Sully, 1913.

Bert Wilson on the Gridiron. New York: Sully, 1914.

Dulack, Thomas J. *Pork: Or, the Day I Lost the Masters.* New York: Dial Press, 1968.

Dunham, Montrew. *Abner Doubleday.* Indianapolis, Ind.: Bobbs-Merrill, 1965.

Dygard, Thomas J. *Point Spread.* New York: Morrow, 1980.

Earl, John Prescott. Pseudonym; see Beth Bradford Gilchrist.

Earll, Frank. "Amos Rusie, Prince of Pitchers; or, the Life and Adventures of the World's Greatest Ball-Player." *Golden Hours,* Nos. 549-553 (6 August–3 September 1898).

Edmunds, Murrell. *Behold, Thy Brother.* New York: Beechhurst, 1950.

Eichler, Alfred. *Big Bruiser.* New York: Phoenix, 1941.

Einstein, Charles (also; pseudonym D. J. Michael).
The Only Game in Town. New York: Dell, 1955. Written by "D. J. Michael."
Win or Else. New York: Blassingame, 1954.

Elderice, J. Raymond.
T. Haviland Hicks, Freshman. New York: Appleton, 1915.
T. Haviland Hicks, Sophomore. New York: Appleton, 1915.
T. Haviland Hicks, Junior. New York: Appleton, 1916.
T. Haviland Hicks, Senior. New York: Appleton, 1916.

Ellis, Edward. "Jack Darcy, the All-Around Athlete; or, Fighting His Way to Fortune." *Golden Hours,* No. 31 (September 1888).

Emery, Russell G.
Wings Over West Point. Philadelphia: Macrae-Smith, 1940.
High, Inside! Philadelphia: Macrae-Smith, 1948.
T Quarterback. Philadelphia: Macrae-Smith, 1949.
Warren of West Point. Philadelphia: Macrae-Smith, 1950.
Gray Line and Gold. Philadelphia: Macrae-Smith, 1951.
Relief Pitcher. Philadelphia: Macrae-Smith, 1953.
Hyland of the Hawks. Philadelphia: Macrae-Smith, 1955.
Rebound. Philadelphia: Macrae-Smith, 1955.
Action at Third. Philadelphia: Macrae-Smith, 1957.

Emmet, R. T. "Dashing Dick, the Young Cadet; or, Four Years at West Point." *The Boys of New York,* No. 690 (3 November 1888).

Brother Ernest, C. S. C. *Captain Johnny Ford.* Evansville, Ind.: Burkert-Walton, 1938.

Etter, Les.
Morning Glory Quarterback. Indianapolis, Ind.: Bobbs-Merrill, 1965.

Bull Pen Hero. Indianapolis, Ind.: Bobbs-Merrill, 1966.

Golden Gloves Challenger. New York: Hastings House, 1967.

Big Down Gamble. New York: Hastings House, 1968.

Cool Man on the Court. New York: Hastings House, 1969.

Fast Break Forward. New York: Hastings House, 1969.

Soccer Goalie. New York: Hastings House, 1969.

Get Those Rebounds! New York: Hastings House, 1978.

Everett, William.

Changing Base. Boston: Lee & Shepard, 1868.

Double Play. Boston: Lee & Shepard, 1871.

Thine Not Mine. Boston: Robert Brothers, 1891.

Exley, Frederick. *A Fan's Notes.* New York: Harper & Row, 1968.

Fadiman, Edwin, Jr. *The Professional.* New York: McKay, 1973.

"Fearnot, Fred." "Fred Fearnot's Defeat; or A Fight Against Great Odds." *Work and Win,* No. 19 (14 April 1899).

Felson, Henry. *Bertie Comes Through.* New York: Dutton, 1947.

Fenner, Phyllis R. *Crack of the Bat.* New York: Knopf, 1952.

Ferguson, B. M. *The Dumb-Bell.* New York: Chelsea House, 1927.

Ferguson, Charles W. *Pigskin.* Garden City, N.Y.: Doubleday, Doran, 1929.

Ferguson, W. B. M. *A Man's Code.* New York: Dillingham, 1915.

Ferndenzi, Til. Joint author, see Yogi Berra.

Finn, Francis J., S. J. *That Football Game and What Came of It.* Cincinnati, Ohio: Benziger Brothers, 1897.

Fishel, D. *Terry and Bunky Play Baseball.* New York: Putnam, 1947.

Fitch, George.

The Big Strike at Siwash. New York: Doubleday, Page, 1909.

At Good Old Siwash. Boston: Little, Brown, 1910.

Fitzgerald, Ed.

The Turning Point. New York: Barnes, 1948.

College Slugger. New York: Barnes, 1950.

Yankee Rookie. New York: Barnes, 1952.

The Ballplayer. New York: Barnes, 1957.

Fitzpatrick, Burgess. *Casey's Redemption.* New York: Greenwich Book Publishing Company, 1958.

Fitzsimmons, Cortland.

70,000 Witnesses. New York: McBride, 1931.

Death on the Diamond. New York: Stokes, 1934.

Crimson Ice. New York: Stokes, 1935.

Fliegal, Dorian. *The Fix.* Boston: Houghton Mifflin, 1978.

Flood, Richard T.

Pass That Puck! Boston: Houghton Mifflin, 1948.

The Point After. Boston: Houghton Mifflin, 1951.

The Fighting Shortstop. Boston: Houghton Mifflin, 1954.

Penalty Shot. Boston: Houghton Mifflin, 1955.

Foley, Louise M.

Somebody Stole Second. New York: Delacorte, 1972.

Tackle Twenty-Two. New York: Delacorte, 1978.

Forbes, Graham B.

The Boys of Columbia High on the Gridiron. New York: Grosset & Dunlap, 1911.

Frank Allen and His Rivals. Garden City, N.Y.: Garden City Publishing, 1926.

Frank Allen—Captain of the Team. Garden City, N.Y.: Garden City Books, 1926.

Frank Allen in Camp. Garden City, N.Y.: Garden City Books, 1926.

Frank Allen in Winter Sports. Garden City, N.Y.: Garden City Books, 1926.

Frank Allen—Pitcher. Garden City, N.Y.: Garden City Books, 1926.

Frank Allen Playing to Win. Garden City, N.Y.: Garden City Books, 1926.

Frank Allen's Schooldays. Garden City, N.Y.: Garden City Books, 1926.

Ford, Whitey and Jack Lang. *The Fighting Southpaw.* Larchmont, N.Y.: Argonaut, 1962.

Foreman, Harry. *Awk.* Philadelphia: Westminster, 1970.

Forrest, Frank. "Dick Daresome's Mistake; or, Losing a Game to Belleville." *Wide Awake Weekly,* No. 160 (7 May 1909).

Foster, Alan S. *Goodbye, Bobby Thomson! Goodbye, John Wayne!* New York: Simon & Schuster, 1973.

Francis, H. D.
 Double Reverse. Garden City, N.Y.: Doubleday, 1958.
 Football Flash. New York: Hastings House, 1961.
 Basketball Bones. New York: Hastings House, 1962.
 Big Swat. Chicago: Follett, 1963.

Frankel, Haskel. *Pro Football Rookie.* Garden City, N.Y.: Doubleday, 1964.

Frederick, Mike.
 Freshman Quarterback. Austin, Tex.: Nova, 1964.
 Frank Merriwell, Quarterback. New York: Award, 1965.
 Frank Merriwell Returns. New York: Award, 1965.

French, Michael. *The Throwing Season.* New York: Delacorte, 1980.

Frick, C. H. Pseudonym; see Constance H. Irwin.

Friend, Alona. *Mixed Doubles.* New York: Greystone, 1940.

Friendlich, Dick.
 Pivot Man. Philadelphia: Westminster, 1949.
 Warrior Forward. Philadelphia: Westminster, 1950.
 Goal Line Stand. Philadelphia: Westminster, 1951.
 Line Smasher. Philadelphia: Westminster, 1952.
 Play Maker. Philadelphia: Westminster, 1953.
 Baron of the Bullpen. Philadelphia: Westminster, 1954.
 Left End Scott. Philadelphia: Westminster, 1955.
 Clean Up Hitter. Philadelphia: Westminster, 1956.
 Gridiron Crusader. Philadelphia: Westminster, 1958.
 Lead-Off Man. Philadelphia: Westminster, 1959.
 Backstop Ace. Philadelphia: Westminster, 1961.
 Full Court Press. Philadelphia: Westminster, 1962.
 All-Pro Quarterback. Philadelphia: Westminster, 1963.
 Relief Pitcher. Philadelphia: Westminster, 1964.
 Pinch Hitter. Philadelphia: Westminster, 1965.
 Touchdown Maker. Garden City, N.Y.: Doubleday, 1966.
 Fullback from Nowhere. Philadelphia: Westminster, 1967.

The Sweet Swing. Garden City, N.Y.: Doubleday, 1968.
Fuller, Samuel R. (pseudonym Norman Brainerd).
  Winning His Shoulder Straps. Boston: Lothrop, Lee &
  Shepard, 1909.
  Winning the Eagle Prize. Boston: Lothrop, Lee & Shep-
  ard, 1910.
  Winning the Junior Cup. Boston: Lothrop, Lee & Shep-
  ard, 1911.
  Winning His Army Blue. Boston: Lothrop, Lee & Shep-
  ard, 1917.
Fullerton, Hugh S.
  Jimmy Kirkland and the Plot for the Pennant. Philadel-
  phia: Winston, 1915.
  Jimmy Kirkland of the Cascade College Team. Philadel-
  phia: Winston, 1915.
  Jimmy Kirkland of the Shasta Boys' Team. Philadel-
  phia: Winston, 1915.
Fulton, Reed.
  Lardy the Great. Garden City, N.Y.: Doubleday, Doran,
  1932.
  Rookie Coach. Garden City, N.Y.: Doubleday, 1955.
Gallico, Paul.
  Golf Is a Friendly Game. New York: Knopf, 1942.
  Matilda. New York: Coward-McCann, 1970.
Gardner, Leonard. *Fat City.* New York: Farrar, Straus & Gi-
  roux, 1969.
Gardner, Lillian. *Somebody Called Booie.* New York: Watts,
  1955.
Garris, Howard. *Dick Hamilton's Football Team.* New York:
  Grosset & Dunlap, 1912.
Gartner, John F.
  Rock Taylor, Football Coach. New York: Dodd, Mead,
  1951.
  Ace Pitcher. New York: Dodd, Mead, 1953.
  Cager's Challenge. New York: Dodd, Mead, 1955.
  Sons of Mercury. New York: Dodd, Mead, 1956.
Gault, William C.
  Mr. Fullback. New York: Dutton, 1953.
  Day of the Rain. New York: Random House, 1956.
  Bruce Benedict, Halfback. New York: Dutton, 1957.

Through the Line. New York: Dutton, 1961.

Little Big Foot. New York: Dutton, 1963.

Backfield Challenge. New York: Dutton, 1967.

The Lonely Mound. New York: Dutton, 1967.

Stubborn Sam. New York: Dutton, 1969.

Quarterback Gamble. New York: Dutton, 1970.

Trouble at Second. New York: Dutton, 1973.

Wild Willie, Wide Receiver. New York: Dutton, 1974.

The Big Stick. New York: Dutton, 1975.

Underground Skipper. New York: Dutton, 1975.

Showboat in the Backcourt. New York: Dutton, 1976.

Cut-Rate Quarterback. New York: Dutton, 1977.

Thin Ice. New York: Dutton, 1978.

Gelman, Steve.

Baseball Bonus Kid. Garden City, N.Y.: Doubleday, 1961.

Football Fury. Garden City, N.Y.: Doubleday, 1962.

Evans of the Army. Garden City, N.Y.: Doubleday, 1964.

Gent, Peter.

North Dallas Forty. New York: Morrow, 1973.

Texas Celebrity Turkey Trot. New York: Morrow, 1978.

Gerson, Noel B. *The Sunday Heroes.* New York: Morrow, 1972.

Ghiselli, Mario James (pseudonym Matty Mario). *Bad Boy.* ed. Harry T. McHugh. New York: Broadway, 1939.

Gilchrist, Beth Bradford (pseudonym John P. Earl).

On the School Team. Philadelphia: Penn, 1908.

The School Team in Camp. Philadelphia: Penn, 1909.

Captain of the School Team. Philadelphia: Penn, 1910.

The School Team on the Diamond. Philadelphia: Penn, 1911.

Goldfrank, Mrs. Herbert (pseudonym Helen Kay). *The Magic Mitt.* New York: Hastings House, 1959.

Graham, Carroll and Graham, Garrett. *Only Human.* New York: Vanguard, 1932.

Graham, John Alexander. *Babe Ruth Caught in a Snowstorm.* Boston: Houghton Mifflin, 1973.

Grantham, Kenneth L. *Baseball's Darkest Days.* New York: Exposition, 1965.

Gray, Charles Wright. *The Sporting Spirit.* New York: Holt, 1925.

Green, Fitzhugh.

Won for the Fleet. New York: Dutton, 1922.

Fought for Annapolis. New York: Appleton, 1925.

Hold 'em Navy! New York: Appleton, 1926.

Greenfield, Robert. *Hayman's Crowd.* New York: Summit, 1978.

Grey, Zane.

The Short-Stop. Chicago: McClurg, 1909.

The Young Pitcher. New York: Harper & Brothers, 1911.

The Red-Headed Outfield and Other Baseball Stories. New York: Grosset & Dunlap, 1915.

Griffith, Peggy. *The New Klondike.* New York: Harper & Brothers, 1911.

Grosscup, Clyde.

The Winning Spirit. New York: Barnes, 1953.

Pro Rookie. New York: Grosset & Dunlap, 1965.

Pro Passer. New York: Grosset & Dunlap, 1966.

Pro Champion. New York: Grosset & Dunlap, 1966.

Throw the Bomb. New York: Grosset & Dunlap, 1967.

Haines, Donal H.

The Southpaw. New York: Rinehart, 1931.

Toss-Up. New York: Farrar & Rinehart, 1932.

Triple Threat. New York: Rinehart, 1933.

Team Play. New York: Farrar & Rinehart, 1934.

Sporting Chance. New York: Farrar & Rinehart, 1935.

Blaine of the Backfield. New York: Farrar & Rinehart, 1937.

Pro Quarterback. New York: Farrar & Rinehart, 1940.

Hale, Harry. *Jack Race's Baseball Nine.* New York: Hearst's International Library, 1915.

Hall, Holworthy. Pseudonym; see Harold Everett Porter.

Hall, Oakley. *The Corpus of Joe Bailey.* New York: Viking, 1953.

Hamill, Pete. *Flesh and Blood.* New York: Random House, 1977.

Hamilton, J. S. *Butt Chandler, Freshman.* New York: Appleton, 1910.

Hancock, Harrie I.

"The Young West Pointer; or, the Cadet Life of Ben Burgess." *Golden Hours,* No. 275 (6 May 1893).

The High School Captain of the Team. Philadelphia: Altemus, 1910.

The High School Freshman. Philadelphia: Altemus, 1910.

The High School Left End. Philadelphia: Altemus, 1910.

The High School Pitcher. Philadelphia: Altemus, 1910.

The Grammar School Boys in Summer Athletics. Philadelphia: Altemus, 1911.

Hano, Arnold.

The Big Out. New York: Barnes, 1951.

A Day in the Bleachers. New York: Crowell, 1955.

Hare, T. Truxtun.

Making the Freshman Team. Philadelphia: Penn, 1907.

A Sophomore Half-Back. Philadelphia: Penn, 1908.

A Junior on the Line. Philadelphia: Penn, 1909.

A Senior Quarter-Back. Philadelphia: Penn, 1910.

A Graduate Coach. Philadelphia: Penn, 1911.

Phillip Kent. Philadelphia: Penn, 1914.

Phillip Kent in the Lower School. Philadelphia: Penn, 1916.

Phillip Kent in the Upper School. Philadelphia: Penn, 1918.

Kent of Malvem. Philadelphia: Penn, 1919.

Harkins, Philip.

Lightning on Ice. New York: Morrow, 1946.

The Big Silver Bowl. New York: Morrow, 1947.

Touchdown Twins. New York: Morrow, 1947.

Southpaw from San Francisco. New York: Morrow, 1948.

Punt Formation. New York: Morrow, 1949.

Knockout. New York: Morrow, 1950.

Son of the Coach. New York: Holiday House, 1950.

Center Ice. New York: Holiday House, 1952.

Game, Carol Canning! New York: Morrow, 1958.

Breakaway Back. New York: Morrow, 1959.

Fight Like a Falcon. New York: Morrow, 1961.

No Head for Soccer. New York: Morrow, 1964.

Harmon, A. W. *Base Hit.* Philadelphia: Lippincott, 1970.

Harris, Jeff. Joint author; see Willie Mays.

Harris, Mark.
>   *The Southpaw.* Indianapolis, Ind.: Bobbs-Merrill, 1953.
>   *Bang the Drum Slowly.* New York: Knopf, 1956.
>   *A Ticket for a Seamstitch.* New York: Knopf, 1957.
>   *It Looked Like For Ever.* New York: McGraw-Hill, 1979.

Harris, Thomas. *Black Sunday.* New York: Putnam, 1975.

Hart, Frank J. *The Speed Boy.* Chicago: Lakewood House, 1938.

Heavlin, Jay. *Fastball Pitcher.* Garden City, N.Y.: Doubleday, 1965.

Heinz, W. C. *The Professional.* New York: Harper & Brothers, 1958.

Hemphill, Paul. *Long Gone.* New York: Viking, 1979.

Hemyng, Bracebridge.
>   "The Captain of the Club; or, the Young Rival Athletes." *Beadle's Half-Dime Library* No. 91 (22 April 1879).
>   "The Left-Hand Athlete; or, the Rival School Sports." *Beadle's Half-Dime Library* No. 1062 (30 November 1897). (Hemyng was British, but wrote for American audiences in American dime novels.)

Henderley, Brooks.
>   *The Y.M.C.A. Boys of Clifford.* New York: Cupples & Leon, 1916.
>   *The Y.M.C.A. Boys at Football.* New York: Cupples & Leon, 1917.

Henderson, Legrand (pseudonym Legrand).
>   *How Baseball Began in Brooklyn.* New York: Abingdon, 1958.
>   *How Basketball Began.* New York: Abingdon, 1962.

Hendryx, James B. *Without Gloves.* New York: Putnam, 1924.

Herrin, Lamar. *The Rio Loja Ringmaster.* New York: Viking, 1977.

Herskowitz, Mickey. *Letters from Lefty.* Houston: Houston Post, 1966.

Heuman, William.
>   *Fighting Five.* New York: Morrow, 1950.
>   *Wonder Boy.* New York: Morrow, 1951.

Junior Quarterback. New York: Morrow, 1952.
Little League Champs. Philadelphia: Lippincott, 1953.
Strictly from Brooklyn. New York: Morrow, 1956.
Rocky Malone. Austin, Tex.: Steck, 1957.
Left End Luisetti. Austin, Tex.: Steck, 1958.
Second String Hero. Austin, Tex.: Steck, 1959.
Backcourt Man. New York: Dodd, Mead, 1960.
Rookie Backstop. New York: Dodd, Mead, 1962.
The Wonder Five. New York: Dodd, Mead, 1962.
Powerhouse Five. New York: Dodd, Mead, 1963.
City High Five. New York: Dodd, Mead, 1964.
The Horse That Played the Outfield. New York: Dodd, Mead, 1964.
Horace Higby and the Field Goal Formula. New York: Dodd, Mead, 1965.
Hillbilly Hurler. New York: Dodd, Mead, 1966.
Tall Team. New York: Dodd, Mead, 1966.
Scrambling Quarterback. New York: Dodd, Mead, 1967.
Backup Quarterback. Austin, Tex.: Steck-Vaughn, 1968.
Horace Higby and the Scientific Pitch. New York: Dodd, Mead, 1968.
City High Champions. New York: Dodd, Mead, 1969.
The Goofer Pitch. New York: Dodd, Mead, 1969.
Gridiron Stranger. Philadelphia: Lippincott, 1970.
Home Run Henri. New York: Dodd, Mead, 1970.
Horace Higby and the Gentle Fullback. New York: Dodd, Mead, 1970.
Fastbreak Rebel. New York: Dodd, Mead, 1971.
Little League Hot Shots. New York: Dodd, Mead, 1972.
Heyliger, William (also, pseudonym Hawley Williams).
Bartley, Freshman Pitcher. New York: Appleton, 1911.
Bucking the Line. New York: Appleton, 1912.
Strike Three! New York: Appleton, 1913.
Off Side. New York: Appleton, 1914.
Against Odds. New York: Appleton, 1915.
Captain Fair-and-Square. New York: Appleton, 1916.
The Captain of the Nine. New York: Appleton, 1917.
The County Pennant. New York: Appleton, 1917.
Fighting for Fairview. New York: Appleton, 1918.
Bean-Ball Bill and Other Stories. New York: Grosset &

Dunlap, 1920.

The Fighting Captain, and Other Stories. New York: Appleton, 1926.

Big Leaguer. Chicago: Goldsmith, 1928.

The Macklin Brothers. New York: Appleton, 1928.

Bill Darrow's Victory. New York: Grosset & Dunlap, 1930.

Quarterback Hot-Head. New York: Grosset & Dunlap, 1931.

The Gallant Crosby. New York: Appleton, 1933.

Backfield Comet. New York: Appleton-Century, 1934.

Fighting Blood. Chicago: Goldsmith, 1936.

Stan Kent, Freshman Fullback. Chicago: Goldsmith, 1936.

Stan Kent, Varsity Man. Chicago: Goldsmith, 1936.

The Loser's End. Chicago: Goldsmith, 1937.

Backfield Play. New York: Appleton-Century, 1938.

Gridiron Glory. New York: Appleton-Century, 1940.

Top Lineman. New York: Appleton-Century, 1943.

Written by "Hawley Williams."

Batter Up. New York: Appleton, 1912.

Quarterback Reckless. New York: Appleton, 1912.

Five Yards to Go! New York: Appleton, 1913.

Johnson of Lansing. New York: Appleton, 1914.

The Winning Hit. New York: Appleton, 1914.

Fair Play! New York: Appleton, 1915.

Straight Ahead! New York: Appleton, 1917.

Dorset's Twister. New York: Appleton, 1926.

Higdon, Hal.

The Horse That Played Center Field. New York: Holt, Rinehart & Winston, 1969.

The Electronic Olympics. New York: Holt, Rinehart & Winston, 1971.

Hill, Frank E. Joint author, see Bob Allison.

Hirshberg, Al.

The Battery for Madison High. Boston: Little, Brown, 1955.

Varsity Double Play. Boston: Little, Brown, 1956.

Hoagland, Edward. *The Circle Game.* New York: Crowell, 1960.

Hoff, Syd. *Baseball Mouse*. New York: Putnam, 1969.

Holaday, A. May. *On the Sidelines*. New York: Century, 1925.

Holland, Clarence Fowler. *Playing the Game*. Little Rock, Ark.: Democrat Printing and Litho, 1923.

Holland, Robert E. *Reardon Rah!* Cincinnati, Ohio: Benziger Brothers, 1923.

Honig, Donald.
  Fury on Skates. New York: Four Winds, 1971.
  Johnny Lee. New York: McCall, 1971.
  Way to Go, Teddy. New York: Watts, 1973.
  Breaking In. New York: Educational Services, 1974.
  Coming Back. New York: Educational Services, 1974.
  Playing for Keeps. New York: Educational Services, 1974.
  The Professional. New York: Educational Services, 1974.
  Going the Distance. New York: Watts, 1976.

Hood, Robert. *Let's Go to a Baseball Game*. New York: Putnam, 1973.

Hoppe, Art. *The Tiddling Tennis Theorem*. New York: Viking, 1977.

Hopper, James.
  The Freshman. New York: Moffat, Yard, 1912.
  Coming Back with the Spitball. New York: Harper & Brothers, 1914.

Hopton, Dr. Ralph Y., and Ann Balliol. *Pink Pants*. New York: Vanguard, 1935.

Houghton, Everett. Joint author, see Paul Dietzel.

Hughes, Rupert.
  "The Lakerim Athletic Club." *St. Nicholas,* 25 (November 1897-April 1898).
  The Patent Leather Kid and Several Others. New York: Grosset & Dunlap, 1927.

Hunting, Gardner. *Touchdown—And After*. New York: Macmillan, 1920.

Hurne, Ralph. *The Yellow Jersey*. New York: Simon & Schuster, 1973.

Hutto, Nelson.
  Breakaway Back. New York: Morrow, 1963.
  Goal Line Bomber. New York: Harper & Row, 1964.
  Victory Volley. New York: Harper & Row, 1967.

Hyland, Dick. *The Diary of a Line Smasher.* Chicago: McClurg, 1932.

Idell, Albert. *Pug.* New York: Greystone, 1941.

Irwin, Constance H. (pseudonym C. H. Frick).

> *Tourney Team.* New York: Harcourt, Brace, 1954.
>
> *Five Against the Odds.* New York: Harcourt, Brace, 1955.
>
> *Patch.* New York: Harcourt, Brace, 1957.
>
> *The Comeback Guy.* New York: Harcourt, Brace, 1961.

Jackson, C. Paul (also pseudonyms Caary Jackson, Colin Lochlons, Jack Paulson; and some written with O.B. Jackson).

> *All-Conference Tackle.* New York: Crowell, 1947.
>
> *Tournament Forward.* New York: Crowell, 1948.
>
> *Rose Bowl All-American.* New York: Crowell, 1949.
>
> *Rookie First Baseman.* New York: Crowell, 1950.
>
> *Shorty Makes First Team.* Chicago: Wilcox & Follett, 1950.
>
> *Rose Bowl Line Backer.* New York: Crowell, 1951.
>
> *Shorty at Shortstop.* Chicago: Wilcox & Follett, 1951.
>
> *Clown at Second Base.* New York: Crowell, 1952.
>
> *Dub, Halfback.* New York: Crowell, 1952.
>
> *Little Leaguer's First Uniform.* New York: Crowell, 1952.
>
> *Shorty Carries the Ball.* Chicago: Wilcox & Follett, 1952.
>
> *Giant in the Midget League.* New York: Crowell, 1953.
>
> *Shorty at the State Tournament.* Chicago: Wilcox & Follett, 1955.
>
> *Spice's Football.* New York: Crowell, 1955.
>
> *Buzzy Plays Midget League Football.* Chicago: Follett, 1956.
>
> *Bud Plays Junior High Football.* New York: Hastings House, 1957.
>
> *Bud Plays Junior High Basketball.* New York: Hastings House, 1959.
>
> *The Jamesville Jets.* Chicago: Follett, 1959.
>
> *Little League Tournament.* New York: Hastings House, 1959.
>
> *Bud Baker, T Quarterback.* New York: Hastings House, 1960.
>
> *World Series Rookie.* New York: Hastings House, 1960.

Bullpen Bargain. New York: Hastings House, 1961.

Pro Hockey Comeback. New York: Hastings House, 1961.

Bud Baker, Racing Swimmer. New York: Hastings House, 1962.

Pro Football Rookie. New York: Hastings House, 1962.

Chris Plays Small Fry Football. Chicago: Follett, 1963.

Little Major Leaguer. New York: Hastings House, 1963.

Bud Plays Senior High Basketball. New York: Hastings House, 1964.

Pee Wee Cook of the Midget League. New York: Hastings House, 1964.

Fullback in the Large Fry League. New York: Hastings House, 1965.

Junior High Freestyle Swimmer. New York: Hastings House, 1965.

Minor League Shortstop. New York: Hastings House, 1965.

Midget League Catcher. Chicago: Follett, 1966.

Rookie Catcher with the Atlanta Braves. New York: Hastings House, 1966.

Bud Baker, High School Pitcher. New York: Hastings House, 1967.

Tim, the Football Nut. New York: Hastings House, 1967.

Big Play in the Small League. New York: Hastings House, 1968.

Hall of Fame Flankerback. New York: Hastings House, 1968.

Second Time Around Rookie. New York: Hastings House, 1968.

Pennant Stretch Drive. New York: Hastings House, 1969.

Stepladder Steve Plays Basketball. New York: Hastings House, 1969.

Bud Baker, College Pitcher. New York: Hastings House, 1970.

Pass Receiver. New York: Hastings House, 1970.

Rose Bowl Pro. New York: Hastings House, 1970.

Tim Mosely, Midget Leaguer. New York: Hastings House, 1971.

Halfback! New York: Hastings House, 1971.

Eric and Dud's Football Bargain. New York: Hastings House, 1972.

Fifth Inning Fadeout. New York: Hastings House, 1972.

Beginner Under the Backboard. New York: Hastings House, 1974.

Written by "Caary Jackson."

A Uniform for Harry. Chicago: Follett, 1962.

Haunted Halfback. Chicago: Follett, 1969.

Written by "Colin Lochlons."

Stretch Smith Makes a Basket. New York: Crowell, 1949.

Squeeze Play. New York: Crowell, 1950.

Three-and-Two Pitcher. New York: Crowell, 1951.

Triple Play. New York: Crowell, 1952.

Barney of the Babe Ruth League. New York: Crowell, 1954.

Written by "Jack Paulson."

Fourth Down Pass. Philadelphia: Winston, 1950.

Match Point. Philadelphia: Westminster, 1956.

Side Line Victory. Philadelphia: Westminster, 1957.

Written with O. B. Jackson.

Star Kicker. New York: Whittlesey House, 1955.

Basketball Clown. New York: Whittlesey House, 1956.

Hillbilly Pitcher. New York: Whittlesey House, 1956.

Puck Grabber. New York: Whittlesey House, 1957.

Freshman Forward. New York: McGraw-Hill, 1959.

The Short Guard. New York: Whittlesey House, 1961.

High School Backstop. New York: Whittlesey House, 1963.

Jackson, David. *Gridiron Gambler.* Philadelphia: Dorrance, 1943.

Jackson, O. B.

Basketball Comes to North Island. New York: McGraw-Hill, 1963.

Southpaw in the Mighty Mite League. New York: McGraw-Hill, 1965.

Joint author, see C. Paul Jackson.

Jacobs, Helen Hull.

Laurel for Judy. New York: Dodd, Mead, 1945.

Center Court. New York: Barnes, 1950.

Judy, Tennis Ace. New York: Dodd,Mead,1951.

Proudly She Serves! New York: Dodd, Mead, 1953.

Jenkins, Dan.

Semi-Tough. New York: Atheneum, 1972.

Dead Solid Perfect. New York: Atheneum, 1974.

Jenks, George C.

"Double-Curve Dan, the Pitcher Detective; or, Against Heavy Odds," *Beadle's Half-Dime Library,* No. 581 (11 September 1888).

"The Pitcher Detective's Toughest Tussle; or, Double-Curve Dan's Double Play," *Beadle's Half-Dime Library,* No. 608 (12 August 1889).

"The Pitcher Detective's Foil; or, Double-Curve Dan's Dead Ball." *Beadle's Half-Dime Library,* No. 681 (12 August 1890).

Johnson, Owen.

The Humming Bird. New York: Baker & Taylor, 1910.

Stover at Yale. New York: Grosset & Dunlap, 1912.

Jones, Jack. *The Animal.* New York: Morrow, 1975.

Jorgensen, Nels L. *Dave Palmer's Diamond Mystery.* New York: Cupples & Leon, 1954.

Kahler, Hugh McNair. *The Big Pink.* New York: Farrar & Rinehart, 1932.

Karlins, Marvin. *The Last Man Is Out.* Englewood Cliffs, N.J.: Prentice-Hall, 1969.

Karney, Jack. *There Goes Shorty Higgins.* New York: Morrow, 1945.

Kay, Helen. Pseudonym, see Mrs. Herbert Goldfrank.

Keating, Lawrence.

False Start. Philadelphia: Westminster, 1955.

Kid Brother. Philadelphia: Westminster, 1956.

Freshman Backstop. Philadelphia: Westminster, 1957.

Junior Miler. Philadelphia: Westminster, 1958.

Senior Challenge. Philadelphia: Westminster, 1959.

Runner-Up. Philadelphia: Westminster, 1961.

Wrong-Way Neelen. Philadelphia: Westminster, 1963.

Ace Rebounder. Philadelphia: Westminster, 1964.

The Comeback Year. Philadelphia: Westminster, 1966.

Keifetz, Norman. *The Sensation.* New York: Atheneum, 1975.

Kennedy, Lucy. *The Sunlit Field*. New York: Crown, 1950.

Kessler, Leonard.

Here Comes the Strikeout. New York: Harper & Row, 1956.

Kick, Pass, and Run. New York: Harper & Row, 1966.

On Your Mark, Get Set, Go. New York: Harper & Row, 1972.

Key, Ed. *Phyllis*. New York: Dutton, 1951.

Knipe, Alden.

Captain of the Eleven. New York: Harper & Brothers, 1910.

The Last Lap. New York: Harper & Brothers, 1911.

Bunny Plays the Game. New York: Harper & Brothers, 1925.

Knott, Bill (pseudonym Bill J. Carol).

Junk Pitcher. Chicago: Follett, 1963. (Published under his own name.)

Backboard Scrambler. Austin, Tex.: Steck, 1963.

Circus Catch. Austin, Tex.: Steck-Vaughn, 1963.

Clutch Single. Austin, Tex.: Steck-Vaughn, 1964.

Scatback. Austin, Tex.: Steck-Vaughn, 1964.

Full-Court Pirate. Austin, Tex.: Steck-Vaughn, 1965.

Hit Away! Austin, Tex.: Steck-Vaughn, 1965.

Hard Smash to Third. Austin, Tex.: Steck-Vaughn, 1965.

Long Pass. Austin, Tex.: Steck-Vaughn, 1966.

Inside the Ten. Austin, Tex.: Steck-Vaughn, 1967.

Lefty's Long Throw. Austin, Tex.: Steck-Vaughn, 1967.

Lefty Finds a Catcher. Austin, Tex.: Steck-Vaughn, 1968.

Touchdown Duo. Austin, Tex.: Steck-Vaughn, 1968.

Crazylegs Merrill. Austin, Tex.: Steck-Vaughn, 1969.

Lefty Plays First. Austin, Tex.: Steck-Vaughn, 1969.

Sandy Plays Third. Austin, Tex.: Steck-Vaughn, 1970.

Stop that Pass. Austin, Tex.: Steck-Vaughn, 1970.

Linebacker Blitz. Austin, Tex.: Steck-Vaughn, 1971.

Squeeze Play. Austin, Tex.: Steck-Vaughn, 1971.

Fullback Fury. Austin, Tex.: Steck-Vaughn, 1972.

High Fly to Center. Austin, Tex.: Steck-Vaughn, 1972.

Double-Play Ball. Austin, Tex.: Steck-Vaughn, 1973.

Flare Pass. Austin, Tex.: Steck-Vaughn, 1973.

Blocking Back. Austin, Tex.: Steck-Vaughn, 1974.

Single to Center. Austin, Tex.: Steck-Vaughn, 1974.

Knox, Jackson. "Shortstop Maje, the Diamond Field Detective; or, Old Falcon's Master Game." *Beadle's Dime Library,* No. 515 (5 September 1888).

Knudson, R. R.

Zanballer. New York: Delacorte, 1972.

Fox Running. New York: Harper & Row, 1975.

Zanbanger. New York: Harper & Row, 1977.

Zanboomer. New York: Harper & Row, 1978.

Koch, Tom. *Tournament Trail.* New York: Lothrop, Lee & Shepard, 1950.

Kohler, Julilly. *Football Trees.* Chicago: Children's Press, 1947.

Konigsburg, E. L. *About the B'nai Bagels.* New York: Atheneum, 1969.

Koperwas, Sam. *Westchester Bull.* New York: Simon & Schuster, 1976.

Kramer, George.

The Left Hander. New York: Putnam, 1964.

Kid Battery. New York: Putnam, 1968.

Laflin, Jack. *Throw the Long Bomb.* Racine, Wis.: Whitman, 1967.

LaFountaine, George. *Two-Minute Warning.* New York: Coward, McCann & Geoghegan, 1975.

Lambert, Reita. *The Noble Art.* Garden City, N.Y.: Doubleday, Doran, 1935.

Lamers, William. *Joe McGuire, Freshman.* Milwaukee, Wis.: Bruce, 1932.

Lampell, Millard. *The Hero.* New York: Messner, 1949.

Lang, Jack. Joint author, see Whitey Ford and Bill Skowran.

Lardner, Ring.

You Know Me Al. New York: Scribner's, 1916.

Lose with a Smile. New York: Scribner's, 1933.

Larner, Jeremy. *Drive, He Said.* New York: Delacorte, 1964.

Lawton, Charles. Pseudonym, see Noel Sainsbury.

Lear, Peter. *Goldengirl.* Garden City, N.Y.: Doubleday, 1978.

Leckie, Robert (pseudonym Mark Porter).

Duel on the Cinders. New York: Simon & Schuster, 1960.

Keeper Play. New York: Simon & Schuster, 1960.

Overtime Upset. New York: Simon & Schuster, 1960.

Set Point. New York: Simon & Schuster, 1960.

Slashing Blades. New York: Simon & Schuster, 1960.

Winning Pitcher. New York: Grosset & Dunlap, 1962.

Legrand. Pseudonym; see Legrand Henderson.

Leonard, Burgess.

Victory Pass. Philadelphia: Lippincott, 1950.

Rookie Southpaw. Philadelphia: Lippincott, 1951.

Phantom of the Foul-Lines. Philadelphia: Lippincott, 1952.

One-Man Backfield. Philadelphia: Lippincott, 1953.

Second-Season Jinx. Philadelphia: Lippincott, 1953.

Stretch Bolton Comes Back. Philadelphia: Lippincott, 1953.

The Rookie Fights Back. Philadelphia: Lippincott, 1954.

Stretch Bolton's Rookies. Philadelphia: Lippincott, 1961.

Rebound Man. New York: Watts, 1962.

Stretch Bolton: Mr. Shortstop. Philadelphia: Lippincott, 1963.

Levitt, Leonard. *The Long Way Round.* New York: Saturday Review Press, 1972.

Levy, Elizabeth.

Something Queer at the Ballpark. New York: Delacorte, 1975.

The Tryouts. New York: Winds Press, 1979.

Lipsyte, Robert. *The Contender.* New York: Harper & Row, 1967.

Liss, Howard. Joint author, see Y. A. Tittle.

Lochlons, Colin. Pseudonym; see C. Paul Jackson.

Loken, Chris. *Come Monday Morning.* New York: Evans, 1974.

London, Jack.

The Game. New York: Grosset & Dunlap, 1905.

The Abysmal Brute. New York: Century, 1913.

Lord, Beman.

The Trouble with Francis. New York: Walck, 1958.

Quarterback's Aim. New York: Walck, 1960.

Bats and Balls. New York: Walck, 1962.

Rough Ice. New York: Walck, 1963.

Mystery Guest at Left End. New York: Walck, 1965.

The Perfect Pitch. New York: Walck, 1965.

Shot-Put Challenge. New York: Walck, 1969.

Lowry, Robert. *The Violent Wedding*. Garden City, N.Y.: Doubleday, 1953.

Lunemann, Evelyn.

Fairway Danger. Westchester, Ill.: Benefic Press, 1969.

No Turning Back. Westchester, Ill.: Benefic Press, 1969.

Ten Feet Tall. Westchester, Ill.: Benefic Press, 1969.

Tip Off. Westchester, Ill.: Benefic Press, 1969.

Face-Off. Westchester, Ill.: Benefic Press, 1972.

Pitcher's Choice. Westchester, Ill.: Benefic Press, 1972.

Swimmer's Mark. Westchester, Ill.: Benefic Press, 1972.

Tennis Champ. Westchester, Ill.: Benefic Press, 1972.

Lynde, Francis. *Dick and Larry, Freshmen*. New York: Scribner, 1922.

Lyons, Kennedy. Pseudonym; see Paschal N. Strong.

McCormick, Wilfred.

Legion Tourney. New York: Putnam, 1948.

The Three-Two Pitch. New York: Putnam, 1948.

Fielder's Choice. New York: Putnam, 1949.

Flying Tackle. New York: Putnam, 1949.

Bases Loaded. New York: Putnam, 1950.

Rambling Halfback. New York: Putnam, 1950.

Grand-Slam Homer. New York: Putnam, 1951.

Quick Kick. New York: Putnam, 1951.

First and Ten. New York: Putnam, 1952.

The Man on the Bench. New York: McKay, 1955.

The Captive Coach. New York: McKay, 1956.

The Big Ninth. New York: Putnam, 1958.

The Bigger Game. New York: McKay, 1958.

The Hot Corner. New York: McKay, 1958.

Five Yards to Glory. New York: McKay, 1959.

The Proud Champions. New York: McKay, 1959.

The Automatic Strike. New York: McKay, 1960.

The Last Put-Out. New York: Putnam, 1960.

One O'Clock Hitter. New York: McKay, 1960.

Stranger in the Backfield. New York: McKay, 1960.

Too Many Forwards. New York: McKay, 1960.

The Bluffer. New York: McKay, 1961.

Man in Motion. New York: McKay, 1961.

The Play for One. New York: McKay, 1961.

The Double Steal. New York: McKay, 1962.

The Five Man Break. New York: McKay, 1962.

Rebel with a Glove. New York: McKay, 1962.

Too Late to Quit. New York: McKay, 1962.

Home Run Harvest. New York: McKay, 1963.

Once a Slugger. New York: McKay, 1963.

The Phantom Shortstop. New York: McKay, 1963.

Rough Stuff. New York: McKay, 1963.

The Starmaker. New York: Speller, 1963.

The Two-One-Two Attack. New York: McKay, 1963.

The Long Pitcher. New York: Duell, Sloan & Pearce, 1964.

The Pro Toughback. New York: Duell, Sloan & Pearce, 1964.

The Right-End Option. New York: McKay, 1964.

The Throwing Catcher. New York: McKay, 1964.

Wild on the Bases. New York: Duell, Sloan & Pearce, 1964.

The Go-Ahead Runner. New York: McKay, 1965.

Seven in Front. New York: McKay, 1965.

Touchdown for the Enemy. New York: Putnam, 1965.

No Place for Heroes. Indianapolis, Ind.: Bobbs-Merrill, 1966.

Tall at the Plate. Indianapolis, Ind.: Bobbs-Merrill, 1966.

The Incomplete Pitcher. Indianapolis, Ind.: Bobbs-Merrill, 1967.

One Bounce Too Many. Indianapolis, Ind.: Bobbs-Merrill, 1967.

Rookie on First. New York: Putnam, 1967.

Fullback in the Rough. Englewood Cliffs, N.J.: Prentice-Hall, 1969.

McDowell, Edwin. *Three Cheers and a Tiger.* New York: Macmillan, 1966.

McIntosh, Burr. *Football and Love.* New York: Transatlantic Publishing, 1895.

MacKellar, William.

Kickoff. New York: Whittlesey House, 1955.

The Team That Wouldn't Quit. New York: Whittlesey

House, 1956.

A Goal for Greg. New York: McKay, 1958.

Score! New York: McKay, 1967.

Mound Menace. Chicago: Follett, 1969.

The Soccer Orphans. New York: Dodd, Mead, 1979.

McKenna, Edward L. *The Bruiser.* New York: McBride, 1929.

McKone, Jim.

Lone Star Fullback. New York: Vanguard, 1966.

To Win in November. New York: Vanguard, 1971.

Magnuson, James. *The Rundown.* New York: Dial, 1977.

Malamud, Bernard. *The Natural.* New York: Harcourt, Brace and Company, 1952.

Manchester, William. *The Long Gainer.* Boston: Little, Brown, 1961.

Mann, Arthur (also, pseudonym A. R. Thurman).

Bob White: Bonus Player. New York: McKay, 1952.

Bob White: Farm Club Player. New York: McKay, 1952.

Written by "A. R. Thurman."

Money Pitcher. New York: McKay, 1952.

Goal in Sight. New York: McKay, 1953.

March, Joseph Moncure. *The Set-Up.* New York: Covici-Friede, 1928.

Mario, Matty. Pseudonym; see Mario James Ghiselli.

Maris, Roger and Jack Ogle. *Slugger in Right.* Larchmont, N.Y.: Argonaut, 1963.

Marks, Percy. *The Unwilling God.* New York: Harper & Brothers, 1929.

Marx, Arthur. *The Ordeal of Willie Brown.* New York: Simon & Schuster, 1951.

Mathewson, Christy (ghostwritten by John Wheeler).

Won in the Ninth. New York: Bodner, 1910.

Catcher Craig. New York: Dodd, Mead, 1915.

First Base Faulkner. New York: Dodd, Mead, 1916.

Pitcher Pollock. New York: Dodd, Mead, 1916.

Second Base Sloan. New York: Dodd, Mead, 1917.

Maule, Hamilton ("Tex").

Footsteps. New York: Random House, 1961.

The Rookie. New York: McKay, 1961.

The Quarterback. New York: McKay, 1962.

The Shortstop. New York: McKay, 1962.

Beatty of the Yankees. New York: McKay, 1963.

The Last Out. New York: McKay, 1964.

The Linebacker. New York: McKay, 1965.

The Running Back. New York: McKay, 1966.

The Corner Back. New York: McKay, 1967.

The Receiver. New York: McKay, 1969.

Maxwell, William. *The Folded Leaf*. New York: Harper & Brothers, 1945.

Maynard, Colton. *The School Days of Elliott Gray, Jr.* New York: Grosset & Dunlap, 1911.

Mays, Willie and Jeff Harris. *Danger in Center Field*. Larchmont, N.Y.: Argonaut, 1963.

Meader, Stephen.

The Will to Win and Other Stories. New York: Harcourt, Brace & World, 1936.

Sparkplug of the Hornets. New York: Harcourt, Brace & World, 1953.

Lonesome End. New York: Harcourt, Brace & World, 1968.

Meincke, William. *Rose Bowl*. New York: Speller, 1936.

Mellett, John C. (pseudonym Jonathan Brooks).

Jimmy Makes the Varsity. Indianapolis, Ind.: Bobbs-Merrill, 1928.

Pigskin Soldier. Garden City, N.Y.: Doubleday, Doran, 1931.

Varsity Jim. Indianapolis, Ind.: Bobbs-Merrill, 1939.

Michael, D. J. Pseudonym, see Charles Einstein.

Miers, Earl Schenk.

The Backfield Feud. New York: Appleton-Century, 1936.

Career Coach. Philadelphia: Westminster, 1941.

Monkey Shines. Cleveland, Ohio: World Publishing, 1952.

Touchdown Trouble. Cleveland, Ohio: World Publishing, 1953.

The Kid Who Beat the Dodgers, and Other Sports Stories. Cleveland, Ohio: World Publishing, 1954.

Ball of Fire. Cleveland: World Publishing, 1956.

Millhauser, Bertram and Beulah Marie Dix. *The Life of Jimmy Dolan*. New York: Macaulay, 1933.

Millholland, Ray. *Lucky Shoes*. Garden City, N.Y.: Doubleday, 1956.

Milton, David S. *The Quarterback*. New York: Dell, 1970.

Minnigerode, Meade. *The Big Year*. New York: Putnam, 1921.

Moffat, William D.

    Belmont College. Cleveland, Ohio: World Syndicate Publishing, no date.

    The Crimson Banner. Cleveland, Ohio: World Syndicate Publishing, 1907.

Molloy, Paul. *A Pennant for the Kremlin*. Garden City, N.Y.: Doubleday, 1964.

Moore, Joseph A. *Hot Shot at Third*. New York: Duell, Sloan & Pearce, 1958.

Morse, Clinton R. ("Brick"). *Jo Dunn, All-American*. Boston: Christopher Publishing, 1941.

Morse, Ray. *Cadets at Kings Point*. New York: Aladdin, 1949.

Muller, Charles.

    The Baseball Detective. New York: Harper & Brothers, 1928.

    Puck Chasers, Incorporated. New York: Harper & Brothers, 1928.

Naidish, Theodore. *Watch Out for Willie Carter*. New York: Scribner's, 1944.

Needham, Henry Beach. *The Double Squeeze*. Garden City, N.Y.: Doubleday, Page, 1915.

Neigoff, Mike.

    Free Throw. Chicago: Whitman, 1967.

    Two on First. Chicago: Whitman, 1967.

    Goal to Go. Chicago: Whitman, 1970.

    Hal, Tennis Champ. Chicago: Whitman, 1971.

    Ski Run. Chicago: Whitman, 1972.

    Playmaker. Chicago: Whitman, 1973.

    Terror on the Ice. Chicago: Whitman, 1974.

    Runner Up. Chicago: Whitman, 1975.

Nemerov, Howard. *The Homecoming Game*. New York: Simon & Schuster, 1957.

Neugeboren, Jay. *Big Man.* Boston: Houghton Mifflin, 1966.

Neville, James M. *Mud and Glory.* New York: Duffield, 1929.

Newman, Edwin. *Sunday Punch.* Boston: Houghton Mifflin, 1979.

Nye, Bud. *Stay Loose.* Garden City, N.Y.: Doubleday, 1959.

O'Connor, Philip F. *Stealing Home.* New York: Knopf, 1979.

O'Cork, Shannon. *Sports Freak.* New York: St. Martin's, 1980.

Odell, Frank I.

> *Larry Burke, Freshman.* Boston: Lothrop, Lee & Shepard, 1911.
>
> *Larry Burke, Sophomore.* Boston: Lothrop, Lee & Shepard, 1911.

Offit, Sidney.

> *The Boy Who Won the World Series.* New York: Lothrop, Lee & Shepard, 1960.
>
> *Cadet Quarterback.* New York: St. Martins, 1961.
>
> *Cadet Command.* New York: St. Martins, 1962.
>
> *Soupbone.* New York: St. Martins, 1963.
>
> *Cadet Attack.* New York: St. Martins, 1964.

Ogle, Jack. Joint author, see Roger Maris.

Oldham, Archie. *A Race Through Summer.* New York: Dell, 1976.

Olgin, Joseph.

> *Little League Champions.* New York: Dutton, 1954.
>
> *Backcourt Rivals.* New York: Dutton, 1955.
>
> *The Scoring Twins.* Scranton: Biddy Basketball, 1956 (with Jay Archer).
>
> *Sports Stories for Boys.* New York: Harvey House, 1956.
>
> *Battery Feud.* Boston: Houghton Mifflin, 1959.

Olsen, Jack.

> *Alphabet Jackson.* Chicago: Playboy, 1974.
>
> *Massy's Game.* Chicago: Playboy, 1976.

Olson, Gene.

> *The Tall One.* New York: Dodd, Mead, 1956.
>
> *The Ballhawks.* Philadelphia: Westminster, 1960.
>
> *Bonus Boy.* New York: Dodd, Mead, 1963.
>
> *Fullback Fury.* New York: Dodd, Mead, 1964.
>
> *Three Men on Third.* Philadelphia: Westminster, 1965.
>
> *Cross-Country Chaos.* Philadelphia: Westminster, 1966.

O'Rourke, Frank.

Flashing Spikes. New York: Barnes, 1948.

The Team. New York: Barnes, 1949.

Bonus Rookie. New York: Barnes, 1950.

The Football Gravy Train. New York: Barnes, 1951.

The Greatest Victory and Other Baseball Stories. New York: Barnes, 1952.

The Heavenly World Series and Other Baseball Stories. New York: Barnes, 1952.

Never Come Back. New York: Barnes, 1952.

Nine Good Men. New York: Barnes, 1952.

The Catcher, and the Manager. New York: Barnes, 1953.

High Dive. New York: Random House, 1954.

Overton, Mark.

Jack Winters' Baseball Team. New York: New York Book, 1919.

Jack Winters' Gridiron Chum. New York: New York Book, 1919.

Paine, Ralph D.

College Years. New York: Scribner's, 1909.

The Head Coach. New York: Scribner's, 1910.

Campus Days. New York: Scribner's, 1912.

Sons of Eli. New York: Scribner's, 1917.

First Down Kentucky! Boston: Houghton Mifflin, 1921.

Pallas, Norvin. *The Baseball Mystery.* New York: Washburn, 1964.

Parker, Charles E. *The Whipper-Snapper.* New York: Stokes, 1926.

Parks, Edd Winfield. *Safe on Second.* Indianapolis, Ind.: Bobbs-Merrill, 1953.

Patten, Gilbert (also pseudonyms Gordon Braddock, Morgan Scott, Burt L. Standish).

The Rockspur Eleven. New York: Street and Smith, 1900.

The Rockspur Nine. New York: Street and Smith, 1900.

The Rockspur Rivals. New York: Street and Smith, 1901.

Bill Bruce of Harvard. New York: Dodd, Mead, 1910.

Cliff Stirling Behind the Line. Philadelphia: McKay, 1910.

Cliff Stirling, Captain of the Nine. Philadelphia: McKay, 1910.

Cliff Stirling, Freshman at Stormbridge. Philadelphia: McKay, 1913.

Boltwood of Yale. New York: Barse and Hopkins, 1914.

The College Rebel. New York: Barse and Hopkins, 1914.

Cliff Stirling, Sophomore at Stormbridge. Philadelphia: David McKay, 1916.

On College Battlefields. New York: Barse and Hopkins, 1917.

Call of the Varsity. New York: Barse and Hopkins, 1920.

Sons of Old Eli. New York: Barse and Hopkins, 1923.

Written by "Gordon Braddock."

Rex Kingdon in the North Woods. New York: Burt, 1914.

Rex Kingdon of Ridgewood High. New York: Burt, 1914.

Rex Kingdon Behind the Bat. New York: Burt, 1916.

Rex Kingdon on Storm Island. New York: Burt, 1917.

Rex Kingdon at Walcott Hall. New York: Burt, n.d.

Written by "Morgan Scott."

Ben Stone at Oakdale. New York: Burt, 1911.

Boys of Oakdale Academy. New York: Barse and Hopkins, 1911.

Rival Pitchers of Oakdale. New York: Burt, 1911.

Great Oakdale Mystery. New York: Burt, 1912.

Oakdale Boys in Camp. New York: Burt, 1912.

New Boys at Oakdale. New York: Burt, 1913.

The Frank Merriwell series by "Burt L. Standish." (The Frank Merriwell stories were originally published weekly in the *Tip Top Library,* later *Tip Top Weekly,* from 18 April 1896 until 6 March 1915. Patten wrote the stories through 27 July 1912, after which the series was continued by other writers who retained the Standish pseudonym. The stories were also bound, three or four to a volume, and published by Street and Smith between 1900 and 1933; and the first twenty-eight were issued in hardcover by A. L. Burt Company between 1915 and 1925. The following is a list of the 217 paperbound Merriwell volumes published by Street and Smith. I am unable to identify the precise year of publication between 1900 and 1933 for each volume, and I make no effort to differentiate those stories that are concerned particularly with sport from those that are not. The entire series describes the career

of America's pre-eminent fictional sports hero. The source
for this list is John L. Cutler, "Gilbert Patten and His Frank
Merriwell Saga," *University of Maine Studies,* 31 (1934), pp.
112-14.)

Frank Merriwell's School Days
Frank Merriwell's Chums
Frank Merriwell's Foes
Frank Merriwell's Trip West
Frank Merriwell Down South
Frank Merriwell's Bravery
Frank Merriwell's Hunting Tour
Frank Merriwell in Europe
Frank Merriwell at Yale
Frank Merriwell's Sports Afield
Frank Merriwell's Races
Frank Merriwell's Party
Frank Merriwell's Bicycle Tour
Frank Merriwell's Courage
Frank Merriwell's Daring
Frank Merriwell's Alarm
Frank Merriwell's Athletes
Frank Merriwell's Skill
Frank Merriwell's Champions
Frank Merriwell's Return to Yale
Frank Merriwell's Secret
Frank Merriwell's Danger
Frank Merriwell's Loyalty
Frank Merriwell in Camp
Frank Merriwell's Vacation Cruise
Frank Merriwell's Cruise
Frank Merriwell's Chase
Frank Merriwell in Maine
Frank Merriwell's First Job
Frank Merriwell's Opportunity
Frank Merriwell's Hard Luck
Frank Merriwell's Protégé
Frank Merriwell on the Road
Frank Merriwell's Own Company
Frank Merriwell's Fame
Frank Merriwell's College Chums

Frank Merriwell's Problem
Frank Merriwell's Fortune
Frank Merriwell's New Comedian
Frank Merriwell's Prosperity
Frank Merriwell's Stage Hit
Frank Merriwell's Great Scheme
Frank Merriwell in England
Frank Merriwell on the Boulevards
Frank Merriwell's Duel
Frank Merriwell's Double Shot
Frank Merriwell's Baseball Victories
Frank Merriwell's Confidence
Frank Merriwell's Auto
Frank Merriwell's Fun
Frank Merriwell's Generosity
Frank Merriwell's Tricks
Frank Merriwell's Temptation
Frank Merriwell on Top
Frank Merriwell's Luck
Frank Merriwell's Mascot
Frank Merriwell's Reward
Frank Merriwell's Phantom
Frank Merriwell's Faith
Frank Merriwell's Victories
Frank Merriwell's Iron Nerve
Frank Merriwell in Kentucky
Frank Merriwell's Power
Frank Merriwell's Shrewdness
Frank Merriwell's Set Back
Frank Merriwell's Search
Frank Merriwell's Club
Frank Merriwell's Trust
Frank Merriwell's False Friend
Frank Merriwell's Strong Arm
Frank Merriwell as Coach
Frank Merriwell's Brother
Frank Merriwell's Marvel
Frank Merriwell's Support
Dick Merriwell at Fardale
Dick Merriwell's Glory

Dick Merriwell's Promise
Dick Merriwell's Rescue
Dick Merriwell's Narrow Escape
Dick Merriwell's Racket
Dick Merriwell's Revenge
Dick Merriwell's Ruse
Dick Merriwell's Delivery
Dick Merriwell's Wonders
Frank Merriwell's Honor
Dick Merriwell's Diamond
Frank Merriwell's Winners
Dick Merriwell's Dash
Dick Merriwell's Ability
Dick Merriwell's Trap
Dick Merriwell's Defense
Dick Merriwell's Model
Dick Merriwell's Mystery
Frank Merriwell's Backers
Dick Merriwell's Backstop
Dick Merriwell's Western Mission
Frank Merriwell's Rescue
Frank Merriwell's Encounter
Dick Merriwell's Market Money
Frank Merriwell's Nomads
Dick Merriwell on the Gridiron
Dick Merriwell's Disguise
Dick Merriwell's Test
Frank Merriwell's Trump Card
Frank Merriwell's Strategy
Frank Merriwell's Triumph
Dick Merriwell's Grit
Dick Merriwell's Assurance
Dick Merriwell's Long Slide
Frank Merriwell's Rough Deal
Dick Merriwell's Threat
Dick Merriwell's Persistence
Dick Merriwell's Day
Frank Merriwell's Peril
Dick Merriwell's Downfall
Frank Merriwell's Pursuit

Dick Merriwell Abroad
Frank Merriwell in the Rockies
Dick Merriwell's Pranks
Frank Merriwell's Pride
Frank Merriwell's Challengers
Frank Merriwell's Endurance
Dick Merriwell's Cleverness
Frank Merriwell's Marriage
Dick Merriwell, the Wizard
Dick Merriwell's Stroke
Dick Merriwell's Return
Dick Merriwell's Resource
Dick Merriwell's Five
Frank Merriwell's Tigers
Dick Merriwell's Polo Team
Frank Merriwell's Pupils
Frank Merriwell's New Boy
Dick Merriwell's Home Run
Dick Merriwell's Dare
Frank Merriwell's Son
Dick Merriwell's Team Mate
Frank Merriwell's Leaguers
Frank Merriwell's Happy Camp
Dick Merriwell's Influence
Dick Merriwell, Freshman
Dick Merriwell's Staying Power
Dick Merriwell's Joke
Frank Merriwell's Talisman
Frank Merriwell's Horse
Dick Merriwell's Regret
Dick Merriwell's Magnetism
Dick Merriwell's Backers
Dick Merriwell's Best Work
Dick Merriwell's Distrust
Dick Merriwell's Debt
Dick Merriwell's Mastery
Dick Merriwell Adrift
Frank Merriwell's Worst Boy
Dick Merriwell's Close Call
Frank Merriwell's Air Voyage

Dick Merriwell's Black Star
Frank Merriwell in Wall Street
Frank Merriwell Facing His Foes
Dick Merriwell's Stanchness
Frank Merriwell's Hard Case
Dick Merriwell's Stand
Dick Merriwell Doubted
Frank Merriwell's Steadying Hand
Dick Merriwell's Example
Dick Merriwell in the Wilds
Frank Merriwell's Ranch
Dick Merriwell's Way
Frank Merriwell's Lesson
Dick Merriwell's Reputation
Frank Merriwell's Encouragement
Dick Merriwell's Honors
Frank Merriwell's Wizard
Dick Merriwell's Race
Dick Merriwell's Star Play
Frank Merriwell at Phantom Lake
Dick Merriwell a Winner
Dick Merriwell at the County Fair
Frank Merriwell's Grit
Dick Merriwell's Power
Frank Merriwell in Peru
Frank Merriwell's Long Chance
Frank Merriwell's Old Form
Frank Merriwell's Treasure Hunt
Dick Merriwell Game to the Last
Dick Merriwell, Motor King
Dick Merriwell's Tussle
Dick Merriwell's Aero Dash
Dick Merriwell's Intuition
Dick Merriwell's Placer Find
Dick Merriwell's Fighting Chance
Frank Merriwell's Tact
Frank Merriwell's Puzzle
Frank Merriwell's Mystery
Frank Merriwell, the Lion-hearted
Frank Merriwell's Tenacity

Dick Merriwell's Perception
Dick Merriwell's Detective Work
Dick Merriwell's Commencement
Dick Merriwell's Decision
Dick Merriwell's Coolness
Dick Merriwell's Reliance
Frank Merriwell's Young Warriors
Frank Merriwell's Lads
Dick Merriwell in Panama
Dick Merriwell in South America
Dick Merriwell's Counsel
Others written by "Burt L. Standish."

Lefty o' the Big League. New York: Barse and Hopkins, 1914.

Lefty o' the Blue Stockings. New York: Barse and Hopkins, 1914.

Lefty o' the Bush. New York: Barse and Hopkins, 1914.

Lefty o' the Training Camp. New York: Barse and Hopkins, 1914.

Lefty Locke, Pitcher-Manager. New York: Barse and Hopkins, n.d.

Brick King, Backstop. New York: Barse and Hopkins, 1914.

Courtney of the Center Garden. New York: Barse and Hopkins, 1915.

Covering the Look-in Corner. New York: Barse and Hopkins, 1915.

The Making of a Big Leaguer. New York: Barse and Hopkins, 1915.

Guarding the Keystone Sack. New York: Barse and Hopkins, 1917.

Man on First. New York: Barse and Hopkins, 1920.

Lego Lamb, Southpaw. New York: Barse and Hopkins, 1923.

The Grip of the Game. New York: Barse and Hopkins, 1924.

Lefty Locke, Owner. New York: Barse and Hopkins, 1925.

Crossed Signals. New York: Barse and Hopkins, 1928.

Paulson, Jack. Pseudonym; see C. Paul Jackson.

Perry, Lawrence.
    The Big Game. New York: Scribner's, 1918.
    For the Game's Sake. New York: Scribner's, 1920.
    The Fullback. New York: Scribner's, 1924.
    Touchdowns. New York: Scribner's, 1924.
Philbrook, Clem.
    The Magic Bat. New York: Macmillan, 1954.
    Skimeister. New York: Macmillan, 1955.
    Ollie's Team and the Baseball Computer. New York: Hastings House, 1967.
    Ollie's Team and the Football Computer. New York: Hastings House, 1968.
    Ollie's Team and the Basketball Computer. New York: Hastings House, 1969.
    Ollie, the Backward Forward. New York: Hastings House, 1970.
    Ollie's Team Plays Biddy Baseball. New York: Hastings House, 1970.
    Ollie's Team and the Alley Cats. New York: Hastings House, 1971.
    Ollie's Team and the Two-Hundred Pound Problem. New York: Hastings House, 1972.
    Ollie's Team and the Million Dollar Mistake. New York: Hastings House, 1973.
Pickens, Arthur E. *The Golf Bum.* New York: Crown, 1970.
Pier, Arthur Stanwood.
    The Triumph. New York: McClure Phillips, 1903.
    Boys of St. Timothy's. New York: Scribner's, 1904.
    The Jester of St. Timothy's. Boston: Houghton Mifflin, 1906.
    Harding of St. Timothy's. Boston: Houghton Mifflin, 1906.
    The New Boy. Boston: Houghton Mifflin, 1908.
    The Crashaw Brothers. Boston: Houghton Mifflin, 1910.
    Grannis.of the Fifth. Boston: Houghton Mifflin, 1914.
    Dormitory Days. Boston: Houghton Mifflin, 1919.
    David Ives. Boston: Houghton Mifflin, 1922.
    Friends and Rivals. Boston: Houghton Mifflin, 1925.
    The Coach. Philadelphia: Penn, 1928.
    The Captain. Philadelphia: Penn, 1929.

The Rigor of the Game. Boston: Houghton Mifflin, 1929.
The Cheer Leader. Philadelphia: Penn, 1930.
The Champion. Philadelphia: Penn, 1931.

Pierrot, George. *Yea, Sheriton.* Garden City, N.Y.: Double-day, Page, 1925.

Pillitteri, Joseph. *Two Hours on Sunday.* New York: Dial, 1971.

Platt, Ken. *The Screwball King Murder.* New York: Random House, 1978.

Playfair, Robert.
The Crimson Road. Boston: Houghton Mifflin, 1938.
Fuller at Harvard. Boston: Houghton Mifflin, 1939.
Colonel of the Crimson. Boston: Houghton Mifflin, 1940.

Porter, Harold Everett (pseudonym Holworthy Hall).
Dormie One and Other Golf Stories. New York: Century, 1917.
Colossus. New York: Sears, 1930.

Porter, Mark. Pseudonym; see Robert Leckie.

Pye, Lloyd. *That Prosser Kid.* New York: Arbor House, 1977.

Quandt, Albert (pseudonym Barry DeForest). *Pushover.* New York: Phoenix, 1936.

Quigley, Martin. *Today's Game.* New York: Viking, 1965.

Quirk, Leslie.
Baby Elton, Quarterback. New York: Century, 1904.
"Midget Blake," Pitcher. New York: McLoughlin Brothers, 1906.
Freshman Dorn, Pitcher. New York: Century, 1911.
The Fourth Down. Boston: Little, Brown, 1912.
Tackle and Quarterback and Other Athletic Stories. New York: McLoughlin Brothers, 1912.
The Third Strike. Boston: Little, Brown, 1914.
Playing the Game. Chicago: Donahue, 1915.

Rand, Addison. Pseudonym, see Adolph C. Regli.

Reck, Franklin. *Varsity Letter.* New York: Crowell, 1942.

Redgate, John. *The Last Decathlon.* New York: Delacorte, 1979.

Reed, Kit. *Captain Grownup.* New York: Dutton, 1976.

Regli, Adolph C. (pseudonym Addison Rand). *Southpaw Fly Hawk.* New York: Longmans Green, 1952.

Renick, Marion (also, some written with James L. Renick).
    Champion Caddy. New York: Scribner's, 1943.
    Skating Today. New York: Scribner's, 1945.
    Swimming Fever. New York: Scribner's, 1947.
    A Touchdown for Doc. New York: Scribner's, 1948.
    The Dooleys Play Ball. New York: Scribner's, 1949.
    Nicky's Football Team. New York: Scribner's, 1951.
    Jimmy's Own Basketball. New York: Scribner's, 1952.
    Pete's Home Run. New York: Scribner's, 1952.
    The Heart for Baseball. New York: Scribner's, 1953.
    Bats and Gloves of Glory. New York: Scribner's, 1956.
    Young Mr. Football. New York: Scribner's, 1957.
    The Tail of the Terrible Tiger. New York: Scribner's, 1959.
    Boy at Bat. New York: Scribner's, 1961.
    The Big Basketball Prize. New York: Scribner's, 1963.
    Football Boys. New York: Scribner's, 1967.
    Ricky in the World of Sport. New York: Scribner's, 1967.
    Take a Long Jump. New York: Scribner's, 1971.
    Five Points for Hockey. New York: Scribner's, 1973.
    Sam Discovers Soccer. New York: Scribner's, 1975.
    Famous Forward Pass Pair. New York: Scribner's, 1977.
Written with James L. Renick.
    David Cheers the Team. New York: Scribner's, 1941.
    Tommy Carries the Ball. New York: Scribner's, 1941.
    Steady. New York: Scribner's, 1942.
Richard, J. R. Pseudonym; see Robert S. Bowen.
Rockne, Knute. *The Four Winners*. New York: Devin-Adair, 1925.
Rosen, Charles.
    Have Jump Shot, Will Travel. New York: Arbor House, 1975.
    A Mile Above the Rim. New York: Arbor House, 1976.
Roth, Philip. *The Great American Novel*. New York: Holt, Rinehart & Winston, 1973.
Rothweiler, Paul R.
    The Sensuous Southpaw. New York: Putnam, 1976.
    Blood Sports. New York: Jove, 1980.
Rowell, Adelaide C. *Touchdown*. New York: Dutton, 1942.
Ruth, Babe. *The "Home-Run King."* New York: Burt, 1920.
Sainsbury, Noel (also, pseudonym Charles Lawton).

Cracker Stanton. New York: Cupples & Leon, 1934.
The Fighting Five. New York: Cupples & Leon, 1934.
Gridiron Grit. New York: Cupples & Leon, 1934.

Written by "Charles Lawton."
    Ros Hackney, Halfback. New York: Cupples & Leon, 1937.
    Clarksville's Battery. New York: Cupples & Leon, 1938.
    The Winning Forward Pass. New York: Cupples & Leon, 1940.
    Home Run Hennessy. New York: Cupples & Leon, 1941.
    Touchdown to Victory. New York: Cupples & Leon, 1942.

Sampson, Arthur.
    The Two Quarterbacks. Boston: Houghton Mifflin, 1939.
    Football Coach. Boston: Houghton Mifflin, 1946.

Sangree, Allen. *The Jinx.* New York: Dillingham, 1911.

Sawyer, Walter L. (pseudonym Winn Standish).
    Captain Jack Lorimer. Boston: Page, 1906.
    Jack Lorimer's Champions. Boston: Page, 1907.
    Jack Lorimer's Holidays. Boston: Page, 1908.
    Jack Lorimer's Substitute. Boston: Page, 1909.
    Jack Lorimer, Freshman. Boston: Page, 1912.

Sayles, John. *Pride of the Bimbos.* Boston: Atlantic-Little, Brown, 1975.

Sayre, Joel. *Rackety Rax.* New York: Knopf, 1932.

Schayer, E. Richard. *The Good Loser.* Philadelphia: McKay, 1917.

Schley, Sturges Mason. *Deepening Blue.* Garden City, N.Y.: Doubleday, Doran, 1935.

Scholefield, Edmund O. Pseudonym; see William E. Butterworth.

Scholtz, Jackson V.
    Split Seconds. New York: Morrow, 1927.
    Soldiers at Bat. New York: Morrow, 1942.
    Pigskin Warriors. New York: Morrow, 1944.
    Goal to Go. New York: Morrow, 1945.
    Batter Up. New York: Morrow, 1946.
    Gridiron Challenge. New York: Morrow, 1947.
    Fielder from Nowhere. New York: Morrow, 1948.
    Johnny King, Quarterback. New York: Morrow, 1949.

Keystone Kelly. New York: Morrow, 1950.
Fullback for Sale. New York: Morrow, 1951.
Deep Short. New York: Morrow, 1952.
One-Man Team. New York: Morrow, 1953.
End Zone. New York: Morrow, 1954.
Base Burglar. New York: Morrow, 1955.
Fighting Chance. New York: Morrow, 1956.
Man in a Cage. New York: Morrow, 1957.
Bench Boss. New York: Morrow, 1958.
Little League Town. New York: Morrow, 1959.
The Perfect Game. New York: Morrow, 1959.
The Football Rebels. New York: Morrow, 1960.
Center-Field Jinx. New York: Morrow, 1961.
Halfback on His Own. New York: Morrow, 1962.
Dugout Tycoon. New York: Morrow, 1963.
Fairway Challenge. New York: Morrow, 1964.
Rookie Quarterback. New York: Morrow, 1965.
Sparkplug at Short. New York: Morrow, 1966.
Backfield Buckaroo. New York: Morrow, 1967.
The Big Mitt. New York: Morrow, 1968.
Fullback Fever. New York: Morrow, 1969.
Hot-Corner Hank. New York: Morrow, 1970.
Backfield Blues. New York: Morrow, 1971.

Schulberg, Budd. *The Harder They Fall.* New York: Random House, 1947.

Scott, Everett ("Deacon"). *Third Base Thatcher.* New York: Dodd, Mead, 1923.

Scott, Leroy. *The Trail of Glory.* Boston: Houghton Mifflin, 1926.

Scott, Morgan. Pseudonym; see Gilbert Patten.

Scribner, Robert. *The Eggheads in the Endzone.* New York: Exposition Press, 1957.

Segal, Fred. *The Broken-Field Runner.* New York: New American Library, 1967.

Severance, Mark. *Hammersmith: His Harvard Days.* Boston: Houghton, Osgood, 1878.

Shaara, Michael. *The Broken Place.* New York: New American Library, 1968.

Shackleford, H. K. "'King of the Bat; or, the Boy Champion of the Pequod Nine." *Happy Days,* No. 32 (25 May 1895).

Shainberg, Lawrence. *One on One.* New York: Holt, Rinehart & Winston, 1970.

Shaw, Irwin. *Voices of a Summer Day.* New York: Delacorte, 1965.

Shea, Cornelius. "Archie Atwood, All-Around Athlete." *Golden Hours,* Nos. 509-518 (30 October 1897–6 January 1898).

Sheldon, Charles M. *The Captain of the Orient Baseball Nine.* 1882.

Sheppard, W. Crispin.

  The Rambler Club's Ball Nine. Philadelphia: Penn, 1913.
  The Rambler Club's Football Team. Philadelphia: Penn, 1914.

Sheridan, Frank. "Jack, the Pride of the Nine; or, How He Won and Wore the Belt." *Golden Hours,* No. 131 (2 August 1890).

Sherman, Harold M.

  Fight 'em, Big Three. New York: Appleton, 1926.
  Mayfield's Fighting Five. New York: Appleton, 1926.
  One Minute to Play. New York: Grosset & Dunlap, 1926.
  Get 'em, Mayfield. New York: Appleton, 1927.
  Touchdown! New York: Grosset & Dunlap, 1927.
  Bases Full! New York: Grosset & Dunlap, 1928.
  Block That Kick! New York: Grosset & Dunlap, 1928.
  Safe! New York: Grosset & Dunlap, 1928.
  Flashing Steel. New York: Grosset & Dunlap, 1929.
  Hit and Run! New York: Grosset & Dunlap, 1929.
  Over the Line. Chicago: Goldsmith, 1929.
  Batter Up! New York: Grosset & Dunlap, 1930.
  Flying Heels and Other Hockey Stories. New York: Grosset & Dunlap, 1930.
  Hold That Line! New York: Grosset & Dunlap, 1930.
  Number 44 and Other Football Stories. New York: Grosset & Dunlap, 1930.
  Shoot That Ball! And Other Basketball Stories. New York: Grosset & Dunlap, 1930.
  Goal to Go! New York: Grosset & Dunlap, 1931.
  It's a Pass! Chicago: Goldsmith, 1931.
  Slashing Sticks and Other Hockey Stories. New York: Grosset & Dunlap, 1931.
  Strike Him Out! Chicago: Goldsmith, 1931.

Crashing Through! New York: Grosset & Dunlap, 1932.

Double Play! And Other Baseball Stories. New York: Grosset & Dunlap, 1932.

Down the Ice and Other Winter Sports Stories. Chicago: Goldsmith, 1932.

Interference and Other Football Stories. Chicago: Goldsmith, 1932.

The Tennis Terror and Other Tennis Stories. New York: Goldsmith, 1932.

Under the Basket and Other Basketball Stories. New York: Goldsmith, 1932.

Captain of the Eleven. Chicago: Goldsmith, 1933.

Shulman, Irving. *The Square Trap.* Boston: Little, Brown, 1953.

Shurtleff, Bertrand. *Flying Footballs.* Indianapolis, Ind.: Bobbs-Merrill, 1953.

Silliman, Leland. *The Purple Tide.* Philadelphia: Winston, 1949.

Silvers, Earl Reed.

Dick Arnold of Raritan College. New York: Appleton, 1920.

Dick Arnold Plays the Game. New York: Appleton, 1920.

Dick Arnold of the Varsity. New York: Appleton, 1921.

At Hillsdale High. New York: Appleton, 1922.

Ned Beals, Freshman. New York: Appleton, 1922.

Jackson of Hillsdale High. New York: Appleton, 1923.

Ned Beals Works His Way. New York: Appleton, 1923.

Barry, the Undaunted. New York: Appleton, 1924.

Barry and Budd. New York: Appleton, 1925.

Barry Goes to College. New York: Appleton, 1925.

The Hillsdale High Champions. New York: Appleton, 1925.

The Spirit of Menlo. New York: Appleton, 1926.

The Red-Headed Halfback. New York: Appleton, 1929.

Team First. New York: Appleton, 1929.

The Scarlet of Avalon. New York: Appleton, 1930.

The Glory of Glenwood. New York: Appleton, 1931.

Code of Honor. New York: Appleton, 1932.

Skene, Don. *The Red Tiger.* New York: Appleton-Century, 1932.

Skowran, Bill, and Jack Long. *New Blood on First.* Larchmont, N.Y.: Argonaut, 1963.

Slote, Alfred.

Stranger on the Ball Club. Philadelphia: Lippincott, 1966.

Jake. Philadelphia: Lippincott, 1971.

The Biggest Victory. Philadelphia: Lippincott, 1972.

My Father, the Coach. Philadelphia: Lippincott, 1972.

Hang Tough. Philadelphia: Lippincott, 1973.

Tony and Me. Philadelphia: Lippincott, 1974.

Matt Gargan's Boy. Philadelphia: Lippincott, 1975.

The Hotshot. New York: Watts, 1977.

Smith, Doris Buchanan. *Up and Over.* New York: Morrow, 1976.

Smith, H. Allen. *Rhubarb.* Garden City, N.Y.: Doubleday, 1946.

Smith, Robert.

Football Twins. New York: Barnes, 1953.

Little League Catcher. New York: Barnes, 1953.

Standish, Burt L. Pseudonym, see Gilbert Patten.

Standish, Winn. Pseudonym, see Walter L. Sawyer.

Stevens, Maurice.

"Jack Lightfoot's Trump Curve; or, the Wizard Pitcher of the Four Town League." *All Sports Library,* No. 6 (18 March 1905).

Jack Lightfoot in the Box. New York: Street and Smith, 1905.

Jack Lightfoot's Decision. New York: Street and Smith, 1905.

Stevenson, James. *Do Yourself a Favor, Kid.* New York: Macmillan, 1962.

Stoddard, Henry B. "Charlie Skylark, the Sport; a Story of Schoolday Scrapes and College Capers." *Beadle's Pocket Library,* No. 391 (8 July 1891).

Stoddard, W. O.

Winter Fun. New York: Scribner's, 1885.

The Village Champion. Philadelphia: Jacobs, 1903.

Zeb, a New England Boy. Philadelphia: Jacobs, 1904.

Stokes, Roy. *Andy at Yale.* New York: Sully & Kleinteich, 1914.

Stone, David.

Yank Brown, Forward. New York: Barse & Hopkins, 1921.

Yank Brown, Halfback. New York: Barse & Hopkins, 1921.

Yank Brown, Miler. New York: Barse & Hopkins, 1923.

Yank Brown, Pitcher. New York: Barse & Hopkins, 1924.

Yank Brown, Honor Man. New York: Barse & Hopkins, 1925.

Stone, Raymond.

Tommy Tiptop and His Baseball Nine. New York: Graham & Matlack, 1912.

Tommy Tiptop and His Football Eleven. New York: Graham & Matlack, 1912.

Tommy Tiptop and His Winter Sports. New York: Graham & Matlack, 1912.

Strange, John S. *Murder on the Ten-Yard Line.* Garden City, N.Y.: Doubleday, Doran, 1931.

Stratemeyer, Edward (also, pseudonyms Captain Ralph Bonehill, Lester Chadwick, Frank V. Webster, Arthur M. Winfield, and Clarence Young. These are all pseudonyms used by the Stratemeyer *Syndicate,* which employed numerous writers.)

Dave Porter at Oak Hall. Boston: Lothrop, Lee & Shepard, 1905.

Dave Porter's Return to School. Boston: Lothrop, Lee & Shepard, 1907.

The Baseball Boys of Lakeport. Boston: Lothrop, Lee & Shepard, 1908.

The Football Boys of Lakeport. Boston: Lothrop, Lee & Shepard, 1909.

Dave Porter and His Classmates. Boston: Lothrop, Lee & Shepard, 1909.

Dave Porter and His Rivals. Boston: Lothrop, Lee & Shepard, 1911.

Written by "Captain Ralph Bonehill."

The Winning Run. New York: Barnes, 1905.

Written by "Lester Chadwick."

A Quarterback's Pluck. New York: Cupples & Leon, 1910.

The Rival Pitchers. New York: Cupples & Leon, 1911.

Batting to Win. New York: Cupples & Leon, 1911.

The Winning Touchdown. New York: Cupples & Leon, 1911.

For the Honor of Randall. New York: Cupples & Leon, 1912.

Baseball Joe of the Silver Stars. New York: Cupples & Leon, 1912.

Baseball Joe on the School Nine. New York: Cupples & Leon, 1912.

Baseball Joe at Yale. New York: Cupples & Leon, 1913.

Baseball Joe in the Central League. New York: Cupples & Leon, 1914.

Baseball Joe in the Big League. New York: Cupples & Leon, 1915.

Baseball Joe on the Giants. New York: Cupples & Leon, 1916.

Baseball Joe Around the World. New York: Cupples & Leon, 1918.

Baseball Joe, Home Run King. New York: Cupples & Leon, 1922.

Baseball Joe, Saving the League. New York: Cupples & Leon, 1923.

Baseball Joe, Captain of the Team. New York: Cupples & Leon, 1924.

Baseball Joe, Champion of the League. New York: Cupples & Leon, 1925.

Baseball Joe, Club Owner. New York: Cupples & Leon, 1926.

Baseball Joe, Pitching Wizard. New York: Cupples & Leon, 1928.

Written by "Frank V. Webster."

The High School Rivals. New York: Cupples & Leon, 1911.

Harry Watson's High School Days. New York: Cupples & Leon, 1912.

Written by "Arthur M. Winfield."

> *The Rover Boys at School.* New York: Mershon, 1899.
>
> *The Putnam Hall Cadets.* New York: Stitt Publishing Company, 1905.
>
> *The Putnam Hall Rivals.* New York: Grosset & Dunlap, 1908.
>
> *The Putnam Hall Champions.* New York: Grosset & Dunlap, 1908.
>
> *The Rover Boys at Colby Hall.* New York: Grosset & Dunlap, 1910.
>
> *The Rover Boys at College.* New York: Grosset & Dunlap, 1910.

Written by "Clarence Young."

> *Jack Ranger's Schooldays.* New York: Cupples & Leon, 1907.
>
> *Jack Ranger's School Victories.* New York: Cupples & Leon, 1908.

Streatfeild, Noel. *Tennis Shoes.* New York: Random House, 1938.

Strong, Paschal N. (also, pseudonym Kennedy Lyons).

> *West Point Wins.* Boston: Little, Brown, 1930.

Written by "Kennedy Lyons."

> *West Pointers on the Gridiron.* Akron, Ohio: Saalfield, 1936.

Summers, James. *Tiger Terwilliger.* Philadelphia: Westminster, 1963.

Summers, Richard. *Ball-Shy Pitcher.* Austin, Tex.: Steck-Vaughn, 1970.

Sylvester, Harry. *Big Football Man.* New York: Farrar & Rinehart, 1933.

Talbot, Charles R. *The Imposter.* Boston: Lothrop, 1895.

Taves, Isabella. *Not Bad for a Girl.* New York: Evans, 1972.

Taylor, Robert Lewis. *Professor Fodorski.* Garden City, N.Y.: Doubleday, 1950.

"Teaser, Tom."

> "Muldoon's Base Ball Club in Boston." *Five Cent Wide Awake Library,* No. 953 (10 May 1890).
>
> "Muldoon's Base Ball Club in Philadelphia." *Five Cent Wide Awake Library,* No. 971 (7 June 1890).

Temple, Willard H. *Pitching for Pawling.* New York: Farrar & Rinehart, 1940.

Thurman, A.R. Pseudonym; see Arthur Mann.

Tilden, William.

It's All in the Game and Other Tennis Tales. Garden City, N.Y.: Doubleday, Doran, 1922.

Glory's Net. Garden City, N.Y.: Doubleday, Doran, 1930.

Tittle, Y. A., and Howard Liss. *Pro Quarterback.* Larchmont, N.Y.: Argonaut, 1963.

Tomlinson, Everett.

Ward Hill at Weston. Philadelphia: Rowland, 1897.

Ward Hill—The Senior. Philadelphia: Rowland, 1898.

Ward Hill at College. Philadelphia: Rowland, 1902.

The Winner. Philadelphia: Griffith & Rowland, 1903.

Winning His "W." Philadelphia: Griffith & Rowland, 1904.

Captain Don Richards. Philadelphia: Griffith & Rowland, 1909.

The Pennant. Philadelphia: Griffith & Rowland, 1912.

Carl Hall of Tait. Philadelphia: Griffith & Rowland, 1914.

Towers, Walter Kellogg. *Letters from Brother Bill, Varsity Sub, to Tad, Captain of the Beechville High School Eleven.* New York: Crowell, 1915.

Towne, Mary. *First Serve.* New York: Athaneum, 1976.

Tracy, Don. *Second Try.* Philadelphia: Westminster Press, 1954.

Treat, Roger. *Duke of the Bruins.* New York: Messner, 1950.

Tully, Jim.

The Bruiser. New York: Greenberg, 1936.

Emmett Lawler. New York: Harcourt, Brace, 1942.

Tunberg, Karl. *While the Crowd Cheers.* New York: Macaulay, 1935.

Tunis, John R.

The Tennis Racket. New York: Brewer and Warren, 1930.

Iron Duke. New York: Harcourt, Brace, 1939.

The Duke Decides. New York: Harcourt, Brace, 1939.

The Kid from Tompkinsville. New York: Harcourt, Brace, 1940.

Champion's Choice. New York: Harcourt, Brace, 1941.

World Series. New York: Harcourt, Brace, 1941.

All-American. New York: Harcourt, Brace, 1942.

Keystone Kids. New York: Harcourt, Brace, 1943.

Rookie of the Year. New York: Harcourt, Brace, 1944.

Yea! Wildcats! New York: Morrow, 1944.

The Kid Comes Back. New York: Morrow, 1946.

Highpockets. New York: Morrow, 1948.

Young Razzle. New York: Morrow, 1949.

The Other Side of the Fence. New York: Morrow, 1953.

Go, Team, Go! New York: Morrow, 1954.

Buddy and the Old Pro. New York: Morrow, 1955.

Schoolboy Johnson. New York: Morrow, 1958.

Turner, Morrie. *Nipper.* Philadelphia: Westminster, 1970.

Tuttle, Anthony. *Drive for the Green.* Garden City, N.Y.: Doubleday, 1969.

Uniack, John R. *Making the Eleven at St. Michael's.* Cincinnati, Ohio: Benziger Brothers, 1926.

Updike, John.

Rabbit, Run. New York: Knopf, 1960.

Rabbit, Redux. New York: Knopf, 1971.

Urnston, Mary. *Larry's Luck.* Garden City, N.Y.: Doubleday, 1952.

Van Loan, Charles E.

The Big League. Boston: Small, Maynard, 1911.

The Ten-Thousand-Dollar Arm and Other Tales of the Big League. Boston: Small, Maynard, 1912.

Inside the Ropes. Boston: Small, Maynard, 1913.

The Lucky Seventh. Boston: Small, Maynard, 1913.

Taking the Count. New York: George H. Doran, 1915.

Fore! New York: Doran, 1918.

Score by Innings. New York: Doran, 1919.

Van Riper, Guernsey, Jr.

Lou Gehrig, Boy of the Sandlots. Indianapolis, Ind.: Bobbs-Merrill, 1949.

Knute Rockne, Young Athlete. Indianapolis, Ind.: Bobbs-Merrill, 1952.

Babe Ruth, Baseball Boy. Indianapolis, Ind.: Bobbs-Merrill, 1954.

Jim Thorpe, Indian Athlete. Indianapolis, Ind.: Bobbs, Merrill, 1956.

Verrall, Charles Spain.
Captain of the Ice. New York: Crowell, 1953.
Champion of the Court. New York: Crowell, 1954.
The Wonderful World Series. New York: Crowell, 1956.
The King of the Diamond. New York: Crowell, 1960.
The Winning Quarterback. New York: Crowell, 1960.

Walden, Amelia Elizabeth.
Queen of the Courts. Philadelphia: Westminster, n.d.
Victory for Jill. New York: Morrow, 1953.
Three Loves Has Sandy. New York: Whittlesey House, 1955.
My Sister Mike. New York: Whittlesey House, 1956.
Basketball Girl of the Year. New York: McGraw-Hill, 1970.
Play Ball, McGill. Philadelphia: Westminster Press, 1972.
Go, Philips, Go! Philadelphia: Westminster Press, 1974.
Escape on Skis. Philadelphia: Westminster Press, 1975.
Heartbreak Tennis. Philadelphia: Westminster Press, 1977.

Waldman, Frank (also, pseudonym Joe Webster).
Giant Quarterback. Boston: Houghton Mifflin, 1950.
Bonus Pitcher. Boston: Houghton Mifflin, 1951.
Delayed Steal. Boston: Houghton Mifflin, 1952.
Basketball Scandal. New York: Ariel, 1953.
Glory Boy. New York: Ariel, 1953.
The Challenger. Cleveland, Ohio: World, 1955.
Lucky Bat Boy. Cleveland, Ohio: World, 1956.

Written by "Joe Webster."
Dodger Doubleheader. New York: Ariel, 1952.
The Rookie from Junction Flats. New York: Ariel, 1952.

Wallace, Francis.
Huddle! New York: Farrar & Rinehart, 1930.
O'Reilly of Notre Dame. New York: Farrar & Rinehart, 1931.
Stadium. New York: Farrar & Rinehart, 1931. 1931.
That's My Boy. New York: Farrar & Rinehart, 1932.
Big Game. Boston: Little, Brown, 1936.

Kid Galahad. Boston: Little, Brown, 1936.

Autumn Madness. Philadelphia: Macrae-Smith, 1937.

Razzle-Dazzle. New York: Mill, 1938.

Little Hercules. New York: Mill, 1939.

Big League Rookie. Philadelphia: Westminster Press, 1950.

Front Man. New York: Rinehart, 1952.

Wallop, Douglas.
> *The Year the Yankees Lost the Pennant*. New York: Norton, 1954.
>
> *So This Is What Happened to Charlie Moe*. New York: Norton, 1965.
>
> *Mixed Singles*. New York: Norton, 1977.

Walton, Todd. *Inside Moves*. Garden City, N.Y.: Doubleday, 1978.

Ward, Millard. *Brute*. New York: Appleton-Century, 1935.

Warfield, Nicole. *Superball*. New York: Bantam, 1974.

Warner, Frank.
> *Bobby Blake on the School Nine*. New York: Barse & Hopkins, 1917.
>
> *Bobby Blake on the School Eleven*. New York: Barse & Hopkins, 1921.

Warren, Patricia Nell. *The Front Runner*. New York: Morrow, 1964.

Wayne, Richard. Pseudonym; see Duane Decker.

Weaver, Robert. *Nice Guy, Go Home*. New York and Evanston: Harper & Row, 1968.

Webster, Frank V. Pseudonym; see Edward Stratemeyer.

Webster, Joe. Pseudonym; see Frank Waldman.

Weeks, Jack.
> *The Hard Way*. New York: Barnes, 1953.
>
> *The Take-Charge Guy*. New York: Barnes, 1955.

Weller, George Anthony. *Not to Eat, Not for Love*. New York: Smith and Haas, 1933.

Wellman, Manly. *Third String Center*. New York: Washburn, 1960.

Wells, Robert W.
> *Five-Yard Fuller*. New York: Putnam, 1964.
>
> *Five-Yard Fuller of the N. Y. Giants*. New York: Putnam, 1967.

The Saga of Shorty Gone. New York: Putnam, 1969.

Wetmore, William. *Here Comes Jamie*. Boston: Little, Brown, 1970.

Wheeler, Edward L. "High Hat Harry, the Baseball Detective; or, the Sunken Treasure." *Beadle's Half-Dime Library*, No. 416 (14 July 1885).

Wheeler, John. See Christy Matthewson.

Whitehead, James. *Joiner*. New York: Knopf, 1971.

Wilder, Robert. *Autumn Thunder*. New York: Putnam, 1952.

Williams, Eustace. *The Substitute Quarterback*. Boston: Estes, 1900.

Williams, Hawley. Pseudonym; see William Heyliger.

Winnfield, Arthur M. Pseudonym; see Edward Stratemeyer.

Winston, Peter. *Luke*. New York: Manor, 1976.

Witwer, H. C.

> *From Baseball to Boches*. Boston: Small, Maynard, 1918.
>
> *Alex the Great*. Boston: Small, Maynard, 1919.
>
> *Kid Scanlon*. Boston: Small, Maynard, 1920.
>
> *No Base Like Home*. Garden City, N.Y.: Doubleday, Page, 1920.
>
> *The Leather Pushers*. New York: Putnam, 1921.
>
> *Fighting Blood*. New York: Putnam, 1923.
>
> *Fighting Back*. New York: Grosset & Dunlap, 1924.
>
> *Bill Grimm's Progress*. New York: Putnam, 1926.

Wolf, Gary K. *Killerbowl*. Garden City, N.Y.: Doubleday, 1976.

Wright, Elsie (pseudonym Jack Wright).

> *On the Forty Yard Line*. Cleveland, Ohio: World Syndicate, 1932.
>
> *Champs on Ice*. Cleveland, Ohio: World, 1940.

Yates, Brock. *Dead in the Water*. New York: Farrar, Straus & Giroux, 1975.

Young, Al. *Ask Me Now*. New York: McGraw-Hill, 1980.

Young, Clarence. Pseudonym, see Edward Stratemeyer.

Young, Isador S.

> *A Hit and a Miss*. Chicago: Wilcox & Follett, 1952.
>
> *The Two-Minute Dribble*. Chicago: Wilcox & Follett, 1964.
>
> *Carson at Second*. Chicago: Wilcox & Follett, 1966.
>
> *Quarterback Carson*. Chicago: Wilcox & Follett, 1967.

Carson's Fast Break. Chicago: Wilcox & Follett, 1969.

Young, Scott.

Scrubs on Skates. Boston: Little, Brown, 1952.

Boy on Defense. Boston: Little, Brown, 1953.

Zanger, Jack.

The Long Reach. Garden City, N.Y.: Doubleday, 1962.

Baseball Sparkplug. Garden City, N.Y.: Doubleday, 1964.

Hi Packett, Jumping Center. Garden City, N.Y.: Doubleday, 1965.

Zinberg, Leo. *Walk Hard—Talk Loud.* Indianapolis, Ind.: Bobbs-Merrill, 1940.

Zuckerman, George. *Farewell, Frank Merriwell.* New York: Dutton, 1973.

Notes

Chapter 1. Introduction: The Field Defined

1. William O. Johnson, Jr., *Super Spectator and the Electric Lilliputians* (Boston: Little, Brown, 1971), pp. 18-21. This book is a useful study of the impact of television on organized sports.
2. Information provided by A. C. Nielson Company.
3. James P. Forkan, "TD Club: Nets Run Up the Score with Key Football Sales," *Advertising Age,* 23 June 1980, p. 3.
4. Figures compiled from Don Pierson, "Look Behind the Stadium Boom," *Mainliner* 19 (November 1975): 55.
5. Information provided by the National Football League.
6. Information provided by the National Basketball Association.
7. Information provided by Major League Baseball.
8. John Rickards Betts, *America's Sporting Heritage: 1850-1950* (Menlo Park, Calif.: Addison-Wesley, 1974), p. 88. This is the best history of American sport.
9. William Bradford, *Bradford's History "Of Plimoth Plantation"* (Boston, 1898). Quoted in Betts, *America's Sporting Heritage,* p. 4. See also Peter McIntosh, *Sport in Society* (London: C. A. Watts, 1963) for a discussion of Calvinist aversion to sport.
10. John A. Lucas and Ronald A. Smith, *Saga of American Sport* (Philadelphia: Lea & Febiger, 1977), pp. 8 and 40.
11. Betty Spears and Richard A. Swanson, *History of Sport and*

Physical Activity in the United States (Dubuque, Iowa: Wm. C. Brown, 1979), p. 45.

12. William Penn, *No Cross, No Crown* (New York: Collins, 1845), p. 69. Quoted in Lucas and Smith, *Saga of American Sport,* p. 23.

13. W. J. Cash, *The Mind of the South* (New York: Knopf, 1941), repeatedly emphasizes these two tendencies as the principal components of the Southern character.

14. One must be careful not to imply too strict a division between Northern and Southern attitudes toward games. For example, the Dutch in New York were very sports-minded—"a most tolerant people, possessing a sense of world-mindedness that looked upon sport, revelry, and certain intemperance as a natural carryover from their lives in the old country." They engaged readily in a variety of sports year round. See Lucas and Smith, *Saga of American Sport,* p. 21.

15. Betts, *America's Sporting Heritage,* pp. 5-6.

16. Discussions of these early forms of baseball can be found in any reputable history of baseball. The best of these are Harold Seymour, *Baseball,* 2 vols. (New York: Oxford University Press, 1960 and 1971); and David Quentin Voigt, *American Baseball,* 2 vols. (Norman: University of Oklahoma Press, 1966 and 1970).

17. See, for example, Charles A. Peverelly, *The National Game* (New York, 1866), a book on baseball cited by Betts, *America's Sporting Heritage,* p. 95.

18. For a reliable history of college football, see Allison Danzig, *The History of American Football* (Englewood Cliffs, N. J.: Prentice-Hall, 1956). For the pro game, see Roger Treat, *The Encyclopedia of Football* (New York: Barnes, 1976). Football has not received the scholarly attention that baseball has.

19. See McIntosh, *Sport in Society.* This is also an excellent text on the British influence on American sport.

20. Ibid., p. 87.

21. See Alexander Johnston, *Ten—and Out!* (New York: Washburn, 1970), for a history of boxing in America.

22. Basketball is also the least satisfactorily chronicled of American sports, but see Neil D. Isaacs, *All the Moves: A History of College Basketball* (New York: Lippincott, 1975).

23. Johan Huizinga, *Homo Ludens: A Study of the Play-Element in Culture* (1944; Boston: Beacon Press, 1955).

24. Roger Caillois, *Man, Play and Games,* translated by Meyer Barash (1958; New York: Free Press of Glencoe, 1961).

25. Irving Howe, *Politics and the Novel* (Cleveland: World Publishing, 1964), p. 17.

26. The five leading states in the per capita production of professional football players are all Southern: Mississippi, Louisiana, Texas, Alabama, and Georgia, in that order. See John F. Rooney, *A Geography of American Sport* (Menlo Park, Calif.: Addison-Wesley, 1974), p. 134.

27. A few examples of these possibilities are Bernard Malamud, *The Natural* (New York: Harcourt, Brace, 1952), in which the story is divided into two sections: "Pre-Game" and "Batter Up!"; Albert Idell, *Pug* (New York: Greystone Press, 1941), which has three sections: "Prelims," "Semi-Final," and "Main Go"; and Peter Gent, *North Dallas Forty* (New York: Morrow, 1973), which has a chapter for each day in a single week of preparation for a football game. Even the eight chapters of Robert Coover, *The Universal Baseball Association* (New York: Random House, 1968), can be viewed as eight "innings" in life, with the ninth yet to be played.

28. Pre-1896 (the date of the beginning of the Frank Merriwell series) dime novel and boys' weekly sports stories include: "Bill Boxer," "Captain Billy Nash; or, the Doings of the Famous Third Baseman," *New York Five Cent Library*, No. 86 (23 June 1894); "Bill Boxer," "King Kelly, the Famous Catcher; or, the Life and Adventures of the $10,000 Ball-Player," *New York Five Cent Library*, No. 85 (16 June 1894); "Bill Boxer," "Yale Murphy, the Great Short-Stop; or, the Little Midget of the Giant New York Team," *New York Five Cent Library*, No. 87 (30 June 1894); Noah Brooks, "The Fairport Nine," *St. Nicholas,* 7 (May-October 1880); Edward Ellis, "Jack Darcy, the All-Around Athlete; or, Fighting His Way to Fortune," *Golden Hours,* No. 31 (1 September 1888); R. T. Emmet, "Dashing Dick, the Young Cadet; or, Four Years at West Point," *The Boys of New York,* No. 690 (3 November 1888); Harrie Irving Hancock, "The Young West Pointer; or, the Cadet Life of Ben Burgess," *Golden Hours,* No. 275 (6 May 1893); Bracebridge Hemyng, "Harry Armstrong, the Captain of the Club; or, the Young Athletes, a Romance of Truth and Treachery," *Beadle's Half-Dime Library,* No. 91 (17 February 1879); George Jenks, "Double Curve Dan the Pitcher Detective; or, Against Heavy Odds," *Beadle's Half-Dime Library,* No. 581 (11 September 1888); George Jenks, "The Pitcher Detective's Foil; or, Double Curve Dan's Double Play," *Beadle's Half-Dime Library,* No. 608 (18 March 1889); George Jenks, "The Pitcher Detective's Toughest Tussle; or, Double Curve Dan's Dead Ball," *Beadle's Half-Dime Library,* No. 681 (12 August 1890); Jackson Knox, "Shortstop Maje, the Diamond Field Detective; or, Old Falcon's Master Game," *Beadle's Dime Library,* No. 515 (5 September 1888);

H. K. Shackleford, "King of the Bat; or, the Boy Champion of the Pequod Nine," *Happy Days*, No. 32 (25 May 1895); Frank Sheridan, "Jack, the Pride of the Nine; or, How He Won and Wore the Belt," *Golden Hours,* No. 131 (2 August 1890); Henry B. Stoddard, "Charley Skylark, the Sport; a Story of Schoolday Scrapes and College Capers," *Beadle's Pocket Library,* No. 391 (8 July 1891); "Tom Teaser," "Muldoon's Base Ball Club in Philadelphia," *Five Cent Wide Awake Library,* No. 971 (7 June 1890); Edward Wheeler, "High Hat Harry, the Baseball Detective; or, the Sunken Treasure," *Beadle's Half-Dime Library,* No. 416 (14 July 1885). Dime novel sports stories were characterized in general by the author's lack of understanding of the games, and by the greater importance of mystery. My source for many of these dime sports novels is Christian Karl Messenger, "Sport in American Literature (1830-1930)" (Ph.D. dissertation, Northwestern University, 1974), an excellent piece of scholarship on the earliest nineteenth-century sports fiction.

29. The absence of boxing from dime novels is noted by Messenger, "Sport in American Literature," p. 205.

30. This is Patten's own estimate in *Frank Merriwell's Father: An Autobiography of Gilbert Patten* ("Burt L. Standish"), edited by Harriet Hinsdale (Norman: University of Oklahoma Press, 1964), p. 181. Sales figures were not recorded.

31. Arthur Mizener, *The Far Side of Paradise* (New York: Vintage Books, 1959), p. 19.

32. Stewart Rodnon, "Sports, Sporting Codes, and Sportsmanship in the Work of Ring Lardner, James T. Farrell, Ernest Hemingway, and William Faulkner" (Ph.D. dissertation, New York University, 1961), p. 69.

33. Ibid., p. 69.

34. See Ibid. for even the most minute uses of sport in the works of Lardner, Farrell, Hemingway, and Faulkner.

35. Donald Elder, Lardner's excellent biographer, reports in *Ring Lardner* (Garden City, N.Y.: Doubleday, 1956), p. 293, that in 1926 Lardner was among the ten most famous men in the United States. And Peter Schwed and Herbert Warren Wind, editors of *Great Stories from the World of Sport,* 3 vols. (New York: Simon & Schuster, 1958), 2:129, claim that in 1911 London was the most widely read author in the world.

36. F. Scott Fitzgerald's comment is typical: "Ring moved in the company of a few dozen illiterates playing a boy's game. A boy's game, with no more possibilities in it than a boy could master, a game bounded by walls which kept out novelty or danger, change or adventure.... However Ring might cut into it, his

cake had exactly the diameter of Frank Chance's diamond." F. Scott Fitzgerald, *The Crack Up* (New York: New Directions, 1956), p. 36.

37. "Mark Harris: An Interview," *Wisconsin Studies in Contemporary Literature,* 6 (Winter-Spring 1965): 15-26.

38. Philip Roth, "Reading Myself," *Partisan Review,* 40 (1973): 412-13.

39. Jim Bouton, *Ball Four* (New York: World, 1970).

40. See, for example, Betts, *America's Sporting Heritage;* Jack Scott, *The Athletic Revolution* (New York: Free Press, 1971); Harry Edwards, *The Revolt of the Black Athlete* (New York: Free Press, 1969); Arnold Beisser, *The Madness in Sports* (New York: Appleton-Century-Crofts, 1967); Susan Dorcas Butts, *Psychology of Sport* (New York: Van Nostrand Reinhold, 1976); Paul Weiss, *Sport: A Philosophic Inquiry* (Carbondale: Southern Illinois University Press, 1969); and Michael Novak, *The Joy of Sports* (New York: Basic Books, 1976).

41. Messenger, "Sport in American Literature," makes an impressive, although perhaps overstated case for the influence of such writers as Augustus Longstreet, George Washington Harris, Johnson Jones Hooper, and Joseph G. Baldwin on twentieth-century writers of sports fiction. My claim, stated more fully in chapter 2, is that the tradition of the juvenile athlete-hero is by far the strongest on subsequent adult sports fiction. But there is no question that the frontier had a large impact on the rise of American sport (see my chapter 3) and that the frontier roarer is an important figure in the history of the "natural" in America. Like Messenger, then, I recognize two traditions in American sports fiction, but I identify them as the more general figures, the self-made man and the natural. Messenger's school sports hero and frontier hero are the most immediate examples of those two figures antecedent to the actual writing of sports fiction.

42. Hugh Fullerton, "The Fellows Who Made the Game," *Saturday Evening Post* 200 (12 April 1928): 18.

43. Owen Johnson, *The Humming Bird* (New York: Baker and Taylor, 1910).

44. James T. Farrell, "Baseball as It's Played in Books—Some Cheers, Jeers and Hopes," *New York Times Book Review* (10 August 1958): 5.

45. See Coulton Waugh, *The Comics* (New York: Macmillan, 1947), and Stephen Becker, *Comic Art in America* (New York: Simon & Schuster, 1959), for discussions of sports comic strips. Betts, *America's Sporting Heritage,* pp. 362-63, also discusses this topic briefly. In addition to the sports comic strips, a number

of sports cartoonists have published in newspapers and maga-
zines around the country. Among these are Tad Dorgan, Bob
Edgren, Edward Windsor Kemble, Rube Goldberg, Hype Igoe,
Robert Ripley, Walter Hoban, Jimmy Hatlo, Tom Webster,
Burris Jenkins, Jr., William Crawford, Karl Hubenthal, Pete
Llanuza, Willard Mullin, Lou Darvas, Tom Paprocki, Murray
Olderman, Al Vermeer, Allen Maurer, Howard Bodie, and John
Pierotti.

46. See Robert Cantwell, "Sport Was Box Office Poison," *Sports
Illustrated,* 31 (15 September 1969): 108-16, and Betts, *America's
Sporting Heritage,* pp. 243-44 and 366-68, for discussions of sports
movies.

47. See Robert Cantwell, "The Music of Baseball," *Sports Illustrated,* 12 (3 October 1960): 82-92, for a discussion of the history
of baseball music; Betts, *America's Sporting Heritage,* pp. 235-36
and 244-46, also offers a brief discussion of sports music. Football fight songs are not included in these discussions but are actually the most memorable examples of sports music.

48. See Betts, *America's Sporting Heritage,* p. 243, for a very
brief discussion of sport in the theater.

49. Other painters include Arthur Frost, Philip Hale, Currier &
Ives, James Chapin, Robert Riggs, James Montgomery Flagg,
Howard Chandler Christy, John Steuart Curry, Joseph W. Golin-
kin, Paul L. Clemens, Mrs. Marjorie Phillips, Douglass Crock-
well, Benton Spruance, and Isabelle Bishop. Other sculptors include John McNamee, Janet Scudder, Paul Landowski, Mahonri
Young, Carl Hallsthammer, and Beatrice Fenton. Again, the
source for these lists is Betts, *America's Sporting Heritage,* pp.
234-35 and 357-60.

50. There are at least two collections of sports poems: Lillian
Morrison, ed., *Sprints and Distances* (New York: Crowell, 1965);
and R. R. Knudson and P. K. Ebert, eds., *Sports Poems* (New
York: Dell, 1971).

51. Novak, *Joy of Sports,* pp. 18-34.

Chapter 2. Frank Merriwell's Sons:
The American Athlete-Hero

1. Stanley T. Williams makes this claim in *Studies in Victorian
Literature* (New York: Dutton, 1923), p. 283.

2. Edward L. Wheeler, "High Hat Harry, the Baseball Detective;
or, The Sunken Treasure," *Beadle's Half-Dime Library,* No. 416

(14 July 1885). George C. Jenks, "Double-Curve Dan, the Pitcher Detective; or, Against Heavy Odds," *Beadle's Half-Dime Library,* No. 581 (11 September 1888). George C. Jenks, "The Pitcher Detective's Foil; or, Double-Curve Dan's Double Play," *Beadle's Half-Dime Library,* No. 608 (26 March 1889). George C. Jenks, "The Pitcher Detective's Toughest Tussle; or, Double-Curve Dan's Dead Ball," *Beadle's Half-Dime Library,* No. 681 (12 August 1890). For a complete list of early sports fiction see footnote 28 of chapter 1.

3. For a complete list of titles, see the checklist following this text. The list is taken from John L. Cutler, "Gilbert Patten and His Frank Merriwell Saga," *Maine University Studies* 31 (1934): 1-123.

4. For a more extensive summary of the saga, see Cutler, "Gilbert Patten," pp. 84-100. For firsthand information, all the original stories are located in the Huntington Library, San Marino, California.

5. My sample includes Ralph Henry Barbour, *The Half-Back* (New York: Appleton, 1899); *Left End Edwards* (New York: Dodd, Mead, 1914); and *Left Half Harmon* (New York: Dodd, Mead, 1921); Bill J. Carol, *Single to Center* (Austin, Tex.: Steck-Vaughn, 1974); Lester Chadwick, *Baseball Joe of the Silver Stars* (New York: Cupples & Leon, 1912); Elmer Dawson, *Garry Grayson's Hill Street Eleven* (New York: Grosset & Dunlap, 1926); Duane Decker, *Third-Base Rookie* (New York: Morrow, 1959); Julian DeVries, *The Strikeout King* (New York: World Publishing, 1940); Albertus True Dudley, *With Mask and Mitt* (Boston: Lothrop, Lee & Shepard, 1906); J. W. Duffield, *Bert Wilson's Fadeaway Ball* (New York: Sully, 1913); Zane Grey, *The Short-Stop* (Chicago: A. C. McClurg, 1909); Philip Harkins, *Punt Formation* (New York: Morrow, 1949); William Heyliger, *The Captain of the Nine* (New York: Appleton, 1912) and *The Loser's End* (Chicago: Goldsmith, 1937); Owen Johnson, *Stover at Yale* (New York: Grosset & Dunlap, 1912); Wilfred McCormick, *Legion Tourney* (New York: Putnam, 1948); Tex Maule, *The Last Out* (New York: McKay, 1964); Frank O'Rourke, *Flashing Spikes* (New York: A. S. Barnes, 1948); Noel Sainsbury, *Cracker Stanton* (New York: Cupples & Leon, 1934); Harold M. Sherman, *Safe!* (New York: Grosset & Dunlap, 1928) and *Strike Him Out!* (Chicago: Goldsmith, 1931); Burt L. Standish, *Frank Merriwell's Schooldays,* edited by Jack L. Rudman (New York: Smith Street Publications, 1971) and *Lefty o' the Training Camp* (New York: Barse and Hopkins, 1914); John R. Tunis, *Iron Duke* (New York: Harcourt Brace, 1939) and *The Kid Comes Back* (New York: Morrow, 1946).

6. Vladimir Propp, *Morphology of the Folktale* (Bloomington: Indiana University Press, 1958).

7. These categories are defined by Tristram P. Coffin, *The Old Ball Game* (New York: Herder and Herder, 1971), p. 79.

8. Harold M. Sherman, *Strike Him Out!* (Chicago: Goldsmith, 1931).

9. Marshall Fishwick, *American Heroes, Myth and Reality* (Washington, D.C.: Public Affairs Press, 1954), p. 190.

10. Walter Evans includes these figures in his list of characters in "The All-American Boys: A Study of Boys' Sports Fiction," *Journal of Popular Culture* 6 (Summer 1972): 104-21.

11. These two primary types are defined by Walter Blair, *Native American Humor (1800-1900)* (New York: American Book Company, 1937).

12. During the past century, several scholars have attempted to discover the recurring patterns in the important myths of the heroes of diverse cultures. Among the foremost are Otto Rank, *The Myth of the Birth of the Hero*, trans. Dr. F. Robbins and Dr. Smith Ely Jelliffe (New York: Brunner, 1952); Fitz Roy Richard Somerset Raglan, *The Hero: A Study in Tradition, Myth, and Drama* (1936. Reprint. London: Watts, 1949). Joseph Campbell, *The Hero with a Thousand Faces* (1949. Reprint. Cleveland: World Publishing, 1963). There is much overlapping and correspondence in all of these and since it is not relevant to my purposes to weigh the relative merits of each, I have chosen Campbell's, the most recent and apparently most comprehensive, as my model.

13. Campbell, *Hero with a Thousand Faces,* pp. 3 and 41.

14. One explicit statement of this idea is made by Anthony Storr, *Human Aggression* (New York: Atheneum, 1968), p. 48.

15. Campbell, *Hero with a Thousand Faces,* pp. 36-37.

16. Ibid., p. 38.

17. Ibid., pp. 245-46.

18. Rank, *Myth of the Birth of the Hero,* pp. 61-68.

19. George Orwell claims in his 1939 essay, "Boys' Weeklies," in *A Collection of Essays* (1946, Garden City, N.Y.: Doubleday, 1954), p. 291, that "there are extremely few school stories in foreign languages." If he is correct, then the American athlete-hero may be unique, as well, in world literature.

20. John R. Tunis, *Iron Duke* (New York: Harcourt, Brace & World, 1938), p. 263.

21. A second "classic" British schoolboy novel, *Stalky & Company*, by Rudyard Kipling (New York: Dell, 1968), reduces the importance of winning, as well as the rest of traditional sports

ethic, to such a degree that this novel has *no* common interest with American schoolboy stories. The heroes are rebellious, delinquent, even cruel at times, and decidedly anti-athletic.

22. Orwell, "Boys' Weeklies," p. 302.

23. Ibid., pp. 294-95.

24. In *School and Adventure Stories for Boys* (London: Epworth Press, 1927).

25. For an excellent discussion of British sporting traditions, see P. C. McIntosh, *Sport in Society* (London: Watts, 1968).

26. The most extensive treatment of the dime novel is Albert Johannsen, *The House of Beadle and Adams* (Norman: University of Oklahoma Press, 1950). See also Merle Curti, "Dime Novels in the American Tradition," *Yale Review*, 26 (Summer 1937); Philip Durham, "Dime Novels: An American Heritage," *Western Humanities Review*, 60 (Winter 1954-55); Philip Durham, "A General Classification of 1,531 Dime Novels," *Huntington Library Quarterly*, 17 (May 1954); and Henry Nash Smith, *Virgin Land* (New York: Knopf, 1950).

27. Durham, "A General Classification."

28. Russel B. Nye, *The Unembarrassed Muse* (1970. Reprint. New York: Dial Press, 1971), pp. 209-10.

29. Johannsen, *House of Beadle and Adams,* I: 4.

30. Dixon Wector, *The Hero in America* (New York: Scribner, 1941), p. 341.

31. Nye, *Unembarrassed Muse,* p. 203.

32. Albertus True Dudley, *With Mask and Mitt* (Boston: Lothrop, Lee & Shepard, 1906), p. vii.

33. Ralph D. Gardner, *Horatio Alger, or the American Hero Era* (Mendota, Ill.: The Wayside Press, 1964), p. 346.

34. Ibid., pp. 311-12.

35. Nye, *Unembarrassed Muse,* p. 71.

36. Ibid., p. 71.

37. Burt L. Standish, "Frank Merriwell on the Road," *Tip Top Weekly*, No. 130 (8 October 1898): 15-16.

38. Horatio Alger, *Rugged Dick*, bound with *Mark, the Match Boy* (New York: Collier Books, 1962).

39. Henry Nash Smith, *Virgin Land*, p. 102.

40. Curti, "Dime Novels in the American Tradition," p. 765.

41. Henry Nash Smith specifically refers to Seth Jones as a Leatherstocking-type hero and to Deadwood Dick as a self-made man in *Virgin Land,* pp. 102 and 111.

42. Richard Dorson, *American Folklore* (Chicago: University of Chicago Press, 1959).

43. Marshall Fishwick, *The Hero: American Style* (New York: McKay, 1969).

44. Orrin E. Klapp, *Heroes, Villains, and Fools* (Englewood Cliffs, N. J.: Prentice-Hall, 1962).

45. John G. Cawelti, *Apostles of the Self-Made Man* (Chicago: University of Chicago Press, 1965).

46. Much of the following historical review of the self-made man is taken from Marshall Fishwick, *American Heroes, Myth and Reality,* pp. 141-57.

47. Ibid., p. 149.

48. Elbert Hubbard, *A Message to Garcia* (East Aurora, N.J.: Roycrofters, 1899); William Thayer, *Tact, Push, and Principle* (Boston: Earl, 1880); and Russell Conwell, *Acres of Diamonds* (Philadelphia: Huber, 1890).

49. Dale Carnegie, *How to Win Friends and Influence People* (New York: Simon & Schuster, 1937), and Wayne W. Dyer, *Pulling Your Own Strings* (New York: Crowell, 1978).

50. Editors of *Fortune* magazine, *100 Stories of Business Success* (New York: Simon & Schuster, 1954).

51. Edward Waldo Emerson, ed. *The Complete Works of Ralph Waldo Emerson,* centenary ed. 12 vols. (Boston: Houghton-Mifflin, 1903), 2: 43-90 and 243-64.

52. Theodore Roosevelt, *The Strenuous Life* (New York: The Review of Reviews Company, 1910), p. 137.

53. F. Scott Fitzgerald, *Tender Is the Night* (New York: Scribner, 1934), p. 132.

54. Tony Goodstone, ed., *The Pulps* (New York: Chelsea House, 1970), p. ix.

55. My sample of pulps is severely limited, but in eleven stories I detected an obvious pattern. The eleven stories are Paul Gallico, "The Yellow Twin," in Goodstone, *The Pulps,* pp. 35-43; Eric Rober, "Crucial Game for Pop," T. W. Ford, "Touchdown at Tobruk," and Eugene Pawley, "Tin Ears," all in *Sports Fiction,* 4:6 (Winter 1943-44); and Bill Erin, "Pass 'em Blind!" Ted Stratton, "Satan in Center," Joe Brennan, "Big-League Pigskinner," Don Kingery, "Last Chance for Glory," C. Paul Jackson, "The King of Swap," David C. Cooke, "Basketball Bum," and Marin S. Madancy, "Where There's Smokey, There's a Fireball," all in *Best Sports,* 2:7 (February 1951).

56. Ron Goulart, *An Informal History of the Pulp Magazine* (1972. Reprint. New York: Ace Books, 1973), p. 180.

57. Robert Jackson Higgs, "The Unheroic Hero: A Study of the Athlete in Twentieth Century American Literature" (Ph.D. dissertation, University of Tennessee, 1967), pp. 21-22.

58. Eldridge Cleaver, *Soul on Ice* (New York: McGraw-Hill,

1968), pp. 84-96. As will be explained later, I disagree with Cleaver's claim in this essay that the heavyweight champion is the masculine ideal (I attribute this status to the football player), but I agree with Cleaver's analysis of the racial identity of black champions.

59. Barry Beckham, *Runner Mack* (New York: Morrow, 1972), p. 85.

60. John O. Lyons, *The College Novel in America* (Carbondale: Southern Illinois University Press, 1962), p. 19. It is interesting to note, too, that historian John Hammond Moore characterizes the years 1893-1913 as "football's ugly decades," when professionalism and brutality nearly destroyed the game. See *Smithsonian Journal of History,* 2 (Fall 1967): 49-68. These years span the time of Patten's writing of the Frank Merriwell stories (1896-1913).

61. Robert Daley, *Only a Game* (New York: New American Library, 1967), pp. 83-84.

62. Quoted in the *Portland Oregonian,* 1 March 1977.

63. Ralph Ellison, "The Golden Age, Time Past," in *Shadow and Act* (New York: Random House, 1964), pp. 208-9.

Chapter 3. The Sunlit Field:
Country and City in American Sports Fiction

1. Charles A. Peverelly, *The National Game* (New York, 1866). Cited in John Rickards Betts, *America's Sporting Heritage: 1850-1950* (Menlo Park, Calif.: Addison-Wesley, 1974), p. 93.

2. Betts, *America's Sporting Heritage,* chs. 4 and 5.

3. Alan Trachtenberg et al., *The City* (New York: Oxford University Press, 1971), p. 99.

4. William Bradford, *History of Plymouth Plantation, 1606-1646,* edited by William T. Davis (New York: Scribner's, 1908), p. 96; and Robert Beverley, *The History and Present State of Virginia,* edited by Louis B. Wright (Chapel Hill: University of North Carolina Press, 1947), p. 296. The first of these passages is quoted in Leo Marx, *The Machine in the Garden* (New York: Oxford University Press, 1964), p. 41.

5. Marx, *The Machine in The Garden,* and Henry Nash Smith, *Virgin Land* (New York: Knopf, 1950).

6. Richard Price, *Observations on the Importance of the American Revolution* (London, 1785), pp. 57-58. Quoted in Marx, *Machine in the Garden,* p. 105.

7. J. Hector St. John de Creuecoeur, *Letters from an American*

Farmer (New York: New American Library, 1963); Thomas Jefferson, *Notes on the State of Virginia,* edited by William Peden (Chapel Hill: University of North Carolina Press, 1954); and Alexis de Tocqueville, *Democracy in America,* trans. George Lawrence (Garden City, N.J.: Doubleday, 1969).

8. John Rickards Betts, "The Technological Revolution and the Rise of Sport, 1850-1900," *The Mississippi Valley Historical Review* 40 (September 1953): 231-56.

9. Thorstein Veblen, *The Theory of the Leisure Class* (New York: Macmillan, 1908), pp. 246-75.

10. Frederick L. Paxson, "The Rise of Sport," *The Mississippi Valley Historical Review,* 4 (September 1917): 167.

11. See, for example, Henry Nash Smith, *Virgin Land,* pp. 291-305.

12. R. W. B. Lewis, *The American Adam* (Chicago: University of Chicago Press, 1955), p. 1.

13. Constance Rourke, *American Humor* (New York: Harcourt, Brace, 1931), p. 31.

14. George Fitch, *At Good Old Siwash* (1911; New York: Peter Smith, 1936), p. 13.

15. George Fitch, *The Big Strike at Siwash* (New York: Doubleday, Page, 1909), p. 8.

16. Fitch, *At Good Old Siwash,* p. 16.

17. Ibid. p. 18.

18. Zane Grey, *The Redheaded Outfield and Other Stories* (New York: Grosset & Dunlap, 1915), p. 29.

19. Franklin M. Reck, "The Gawk," in *Varsity Letter* (New York: Crowell, 1942), p. 133.

20. Charles E. Van Loan, "Easy Picking," in *Taking the Count* (New York: Doran, 1915), p. 314.

21. Ibid., p. 314.

22. Jack London, *The Abysmal Brute,* bound with *The Game,* edited by I. O. Evans (London: Arco Publications, 1967), p. 77.

23. Ibid., p. 80.

24. Ibid., pp. 79-80.

25. Ibid., p. 94.

26. Ernest Hemingway, *A Farewell to Arms* (New York: Scribner, 1929), pp. 3, 71, 118, 289, 290.

27. Robert Wilder, *Autumn Thunder* (New York: Putnam, 1952), p. 31.

28. Ibid., p. 49.

29. Donald Elder, *Ring Lardner* (Garden City: Doubleday, 1956), pp. 141-42.

30. Ring Lardner, *You Know Me Al* (New York: Scribner, 1916), p. 10.

31. Page Smith, *As a City Upon a Hill* (New York: Knopf, 1966), pp. 208-9.

32. Lardner, *You Know Me Al,* p. 41.

33. Ibid., p. 10.

34. Maxwell Geismar, *Ring Lardner and the Portrait of Folly* (New York: Crowell, 1972), p. 121.

35. In Harold Stearns, ed.; *Civilization in the United States* (New York: Harcourt, Brace, 1922), p. 461.

36. F. Scott Fitzgerald, *The Crack Up* (New York: New Directions, 1956), p. 36.

37. Virginia Woolf, "American Fiction," in *Collected Essays* (New York: Harcourt, Brace & World, 1967), vol. 2, p. 118.

38. Smith, *As a City Upon a Hill,* pp. 199-200.

39. "Twelve Southerners," *I'll Take My Stand* (New York: Harper & Brothers, 1930).

40. Robert Penn Warren, "Goodwood Comes Back," in *The Circus in the Attic and Other Stories* (New York: Harcourt, Brace & World, 1962), p. 109.

41. Ibid., p. 115.

42. Henry James, *Portrait of a Lady* (Boston: Houghton, Mifflin, 1882).

43. Marx, *Machine in the Garden.*

44. Budd Schulberg, *The Harder They Fall* (New York: Random House, 1947), p. 38-39.

45. Ibid., p. 109.

46. Ibid., p. 185.

47. Ibid., p. 342.

48. W. C. Heinz, *The Professional* (New York: Harper & Row, 1958), p. 238.

49. Ibid., p. 63.

50. Ibid., p. 67.

51. Ibid., p. 147.

52. Ibid., p. 258.

53. Ibid., pp. 58, 75-76, 86, 111, 265, and 284.

54. Ibid., p. 112.

55. Ibid., pp. 75-76.

56. Ibid., p. 97.

57. Leonard Gardner, *Fat City* (New York: Farrar, Straus & Giroux, 1969), pp. 151-52.

58. Ibid., p. 183.

59. Ibid., pp. 143-44.

60. Pete Axthelm, *The City Game* (New York: Harper's Magazine Press, 1970), p. ix.

61. Ibid., p. 10.

62. Charles Rosen, *A Mile Above the Rim* (New York: Arbor House, 1976), p. 46.

63. Jay Neugeboren, *Big Man* (Boston: Houghton Mifflin, 1966), p. 14.

64. Lawrence Shainberg, *One on One* (New York: Holt, Rinehart and Winston, 1970), p. 56.

65. Charles Rosen, *Have Jump Shot Will Travel* (New York: Arbor House, 1975), p. 20.

66. Ibid., p. 30.

67. Ibid., p. 56.

68. Ibid., p. 129.

69. Axthelm, *The City Game,* p. 13.

70. Ibid., p. 47.

71. Ibid., p. 73.

72. Ibid., p. 138.

73. Rosen, *A Mile Above the Rim,* p. 24.

74. Jeremy Larner, *Drive, He Said* (New York: Delacorte, 1964), p. 108.

75. Rosen, *Have Jump Shot Will Travel,* p. 145.

76. Shainberg, *One on One,* p. 38.

77. Rosen, *A Mile Above the Rim,* p. 15.

78. Larner, *Drive, He Said,* p. 15.

79. Shainberg, *One on One,* p. 117.

80. Rosen, *A Mile Above the Rim,* p. 111.

81. Shainberg, *One on One,* p. 152.

82. Larner, *Drive, He Said,* p. 111.

83. Rosen, *Have Jump Shot Will Travel,* p. 149.

84. Rosen, *A Mile Above the Rim,* pp. 3-4.

85. Larner, *Drive, He Said,* pp. 162-63.

86. Shainberg, *One on One,* p. 109.

87. *The Poems of John Dryden,* edited by James Kinsley (Oxford: Clarendon Press, 1958), vol. 1, p. 221.

88. Shainberg, *One on One,* p. 4.

89. Ibid., p. 21.

90. Ibid., 155.

91. Ibid., p. 127.

92. Ibid., p. 127.

93. Ibid., p. 216.

94. Larner, *Drive, He Said,* p. 30.

95. Ibid., p. 26.

Chapter 4. Intimations of Mortality:
Youth and Age in American Sports Fiction

1. Geoffrey Gorer. *The American People* (New York: Norton, 1964), p. 121.
2. Max Lerner, *America as a Civilization* (New York: Simon & Schuster, 1957), pp. 564-65.
3. See particularly Leslie Fiedler, "The Eye of Innocence," in *No! In Thunder* (1960; New York: Stein and Day, 1972).
4. James George Frazer, *The Golden Bough,* abridged ed. (1922; New York: Macmillan, 1963), pp. 308-30.
5. Frazer, *Golden Bough,* p. 309.
6. Jack Olsen, *Alphabet Jackson* (Chicago: Playboy Press, 1974), pp. 274-75.
7. Thorstein Veblen, *The Theory of the Leisure Class* (New York: Macmillan, 1908), pp. 255-56.
8. Quoted in Leverett Smith, "Ty Cobb, Babe Ruth and the Changing Image of the Athlete Hero," in Ray B. Browne et al., *Heroes of Popular Culture* (Bowling Green, Ohio: Bowling Green University Press, 1972), p. 76.
9. Olsen, *Alphabet Jackson,* p. 154.
10. Philip O'Connor, *Stealing Home* (New York: Knopf, 1979).
11. George Zuckerman, *Farewell, Frank Merriwell* (New York: Dutton, 1973), p. 21.
12. Alan S. Foster, *Goodbye, Bobby Thomson! Goodbye, John Wayne!* (New York: Simon & Schuster, 1973), p. 190.
13. See Johan Huizinga, *Homo Ludens* (Boston: Beacon Press, 1970), p. 13, for Huizinga's definition of "play."
14. Jack London, "A Piece of Steak," in *Great Stories from the World of Sport,* 3 vols., ed. Peter Schwed and Herbert Warren Wind (New York: Simon & Schuster, 1958), vol. 2, p. 134.
15. Ibid., pp. 130, 141, 142.
16. Ibid., pp. 137-38.
17. Ibid., pp. 136, 137, 142, 143.
18. Ibid., p. 137.
19. Ibid., p. 135.
20. Gary Cartwright, *The Hundred-Yard War* (Garden City, N.Y.: Doubleday, 1968), pp. 224-25.
21. Ibid., p. 227.
22. Ibid., p. 355.
23. Eliot, Asinof, *Man on Spikes* (New York: McGraw-Hill, 1955), p. 272.

24. Mark Harris, *The Southpaw* (Indianapolis: Bobbs-Merrill, 1953), p. 222.

25. Ibid., p. 27.

26. Ibid,, p. 136.

27. Ibid., p. 205.

28. Ibid., p. 310.

29. Ibid., p. 30.

30. Ibid., p. 42.

31. Ibid., p. 60.

32. Ibid., p. 277.

33. Ibid., p. 116.

34. Ibid., p. 101.

35. Ibid., p. 193.

36. Ibid., p. 330.

37. Ibid., p. 135.

38. Ibid., p. 64.

39. Ibid., p. 348.

40. Ibid., p. 337.

41. Lerner, *America as a Civilization*, p. 618.

42. "Mark Harris: An Interview," *Wisconsin Studies in Contemporary Literature,* 6 (Winter-Spring 1965): 21.

43. Mark Harris, *Bang the Drum Slowly* (New York: Knopf, 1956), p. 6.

44. Ibid., pp. 4-5.

45. Ibid., p. 45.

46. Ibid., p. 140.

47. Ibid., p. 190.

48. Ibid., p. 12.

49. Ibid., p. 159.

50. Ibid., p. 212-13.

51. Ibid., p. 242.

52. Mark Harris, *A Ticket for a Seamstitch* (New York: Knopf, 1957), pp. 86-87.

53. Ibid., p. 111.

54. Mark Harris, *It Looked Like For Ever* (New York: McGraw-Hill, 1979), p. 6.

55. Ibid., p. 3.

56. Ibid., p. 4.

57. Ibid., p. 26.

58. Ibid., p. 49.

59. Ibid., p. 71.

60. Ibid., p. 72.

61. Michael Novak, *The Joy of Sports* (New York: Basic Books, 1976), p. 48.

62. Irwin Shaw, "The Eighty-Yard Run," in *Great Stories from the World of Sport,* 3 vols., edited by Peter Schwed and Herbert Warren Wind (New York: Simon & Schuster, 1958), vol. 2, p. 208.

63. Ibid., p. 219.

64. Ibid., p. 219.

65. Ibid., p. 218.

66. Ibid., p. 208, 220.

67. Ibid., p. 219.

68. John Cheever, "O Youth and Beauty!" in *The Housebreaker of Shady Hill and Other Stories* (New York: Harper, 1958), p. 35.

69. Ibid., p. 62.

70. Ibid., p. 43.

71. Ibid., p. 34, 45.

72. Ibid., p. 46.

73. James Whitehead, *Joiner* (1971; New York: Avon, 1973), p. 431.

74. Edward P. Vargo, *Rainstorms and Fire* (Port Washington, N.Y.: Kennikat Press, 1973), p. 51. See also Gerry Brenner, "*Rabbit, Run*: John Updike's Criticism of the 'Return to Nature,' " *Twentieth Century Literature,* 12 (April 1966): 3-14; Rachael C. Burchard, *John Updike* (Carbondale: Southern Illinois University Press, 1971); Robert Detweiler, *John Updike* (New York: Twayne Publishers, 1972); Alice Hamilton and Kenneth Hamilton, *The Elements of John Updike* (Grand Rapids: William B. Eerdmans Pub. Co.; 1970); Joyce B. Markle, *Fighters and Lovers* (New York: New York University Press, 1973); John C. Stubbs, "The Search for Perfection in *Rabbit, Run,*" *Critique,* 10 (1968): 94-101; J. A. Ward, "John Updike's Fiction," *Critique,* 5 (Spring-Summer 1962): 27-40; for a representative sample of criticism on *Rabbit, Run.*

75. John Updike, "Ace in the Hole," in *The Same Door* (New York: Knopf, 1959), pp. 14-26; and "Ex-Basketball Player," in *The Carpentered Hen and Other Tame Creatures* (New York: Harper, 1958), pp. 2-3.

76. John Updike, *Rabbit, Run* (New York: Knopf, 1960), p. 104.

77. Ibid., p. 105.

78. Ibid., p. 4.

79. Ibid., p. 65.

80. Ibid., pp. 34, 37, 39.

81. Ward, "John Updike's Fiction," p. 34.

82. Updike, *Rabbit, Run,* p. 198.

83. Ibid., p. 142.

84. Ibid., pp. 73, 75.

85. Ibid., pp. 246-47.

86. Ibid., p. 76.
87. Ibid., pp. 133-34.
88. Ibid., p. 130.
89. Ibid., p. 160, 167.
90. Ibid., p. 42.
91. Ibid., p. 20, 89, 233, 244.
92. Ibid., p. 127.
93. Ibid., p. 280.
94. Ibid., p. 171.
95. Ibid., p. 306.
96. Ibid., pp. 9, 52.
97. Ibid., p. 289, 290.
98. Ibid., p. 307.
99. Ibid., p. 149.
100. Ibid., p. 303.
101. Ibid., p. 237.
102. Ibid., p. 301.
103. Ibid., p. 223.
104. Ibid., p. 106.
105. John Updike, *Rabbit Redux* (New York: Knopf, 1971), p. 4.
106. Ibid., p. 53.
107. Ibid., pp. 67-68.
108. Ibid., p. 179.
109. Ibid., pp. 181, 182, 183.
110. Ibid., p. 215.
111. Ibid., p. 228.
112. Ibid., p. 254.

Chapter 5. Men Without Women:
Sexual Roles in American Sports Fiction

1. Erik H. Erikson, *Childhood and Society* (New York: Norton, 1963), p. 291.
2. Jack Olsen, *Alphabet Jackson* (Chicago: Playboy Press, 1974), p. 19.
3. Arnold Beisser, *The Madness in Sports* (New York: Appleton-Century-Crofts, 1967), p. 221.
4. Lionel Tiger, in *Men in Groups* (New York: Random House, 1969), p. 19, defines male bonding as "A particular relationship between two or more males such that they react differently to members of their bonding unit as compared to individuals outside

it." This is a biological need, according to Tiger, that men share with other primates.

5. See, for example, James Whitehead, *Joiner* (New York: Avon, 1971), pp. 24-25.

6. Jack London, *The Game,* bound with *The Abysmal Brute,* edited by I. O. Evans (London: Arco Publications, 1967), p. 17.

7. Ibid., p. 35.

8. Ibid., p. 18.

9. Ibid., pp. 17, 35, 38.

10. Ibid., p. 19.

11. Ibid., p. 40.

12. Ibid., p. 45.

13. Ibid., p. 59.

14. Ibid., p. 61.

15. Ibid., pp. 63-64.

16. Ibid., p. 20.

17. Mac Davis, *Great American Sports Humor* (New York: Dial, 1949), p. 52.

18. Ibid., p. 53.

19. Heywood Broun, *The Sun Field* (New York: Putnam, 1923), p. 43.

20. Ibid., p. 43.

21. Ibid., p. 58.

22. Ibid., p. 65.

23. Ibid., p. 188.

24. Robert Lowry, *The Violent Wedding* (Westport, Conn.: Greenwood Press, 1953), p. 86.

25. Ibid., p. 72.

26. Ibid., pp. 43, 93.

27. Ibid., p. 68.

28. Ibid., p. 83.

29. Ibid., p. 129.

30. Ibid., p. 165.

31. Ibid., p. 199.

32. Ibid., p. 32.

33. Lamar Herrin, *The Rio Loja Ringmaster* (New York: Viking, 1977), p. 220.

34. Ibid., p. 22.

35. Ibid., p. 200.

36. Ibid., p. 241.

37. Ibid., p. 6.

38. Ibid., p. 81.

39. Ibid., p. 256.

40. Ibid., p. 257.

41. Ibid., p. 257.

42. Ibid., p. 267.

43. Eldridge Cleaver, "Lazarus Come Forth," in *Soul on Ice* (New York: McGraw-Hill, 1968), p. 84.

44. Leslie Fiedler, *No! In Thunder*, (1960; New York: Stein and Day, 1971), p. 265.

45. Dan Jenkins, *Semi-Tough* (New York: Atheneum, 1972), p. 152.

46. Ibid., p. 12.

47. Peter Gent, *North Dallas Forty* (New York: Morrow, 1973), pp. 258-59, 275.

48. Ibid., p. 56.

49. Ibid., p. 285.

50. Ibid., p. 5.

51. Ibid., p. 28.

52. Ibid., p. 21.

53. Ibid., p. 211-12.

54. Ibid., p. 194.

55. Ibid., p. 307.

56. Richard Chase, *The American Novel and Its Tradition* (Garden City, N.Y.: Doubleday, 1957).

57. Hamilton Maule, *Footsteps* (New York: Random House, 1961), p. 4.

58. Ibid., p. 198.

59. Ibid., p. 279.

60. William Maxwell, *The Folded Leaf* (New York: Book Find Club, 1945). Maxwell's hero, a timid unathletic boy, painfully reaches maturity only when he can sever his dependence on his athletic friend.

61. Jay Neugeboren, "Something's Rotten in the Borough of Brooklyn," in *Corky's Brother* (New York: Farrar, Straus & Giroux, 1964), p. 146.

62. Beisser, *Madness in Sports*, p. 127.

63. All these expressions of the fan's experience can be found in Marvin Cohen, *Baseball the Beautiful* (New York: Links Books, 1974).

64. Martin Quigley, *Today's Game* (New York: Viking, 1965), and Herrin, *Rio Loja Ringmaster*, are among the novels that express this idea.

65. Beisser, *Madness in Sports*, pp. 128-29.

66. William Heuman, "Brooklyns Lose," in *Great Stories from the World of Sport*, 3 vols., edited by Peter Schwed and Herbert Warren Wind (New York: Simon & Schuster, 1958), vol. 2, p. 182.

67. Frederick Exley, *A Fan's Notes* (New York: Harper & Row, 1968), p. 240.
68. Ibid., p. 99.
69. Anthony Storr, *Human Aggression* (New York: Atheneum, 1968), pp. 72-83, cites these symptoms of blocked aggression.
70. Exley, *A Fan's Notes,* p. 201.
71. Ibid., p. 8.
72. Ibid., p. 232.
73. Ibid., pp. 159-60.
74. Ibid., p. 21.
75. Ibid., p. 357.
76. Ibid., p. 88.

Chapter 6. In Extra Innings:
History and Myth in American Sports Fiction

1. The best discussion of these folklore elements is found in Earl R. Wasserman's article, *"The Natural*: World Ceres," in *Bernard Malamud and the Critics,* edited by Leslie A. Field and Joyce W. Field (New York: New York University Press, 1970), pp. 45-65. Some additions have been made.
2. Bernard Malamud, *The Natural* (New York: Harcourt, Brace, 1952), p. 178.
3. For the identification of Homeric parallels see particularly, Norman Podhoretz, "Achilles in Left Field," *Commentary,* 15 (March 1953): 321-26; and Marcus Klein, *After Alienation: American Novels in Mid-Century* (Cleveland: World Publishing, 1964), pp. 247-93. Nearly every critic discussing the novel has been concerned with identifying the Arthurian parallels. See, for example, Robert Ducharme, *Art and Idea in the Novels of Bernard Malamud* (The Hague: Mouton, 1974); Sidney Richman, *Bernard Malamud* (New York: Twayne, 1966); and Wasserman, *"The Natural*: World Ceres," and Klein, *After Alienation.*
4. Malamud, *The Natural,* p. 233.
5. Ibid., p. 232.
6. Wasserman, *"The Natural*: World Ceres," is the best source here. In fact, this article is the best single explication of the broad range of mythic patterns in the novel.
7. Malamud, *The Natural,* p. 185.
8. Wasserman, *"The Natural*: World Ceres," p. 55.
9. Malamud, *The Natural,* p. 9.
10. Ibid., pp. 83-84, 223.
11. Ibid., p. 156.

12. See Wasserman, *"The Natural*: World Ceres," for a discussion of several of these motifs.

13. Malamud, *The Natural,* p. 29.

14. Max F. Schulz, *Radical Sophistication: Studies in Contemporary Jewish-American Novelists* (Athens: Ohio University Press, 1969), p. 60.

15. Malamud, *The Natural,* p. 154.

16. Roger Angell, *The Summer Game* (1972; New York: Popular Library, 1973), p. 12.

17. Frederick Exley, *A Fan's Notes* (New York: Harper & Row, 1968), p. 346.

18. Lucy Kennedy, *The Sunlit Field* (New York: Crown Publishers, 1950).

19. William Brashler, *The Bingo Long Traveling All-Stars and Motor Kings* (New York: Harper & Row, 1973), p. 77.

20. See Robert W. Peterson, *Only the Ball Was White* (Englewood Cliffs, N.J.: Prentice-Hall, 1970) for a history of the black baseball leagues.

21. Morris R. Cohen, "Baseball," *The Dial,* 67 (26 July 1919): 57.

22. Michael Novak, *The Joy of Sports* (New York: Basic Books, 1976), p. 21.

23. Ibid., pp. 19-20.

24. Ibid., pp. 29-31.

25. Howard S. Slusher, *Man, Sport and Existence: A Critical Analysis* (Philadelphia: Lea & Febiger, 1967), p. 130.

26. Angell, *The Summer Game,* p. 308.

27. Thomas Hornsby Ferril, "Freud, Football and the Marching Virgins," *Readers' Digest,* 105 (September 1974): 72.

28. John Steinbeck, "And Then My Arm Glassed Up," *Sports Illustrated,* 23 (20 December 1965): 99.

29. Slusher, *Man, Sport and Existence,* p. 134.

30. Irwin Shaw, *Voices of a Summer Day* (New York: Delacorte, 1965), p. 12.

31. Ibid., p. 142.

32. Ibid., p. 153.

33. Babs Deal, *The Grail* (New York: David McKay, 1963), p. 7.

34. Philip Roth, "Reading Myself," *Partisan Review,* 40 (1973): 414.

35. Hans Meyerhoff, *Time in Literature* (Berkeley-Los Angeles: University of California Press, 1960), p. 80.

36. Robert Coover, *The Universal Baseball Association, Inc., J. Henry Waugh, Prop.* (New York: Random House, 1968), pp. 34-35.

37. Ibid., p. 19.

38. Ibid., p. 45.

39. Ibid., p. 171.

40. Ibid., p. 35.

41. Ibid., p. 141.

42. Leo J. Hertzel, "What's Wrong with the Christians?" *Critique,* 11 (1969): 12.

43. Coover, *The Universal Baseball Association,* p. 166.

44. Ibid., pp. 47 and 48.

45. Frank W. Shelton, "Humor and Balance in Coover's *The Universal Baseball Association, Inc.,*" *Critique,* 18 (September 1975): 82.

46. Max F. Schultz, *Black Humor Fiction of the Sixties* (Athens: Ohio University Press, 1973), p. 83.

47. Coover, *The Universal Baseball Association,* pp. 17-18.

48. Ibid., p. 9.

49. Ibid., p. 22.

50. Robert Coover, *Pricksongs & Descants* (New York: Dutton, 1969), p. 77.

51. Ibid., p. 79.

52. Coover, *The Universal Baseball Association,* p. 43.

53. Ibid., pp. 202 and 210.

54. Ibid., p. 55.

55. Ibid., pp. 211-12.

56. Ibid., pp. 228-29.

57. Hertzel, "What's Wrong with the Christians?" p. 17.

58. Shelton, "Humor and Balance," p. 85.

59. Coover, *The Universal Baseball Association,* p. 242.

60. Coover, *Pricksongs & Descants,* pp. 77-78.

61. Coover, *The Universal Baseball Association,* p. 49.

62. Don DeLillo, *End Zone* (Boston: Houghton-Mifflin, 1972), pp. 30-31.

63. Ibid., pp. 22 and 30.

64. Ibid., p. 5.

65. Ibid., pp. 36 and 121.

66. Ibid., pp. 233 and 237.

67. Ibid., p. 111.

68. Ibid., p. 112.

69. See Stanley Fogle, " 'And All the Little Typtopies': Notes on Language Theory in the Contemporary Novel," *Modern Fiction Studies,* 20 (Autumn 1974): 328-36, for a discussion of metafiction.

70. DeLillo, *End Zone,* p. 17.

71. Ibid., p. 48.

72. Ibid., p. 231.
73. Ibid., p. 217.
74. Ibid., p. 117.
75. Ibid., p. 118.
76. Ibid., p. 17.
77. Ibid., p. 102.
78. Ibid., p. 187.
79. William P. Alston, *Philosophy of Language* (Englewood Cliffs, N.J.: Prentice-Hall, 1964), pp. 5-6.
80. DeLillo, *End Zone,* p. 25.
81. Ibid., p. 128.
82. Ibid., pp. 23, 25, 50-51, 57, 73, 148.
83. Ibid., p. 92.
84. Ibid., pp. 27-28.
85. Ibid., p. 89.
86. Ibid., p. 234.
87. Ibid., p. 215.
88. Ibid., p. 121.
89. Ibid., p. 82.
90. See Anatol Rapoport, *Fights, Games and Debates* (Ann Arbor: University of Michigan Press, 1960), for a discussion of game theory.
91. DeLillo, *End Zone,* pp. 83 and 87.
92. Ibid., p. 85.
93. Ibid., pp. 69-70.
94. Ibid., p. 229.
95. Ibid., p. 189.
96. Tony Tanner, *City of Words* (London: Jonathan Cape, 1971), p. 16.
97. DeLillo, *End Zone,* p. 45.
98. Ibid., pp. 49 and 77.
99. Edward Sapir, *Language: An Introduction to the Study of Speech* (New York: Harcourt, Brace & World, 1921), p. 116.
100. DeLillo, *End Zone,* p. 112.
101. Ibid., p. 112.
102. Tanner, *City of Words,* p. 17.
103. DeLillo, *End Zone,* pp. 241-42.
104. Ibid., p. 19.
105. Ibid., pp. 167-71.
106. Ibid., p. 113.
107. Roth, "Reading Myself," pp. 404-5.
108. John Leonard, "Cheever to Roth to Malamud," *Atlantic Monthly,* 131 (June 1973), p. 114.
109. Jonathan Raban, "Bad Language: New Novels," *Encounter,* 41 (December 1973), p. 77.

110. For example, Astarte was the West Semitic fertility god and Frenchy Astarte is a dairy farmer; Gofannon is the Celtic craftsman diety and Luke Gofannon has his "magic wand"; Ptah is the Egyptian equivalent of the Greek Hephaestus and Hothead Ptah is a cripple; and elements of the Roland and Gilgamesh stories are obvious in those of their namesakes in the novel.

111. Philip Roth, *The Great American Novel* (New York: Holt, Rinehart & Winston, 1973), p. 124.

112. Ibid., p. 113.

113. Bill Veeck with Ed Linn, *Veeck—As in Wreck* (New York: Putnam, 1962), p. 104.

114. Roth, "Reading Myself," p. 417.

115. Roth, *The Great American Novel,* p. 15.

116. Roth, "Reading Myself," p. 413.

117. Ibid., p. 417.

118. Roth, *The Great American Novel,* pp. 14, 16, 94, 149.

119. Herbert Leibowitz, "Roth Strikes Out," *New Leader,* 56 (14 May 1973): 14.

120. Roth, *The Great American Novel,* pp. 68 and 75.

121. Roth, "Reading Myself," p. 417.

122. Roth, *The Great American Novel,* p. 392.

123. Roth, "Reading Myself," p. 417.

124. Jerome Charyn, *The Seventh Babe* (New York: Arbor House, 1979), p. 328.

125. Paul Hemphill, *Long Gone* (New York: Viking, 1979), pp. 8-9.

126. Ibid., p. 8.

Bibliography

Alger, Horatio. *Ragged Dick*. Bound with *Mark, the Match Boy*. New York: Collier, 1962.

Algren, Nelson. *Never Come Morning*. 1942. New York: Perennial Library, 1965.

Alibrandi, Tom. *Kill Shot*. Los Angeles: Pinnacle, 1979.

Alston, William P. *Philosophy of Language*. Englewood Cliffs, N.J.: Prentice-Hall, 1964.

Anderson, Sherwood. *Beyond Desire*. New York: Liveright, 1932.

————. *Memoirs*. New York: Harcourt, Brace, 1942.

Angell, Roger. *Five Seasons*. New York: Simon and Schuster, 1977.

————. *The Summer Game*. New York: Popular Library, 1973.

Asinof, Eliot. *Man on Spikes*. New York: McGraw-Hill, 1955.

Axthelm, Pete. *The City Game*. New York: Harper's Magazine Press, 1970.

Barbour, Ralph Henry. *The Half-Back*. New York: Appleton, 1899.

Barth, John. *Chimera*. New York: Random House, 1972.

————. *Left End Edwards*. New York: Dodd, Mead, 1914.

————. *Left Half Harmon*. New York: Dodd, Mead, 1921.

Beckham, Barry. *Runner Mack*. New York: Morrow, 1972.

Beisser, Arnold. *The Madness in Sports.* New York: Appleton-Century-Crofts, 1967.

Bell, Marty. *Breaking Balls.* New York: New American Library, 1979.

Berry, Eliot. *Four Quarters Make a Season.* New York: Curtis Brown, 1973.

Betts, John Rickards. *America's Sporting Heritage: 1850-1950.* Menlo Park, Calif.: Addison-Wesley, 1974.

————. "The Technological Revolution and the Rise of Sport, 1850-1900." *The Mississippi Valley Historical Review* 40 (September 1953): 231-56.

Beverley, Robert. *The History and Present State of Virginia.* Ed. Louis B. Wright. Chapel Hill: University of North Carolina Press, 1947.

Blair, Walter, ed. *Native American Humor* (1800-1900). New York: American Book Company, 1937.

Bonner, M. G. *The Dugout Mystery.* New York: Knopf, 1953.

Bouton, Jim. *Ball Four.* New York: World Publishing, 1970.

Boyar, Jane, and Burt Boyer. *World Class.* New York: Random House, 1975.

Braddon, Russell. *The Finalists.* New York: Atheneum, 1977.

Brashler, William. *The Bingo Long Traveling All-Stars and Motor Kings.* New York: Harper & Row, 1973.

Brennan, Joe. "Big League Pigskinner." *Best Sports* 2:7 (February 1951): 112-26.

Brenner, Gerry. "*Rabbit, Run*: John Updike's Criticism of the 'Return to Nature.'" *Twentieth Century Literature* 12 (April 1966): 3-14.

Brinkley, William. *Breakpoint.* New York: Morrow, 1978.

Brooks, Noah. *Our Baseball Club and How It Won the Championship.* New York: Dutton, 1884.

Broun, Heywood. *The Sun Field.* New York: Putnam, 1923.

Burchard, Rachael C. *John Updike: Yea Sayings.* Carbondale, Ill.: Southern Illinois University Press, 1971.

Butts, Susan Dorcas. *Psychology of Sport.* New York: Van Nostrand Reinhold, 1976.

Caillois, Roger. *Man, Play, and Games.* Trans. by Meyer Barash. 1958. New York: Free Press of Glencoe, 1961.

Campbell, Joseph. *The Hero with a Thousand Faces.* 1949. Cleveland: World Publishing, 1963.

Cantwell, Robert. "The Music of Baseball." *Sports Illustrated* 13 (3 October 1960): 82-92.

————. "A Sneering Laugh with the Bases Loaded." *Sports Illustrated* 16 (23 April 1962): 68-76.

————. "Sport Was Box Office Poison." *Sports Illustrated* 31 (15 September 1969): 108-16.

Carnegie, Dale. *How to Win Friends and Influence People.* New York: Simon & Schuster, 1937.

Carol, Bill J. *Single to Center.* Austin, Tex.: Steck-Vaughn, 1974.

Cartwright, Gary. *The Hundred-Yard War.* Garden City, N.Y.: Doubleday, 1968.

Cash, W. J. *The Mind of the South.* New York: Knopf, 1941.

Cawelti, John G. *Apostles of the Self-Made Man.* Chicago: University of Chicago Press, 1965.

Chadwick, Lester. *Baseball Joe of the Silver Stars.* New York: Cupples & Leon, 1912.

Charyn, Jerome. *The Seventh Babe.* New York: Arbor House, 1979.

Chase, Richard. *The American Novel and Its Tradition.* Garden City, N.Y.: Doubleday, 1957.

Cheever, John. "O Youth and Beauty!" In *The Housebreaker of Shady Hill and Other Stories.* New York: Harper, 1958.

Chute, B. J. *Blocking Back.* New York: Macmillan, 1938.

Cleaver, Eldridge. *Soul on Ice.* New York: McGraw-Hill, 1968.

Coe, Charles Francis. *Knockout.* Philadelphia: Lippincott, 1935.

Coffin, Tristram P. *The Old Ball Game.* New York: Herder and Herder, 1971.

Cohen, Marvin. *Baseball the Beautiful.* New York: Links Books, 1974.

Cohen, Morris R. "Baseball." *The Dial* 67 (26 July 1919): 57.

Commager, Henry Steele. *The American Mind: An Interpretation of American Thought and Character Since the 1880's.* New Haven, Conn.: Yale University Press, 1950.

Conwell, Russell. *Acres of Diamonds.* Philadelphia: Huber, 1890.

Cooke, David C. "Basketball Bum." *Best Sports* 2:7 (February 1951): 59-66.

Coover, Robert. "McDuff on the Mound." *Iowa Review* 2 (Fall 1971): 111-20.

————. *The Origin of the Brunists.* New York: Putnam, 1966.

————. *Pricksongs & Descants.* New York: Dutton, 1969.

————. *The Universal Baseball Association, Inc., J. Henry Waugh, Prop.* New York: Random House, 1968.

————. "Whatever Happened to Gloomy Gus of the Chicago Bears?" *American Review* 22 (1975): 31-111.

de Crevecoeur, J. Hector St. John. *Letters from an American Farmer.* New York: New American Library, 1963.

Cronley. *Fall Guy.* Garden City, N.Y.: Doubleday, 1978.

Curti, Merle. "Dime Novels in the American Tradition." *Yale Review* 26 (Summer 1937): 761-78.

Cutler, John L. "Gilbert Patten and His Frank Merriwell Saga." *Maine University Studies* 31 (1934): 1-123.

Daley, Robert. *Only a Game.* New York: New American Library, 1967.

Danzig, Allison. *The History of American Football: Its Great Teams, Players, and Coaches.* Englewood Cliffs, N.J.: Prentice-Hall, 1956.

Davies, Valentine. *It Happens Every Spring.* New York: Farrar, Straus, 1949.

Davis, Mac. *Great American Sports Humor.* New York: Dial Press, 1949.

Davis, Richard Harding. *Gallegher and Other Stories.* 1891. New York: Scribner, 1906.

———. *Stories for Boys.* New York: Scribner, 1894.

Davis, Terry. *Vision Quest.* New York: Viking, 1979.

Dawson, Elmer A. *Garry Grayson's Hill Street Eleven.* New York: Grosset & Dunlap, 1926.

Deal, Babs. *The Grail.* New York: McKay, 1963.

Decker, Duane. *Third-Base Rookie.* New York: Morrow, 1959.

Deford, Frank. *Cut 'n' Run.* New York: Viking, 1972.

DeLillo, Don. *End Zone.* Boston: Houghton Mifflin, 1972.

———. *Ratner's Star.* New York: Knopf, 1976.

Detweiler, Robert. *John Updike.* New York: Twayne, 1972.

Devries, Julian. *The Strikeout King.* Cleveland, Ohio: World Publishing, 1940.

Dorson, Richard M. *American Folklore.* Chicago: University of Chicago Press, 1959.

Ducharme, Robert. *Art and Idea in the Novels of Bernard Malamud.* The Hague: Mouton, 1974.

Dudley, Albertus True. *With Mask and Mitt.* Boston: Lothrop, Lee & Shepard, 1906.

Duffield, J. W. *Bert Wilson's Fadeaway Ball.* New York: Sully, 1913.

Durham, Philip. "Dime Novels: An American Heritage." *Western Humanities Review* 9 (Winter 1954-55): 33-43.

———. "A General Classification of 1,531 Dime Novels." *Huntington Library Quarterly* 17 (May 1954): 287-91.

Earl, John Prescott. *On the School Team.* Philadelphia: Penn, 1908.

Ebert, P. K., and R. R. Knudson, eds. *Sports Poems.* New York: Dell, 1956.

Edwards, Harry. *The Revolt of the Black Athlete.* New York: Free Press, 1969.

Einstein, Charles. *The Only Game in Town.* New York: Dell, 1955.

Elder, Donald. *Ring Lardner*. Garden City, N.Y.: Doubleday, 1956.

Ellis, Edward S. *Seth Jones; or, The Captives of the Frontier*. Ed. Philip Durham. 1860. New York: Odyssey, 1966.

Ellison, Ralph. *Shadow and Act*. New York: Random House, 1964.

Emerson, Ralph Waldo. "Self-reliance" and "Heroism." In *The Complete Works of Ralph Waldo Emerson*. Ed. by Edward Waldo Emerson. Centenary Edition, 12 vols. Boston: Houghton Mifflin, 1903. Vol. 2, pp. 43-90, 243-64.

Erikson, Erik H. *Childhood and Society*. 2nd ed. New York: Norton, 1963.

Erin, Bill. "Pass 'em Blind!" *Best Sports* 2:7 (February 1951): 6-21, 111.

Evans, Walter. "The All-American Boys: A Study of Boys' Sports Fiction." *Journal of Popular Culture* 6 (Summer 1972): 104-21.

Everett, William. *Changing Base*. Boston: Lee & Shepard, 1868.

Exley, Frederick. *A Fan's Notes*. New York: Harper & Row, 1968.

————. *Pages from a Cold Island*. New York: Random House, 1975.

Farrell, James T. "Baseball as It's Played in Books—Some Cheers, Jeers and Hopes." *New York Times Book Review* 10 August 1958, p. 5.

————. *The Face of Time*. New York: Vanguard, 1940.

————. *Father and Son*. New York: Vanguard, 1940.

————. *My Baseball Diary*. New York: Barnes, 1957.

————. *My Days of Anger*. New York: Vanguard, 1943.

————. *No Star Is Lost*. New York: Vanguard, 1936.

————. *Studs Lonigan: A Trilogy*. New York: Vanguard, 1935.

————. *A World I Never Made*. New York: Vanguard, 1936.

Faulkner, William. *The Hamlet*. New York: Random House, 1940.

————. *Intruder in the Dust*. New York: Random House, 1948.

————. *Sanctuary*. New York: Cape & Smith, 1931.

Ferguson, Charles. *Pigskin*. Garden City, N.Y.: Doubleday, Doran, 1929.

Ferril, Thomas Hornsby. "Freud, Football and the Marching Virgins." *Readers Digest* 105 (September 1974): 71-73.

Fiedler, Leslie. *No! In Thunder*. 1960. New York: Stein and Day, 1971.

Fishwick, Marshall W. *American Heroes, Myth and Reality*. Washington D.C.: Public Affairs Press, 1954.

————. *The Hero: American Style*. New York: McKay, 1969.

Fitch, George. *At Good Old Siwash*. 1911. New York: Peter Smith, 1936.

―――. *The Big Strike at Siwash*. New York: Doubleday, Page, 1909.

Fitzgerald, F. Scott. *The Crack Up*. New York: New Directions, 1956.

―――. "The Freshest Boy." In *The Portable F. Scott Fitzgerald*. New York: Viking, 1945.

―――. *The Great Gatsby*. New York: Scribner's, 1925.

―――. *Tender Is the Night*. New York: Scribner's, 1934.

―――. *This Side of Paradise*. New York: Scribner's, 1920.

Fitzsimmons, Cortland. *Crimson Ice*. New York: Stokes, 1935.

―――. *Death on the Diamond*. New York: Stokes, 1934.

―――. *70,000 Witnesses*. New York: McBride, 1931.

Fogle, Stanley. " 'And All the Little Typtopies': Notes on Language Theory in the Contemporary American Novel." *Modern Fiction Studies* 20 (Autumn 1974): 328-36.

Ford, T. W. "Touchdown at Tobruk." *Sports Fiction* 4:6 (Winter 1943-44): 36-46.

Forkan, James P. "T. D. Club: Nets Run Up Score with Key Football Sales." *Advertising Age*, 23 June 1980, pp. 3 and 9.

Fortune editors. *100 Stories of Business Success*. New York: Simon & Schuster, 1954.

Foster, Alan S. *Goodbye, Bobby Thomson! Goodbye, John Wayne!* New York: Simon & Schuster, 1973.

Francis, H. D. *Double Reverse*. Garden City, N.Y.: Doubleday, 1958.

Frazer, James George. *The Golden Bough: A Study in Magic and Religion*. Abridged ed. 1922. New York: Macmillan, 1963.

Frick, C. H. *Tourney Team*. New York: Harcourt, Brace, 1954.

Fullerton, Hugh. "The Fellows Who Made the Game." *Saturday Evening Post* 200 (21 April 1928): 18-19, 184-86, 188.

Gallico, Paul. *Matilda*. New York: Coward-McCann, 1970.

―――. "The Yellow Twin." In *The Pulps*. Ed. by Tony Goodstone. New York: Chelsea House, 1970.

Gardner, Leonard. *Fat City*. New York: Farrar, Straus and Giroux, 1969.

Gardner, Ralph D. *Horatio Alger, or The American Hero Era*. Mendota, Ill.: Wayside Press, 1964.

Geismar, Maxwell. *Ring Lardner and the Portrait of Folly*. New York: Crowell, 1972.

Gent, Peter. *North Dallas Forty*. New York: Morrow, 1975.

Gerson, Noel B. *The Sunday Heroes*. New York: Morrow, 1972.

Glanville, Brian. *The Olympian*. New York: Coward-McCann, 1969.

Goodstone, Tony, ed. *The Pulps.* New York: Chelsea House, 1970.

Gorer, Geoffrey. *The American People: A Study of National Character.* Rev. ed. New York: Norton, 1964.

Goulart, Ron. *An Informal History of the Pulp Magazine.* 1972; New York: Ace Books, 1973.

Graham, John Alexander. *Babe Ruth Caught in a Snowstorm.* Boston: Houghton Mifflin, 1973.

Greenberg, Martin H., and Joseph D. Olander, eds. *Run to Starlight: Sports Through Science Fiction.* New York: Delacorte, 1975.

Grey, Zane. *The Redheaded Outfield and Other Baseball Stories.* New York: Grosset & Dunlap, 1915.

———. *The Short-stop.* New York: Grosset & Dunlap, 1909.

Grobani, Anton. *Guide to Baseball Literature.* Detroit: Gale Research, 1975.

———. *Guide to Football Literature.* Detroit: Gale Research, 1975.

Hamill, Pete. *Flesh and Blood.* New York: Random House, 1977.

Hamilton, Alice and Kenneth Hamilton. *The Elements of John Updike.* Grand Rapids, Mich.: Erdmans Publishing, 1970.

Harkins, Philip. *Punt Formation.* New York: Morrow, 1949.

Harris, Mark. *Bang the Drum Slowly.* New York: Knopf, 1956.

———. *It Looked Like For Ever.* New York: McGraw-Hill, 1979.

———. *The Southpaw.* Indianapolis: Bobbs-Merrill, 1953.

———. *A Ticket for a Seamstitch.* New York: Knopf, 1957.

Harris, Thomas. *Black Sunday.* New York: Putnam, 1975.

Heinz, W. C. *The Professional.* New York: Harper & Row, 1958.

Hemingway, Ernest. *A Farewell to Arms.* New York: Scribner's, 1929.

———. *For Whom the Bell Tolls.* New York: Scribner's, 1940.

———. *The Old Man and the Sea.* New York: Scribner's, 1952.

———. *The Short Stories of Ernest Hemingway.* New York: Scribner's, 1938.

Hemphill, Paul. *Long Gone.* New York: Viking, 1979.

Herrin, Lamar. *The Rio Loja Ringmaster.* New York: Viking, 1977.

Hertzel, Leo J. "What's Wrong with the Christians?" *Critique* 11 (1969): 11-22.

Heyliger, William. *The Captain of the Nine.* New York: Appleton, 1912.

———. *The Loser's End.* Chicago: Goldsmith, 1937.

Higdon, Hal. *The Horse That Played Center Field.* New York: Holt, Rinehart & Winston, 1969.

Higgs, Robert Jackson. "The Unheroic Hero: A Study of the Athlete in Twentieth Century American Literature." Ph.D. dissertation, University of Tennessee, 1967.

Hoagland, Edward. *The Circle Home.* New York: Crowell, 1960.

Howe, Irving. "The City in Literature." *Commentary* 51 (May 1971): 61-68.

————. *Politics and the Novel.* 1957. Cleveland: World Publishing, 1964.

Hubbard, Elbert. *A Message to Garcia.* East Aurora, N.J.: Roycrofters, 1899.

Hughes, Rupert. *The Patent Leather Kid and Other Stories.* New York: Grosset & Dunlap, 1927.

Hughes, Thomas. *Tom Brown's School Days.* 1857. London: Macmillan, 1974.

Huizinga, Johan. *Homo Ludens: A Study of the Play-Element in Culture.* Boston: Beacon Press, 1955.

Idell, Albert. *Pug.* New York: Greystone, 1941.

Inge, William. *Four Plays.* New York: Random House, 1958.

Isaacs, Neil D. *All the Moves: A History of College Basketball.* Philadelphia: Lippincott, 1975.

Jackson, C. Paul. "The King of Swat." *Best Sports* 2:7 (February 1951): 31-37, 47.

James, Henry. *Portrait of a Lady.* Boston: Houghton, Mifflin, 1882.

Jefferson, Thomas. *Notes on the State of Virginia.* Chapel Hill: University of North Carolina Press, 1954.

Jenkins, Dan. *Semi-Tough.* New York: Atheneum, 1972.

Jenks, George C. "Double-Curve Dan, the Pitcher Detective; or, Against Heavy Odds." *Beadle's Half-Dime Library*, no. 581 (11 September 1888).

————. "The Pitcher Detective's Foil; or, Double-Curve Dan's Double Play." *Beadle's Half-Dime Library, no.* 608 (26 March 1889).

————. "The Pitcher Detective's Toughest Tussel; or, Double-Curve Dan's Dead Ball." *Beadle's Half-Dime Library*, no. 681 (12 August 1890).

Johannsen, Albert. *The House of Beadle and Adams.* 2 vols. Norman: University of Oklahoma Press, 1950.

Johnson, Owen. *The Humming Bird.* New York: Baker and Taylor, 1910.

————. *Stover at Yale.* 1912. New York: Collier Books, 1968.

Johnson, William O., Jr. *Super Spectator and the Electric Lilliputians.* Boston: Little, Brown, 1971.

Johnston, Alexander. *Ten—and Out! The Complete Story of the Prize Ring in America.* 3d rev. ed. New York: Washburn, 1947.

Jones, James. *From Here to Eternity.* New York: Scribner, 1953.

Karlins, Marvin. *The Last Man Is Out.* Englewood Cliffs, N.J.: Prentice-Hall, 1969.

Kennedy, Lucy. *The Sunlit Field.* New York: Crown, 1950.

Kingery, Don. "Last Chance for Glory." *Best Stories* 2:7 (February 1950): 48-58.

Kinsley, James, ed. *The Poems of John Dryden.* Oxford: Clarendon Press, 1958.

Kipling, Rudyard. *Stalky & Company.* New York: Dell, 1968.

Klapp, Orrin E. *Heroes, Villains, and Fools.* Englewood Cliffs, N.J.: Prentice-Hall, 1962.

Klein, Marcus. *After Alienation: American Novels in Mid-Century.* Cleveland, Ohio: World Publishing, 1964.

Knudson, R. R., and P. K. Ebert, eds. *Sports Poems.* New York: Dell, 1971.

Koch, Kenneth. *Ko, or Season on Earth.* New York: Grove, 1959.

Lampell, Millard. *The Hero.* New York: Messner, 1949.

Lardner, Ring. *The Collected Short Stories of Ring Lardner.* New York: Modern Library, no date.

———. *Lose with a Smile.* New York: Scribner, 1933.

———. *You Know Me Al.* New York: Scribner, 1916.

Larner, Jeremy. *Drive, He Said.* New York: Delacorte, 1964.

Leibowitz, Herbert. "Roth Strikes Out." *The New Leader* 56 (19 May 1973): 24-25.

Leonard, John. "Cheever to Roth to Malamud." *Atlantic Monthly* 121 (June 1973): 114-16.

Lerner, Max. *America as a Civilization: Life and Thought in the United States Today.* New York: Simon & Schuster, 1957.

Lewis, R. W. B. *The American Adam: Innocence, Tragedy and Tradition in the Nineteenth Century.* Chicago: University of Chicago Press, 1955.

Lewis, Sinclair. *Elmer Gantry.* New York: Harcourt, Brace, 1927.

Lindsay, Vachel. *The Golden Whales of California.* New York: Macmillan, 1920.

London, Jack. "The Mexican." In *The Bodley Head Jack London.* Ed. by Arthur Calder-Marshall. London: The Bodley Head, 1913.

———. *The Game and the Abysmal Brute.* Ed. by I. O. Evans. Fitzroy Edition. London: Arco Publications, 1967.

Lowry, Robert. *The Violent Wedding*. Westport, Conn.: Greenwood, 1953.

Lucas, John A., and Ronald A. Smith. *Saga of American Sport.* Philadelphia: Lea & Febiger, 1978.

Lyons, John O. *The College Novel in America.* Carbondale: Southern Illinois University Press, 1962.

McGuane, Thomas. *Ninety-Two in the Shade.* New York: Farrar, Straus and Giroux, 1973.

McIntosh, P. C. *Sport in Society.* London: Watts, 1968.

Madancy, Marin S. "Where There's Smokey, There's a Fireball." *Best Sports* 2:7 (February 1951): 105-11.

Malamud, Bernard. *The Natural.* New York: Harcourt, Brace, 1952.

Manchester, William. *The Long Gainer.* Boston: Little, Brown, 1961.

March, Joseph Moncure. *The Set-Up.* New York: Covici-Friede, 1928.

"Mark Harris: An Interview." *Wisconsin Studies in Contemporary Literature* 6 (Winter-Spring 1965): 15-26.

Markle, Joyce B. *Fighters and Lovers: Theme in the Novels of John Updike.* New York: New York University Press, 1973.

Marks, Percy. *The Unwilling God.* New York: Harper & Brothers, 1929.

Marquand, J. P. *H. M. Pulham, Esq.* Boston: Little, Brown, 1941.

Marquez, Gabriel Garcia. *One Hundred Years of Solitude.* Trans. by Gregory Rabasa. New York: Harper & Row, 1970.

Marx, Leo. *The Machine in the Garden: Technology and the Pastoral Ideal in America.* New York: Oxford University Press, 1964.

Maule, Hamilton (Tex). *Footsteps.* New York: Random House, 1961.

————. *The Last Out.* New York: McKay, 1964.

Maxwell, William. *The Folded Leaf.* New York: Book Find Club, 1945.

Menke, Frank G. *The Encyclopedia of Sports.* 3d rev. ed. New York: Barnes, 1963.

Messenger, Christian Karl. "Sport in American Literature (1830-1930)." Ph.D. dissertation, Northwestern University, 1974.

Meyerhoff, Hans. *Time in Literature.* Berkeley: University of California Press, 1960.

Miller, Arthur. *Death of a Salesman.* New York: Viking, 1949.

Miller, Jason. *That Championship Season.* New York: Atheneum, 1972.

Mizener, Arthur. *The Far Side of Paradise: A Biography of F. Scott Fitzgerald.* 1949. New York: Vintage Books, 1959.

Molloy, Paul. *A Pennant for the Kremlin.* Garden City, N.Y.: Doubleday, 1964.

Moore, John Hammond. "Football's Ugly Decades." *Smithsonian Journal of History* 2 (Fall 1967): 49-68.

Morrison, Lillian, ed. *Sprints and Distances: Sports in Poetry and Poetry in Sport.* New York: Crowell, 1965.

Nemerov, Howard. *The Homecoming Game.* New York: Simon & Schuster, 1957.

Neugeboren, Jay. *Big Man.* Boston: Houghton Mifflin, 1966.

————. "Something's Rotten in the Borough of Brooklyn." In *Corky's Brother.* New York: Farrar, Straus, Giroux, 1964.

Newman, Edwin. *Sunday Punch.* Boston: Houghton Mifflin, 1979.

Norris, Frank. *Collected Writing.* Garden City, N.Y.: Doubleday, Doran & Company, 1928.

Novak, Michael. *The Joy of Sports.* New York: Basic Books, 1976.

Nye, Bud. *Stay Loose.* Garden City, N.Y.: Doubleday, 1959.

Nye, Russel B. *The Unembarrassed Muse: The Popular Arts in America.* 1970. New York: Dial Press, 1971.

O'Connor, Philip. *Stealing Home.* New York: Knopf, 1979.

O'Cork, Shannon. *Sports Freak.* New York: St. Martin's, 1980.

Odets, Clifford. *Golden Boy.* In *Three Dramas of American Individualism.* New York: Washington Square, 1961.

Olsen, Jack. *Alphabet Jackson.* Chicago: Playboy, 1974.

O'Neill, Eugene. *Lost Plays.* New York: New Fathoms, 1950.

————. *Nine Plays.* New York: Modern Library, 1941.

O'Rourke, Frank. *Flashing Spikes.* New York: Barnes, 1948.

Orwell, George. "Boys' Weeklies." In *A Collection of Essays.* 1946. Garden City, N.Y.: Doubleday, 1954. Pp. 284-313.

Patten, Gilbert. *Frank Merriwell's "Father": An Autobiography of Gilbert Patten ("Burt L. Standish").* Ed. by Harriet Hinsdale. Norman: University of Oklahoma Press, 1964.

Pawley, Eugene. "Tin Ears." *Sports Fiction* 4:6 (Winter 1943-44): 69-79.

Paxson, Frederick L. "The Rise of Sport." *Mississippi Valley Historical Review* 4 (September 1917): 143-68.

Peterson, Robert W. *Only the Ball Was White.* Englewood Cliffs, N.J.: Prentice-Hall, 1970.

Pierson, Don. "Look Behind the Stadium Boom." *Mainliner* 19 (November 1975): 53-56.

Podhoretz, Norman. "Achilles in Left Field." *Commentary* 15 (March 1953): 321-26.

Propp, Vladimir. *Morphology of the Folktale.* Trans. by Laurence

Scott. Bloomington: Indiana University Press, 1958.

Pye, Lloyd. *That Prosser Kid.* New York: Arbor House, 1977.

Quigley, Martin. *Today's Game.* New York: Viking, 1965.

Raban, Jonathan. "Bad Language: New Novels." *Encounter* 41 (December 1973): 77-79.

Rank, Otto. *The Myth of the Birth of the Hero.* Trans. by Dr. F. Robbins and Dr. Smith Ely Jelliffe. New York: Bruner, 1952.

Rapoport, Anatol. *Fights, Games and Debates.* Ann Arbor, University of Michigan Press, 1960.

Reck, Franklin M. "The Gawk." In *Varsity Letter.* New York: Crowell, 1942.

Redgate, John. *The Last Decathlon.* New York: Delacorte, 1979.

Ribalow, Harold U., ed. *The World's Greatest Boxing Stories.* New York: Twayne, 1952.

Richman, Sidney. *Bernard Malamud.* New York: Twayne, 1966.

Rober, Eric. "Crucial Game for Pop." *Sports Fiction* 4:6 (Winter 1943-44): 10-20.

Rosen, Charles. *Have Jump Shot Will Travel.* New York: Arbor House, 1975.

———. *A Mile Above the Rim.* New York: Arbor House, 1976.

Rodnon, Stewart. "Sports, Sporting Codes, and Sportsmanship in the Work of Ring Lardner, James T. Farrell, Ernest Hemingway, and William Faulkner." Ph.D. dissertation, New York University, 1961.

Rooney, John F. *A Geography of American Sport.* Menlo Park, Calif.: Addison-Wesley, 1974.

Roosevelt, Theodore. *The Strenuous Life.* New York: The Review of Reviews Company, 1910.

Roth, Philip. *Goodbye Columbus.* Cleveland, Ohio: World, 1963.

———. *The Great American Novel.* New York: Holt, Rinehart, Winston, 1973.

———. *Portnoy's Complaint.* New York: Random House, 1969.

———. "Reading Myself." *Partisan Review* 40 (1973): 404-17.

Rourke, Constance. *American Humor.* New York: Harcourt, Brace, 1931.

Runyon, Damon. *More Guys and Dolls.* Garden City, N.Y.: Garden City Books, 1951.

Sackler, Howard. *The Great White Hope.* New York: Dial Press, 1968.

Sainsbury, Noel. *Cracker Stanton.* New York: Cupples & Leon, 1934.

Sapir, Edward. *Language: An Introduction to the Study of Speech.* New York: Harcourt, Brace & World, 1921.

Sayles, John. *The Pride of the Bimbos.* Boston: Little, Brown, 1975.

Sayre, Joel. *Rackety Rax.* New York: Knopf, 1932.

Schlesinger, Arthur. *The Rise of the City, 1878-1898.* New York: Macmillan, 1933.

School and Adventure Stories for Boys. London: Epworth Press, 1927.

Schulberg, Budd. *The Harder They Fall.* New York: Random House, 1947.

Schulz, Max F. *Black Humor Fiction of the Sixties: A Pluralistic Definition of Man and His World.* Athens: Ohio University Press, 1969.

Schwed, Peter, and Herbert Warren Wind, eds. *Great Stories from the World of Sport.* 3 vols. New York: Simon & Schuster, 1958.

Scott, Jack. *The Athletic Revolution.* New York: Free Press, 1971.

Severance, Mark. *Hammersmith: His Harvard Days.* Boston: Houghton, Osgood & Company, 1878.

Seymour, Harold. *Baseball: The Early Years.* New York: Oxford University Press, 1960.

————. *Baseball: The Golden Age.* New York: Oxford University Press, 1971.

Shainberg, Lawrence. *One on One.* New York: Holt, Rinehart & Winston, 1970.

Shaw, Irwin. *Voices of a Summer Day.* New York: Delacorte, 1965.

Shecter, Leonard. *The Jocks.* New York: Warner Books, 1970.

Shelton, Frank W. "Humor and Balance in Coover's *The Universal Baseball Association, Inc.*" *Critique* 17 (September 1975): 78-90.

Sherman, Harold M. *Safe!* New York: Grosset & Dunlap, 1928.

————. *Strike Him Out!* New York: Goldsmith, 1931.

Sherwood, Robert. *The Petrified Forest.* In *Representative American Dramas.* Ed. by Montrose J. Moses and Joseph Wood Krutch. Boston: Little, Brown, 1941.

Shulman, Irving. *The Square Trap.* Boston: Little, Brown, 1953.

Slusher, Howard S. *Man, Sport and Existence: A Critical Analysis.* Philadelphia: Lea & Febiger, 1967.

Smith, H. Allen. *Rhubarb.* Garden City, N.Y.: Doubleday, 1946.

Smith, Henry Nash. *Virgin Land: The American West as Symbol and Myth.* New York: Knopf, 1950.

Smith, Leverett. "Ty Cobb, Babe Ruth and the Changing Image of the Athlete Hero." In *Heroes of Popular Culture.* Ed.

by Ray B. Browne et al. Bowling Green, Ohio: Bowling Green University Popular Press, 1972. Pp. 43-85.

Smith, Page. *As a City Upon a Hill: The Town in American History.* New York: Knopf, 1966.

Smith, Robert. *Baseball.* Rev. ed. New York: Simon & Schuster, 1970.

Spears, Betty and Richard A. Swanson. *History of Sport and Physical Activity in the United States.* Dubuque, Iowa: William C. Brown, 1979.

Standish, Burt L. "Frank Merriwell on the Road." *Tip Top Weekly* 130 (8 October 1898).

————. "Frank Merriwell; or, First Days at Fardale." *Tip Top Library* 1 (18 April 1896).

————. "Frank Merriwell's Brother; or, Training a Wild Spirit." *Tip Top Weekly* 275 (20 July 1901).

————. "Frank Merriwell's Finish; or, Blue Against Crimson." *Tip Top Library* 43 (6 February 1897).

————. "Frank Merriwell's Glory; or, Last Triumphs at Old Yale." *Tip Top Weekly* 273 (6 July 1901).

————. "Frank Merriwell's Great Run; or, Trouncing the Tigers." *Tip Top Library* 45 (20 February 1897).

————. "Frank Merriwell's Marvel; or, Dick Merriwell in the Box." *Tip Top Weekly* 277 (3 August 1901).

————. *Frank Merriwell's Schooldays.* Ed. by Jack L. Rudman. 1901. New York: Smith Street Publications, 1971.

————. *Lefty O' the Training Camp.* New York: Barse & Hopkins, 1914.

Steinbeck, John. "And Then My Arm Glassed Up." *Sports Illustrated* 23 (20 December 1965): 94-102.

————. *Burning Bright.* New York: Viking, 1950.

Storr, Anthony. *Human Aggression.* New York: Atheneum, 1968.

Stratton, Ted. "Satan in Center." *Best Sports* 2:7 (February 1951): 78-97.

Stubbs, John C. "The Search for Perfection in *Rabbit, Run.*" *Critique* 10 (1968):94-101.

Styron, William. *Lie Down in Darkness.* Indianapolis: Bobbs-Merrill, 1951.

Tanner, Tony. *City of Words: American Fiction 1950-1970.* London: Cape, 1971.

Taylor, Larry E. *Pastoral and Anti-pastoral Patterns in John Updike's Fiction.* Carbondale: Southern Illinois University, 1973.

Thayer, William. *Tact, Push, and Principle.* Boston: Earl, 1880.

Tiger, Lionel. *Men in Groups.* New York: Random House, 1969.

de Tocqueville, Alexis. *Democracy in America.* Garden City, N.Y.: Doubleday, 1969.

Trachtenberg, Alan et al., eds. *The City: American Experience.* New York: Oxford University Press, 1971.

Treat, Roger. *The Encyclopedia of Football.* 15th rev. ed. New York: Barnes, 1976.

Tunis, John R. *Iron Duke.* New York: Harcourt, Brace & World, 1938.

————. *The Kid Comes Back.* New York: Morrow, 1946.

Turner, Frederick Jackson. *The Frontier in American History.* New York: Holt, 1920.

"Twelve Southerners." *I'll Take My Stand: The South and the Agrarian Tradition.* New York: Harper, 1930.

Updike, John. "Ace in the Hole." In *The Same Door.* New York: Knopf, 1959.

————. "Ex-Basketball Player." In *The Carpentered Hen and Other Tame Creatures.* New York: Harper & Brothers, 1958.

————. *Rabbit Redux.* New York: Knopf, 1971.

————. *Rabbit, Run.* New York: Knopf, 1960.

Van Loan, Charles. "Excess Baggage." In *Score by Innings.* New York: Doran, 1919.

————. "Easy Picking." In *Taking the Count.* New York: Doran, 1915.

Vargo, Edward P. *Rainstorms and Fire: Ritual in the Novels of John Updike.* Port Washington, N.Y.: Kennikat Press, 1973.

Veblen, Thorstein. *The Theory of the Leisure Class.* New York: Macmillan, 1908.

Veeck, Bill, with Ed Linn. *Veeck—As in Wreck.* New York: Putnam, 1962.

Voigt, David Quentin. *American Baseball: From Gentleman's Sport to the Commissioner System.* Norman: University of Oklahoma Press, 1966.

————. *American Baseball: From the Commissioners to Continental Expansion.* Norman: University of Oklahoma Press, 1970.

Walden, Awelia Elizabeth. *My Sister Mike.* New York: Whittlesey House, 1955.

————. *Queen of the Courts.* Philadelphia: Westminster, n.d.

————. *Victory for Jill.* New York: Morrow, 1953.

Wallop, Douglas. *The Year the Yankees Lost the Pennant.* New York: Norton, 1954.

Ward, J. A. "John Updike's Fiction." *Critique* 5 (Spring-Summer 1962): 27-40.

Warfield, Nicole. *Superball.* New York: Bantam Books, 1974.

Warren, Robert Penn. *All the King's Men.* New York: Grosset & Dunlap, 1946.

————. "Goodwood Comes Back." In *The Circus in the Attic and Other Stories.* New York: Harcourt, Brace & World, 1962.

Wasserman, Earl R. "*The Natural*: World Ceres." In *Bernard Malamud and the Critics.* Ed. by Leslie A. Field and Joyce W. Field. New York: New York University Press, 1970, pp. 45-65.

Waugh, Coulton. *The Comics.* New York: Macmillan, 1947.

Wector, Dixon. *The Hero in America.* New York: Scribner, 1941.

Weiss, Paul. *Sport: A Philosophic Inquiry.* Carbondale: Southern Illinois University Press, 1969.

Wheeler, Edward L. *Deadwood Dick on Deck; or, Calamity Jane, the Heroine of Whoop-Up.* 1878. New York: Odyssey Press, 1966.

————. "High Hat Harry, the Baseball Detective; or, The Sunken Treasure." *Beadle's Half-Dime Library* 416 (14 July 1885).

Whitehead, James. *Joiner.* 1971. New York: Avon, 1973.

Wilder, Robert. *Autumn Thunder.* New York: Putnam, 1952.

Williams, Stanley T. *Studies in Victorian Literature.* New York: Dutton, 1923.

Williams, Tennessee. *Cat on a Hot Tin Roof.* New York: New Directions, 1955.

Wolfe, Thomas. *The Web and the Rock.* New York: Harper & Brothers, 1939.

————. *You Can't Go Home Again.* New York: Harper & Brothers, 1940.

Woolf, Virginia. "American Fiction." In *Collected Essays,* vol. II. New York: Harcourt, Brace & World, 1967.

Wright, Jack. *Champs on Ice.* Cleveland, Ohio: World Publishing, 1940.

Zuckerman, George. *Farewell, Frank Merriwell.* New York:

Index

179-80; history in, 222-24; history of, 6, 8-9, 15-17, 21-23, 211, 258-62; juvenile, 8-9, 11-12; literary advantages of, 7-8, 94, 122; major themes of, 21, 261-62; mysteries, 18-19, 260; myth in, 211-20, 229-58; nonathlete in, 200-9; popularity of, 11-15; prejudice against, 11, 93-94; pulps, 17, 55-57; related to non-sports fiction, 7, 23, 51, 54, 55, 81, 85, 97, 107, 139, 145, 158-59, 205, 235; reputation of, 8; sexual themes in, 175-208; sources of, 5-6; typical characteristics of, 20-21, 131; youth and age in, 133-69. *See also* Baseball fiction; Basketball fiction; Boxing fiction; Football fiction
Sports Freak (O'Cork), 260
Sports hero, 25-27; American contrasted to British, 40-43; in American culture, 36; baseball player as, 59-61; basketball player as, 65-67; boxer as, 58-59; contrasted to mythical heroes, 36-40; female creators of, 179-80; football player as, 61-62; juvenile version of, 27-35; 180; as myth, 211-20; as a natural, 77-97, 98; in pulp magazines, 55-57; as rebel against authority, 130; as representative American hero, 25, 26-27, 43-44, 44-45, 68; as self-made man, 46-51, 98, 198; as sexual ideal, 171-72; as source of cultural value, 20; television's impact on, 27, 55; types of, 57; as victim of sexual ideal, 198, 199-200
Sports history, 2-5, 69-74, 220-24, 259
Sports movies, 18
Sports music, 18
Sports mysteries/thrillers, 18-19, 260
Sports poetry, 19
Sports theater, 11, 18
Sport Story, 17
Square Trap, The (Shulman), 99
"Standish, Burt L." *See* Gilbert Patten
Stay Loose (Nye), 18
Stealing Home (O'Connor), 130-

31, 260
Steinbeck, John, 11, 227
Stengel, Casey, 212
Stories for Boys (Norris), 10
Stover at Yale (Johnson), 30, 32, 40, 41, 133, 179
Strange Interlude (O'Neill), 11
Stratemeyer, Edward, 9, 46
Strike Him Out! (Sherman), 30, 33
Styron, William, 11, 62
Success (magazine), 50
Sullivan, John L., 70
Summer Game, The (Angell), 61
Sun Also Rises, The (Hemingway), 10
Sunday Heroes, The (Gerson), 192
Sunday Punch (Newman), 111, 261
Sun Field, The (Broun), 180, 181-83
Sunlit Field, The (Kennedy), 61, 223
Superball (Warfield), 192
Super Bowl, 1, 190
Super Sports, 17

Tact, Push, and Principle (Thayer), 50
Taking the Count (Van Loan), 80, 81, 183
Tanner, Tony, 249
Tchambuli tribe, 174
Tennis fiction, 259-60
That Championship Season (Miller), 11
That Prosser Kid (Pye), 63, 189
Thayer, Ernest Lawrence, 19
Thayer, William, 50
"This Animal of a Buldy Jones" (Norris), 10
This Side of Paradise (Fitzgerald), 10
This Sporting Life (movie), 18
Thomson, Bobby, 213, 221
Thoreau, Henry, 111
Thrilling Sports, 17
Ticket for a Seamstitch, A (Harris), 12, 138, 150-51
Tinker, Joe, 180, 212
Tip Top Weekly (also *Tip Top Library*), 9, 27-28, 41, 42, 44, 57, 220
"To an Athlete Dying Young" (Housman), 160

de Tocqueville, Alexis, 72
Today's Game (Quigley), 133
Tom Brown's School Days
  (Hughes), 27, 40, 41
"Town ball," 3, 69
"Travis Hallett's Half Back"
  (Norris), 9
Tunis, John R., 11, 29, 30, 40
Tunney, Gene, 85
Turner, Frederick Jackson, 74
Twain, Mark. *See* Samuel Clemens
Two-Minute Warning (LaFoun-
  taine), 19, 260
Typee (Melville), 255

"Unheroic Hero, The" (Higgs), 57
Universal Baseball Association,
  J. Henry Waugh, Prop., The
  (Coover), 14, 17, 222, 231-41
Unwilling God, The (Marks), 63
Updike, John, 17, 21, 43, 67, 122,
  160-69, 171

Vance, Dazzy, 212
Van Loan, Charles E., 15, 16, 22,
  80, 81, 82, 180-81, 183
Vargo, Edward, 164
Varsity Letter (Reck), 80, 81
Veblen, Thorstein, 73, 127
Veeck, Bill, 252-53
Veeck—As in Wreck (Veeck), 253
Violence, 175, 192, 197
Violent Wedding, The (Lowry),
  183-85, 204
Virgin Land (Smith), 81
Vision Quest (Davis), 261
Voices of a Summer Day (Shaw),
  227-29

Waddell, Rube, 61, 78-79, 212
Waitkus, Eddie, 212
Walden, Amelia Elizabeth, 179
Wallace, Robert, 19
Wallop, Douglas, 18
Warfield, Nicole, 192
Warren, Robert Penn, 11, 62, 96-97
Washburn, Leonard, 15

Wasserman, Earl, 215
Web and the Rock, The (Wolfe),
  10
Weiss, Paul, 15
Weston, Jessie, 214
"Whatever Happened to Gloomy
  Gus of the Chicago Bears?"
  (Coover), 13, 19, 232
Whitehead, James, 61, 132, 159-60
Whitman, Walt, 19
Wide Awake Weekly, 8
Wilder, Robert, 85-88
Williams, Roger, 124
Williams, Ted, 61
Williams, Tennessee, 11
Williams, William Carlos, 19
Wills, Harry, 59
Wilson, Edmund, 93
With Mask and Mitt (Dudley), 45
Wolfe, Thomas, 10, 254
Woolf, Virginia, 94
Work and Win, 8
World Class (Boyar), 260
Wright, Elsie (*pseud.* Jack Wright),
  179
Wynn, Early, 253

Yanks 3, Detroit 0, Top of the
  Seventh (Reynolds), 11
Year the Yankees Lost the Pen-
  nant, The (Wallop), 18
You Can't Go Home Again
  (Wolfe), 10
You Know Me Al (Lardner), 17,
  88, 89-90, 91-92, 95
"You Know Me Al" (comic strip),
  17
Young, Al, 260, 261
Young Athlete's Weekly, The, 8
Youth, 109; age contrasted to, 123;
  cult of in America, 123-26, 133;
  as myth, 211, 216; in sports, 126-
  30; the sports novel of, 137-51;
  typical literary portrait of, 133-
  36

Zuckerman, George, 132